KESSIE

KESSIE

JOYCE MARLOW

HODDER AND STOUGHTON
LONDON SYDNEY AUCKLAND TORONTO

British Library Cataloguing in Publication Data
Marlow, Joyce
    Kessie.
    I. Title
    823'.914[F]   PR6063.A65/
    ISBN 0 340 35566 2

For Marabel Hadfield
with affection and gratitude

I am deeply indebted to all those who gave me their love, friendship, help or encouragement in difficult days: to my husband Patrick Connor, my sister Janet Hurrell, my agent Vivienne Schuster, and my editor Maureen Waller; to Jill Craigie, Brigadier Peter Young, DSO, MC, and David Doughan in the research field; and to my friends Joy Rowe, Maggie and Ray Lulham, Bernadette Milnes, Brigid Brophy, Anne Thicknesse, Carole and Richard Fries, Barbara Keogh, Sheila Jerram, Joan Mineau, Elizabeth Thomas, Ruth and Hugh Forbes, Maureen Duffy, Paddy Kitchen and Dulan Barber.

PART ONE

Preface

At the end of April 1905, the following letter appeared in the correspondence columns of Manchester's most famous newspaper:

To the Editor of the *Manchester Guardian*

Dear Sir,

I read twice through the report of the trial of Miss Lily Harrison, to confirm that my eyes had not deceived me upon their first reading; to confirm that in February last a thirteen-year-old child was found collapsed in the snow, with her dead babe not far from her side; to confirm that she was subsequently charged with infanticide; to confirm that she has now been sentenced to be hanged by the neck until she is dead.

Having twice digested this astonishing report, I asked myself whether I am a citizen of the proudest city of the Mother Country of the greatest Empire the world has ever known, a country which boasts of its ancient justice? Or had I, by some temporal trick as imagined by Mr Wells in *The Time Machine*, been transported into seventeenth-century Russia? For, Sir, I venture to assert that not even the present Czar and his despotic Government would have treated a thirteen-year-old child thus.

I beg, Sir, that you will extend me the courtesy of your correspondence columns to announce the setting-up of a campaign to save the poor child from the hangman's noose, to remove the stain that is disfiguring our city and our country by this monstrous travesty of the justice all true-born Britons cherish.

Donations will be gratefully received and should be sent to the following address: The Lily Harrison Defence Committee, c/o Messrs Thorpe and Company Limited, Portland Street, Manchester.

I am, Sir,

Yours truly,

Charles W. Thorpe,

The Laurels,

Whalley Range.

1

With a glow of justified pride, Kessie Thorpe decided that *her* letter to the *Manchester Guardian* had definitely been a good one.

It was only just past midday but already the postman had delivered two sacks of mail to Papa's Portland Street office. The room off the counting-house was awash with donations to the Lily Harrison Defence Fund, offerings both touchingly small and heart-warmingly large, piles of silver farthings, threepenny and sixpenny pieces, of ten shilling, one pound and even five pound notes.

To think that only a few days ago she had been having breakfast at The Laurels, while Papa—who was a law unto himself, reading while he ate—had been buried behind the *Guardian*, smooth from its ironing by the parlour maid, and Kessie had as usual been wondering what to do that day. Accept her friend Muriel's invitation to attend the spring fashion show at the Midland Hotel, stay in town for luncheon and go on to the Ladies' Concert in the afternoon? She had been thinking what a boring prospect that was, watching the sunlight break into rainbow hues as it filtered through the leaded lights of the breakfast-room windows, and wondering if life would be different when she was twenty-one and came into her inheritance, a day nine long months away, when Papa had suddenly let out a loud exclamation.

'Jumping Jehosephat!'

This was his favourite expletive, uttered when his short-fuse temper or sense of outrage, or both, were about to explode, so Kessie had given him her full attention. In view of the newspaper report on Lily Harrison's trial and sentence, it had been both and Papa's bristly ginger moustache which slanted downwards, though not in a full walrus droop, had almost straightened with fury. People said he was 'a card', which was perhaps another way of saying he was unpredictable, always doing what he, not they, thought best and not in the least caring if he trod on tender corns, but Kessie had been very proud of him as he'd flung down his napkin and stormed off to organise the Lily Harrison Defence Committee.

She had followed, catching him in the hall. As he was so busy and she had so little to do, she had suggested that she might write the proposed letter to the *Guardian*. Somewhat to her surprise, Papa had agreed and she'd spent the best part of the day in her study high in the turret of The Laurels, filling a waste-paper basket with discarded pages as she'd tried to make the letter sound like Papa. In the evening, when he had returned from the office, he'd said the letter was first-rate and he particularly liked the reference to the despotic Czar, which Kessie had inserted especially because she knew the Czar was one of Papa's many *bêtes noires*.

While they had been in the dining-room waiting for dinner to be served, Papa had told her that he was clearing the room off the counting-house at his Portland Street office to serve as the campaign headquarters, and that he had hired a barrister to deal with the legal aspects of the appeal for mercy. After the soup arrived, a brilliant idea had struck Kessie.

'Shall I be in charge of the campaign?'

With a spoonful of mutton broth halfway to his mouth, Papa had paused, 'Why not?'

And so now Kessie found herself sitting in the office, issuing instructions for acknowledgments of donations received to two of Papa's lady clerks. How wonderful it was to have a purpose in life, and what a purpose, the saving of a thirteen-year-old child from the hangman's noose!

In the middle of the afternoon, Kessie was having a well-earned cup of tea and nibbling at an Osborne biscuit when the telephone emitted its long insistent trills. Papa approved of the telephone and had had instruments installed here in the office, in the Thorpe family mill up in Mellordale,

12

and also at The Laurels. Lifting the receiver from its hook, she held it close to her ear and said 'Hello' loudly into the mouthpiece. It was a good connection, the only-too-frequent cracklings and distortions were absent, and a pacily crisp female voice said, 'My name is Christabel Pankhurst. To whom am I speaking?'

'This is Miss Thorpe.'

'Good afternoon, Miss Thorpe. I am telephoning on behalf of the Women's Social and Political Union. As an organisation we are deeply shocked by the death sentence meted out to Lily Harrison and we wish to liaise closely with Mr Thorpe's campaign to save the child's life. I am myself studying law and will freely render any legal service I can.'

'Oh, well, my father has already hired a barrister, Miss Pankhurst. . . .'

'I see.' There was a slight pause—of disappointment or annoyance?—before the disembodied voice said briskly, 'My mother and I have full appointment diaries until late tonight, but Miss Whitworth, who is one of our most able and experienced members, is free later this afternoon. Will it be convenient if she calls at your father's office at, say, five-thirty?'

'Well, yes, I think so. . . .'

'Good. We look forward to a successful outcome of our joint efforts to save that wretched, ill-used child. Thank you for your assistance, Miss Thorpe.'

Putting the receiver back in its cradle, Kessie wished she was as coolly composed as Miss Pankhurst! She knew the Pankhurst name vaguely, from the papers. When her father next strode into the office she told him that a Miss Whitworth would be here at five-thirty, on behalf of the Women's Social and Political Union.

'And who might they be?'

Kessie had no idea but she hazarded a guess. 'I think it's run by Mrs Pankhurst.'

'Doctor Pankhurst's widow? If she intends to do anything for women, socially or politically, she'll need to have more about her than he had. Good chap but head stuffed with

Utopian nonsense. But I've no objection to seeing the young woman.' Papa smiled. 'Mustn't ignore the ladies' contribution, eh?'

The rest of the afternoon flew past like an express train and at five-thirty precisely Papa ushered in a young woman. Without staring, which would have been rude, Kessie regarded Miss Whitworth curiously. She was tiny, her skin was unusually dark, a brown tam-o'-shanter sat on her upswept jet-black hair, and the overall impression she gave was of an alert little blackbird. After the introductions had been made, Papa looked quizzically down at her. 'You're very small to be representing the Women's Social and Political Union, Miss Whitworth.'

'Size has nothing to do with strength of purpose, Mr Thorpe.'

'What is your purpose, pray?' If there had been a hint of condescension in Papa's voice, it was gone now.

'We want the vote for women on the same terms as it exists for men, so that as acknowledged equals we may take our rightful place in the world and turn our attention to the many demanding social issues, such as why innocent thirteen-year-old girls have babies and are driven on to the streets to collapse in the snow and are then charged with infanticide.'

Her voice was a surprise, not merely because of its purposefulness, unusual in a woman, but because Miss Whitworth had a Lancashire accent, burring 'r' and flat vowel sounds—she would say *grass* rather than the *grarss* that Kessie had been taught. Moreover, she did not appear to be in the least bothered or embarrassed by her accent, as the lower classes usually were. Anxiously Kessie glanced at her father, but from his expression she knew that he was tickled pink, not angered by Miss Whitworth's forthrightness. 'Ha! And what can we do for you, or you for us, in the matter of the Harrison child?'

In the same sharp, no-time-to-waste manner, Miss Whitworth told him that they in the WSPU thought it would be a good idea to issue a penny pamphlet about Lily Harrison's case; and to have a board erected outside Mr

Thorpe's office, showing how many people had signed the mercy petition. Mr Thorpe was, of course, sending a petition of mercy to the King? Papa said, 'Of course,' and Kessie was enormously impressed by the self-confidence of this *working-class* young woman, for such her clothes and her accent labelled her.

And in the days that followed Kessie went on being impressed.

Miss Whitworth was a school teacher and she came regularly to the Portland Street office after she had finished work with more suggestions as to how the Lily Harrison campaign should be pursued; protest meetings, newspaper publicity, lobbying Members of Parliament, and she brought legal tips from Miss Pankhurst which did not please Papa's barrister. Each evening Kessie and she adjusted the numbers board, and this became quite a local event, with a good-sized crowd gathering to cheer on the pavement outside the soot-blackened City Art Gallery, as the figures mounted into their thousands.

At the end of the most hectic but rewarding week of Kessie's life, Miss Whitworth said, 'Will you call me "Sarah"? I know it isn't usual until you've known somebody for ages but we in the WSPU think it's a good way of breaking down barriers, calling people by their *names*, not their *titles*. Do you mind if I call you "Kessie"?'

'No, please do . . . Sarah.'

Papa looked surprised when he heard their intimate mode of address, but he made no comment.

On the second Tuesday of the campaign, after another liaison meeting, while Kessie was anchoring her large straw hat with a pretty pearl hatpin, Sarah said, 'Would you care to come home with me and have a bite to eat and a natter?'

Although Papa allowed her a great deal of freedom, he was strict about knowing where she was going and with whom, but he liked Sarah. Besides, Tuesdays were one of his evenings out, and probably he wouldn't even need to know about her visit. Unaccustomed to travelling on public transport, Kessie's sense of boldness increased as they waited at the tram-stop in Piccadilly. When the tram arrived it was one of the new electric ones, blue flames flashing from its long pole's contact with the overhead wires. A rush of bodies carried Kessie inside the vehicle, where the wooden benches were already tightly packed with people while others hung on to the straps, but a man offered Kessie his seat and Sarah squeezed in, too. It had been raining and in the confined space the damp clothes smelled to Kessie like mouldering autumn leaves.

At All Saints Church, Sarah said, 'This is our stop.'

Briskly she walked past the dingy shops, while Kessie glanced curiously into the pawnbrokers' windows crammed with every conceivable object, pausing to watch a little Jewish man rehanging suits and dresses on a rail outside his second-hand clothing shop, now that the rain had stopped. Imagine buying clothes that other people had worn!

On Sarah went, deeper into the warren of streets, the entrances to which Kessie had driven past all her life, either in the carriage or in Papa's recently acquired Sunbeam motor car. *Walking* through these bleak geometric rows of squat terraces, narrow streets and back alleyways, ducking her head to avoid the sodden washing hung between the houses, lifting the hem of her skirt over the mounds of rubbish and pools of stagnant water, was an entirely different matter. People were staring at Kessie, pointing at her, and the noise was ear-shattering. Women wrapped in shawls shouted outside public houses, mangy dogs barked, cauliflower-eared cats yowled, clogs clattered over the cobblestones. There were children everywhere, babies in battered perambulators, girls in grubby pinafores and faded bonnets, boys with flat caps worn back to front. A gaggle of them danced behind, their shrill voices swelling derisively. 'Where did you get that 'at? Oh, where did you get that 'at?'

Kessie's new hat was really nothing special, a cartwheel of fine turquoise coloured straw, but here in these streets she felt as if it were a glittering tiara. The blood rushed to her cheeks. But then, in her bossiest school ma'amly voice, Sarah shouted, 'Buzz off, or I'll clip your earholes.'

To Kessie's intense relief, the children fell back. Frankly, without Sarah, she would have been terrified. Still, without Sarah she would never have been here in the first place.

When they reached Sarah's home, that was another shock. What she had expected Kessie could not think, because she knew Sarah hailed from Mellordale. Papa had suddenly realised that she was Amos Whitworth's daughter, a man with whom he had frequently crossed swords, since before his recent death Amos had been a notorious trades unionist in The Dales. What Kessie had *not* expected was that Sarah should live by herself in one room at the top of one of the taller houses which was dark, damp and—Kessie tried unobtrusively to hold her breath as they mounted the stairs—fearfully smelly. The room itself was, oh so bleak, so very different from her own damask-curtained, Wilton-carpeted, walnut-furnished bedroom, sitting-room and study. All that Sarah's single room contained were an iron bedstead, an old table, one chair, a battered wardrobe, and a collection of wooden boxes in which books, crockery and cooking utensils were neatly stacked.

After Sarah had disappeared to fill the kettle—the only water tap apparently was down in the back yard—and had brewed the tea on a small primus stove, they sat on the bed eating what she called 'cheese doorsteps', two hunks of bread with a slab of cheese between them. All the time she talked, but she was such a fascinating companion that Kessie's distaste for her table manners was only slight (Papa might read while he ate, but he would not dream of talking with his mouth full).

'What are your views on the condition of women, Kessie?'

Sarah had a habit of throwing out questions like that, which caught one quite off-balance.

'Oh. Well. Um. . . .'

'You haven't thought about it at all.'

'Well, I have a bit,' Kessie protested, not wishing to be thought an antediluvian little miss, 'I mean we used to have debates at school. Manchester High School isn't stuffy, you know, and—'

17

'Don't worry,' Sarah said soothingly. 'They only hit me a few years ago, the cold hard facts of our situation, though I can tell you the exact moment they did. It was on my seventeenth birthday and I told Dad I wanted to go to Manchester to train properly as a teacher. I'd been half-time teaching since I was twelve, my Dad was allus going on about the rights of man and he was proud of me—"Our Sal's got brains, tha knows",' her voice deepened, her accent broadened, and Kessie giggled, 'so I reckoned he'd be pleased by the news. But not a bit of it. The rights of man didn't include women and he bawled, "No lass of mine's going to Manchester on her lonesome. Who put yon daft notion into yer head? I'll tan his hide off." I said it was my own idea and why should he assume it would be a man, any road? Oo, the rows went on for days, but to cut a long story short, I packed my bag, I came to Manchester and I got my teaching diploma. Then what did I find?'

Kessie hadn't the faintest idea.

'I'll tell you what I found. Women teachers are paid just over half a man teacher's wages for doing exactly the same job and a hundred times better. . . . Well, that really got me thinking. I listened to the Socialist lads saying it was disgusting and women are the equals of men. Do you know what *they* did once we'd finished our discussions? Expected us girls to trot off and make the tea, while they sat on their backsides. I listened to middle-class men saying women are *frail, sensitive, emotional creatures whose place is in the home under male protection*. . . .' Sarah had adopted a swanky accent which made Kessie giggle even more, though actually it was not unlike her own. 'And I wondered what world they lived in. My Mam's dead but she worked all her life, so do all the women in Mellordale. I don't have to tell you, Kessie; you know how many women work in your Dad's mill. Three-quarters of his labour force is female, isn't it?'

Kessie had never thought of this before, but it was true, so she nodded.

'My Dad used to say your grandfather was an old bugger to work for, still, self-made men usually are the hardest on those they've just left behind, and, as far as mill-owners go, your Dad has a good record.'

Kessie was glad to know about her father having a good record, but she blinked to hear her grandpapa openly described as 'a bugger to work for'. Apparently unaware that she might have made a tactless remark, Sarah jumped from the bed and started to pace the bare scrubbed boards.

'Everything was muddled in my head. Then I went to a meeting where I heard Mrs Pankhurst speak. She said we women will have to change things for ourselves and we'll never achieve anything until we have the vote. Oh, it was like a thunderbolt from heaven, Kessie. Of course, the vote's the key. We live in a democracy supposedly run by the people for the people. But how can it be that when half its citizens have no say whatsoever and everything that affects women's lives is cooked up by *male* Members of Parliament elected by *men?*'

Settling into a more comfortable position on the hard lumpy mattress, Kessie listened spellbound as Sarah stalked up and down, the words cascading from her like the waterfall on Mellordale moor. 'The way things are it's no wonder we women have had to fight every inch of the way to get anything. What have we got so far? A privileged few can go to university or become doctors. Even so, will Christabel Pankhurst, however clever she is, be allowed to become a barrister or a judge? No! Do *any* women earn the same money as men? No! Do the children men say are our natural province belong to us in law? Not on your nelly, they don't! Has little Lily Harrison any likelihood of redress from that brute who violated her? Not on your nelly, she hasn't.'

Sarah spun round to face Kessie, her voice rising. 'Most men value us several degrees lower than horses and dogs. And they'll go on treating us like low-grade pets until we stand up and fight for ourselves. By heck, we're going to!'

With the resonance of a cathedral bell, her words reverberated in Kessie's head. In Sarah's presence she was transported to another world, or was it that Sarah opened her mind to the world as it really was? Her relations were always saying that Papa had spoiled her, letting her have far

19

too much of her own way, and she was an uppity miss. Had he? Was she uppity enough? Not by Sarah's standards she wasn't! Might not her own recent feelings of restlessness, her sense of aimlessness, stem from the same root as Sarah's clear-cut anger? A rebellion against a male-dominated society?

'You're so right, Sarah. When I suggested going to university Papa acted just like your father. And I'm afraid I wasn't like you. I submitted.'

'Why don't you join us in the WSPU?'

Kessie was taken aback. Then, before she could answer, the door opened and a man came in saying, 'Sal, me luv, can I sleep on your floor tonight?'

He was tall, a good six feet, and his clothes were shabby and ill-fitting which gave him an extra gangling look. His skin was dark, his eyes were dark, his hair was thick and black, he had a generous mouth and there was a cleft in his determined chin. Half Kessie's mind envied Sarah such a lover, while the other half panicked. What was she doing in the company of a young woman who lived by herself and had lovers who slept on her floor? What would Papa say if he found out?

'Tom!' Sarah ran towards the young man, 'I thought you were in Newcastle. It's grand to see you. Oh, this is Miss Thorpe. She's a new friend and she's joining the WSPU. Kessie, this is my brother Tom who *genuinely* believes that women are the equals of men. Don't you?'

Playfully, Sarah punched him in the stomach and Kessie felt an immense relief, because he wasn't her lover, he was her brother, though apart from the dark hair and skin there was little sibling resemblance. In height, they were certainly the long and the short of it. Tom Whitworth was smiling, holding out his hand, and suddenly Kessie became acutely conscious that she was in the same room with a strange man and a bed. Leaping up, she clasped his hand, his grip was warm and firm, and she noticed the dark hairs under the frayed cuffs on his wrist. Sarah seized the kettle and, saying she'd mash some more tea, bustled from the room. Tom Whitworth bowed slightly, gesturing towards the only chair. His teeth were beautifully even and white against the dark skin, his fingers were long and elegantly shaped, his eyes were riveting. There didn't seem anything else to do until Sarah returned, so Kessie sat down, though she had never been alone with a young man before in her life.

'Did Sarah convert you?'

'Mm?' It was a ridiculous squeak that came from her mouth.

He said, 'To the cause! To the WSPU!'

'I haven't actually joined yet.'

'You must.'

He went on talking. His whole attention was focused on her, and she felt he really wanted to know about her and was impressed by her replies. From time to time, when he ran his left hand through the black locks that fell repeatedly on to his forehead, she saw the hairs on his wrist. She tried not to look at them. As soon as Sarah returned, she jumped up.

'I must go, it must be getting late.'

She looked at her fob-watch and the hands pointed to nine-fifteen. It couldn't be that hour, it could not be, it was long past the dinner hour, and Papa did not know where she was. Sarah understood her panic, quickly putting down the kettle.

'Shall we take Kessie home, Tom?'

He nodded. Frantically, Kessie donned her hat and coat and she saw him eyeing her elegant turquoise headgear; Sarah put on her shabby coat and tam-o'-shanter, and slowly they descended the dark, smelly stairs, Tom Whitworth in the rear. As they reached the first floor landing, from below there was a commotion, a shout of, 'I'll get Sarah'. Somebody flew up the stairs and almost crashed into them.

'I'm here, Florrie, what's up?'

There was a gabbled conversation, the gist of which was that some old woman living downstairs was desperately ill and ought to be in hospital and only Sarah could persuade her to go.

Briskly, Sarah said, 'I must see to it. Tom'll take you home, Kessie. Oh, and explain to Mr Thorpe that it was all my fault that Kessie stayed so long, won't you?'

21

They walked back through the ill-lit streets. Sarah's brother talked easily, but Kessie was rigid with the tension of being alone with this young man. They turned a corner and against the wall of an alleyway two shadowy figures were locked together and the man was thrusting himself against the woman. Hastily Kessie averted her eyes, fixing them on her gloves. She was unclear as to exactly what the man and woman were doing, but it was something that was making Kessie's blood rush from her toes to the roots of her hair.

Breathlessly, she said, 'Sarah said you were in Newcastle, Mr Whitworth. Why was that?'

'I travel all over the north. I'm an organiser for the ILP.' He smiled at her and in the ghostly glare of the street-lamp his teeth shone above the shadowed dimple in his chin. 'The Independent Labour Party, that is.'

'How interesting.' Kessie tried desperately to recall what she knew about the Labour movement and Socialism. Nothing came to mind, so she said, 'You play cricket, don't you?'

'I used to. Still do occasionally.'

'My father said you were a very good fast bowler, good enough to play for Lancashire.' Actually, Papa had said one of the Whitworth brood had been offered a trial by Lancashire County Cricket Club, which was a good job for a working-class lad, but the danged young fool had turned it down.

'I was good enough to play for England, but I didn't choose to be a professional cricketer in a game run by amateur gentlemen.'

The contempt in his voice was like a whiplash and Kessie wished the ground would swallow her up, except she wanted to stay by the side of this young man, so very unlike any she had ever met. They were out of the back streets and had reached Oxford Road, when she saw a hansom cab which she hailed loudly. The horse clopped to a standstill and the driver looked down disrespectfully (women who hailed cabs at this time of night were no better than they should be).

22

'Where to?'

'The Laurels, Whalley Range.'

'Yes, miss.' The driver's manner changed abruptly when he heard the address (some of these modern middle-class misses were decidedly forward). 'Certainly, miss.'

Tom Whitworth opened the cab door, Kessie lifted her skirt, conscious of his eyes on her slim ankles as she climbed inside and he followed. She sat as far away from him as possible, holding on to the leather strap so that she wouldn't fall against him as the horse pulled round the corners.

'Will you be in disgrace when you reach home, Miss Thorpe?'

'My father doesn't know I went to your sister's.'

'I will do my best to explain then.' He talked on, calmly describing his work with the ILP.

His voice had the same distinctive Lancashire pronunciations as Sarah's: *uzz* for *us, wan* for *one*, a peculiar 'u' in words like 'worry', an extra emphasis on the final 'ing', but what did the way he spoke matter, when the deep resonance of his voice was so thrilling and what he said so fascinating? After all, most of her relations, including Papa, had slight Lancashire accents. Perhaps the most astonishing things about Sarah and her brother were their articulateness, the lucidity of their thought, the confidence of their speech.

They clopped through the streets and Kessie sat listening to Tom Whitworth with a breathless pleasure. It had turned into the most beautiful night, the full moon risen high in the sky, casting a silver glow over the rooftops of Moss Side, and as they reached the fields of Whalley Range the grass was glittering in the moonlight and the trees seemed hung with tinsel. When the cab turned through the main gates, trotting past the mass of laurels after which the house had been named, up the circular driveway to the front door, Tom Whitworth's dark eyebrows rose slightly and Kessie saw her home through his eyes. It was very large and very imposing, at least in contrast to the hovels around All Saints, dominated by the tower on whose topmost turret Papa flew the Union Jack, though it was always lowered at sunset by one of the maids. Kessie also realised how peaceful her home was, enclosed by its acre of garden.

The cab halted in front of the double-fronted doors. Almost immediately Papa appeared and Kessie's excitement turned to apprehension, for his back was ramrod straight, his moustache had its furiously erect appearance and in the moonlight his eyes were glinting. It took an agonisingly long time for Tom Whitworth to pay off the cabby, fumbling around in the pockets of his shabby jacket—it did not occur to Kessie that he was in fact having great difficulty finding the fare. And then, the minute the cab disappeared behind the laurel bushes and he turned to her father to make his explanations, he was immediately interrupted.

'Whoever you may be, you are no gentleman because no gentleman would dream of compromising a young lady by being alone with her, and at this time of night. Are you aware, sir, that it is nearly ten o'clock?' On and on he went, barking like a sealion at Belle Vue Zoo, but Kessie dared not interrupt, and Tom Whitworth just stood there, staring up at him. His silence had an insolent quality which she knew was stoking Papa's rage. '. . . and you are never to set eyes on my daughter again. Never! I can only trust that you are sufficiently a gentleman not to have laid so much as a finger on her. . . .'

At that Kessie cried out, 'Please Papa, you don't understand. . . .'

'Be silent! You have created enough mischief for one night, miss. And you, sir, leave my house!'

Tom Whitworth bowed slightly to Kessie and, still without saying a word, disappeared into the night. Why hadn't he tried to explain? She turned towards her father, 'Please, Papa, listen. It wasn't . . .'

'Go to bed, this instant.'

Dear as he was, it was useless to argue when Papa was in a rage, so miserably Kessie went. When she was in bed, lying between the lavender-scented sheets on the soft feather mattress, she could not sleep. Her father was forgotten: in the morning, she felt certain, all would be well again between them. And now the sensations that had crept into

24

her from time to time for as long as she could remember were flooding through her body. In her childhood, although the desire had always been imperative, something she just had to comply with, it had been a deliciously enveloping miasma, but nowadays the physical act of her hand rubbing and rubbing that hard piece of bone between her legs was accompanied by mental images, of her body and men's bodies, doing things together, sweeping together towards that climactic moment, after which she felt blissfully satisfied and usually fell asleep. Recently, these overwhelming, insistent, urgent desires had been occurring more and more frequently, the mental images had become wilder, and she had invented a lover. His name was Rory and he was handsome, intelligent and very, very strong. Sometimes even during the day now the desire would overcome her, so that she stood dreaming of Rory's lips on hers and of Rory taking her in his arms.

Kessie realised that these secret feelings, about which sometimes she felt guilty, though she couldn't stop them— did other girls have them? did Sarah? or was she peculiarly sinful?—were connected with the subject nobody ever mentioned. What men and women did together once they were married which, she thought, made babies, if exactly how she was uncertain. Although—puzzlingly enough—girls could, as poor little Lily Harrison's case had emphasised, have babies even *before* they married.

Tonight, as she lay with her face in the pillow, her body pressing into the softness of the feather mattress, her hand rubbing harder and harder, her breasts moving, her legs straining against the cool cotton of the sheets, it was not Rory's image that filled her mind. It was Tom Whitworth's tall, lean body. His hands, with those dark hairs on the wrists, were caressing her, his wide mouth was kissing her, he was holding her tightly in his arms against the wall of an alleyway, he was thrusting against her as that man had thrust against that woman. She tried to hold on to the images, but they became jumbled in her mind and she could hold them no longer. The supreme rapture overcame her, more rapturous than ever before, and her hand moved

25

limply to her side. But the images of Tom Whitworth stayed with her and as drowsiness numbed her mind she was still seeing his dark eyes smiling into hers, he was holding her in his arms, gently now, the fierce passion spent, and she was stroking the black hairs on his wrist.

2

The Free Trade Hall was packed to capacity and like the buzzing of a disturbed bee-hive the excited anticipation mounted. From her reserved seat in the main arena, immediately below the flower-banked platform, Kessie gazed round the vast auditorium. The idea of a monster rally as the climax of the campaign to save Lily Harrison's life had been suggested by Sarah on behalf of the WSPU, but most of the organisation had fallen on Kessie's shoulders. She had found that she not only enjoyed organising but was good at it. As Papa had observed in some surprise, 'By the left, miss, you know how to get things done.'

The only difficult moment had been when Sarah proposed her brother and Mrs Pankhurst as two of the principal speakers. Papa had raised no objection to Mrs Pankhurst, as many men would have to a woman orator, but he had jibbed at Tom Whitworth. Sarah had protested, 'My brother is a brilliant speaker, well known in the area,' and Papa had said, 'To whom?' But, with Kessie's discreet support, Sarah had won the day.

The rally must be a success, Kessie prayed, and Tom Whitworth had to be a good speaker. Please, dearest God.

The buzzing subsided and there was a ripple of applause as Papa escorted Mrs Pankhurst on to the platform, some shouts from the distant galleries for 'good old Tom', but the real enthusiasm broke as Papa's prize contribution, Mr Lloyd George, walked on. The storming applause gave Kessie time to feast her eyes, not on 'the Welsh Wizard' of politics, nor on Mrs Pankhurst, the lady she had heard so much about from Sarah, but on 'good old Tom'.

Since that disastrous evening when he had escorted her home she had not seen him, but Sarah talked about her brother so much that by now Kessie felt she really knew him. There was quite a gap between the rest of the Whitworth brood and Sarah and Tom, so they'd been particularly close. Tom had actually been born in a mill—not the Thorpe mill, Sarah hastened to reassure her—and he had gone to work in that same mill as a 'half-timer' when he was twelve years old, just as Sarah herself had been a 'half-time' teacher from the same age, both of them spending the mornings at school and the afternoons at work, or vice versa. But they'd attended evening classes and every penny Tom could save he'd spent on books, building up his *own* library. The pride in Sarah's voice as she said this made Kessie realise how completely she had taken for granted the books in Papa's library. Apparently, Tom had been devoted to their dead mother—'Do you know, Kessie, he used to go round Mellordale scooping up the horses' muck and selling it as manure to the gardeners at the posh houses, to earn extra money for Mam.' He had not, however, been a success as a mill-hand—'He's deft with words, is our Tom, but not with his fingers'—and when he was seventeen he'd been sacked from his job as a loom-dresser, for pasting the warp the wrong way and bringing the looms to a grinding halt. Sarah reckoned he'd been thinking about something else entirely; he'd never taken to working in the mill, but it hadn't mattered because by then both he and Sarah were working for the Independent Labour Party. Mr Keir Hardie had secured Tom the job as one of the few paid organisers the ILP could afford. He was the best organiser they'd ever had, and one day he would be a Socialist Member of Parliament like Mr Keir Hardie.

Apart from his endless intellectual and moral virtues, even with the platform between them, Kessie found Tom Whitworth's physical attractions as compulsive as she remembered and as her nocturnal fantasies imagined. Her only regret was that he had done nothing about his clothes which were as shabbily ill-fitting as she also remembered. And she must *not* stare at him!

Papa opened the proceedings with a short no-nonsense speech outlining the facts of Lily Harrison's case. Then Tom Whitworth uncoiled his gangling height, starting to speak quietly as if he were addressing a small room, not a vast hall crammed with people. But his diction was superb and the burring Lancashire voice, growing in power and resonance, carried to the furthest crannies. His mannerism of running his left hand through his black hair, which flopped on to his forehead with increasing vehemence as his anger mounted, gave a passionate spontaneity to his speaking. At the peroration his voice was ringing round the hall, soaring upwards to the roof, and Kessie felt the hairs on her neck prickling. She leapt to her feet, clapping and cheering with an exalted excitement, and she wanted to rush down to Strangeways Gaol to free Lily Harrison with her own hands.

Sarah was right. Her brother was an absolute spellbinder. Why wasn't he famous? Why hadn't she arranged for Mrs Pankhurst to speak before him? It wasn't fair, expecting Mrs Pankhurst to compete, sandwiched between this electrifying, passionate young man and the greatest orator in Britain, David Lloyd George.

Mrs Pankhurst allowed the tumultuous applause almost to die away. Then, rising to catch its ebb, her deep contralto voice throbbed with intensity, carrying as clearly and powerfully as had Tom Whitworth's. When, in her most plangent tones, she said, 'Perhaps, as a woman, I may be permitted to ask the question that nobody has posed—where is the man who gave that poor child the babe she is said to have murdered? What penalty is he suffering?', there was a momentary hush, then a sympathetic roar from the packed auditorium. When she finished, the audience clapped and cheered and stamped as long and as hard as they had for Tom Whitworth. Kessie was again on her feet. What had Papa said? Mrs Pankhurst would need to have more about her than her late husband if she was to do anything for women. My goodness, she certainly had!

For several seconds David Lloyd George, stockily compact, stood completely still as he stared at the thousands of expectant faces. Then, holding his arms out wide, in his most silvery tones which accentuated his Welsh lilt, he said, 'You know, I was born here in Manchester, so I'm just a little bit of a Mancunian myself.'

The audience was his and when *he* sat down the applause positively shook the Free Trade Hall. Afterwards there was a champagne reception in the largest ante-room, paid for by Papa, and among the aspidistras and the massed geraniums euphoria continued to grip Kessie. While she was basking in the repeated congratulations for a superb rally excellently organised, Sarah pushed through to her side.

'Mrs Pankhurst would like to meet you.'

In fact, it took several minutes to attract Mrs Pankhurst's attention, so great was the crush around her, and when Sarah finally caught her eye she held out her hands with the dramatically graceful gesture she had used so effectively on the platform.

'How nice to meet you at last, Miss Thorpe.'

Then, with equally dramatic grace, she turned back to the well-dressed gentleman at her side, 'My dear sir, don't talk to me about all men not yet having the vote. *No* women are allowed to vote.'

For a few seconds Kessie stood on the edge of the group, feeling piqued. Mrs Pankhurst might at least have thanked her for organising the rally that had given her the opportunity to shine so brilliantly. Then Papa called out to her; she turned and saw Mr Lloyd George by his side.

'May I introduce my daughter, sir?'

'Manchester has not ceased to produce beautiful young ladies,' gallantly he took her hand and kissed it, 'among her many other excellent contributions to the world.'

Blushing, Kessie withdrew her hand. Papa and he were talking politics and though he appeared to be focusing his attention on her father, his eyes kept flicking towards her, with a devilish glint, as if they were undressing her. Kessie felt herself blushing again, though he surely couldn't want to do anything like *that*, a man in his forties, with several children? Across the room she saw Tom Whitworth, quietly but vehemently speaking to a group of women, as once he had spoken to her, and she wished she could join them.

'What do you feel, Mr Lloyd George, about this business of women's suffrage that the Pankhursts are so keen on?'

'In the twentieth century, Mr Thorpe, there is no moral or intellectual justification for the withholding of the vote from the fair sex.'

Kessie returned her attention to the two men and to her astonishment she heard herself saying, 'Was there ever any justification, sir?'

Out of the corner of her eyes she saw Papa's startled expression, but Mr Lloyd George smiled impishly.

'Don't tell me you're a lady suffragist, Miss Thorpe. No, of course there never was. But those who have like to hold. It's an elemental human characteristic.' He took out his watch, inspected it, bowed. 'And now, I regret to say, I must take my leave of you.'

As they escorted Mr Lloyd George from the room, they passed Tom Whitworth. With a curt nod of the head Papa said, 'Well done. You know how to hold an audience.'

'Thank you, Mr Thorpe.' He did not sound grateful.

Mr Lloyd George regarded him thoughtfully. 'You could have a future in politics, young man. Why not come and see me if you're in London?'

'I already have a party. The Independent Labour Party.'

Papa and Mr Lloyd George both laughed and the Welsh-man said, 'Hardly a serious political party, young fellow me lad.'

When they were gone, Kessie edged herself to the young man's side and took a deep breath. 'I thought your speech was superb, Mr Whitworth.'

He inclined his head, the black hair fell forward, and her stomach lurched. 'Thank *you*, Miss Thorpe.'

'The whole meeting was wonderful, wasn't it? I love the atmosphere of the Free Trade Hall when it's crammed to capacity, don't you?' She realised she was babbling, and stopped short.

'The dear old Free Trade Hall.' His dark eyes looked

straight into hers. 'Do you know how an American once described Free Trade? As a system invented by the English to plunder the world.'

His manner was distant, with a spiked edge. He was treating her as if she were pampered and stupid. All those imagined discussions, all those witty comments, all those devastatingly intelligent remarks she had impressed him with, froze in her mind. Presumably he had neither forgiven nor forgotten Papa's attitude and her spineless behaviour on *that* night. Or was she perhaps overestimating her attractions and his previous interest in her? Whichever was the answer, she felt desolate and had to fight back her tears as she watched him walk away into the crowd.

A fortnight later, the Lily Harrison Defence Committee received a letter from His Majesty's Secretary of State for Home Affairs informing them that he was recommending to His Majesty King Edward VII that the death sentence on Miss Harrison be commuted to life imprisonment.

'We did it!' In the office, in front of everybody, Kessie threw her arms around Sarah's neck. 'We did it! We saved her!'

At the celebration party at the Midland Hotel to which all the campaigners were invited by Papa, Christabel Pankhurst made a point of coming over to Kessie.

'I think it's time we became acquainted, don't you, seeing we've had so many conversations over the telephone?'

Privately, Kessie thought it was past time, but in Christabel's actual presence she found it difficult to nurse resentment. How like her mother Miss Pankhurst was, the same slight build, the same average height, the same neat features and retroussé nose. Her slightly slanted eyes were less beautiful than Mrs Pankhurst's lustrous violet ones, and her hair curled less prettily, but when she smiled her whole face lit up, and she had the most glorious English rose complexion. Like her mother, Christabel had something else, that intangible quality called personality.

'Sarah tells us you're thinking of joining us in the WSPU. I should like you to.'

To be invited personally by Miss Pankhurst was as good

31

as a royal command, but Kessie had not yet come to a decision, so she prevaricated. 'Thank you. Well, I am seriously considering it.'

Smiling briefly, Miss Pankhurst walked away towards Sarah (whose brother, alas, was unable to be present), her irritation with those who could not make up their minds only too evident. Kessie wanted to run after her, to regain her favour, but to join the WSPU would be a momentous act with all manner of implications, so instead she turned to her father who was discussing with the barrister what should now be done with the surplus money raised in the Harrison campaign. Papa said he thought a trust fund would be the best idea so that when, or if, they obtained a free pardon for the Harrison girl there would be a decent sum awaiting her.

'What happens,' Kessie asked, 'if Lily doesn't get a free pardon?'

'She will serve her sentence, Miss Thorpe,' the barrister said. 'A life sentence means just that. But there have been reforms in the penal law recently from which Miss Harrison may benefit.'

'Lily's only thirteen!' Kessie cried passionately. 'She could live to be seventy!'

Most of that night she lay awake, for once not thinking of Tom Whitworth, but of Lily Harrison alone in her cell and the appalling future should they not obtain a free pardon for her. Kessie also thought about the Pankhursts and Sarah and what she had learned about life in the last hectic weeks, particularly about the condition of women. Towards dawn she fell asleep, and in consequence she was late for breakfast.

As she entered the breakfast-room, Papa had already started eating and his eyebrows rose disapprovingly, but she marched firmly to his side. 'I'm joining the Women's Social and Political Union,' she announced.

Her father half-choked on a piece of kipper. 'Are you, by gad? Sit down and have your breakfast first.'

Kessie sat down and hoped her eyes were boring into Papa's head, bent over his plate. After a decent silence, to allow him to recover from his shock, she said, 'You've always told me I'm as good as any man.'

'So you are. Better than most.'

'I shan't have the opportunity of proving my worth until I have the vote.'

'Stuff and nonsense.'

'It's not just I, Papa, it's women everywhere.' Purposefully Kessie smashed the top of her boiled egg. 'Many of them don't have any opportunities and they won't until we obtain the vote, which is when men will begin to take us seriously and then we can . . .'

'You sound like Miss Whitworth's parrot.'

Charles Thorpe regarded his only child with some perplexity. He loved her more than anybody in the world. Dear, eager, affectionate, motherless Kessie—even when her mother had been alive she had never, alas, loved her. A sick woman for many years, she had blamed the child for wrecking her health and her life. In consequence, he had always striven to make up for the affection denied by her mother, to let Kessie have her head, to give her everything that was in his power.

Thoughtfully he buttered a piece of toast. Then: 'If you feel you must join Mrs Pankhurst's gang, I shall not stand in your way.'

'Oh.' Kessie was deflated. She had been about to hurl at her father the speech she had rehearsed while Effie, her maid, had put her hair up, including the final defiance, 'If you won't let me join the wspu, if you won't give me your blessing, I shall leave home!' She had imagined living by herself in one room like Sarah's, with steadfast courage. Still, it was much nicer that Papa did not object. Really. She supposed. 'Thank you, Papa. In that case I shall join on Monday morning.'

The other thought in Kessie's mind, that by joining the wspu she would see more of Sarah and thereby, probably, of her brother, was quickly pushed away. In the first place, Tom Whitworth was seldom in Manchester these days, and secondly she was plunged into a world filled with heroic *women*, a whole world that had been pulsating with activity while she had been moping about doing those things adjudged seemly for a well-bred young lady, such as playing

33

the piano, keeping a diary, shopping, arranging flowers. The high points of her former life had been bicycling round Lancashire and Cheshire with certain approved friends and learning how to drive Papa's motor car.

For Kessie the focal point of this new, amazing, wonderful female world was the Pankhursts' home at number sixty-two Nelson Street. The house was a fair size, with rooms that you *could* swing a cat in (as Papa would say), but it was at the end of a terraced row in the 'wrong', meaning lower-middle-class, area of Rusholme. Kessie was astonished that they should live there, until Sarah told her that Doctor Pankhurst (a doctor of law, not medicine) had left his family virtually penniless. Shattered as they were by his sudden death, had they collapsed with the vapours? Not a bit of it! Mrs Pankhurst had taken a job; Christabel was following in her father's footsteps by studying for her law degree at the nearby Owen's College, one of the handful of women in the entire British Isles to be so daring; her sister Sylvia was studying art in London; and the whole family, including Adela and young Harry, still in his teens, were working for the cause of women's suffrage. Harry was a dear, lolloping around like an overgrown colt, eager to earn a pat on the muzzle from his mother, though actually he seemed over-whelmed by his womenfolk.

Then so was Kessie. In truth, she found Mrs Pankhurst—though they indeed used Christian names in the WSPU, nobody dreamed of calling her 'Emmeline'—formidable, and she reminded Kessie of the headmistress at Manchester High School, a woman full of energy, passionately con-cerned about her girls, but a distant, august personage. Christabel, however, was different, the shining head girl whom everybody worshipped but who remained ap-proachable. At least Kessie found her so, though Sarah said, 'You're honoured, I'd say. She's taken to you, and no mistake.'

Did dear Sarah sound just the slightest bit miffed?

Papa, on the other hand, said, 'If you absorb every word she utters as if it's the Holy Writ, I'm not surprised she likes you.'

Kessie dismissed that interpretation of their friendship. She had to admit, though, that listening to Christabel was exciting and instructive. Her head was simply stuffed with facts and figures which she withdrew as easily as taking a handkerchief from a drawer.

'Did you know,' she said as she and Kessie met outside Owen's College, a habit they had fallen into if not otherwise engaged, 'that women nail-makers earn only five shillings a week?'

Kessie didn't even know there were women nail-makers but she was outraged by the information because Papa paid his lowliest workers fifteen shillings a week and her personal allowance was two pounds.

On a beautiful sunny afternoon in June she was waiting outside Owen's College when Christabel emerged, and arm-in-arm they walked up Oxford Road to the Nelson Street house where the front parlour was already filled with women for the weekly meeting. As usual Mrs Pankhurst was pacing restlessly up and down, fulminating against the useless gang of women suffragists in London who imagined that if they kept on asking nicely for the vote, the odious politicians would give it to them.

'Deeds, not words, is what we want.'

Everybody cheered loudly and Christabel said, 'Yes mother, and it's about time we acted more decisively.' She already had her notepad and pencil on her knee, checking through the list of speakers for next week. 'Can you do the Women's Trades Union League in Bury for us, Kessie, on Saturday afternoon?'

For a couple of seconds Kessie did not absorb the casual question, but then she stammered, 'Oh, I don't think so, I mean, I've never spoken in public, I mean, I might let you down.'

'Nonsense,' Mrs Pankhurst swung round. 'We are all nervous to begin with. You have a lovely speaking voice. It will be a pleasure for them to listen to you. Remember to give your audience time to grasp what you are saying, but do not allow them time to interrupt. And speak *up*. There is nothing worse than inaudibility.'

With those brief words of advice, Mrs Pankhurst moved on to other topics.

Kessie spent hours in her study, drafting and redrafting her speech.

Once she was standing on the platform of the dingy hall in Bury, however, most of it went from her head and she had only the haziest idea of what she said to her audience of eager mill-girls, none of whom interrupted. Afterwards they told her how much they had enjoyed her talk and how much they had learned about women's suffrage. Kessie felt absurdly pleased with herself.

On her return to The Laurels, just before dinner-time on the Saturday evening, Sheba was waiting to intercept her in the hall. Dear Sheba of the ridiculously inapposite name, the large-boned, forthright woman from Mellordale who had looked after the Thorpe household for the last twenty years and had been her surrogate mother.

'Ah hope you're not feeling hungry because we shan't be eating until midnight, ah reckon. The family arrived an hour ago. News travels fast in these parts and they've found out what you've been oop to this afternoon. They're all in the library with your Dad now, your aunts, your uncles and your cousins.'

'Oh.' The jubilation drained from Kessie.

'Proper conference it is. Right noisy one, too. A well-bred young lady like you standing oop in public! They've never heard owt like it! And your Dad's to put a stop to it this minute! If ah was you, lass, for the time being ah'd mek meself scarce.'

Gratefully, Kessie squeezed Sheba's hand and went up to her study where she stood at the window, looking down on the rows of dying tulips, their colours glowing in the evening sunlight. Oh heavens, what would happen now? A show-down with Papa? Would she be forced to leave home, after all? She certainly had no intention of abandoning her work for the cause. Where would she live? Would she actually be able to fend for herself?

Grave as the situation was, Kessie found herself unable

to focus her thoughts on the crisis. They would keep returning to the casual invitation Sarah had thrown out the
previous evening: 'Tom should be in Manchester any day
now. Why don't you come and have supper with us one
night?'

3

Only two hundred and fifty miles away, but in a different
England, Alice Hartley surveyed herself in the full-length
mirror of the bedroom of her brother-in-law's ancestral
home, Frensham Manor, in Sussex.

'Is that tight enough, Miss Hartley?'

'Give it another pull, Gertie.'

Obediently, her personal maid tugged on the lacing
of her corsets, and Alice nodded. Yes, that was fine. She
could span her hands easily round her waist, yet she could
still breathe. Gertie fetched her underskirt, she stepped
into it, then into her afternoon gown. Gertie pulled the
garment slowly upwards, adjusting the shoulder line and
gingerly doing up the 'zipper'. Back home in New York
'zippers' were all the rage but Gertie, whom she had
engaged in London, treated them as if they would bite
her.

After Gertie had anchored her large white folded straw
hat—the one trimmed with scarlet poppies—Alice stood in
front of the mirror again. Yes, the effect was divine, or 'divi'
as the English society slang had it. Momma should be
pleased.

Alice knew why her mother had wanted her to come
to England. Her sister Verena was already married to
an Englishman, Sir Lionel Mainwaring, pronounced
'Mannering', goodness knew why but the English were like
that. Alice herself was twice as attractive as Verena, so

Momma thought she could land a duke, and with both her daughters married into the English aristocracy, Momma hoped to crash through the upper barriers of New York society. To be frank, Alice neither wanted to marry a duke nor cared about New York society. Still, being in England was fun, and without doubt the English had style. Alice set great store by style.

Selecting an ivory fan trimmed with scarlet lace, to match the poppies on her hat, she wandered down the oak staircase and across the hall. Franklin Adams had style—after all, he was one of the Boston Adams—and meeting him on the Atlantic crossing had proved useful, because his circle of English friends was far wider and more interesting than the Mainwarings'. Through him Alice and her mother had met an impressive cross-section of London society, including Mr and Mrs Asquith. And everybody said that Mr Asquith would soon be the Prime Minister.

It was a heavenly day, the sun shimmering across the green parkland, over the patchwork quilt English landscape with its neatly hedged fields, and the rolling chalky Downs. On the flagged terrace of Frensham Manor the butler was issuing orders with curt waves of the hand, the maids were scurrying in and out loaded with trays, the ribbons of their caps flapping in the gentle breeze. Alice wondered why her sister bothered, eating out of doors was a bore, all those wasps swooping on the food, but dearest Verena was growing more English than the English. As they saw the sun so infrequently, she supposed they had to make obeisance when it appeared in all its glory.

Drifting through the rose garden, Alice settled herself comfortably in the chaise longue that one of the manservants had carried out. Beyond the rose garden, white figures were leaping around the immaculate green of the tennis court, and she heard Lord Algernon Hereford's braying voice, 'Well played, jolly good shot!' Why people were so obsessed with hitting balls across a net, or banging them along a golf course, Alice could not imagine.

Suffering rattlesnakes, that must have been the last shot because Lord Algy was lolloping towards her like an off-balance giraffe. Languidly, Alice fanned herself. 'Did you have a good game?'

'Tophole. Been even jollier if you had been my partner, what? I say, Miss Hartley, you *are* a picture, lyin' there like that. More beauteous than the most beauteous rose, what?'

The drawlin' noises that emanated from the mouths of some Englishmen truly were extraordinary. They never sounded a final 'g'. It was presumably to catch an idiot like him that Momma had brought her to England, for if not a duke, Lord Algy was the younger son of one.

'Off to change out of the old bags. See you at luncheon, eh?'

At luncheon she made sure she was not sitting next to Lord Algy, despite Momma's efforts, and concentrated her attention on the food. Verena had an excellent cook and it was a superb cold buffet, laid out in a manner to delight the eye as much as the stomach. Also, and surprisingly, the sun still shone.

The pigeon and raised game pies lay on silver salvers, hedged by mustard and cress, fronded lettuce leaves and scalloped tomatoes, while the rest of the main dishes looked down from silver pedestal plates; cold cutlets banking a mound of sweet garden peas, prawns *en bouquet* appearing like pink petals from their shrubbery of green vegetables, tumbler shapes of galantined cream chicken rising like futuristic buildings, plovers' eggs piled in a pyramid, larks *farcie* in an elaborate cake structure, ham piped with orange and lemon slices, boned capon feathery with glazed patterns. Topping the dishes were spouts of celery sculpted into the Prince of Wales's feathers. On a nearby table lay the bowls of trifle, the plates of meringues and éclairs, the fruit pies, the jugs of cream and mounds of fruit, kept fresh in constantly replenished ice.

'It's a question of hands, doncher know, how you touch, how you hold, that's what they respond to.' Franklin Adams glanced uneasily at Algy Hereford, and then gave Alice a conspiratorial smile—they were two Americans holding the fort in a friendly, yet alien, land. Algy Hereford's remarks could have connotations unsuitable for a mixed luncheon party, though with him presumably they referred to horses. 'Light hands, light control, that's the secret. Miss Hartley knows it well. What?'

Alice nodded demurely, though she was, Franklin by now appreciated, about as truly demure as an English sergeant-major. The first time he had seen her, standing against the *Oceanic*'s rail, waving 'goodbye' as the great liner slipped slowly from the berth at the North River pier on the stroke of midnight, a shaft of light had caught her exquisite profile and his pulse rate had quickened. Discreet enquiries of a steward had revealed that she was Miss Alice Hartley, a daughter of the man who owned a chain of cheap garment stores in New York and other eastern cities. Franklin had managed to effect an introduction—not a difficult feat as the mother was one of those dreadful matrons his country all too often bred, alas, a snob of the worst kind, trundling around like a very short-sighted rhinoceros, shouting at the top of her voice as if everyone else was deaf.

But Alice herself, ah, she was a different matter, her golden hair piled high, her laughter pealing out like golden bells, a high-spirited young foal who had no idea there were such things in the world as saddles, bits, bridles, reins or whips. For some months now, Franklin's mother had been reminding him that he was twenty-six and the moment had come for him to find a wife, rear a family and give thought to the Adams' long tradition of public service. Franklin had given himself until he was thirty to think of such things, but Alice Hartley might make a man change his mind. Apart from her stunning physical beauty, she had a touch of the outrageous in her personality—that hat on anybody but her would be downright vulgar—and breaking her in truly would be an enjoyable process.

Mrs Hartley's voice held forth with stentorian blast. It had been grinding away throughout the meal, boring the guests with her surprising hobby-horse, women's suffrage, regaling them with the contents of various letters received by the second post, and Franklin had been doing his best to ignore the unpleasant sound.

'Alice, my dear, I have made up my mind. We shall travel to Man-chest-er next weekend.' She gave the syllables equal stress, while the assembled party regarded her with expressions as glazed as the boned capon. 'That last letter of Miss Pankhurst's has convinced me. Without doubt, the worthwhile activity in the women's movement in this country is occurring not, as you might imagine, in London, but in Man-chest-er.'

Alice did not care where it was occurring. From her earliest conscious moments she had been dragged to rights-of-women tea parties, soirées, conventions and fund-raising parties, not forgetting their annual visit to Pilgrim *Mother's* Day. Alice had never met so many boring, earnest, humourless people as women suffragists and personally she did not give a fig about the vote.

'No thank you, Momma, I don't wish to come with you. In any case, I have been invited to Chadburn Hall next weekend.'

Franklin's sister was married to a duke, the Duke of Derbyshire, and she had issued the invitation.

Momma's podgy hand swept the air, stunning a fly which fell into a bowl of trifle, to emphasise her horror that her daughter should dare to disagree with her, and in front of their English friends! Before Alice could speak Frankie cut in fast, his Boss-town Bostonian accents at their bossiest.

'Why do we not all travel north next weekend? I am sure my sister will be delighted to have you join her guests, Mrs Hartley. Chadburn Hall is not far from Manchester. I am driving up in my motor car, as our friends over here call the automobile, so I can act as your chauffeur.'

A keen motorist, Franklin drove his own automobile, a Lanchester he had bought in London. Watching Momma's face, Alice saw the thought of staying with a real live duchess fighting the desire to keep her away from Franklin Adams, and correctly guessed which would win.

'Thank you, Mr Adams. We accept your kind offer.'

Bless Frankie! Alice returned her spoon to a bowl of strawberries and cream and he winked at her, the naughty man, so she winked back, acknowledging that he would

41

not allow her to be trapped into a visit to boring women suffragists in Manchester.

The evening sunlight was filtering through the layers of sooty smoke and after the long hot day the atmosphere in the narrow crowded streets was like a disgusting Turkish bath. Even walking the short distance from the tram-stop at All Saints to Sarah's lodgings had made the fine muslin of Kessie's dress cling to her body like glue.

As she climbed the stairs up to Sarah's room, yet again Kessie thought what a slice of luck the family's descent on The Laurels had been. For if Papa was unenthusiastic about her increasing involvement with the WSPU, he was even less keen on being told what he should do about his own daughter, so that the anticipated ban on Kessie's activities had not materialised. At the meeting she had just attended in Nelson Street, Mrs Pankhurst had told them they might be having American visitors, a Mrs and Miss Hartley, which everybody had agreed would be most interesting. When she reached the top landing, the key which, if she was out, Sarah normally left on the lintel, was missing, so Kessie tried the handle and the door opened.

It was Tom Whitworth, not his sister, who was inside the room. That he should be here was a surprise because he had not turned up in Manchester to have supper after all. The shock of his actual physical condition was electric. He was stripped to the waist, his shirt on the floor, his vest and braces hanging down his trousers, washing his naked torso in a tin bowl on the table. As Kessie came into the room he ducked his lathered face into the bowl and held out his left hand, 'Hello luv, give us the towel, will you?'

A threadbare towel was hanging on the back of the chair and silently Kessie passed it to him. He rubbed his face and hair and said, 'We're going to have to take positive action, Sal. There are now fifty thousand people on the verge of starvation in the Manchester area alone. We're the richest country in the world and those fat overfed gentlemen in the House of Commons can't find the time to pass the Unemployment Relief Bill. They're too busy debating the vital issue of a doctrinal dispute between the Scottish Free Churches and the United Free Churches of Scotland. . . .'

Kessie's brain was hearing his words but it was not absorbing them. No more than three feet away from him she stood, staring, staring, for she had never in her life seen a naked man. She had seen statues of naked men when Papa had taken her on a Continental tour to ease the pain of Mama's death, but they had been smooth, cold and white. Tom Whitworth's skin was warm—she could almost feel the heat of his body—brown and far from smooth. Kessie knew he had hairs on his wrists but now she saw that they extended up to his elbows and that he had hairs on his chest, too, fine black hairs that started just below his throat, fanning out to cover the curve of his breastbone, thick round his nipples, tapering to a silky black line round his navel, exposed by the slackness of his trousers.

At the back of her mind Kessie heard her friend Muriel's voice, giggling and secretive in their days at Manchester High School, 'I know something you don't know. My cousin told me. I know how to tell common men from gentlemen. Gentlemen have smooth soft skins. Common men have hairs on their chests.'

By that definition Tom Whitworth was no gentleman, but still Kessie watched, mesmerised, as he towelled himself. If she put out her hand she could touch the smooth parts of his brown flesh, the muscles rippling over his rib-cage as he rubbed his hair vigorously, the black hairs glittering in the evening sunlight.

Throwing down the towel, he opened his eyes and the wide welcoming smile slowly disappeared. Wildly, idiotically, Kessie thought of the Cheshire Cat, except he was a Lancashire tom-cat. For a few seconds she went on staring at him, his lips were half open, his tongue was running over his white even teeth and his dark eyes were travelling up and down her body. The blood was pumping through Kessie's veins, the muscles in her groin were contracting, the lurching sensations were turning her stomach over, she was incredibly conscious of her nipples, and she felt as if she were an iron filing being drawn irresistibly towards the magnet that was

Tom Whitworth. Every coherent thought had gone from her head, she knew only that she wanted to be in his arms, she wanted him to hold her, tightly, tightly, she wanted to feel his mouth on hers, she wanted him to touch every part of her body, and the sensations were so powerful, so all-enveloping, she thought she might faint and if he did touch her, if he moved towards her. . . .

Clasping her gloved hands in front of her, Kessie closed her eyes, waiting, wanting. Then she heard him saying, 'I'm sorry, Miss Thorpe, I should have locked the door.'

Opening her eyes, she saw him pulling up the grey vest and fastening the buttons at the neck, before bending down to pick up his flannel shirt and pull it over his head. Those incredible sensations were ebbing away and breathlessly Kessie said, 'I didn't realise you would be here, Mr Whitworth. I came to leave some books for Sarah.'

'I'll take them.' He had his braces back over his shoulders but the black hairs on his lower arms were still visible beneath the unbuttoned sleeve of the shirt. Even more breathlessly, Kessie said, 'Tell Sarah I'll see her in Mellordale tomorrow at the fair.'

She ran towards the door and shut it so hard that it flew open behind her, but she went on running down the dark stairs. Tom listened to the fading sound of her footsteps.

Briefly, he stood still, before crossing to the door which he shut and locked. Walking slowly back to the table, he ducked his head hard into the bowl again, letting the cold water drip down his face. Having re-towelled his hair, he threw himself on to Sarah's narrow bed and with his hands behind his neck stared up at the ceiling. Jesus! He'd wanted her and, by heck, he could have had her, there and then! Nice middle–class Miss Thorpe, standing staring at him like that.

From the moment they had met, nearly three months ago, in this room, Tom had been attracted to Kessie. Strictly speaking, she was not beautiful because her nose was too aquiline (like her father's), her chin too sharp, but she had a lovely complexion, her wide hazel eyes sparkled, her voice was delightfully husky and a woman's crowning glory was a softly upswept chestnut mass, with tendrils escaping past the lobes of her deliciously biteable ears. As for her figure, that was calculated to raise the blood pressure in any male, tall and slender, with a full rounded bosom swelling the folds of her blouses and dresses. There was something else, too, something extra, something different about Miss Kessie Thorpe. Perhaps it was her eagerness, or perhaps it was the mixture of assurance and shyness, of intelligence and naivety.

Lying on the bed, he imagined shagging her, and how fine it would be . . . but then he heard the tap-athump of heels and soles on the bare wooden stairs and at that pace it had to be Sarah. Rapidly, Tom buttoned up his shirt, knotted his tie, put on his jacket, and unlocked the door. When his sister came into the room, he was sitting reading from the beautiful leather-bound copy of *The Poetical Works of Percy Bysshe Shelley* that Kessie Thorpe had thrown on to the orange box. The book had fallen open at 'Peter Bell the Third' and Tom's eyes went to the bottom of the page:

> To believe their minds are given
> To make this ugly Hell a Heaven;
> In which faith they live and die.

How very apt! The world was before him, waiting to be changed by Tom Whitworth, future Member of Parliament —future Prime Minister? Kessie Thorpe had got under his skin but he would have to get her out because there was no place in his ambitions for an expensive, middle-class miss who had a father who would kill him as soon as look.

After he had explained about Kessie bringing the book, if not the precise circumstances, Sarah said, 'What are your plans for the weekend, Tom?'

'Why?'

'We've a big meeting at the Wakes Week fair tomorrow. There was trouble last week in Rawtenstall, so we could do with another strong arm. And you should hear Kessie. She's developing into a really fine speaker. You do like her, don't you? She's a spunky girl, if she is a bit posh.'

Tom said, yes, he thought Kessie Thorpe was a very spunky girl and—just to oblige his sister—he'd see about staying over for the fair.

4

By midday the sun was high in the sky, spreading a warm hazy light over Mellordale, glinting on the many-windowed cotton mills, softening the outlines of the tall chimney stacks and the rows of squat houses crammed into the valley. Kessie shut the wooden gate in the back garden of Aunt Ada's small house at the end of Milnrow, and climbed steadily up the lane to the fairground on the edge of the moor.

Aunt Ada was one of Papa's sisters and for years she had worked as a book-keeper in the family mill, but when Grandpapa Thorpe had suffered a stroke, as the only un-married daughter naturally she had left the mill to look after him. Three years ago Grandpapa had finally died, but instead of continuing to live in his big house by the mill, with the money he had left her Aunt Ada had bought herself a property in Milnrow. Everybody said that was most queer, living by yourself in a poky little house at the wrong end of town, but Aunt Ada had always kept herself to herself and Kessie suspected that after years of caring for Grandpapa—who had not been the best-tempered of invalids—her aunt was at last savouring her independence. She liked Aunt Ada, she presumed her aunt liked her because she was the only member of the family to be invited regularly to Milnrow, and she always came up for the Wakes Week fair.

Wakes Weeks were peculiar to Lancashire, their origins lost in the mists of pagan festivals and later hiring fairs, but nowadays in turn the Pennine cotton towns more or less shut up shop for a week each year and made merry. Of all the Wakes Weeks fairs, that of The Dales—the three towns

46

of Upperdale, Mellordale and Lowtondale were known collectively as The Dales—held on the moor above Mellordale, was the biggest. But the knowledge that she was not attending today solely to enjoy herself was making Kessie tense, and the hope or fear that Tom Whitworth might be here even tenser. What would she say to him if he was? What must he have thought of her, standing there looking at him practically naked?

Long before she reached the gap in the stone-piled wall that led on to Mellordale moor, she heard the jolly repetitive strains of the steam-organs and the stirring brass of the Salvation Army band. As she turned through the gap, the tambourines were rattling and the Army lads and lasses were beating out their version of 'Champagne Charlie'— 'Bless His name and He sets me free . . .' Kessie's spirits rose. For the last thirty years, the Salvation Army had been fighting the good fight, taking its message to the people, and now the WSPU was doing the same—though not, she hoped, for thirty years!

The fair was spread wide across the hassocky grey-green moorland, stalls, booths, amusements, the crowds were gathering and the voices of the fairground people were rising in competition. On the merry-go-rounds the children were clutching the iron poles that transfixed the brightly painted horses, shouting with pleasure as the wooden animals whirled in their circle, stiffly yet smoothly, up and down, up and down, the punt-shaped swings were sailing high into the warm air and the muffin man was pushing his way through the throngs. Balancing his tray on his head, he was ringing his bell and the children were following him, holding stones on their heads and shouting, 'Ding dong! Ding dong!'

'Kessie!'

Sarah's small figure came towards her and, oh joy, behind her was her brother, his black hair untidy in the breeze (flouting convention, he never wore a hat). Kessie felt herself blushing, but he greeted her as if nothing had happened in Sarah's room, which actually she found a bit disappointing. The children deserted the muffin man, flocking towards

Tom: 'Coom and 'ave a game of cricket, Tom.' Shaking his head, he laughed and the black locks tumbled further on to his forehead, and Kessie forgot her disappointment, delighted by his obvious popularity.

As they wandered round the delights of the fair, the children followed him like the Pied Piper. He joked and chatted to them (Kessie could never think what to say to children), he even picked a crying baby from its mother's arms and made it chuckle. He took a sixpence from his pocket and spun it in the air, catching it in his left hand, 'Heads or tails?' Half the children shouted 'Heads', the other half, 'Tails', he gave the sixpenny piece to them and they rushed to the food stalls. Except that several of them, Kessie saw, were left behind because they had braces on their legs or their feet in ugly surgical boots. She took a half crown from her reticule and gave it to the most crippled little girl, who looked at the coin as if it frightened her. 'Share it among your friends.' The children stuffed themselves with Bakewell tarts and Maids of Honour and parkin and treacle toffee and mint humbugs and sherbet dips and Sarah said she shouldn't have given them so much, they'd be sick. Kessie admitted that she had never noticed before how many children were crippled.

She saw Tom stiffen. 'Have you not, Miss Thorpe? They're suffering from rickets because their mothers' bodies were under-nourished and now they are too.' They were walking past the ranks of lay preachers standing on their soap-boxes shouting that damnation and the eternal roasting fires of hell awaited all who did not repent of their evil ways and come to Jesus, and Tom looked up and said, 'It's not the hell in the next world that concerns me. It's the hell in this.'

Then he relaxed and smiled at her. 'That's why I'm a Socialist, Miss Thorpe. I know what it's like to be at the bottom of the heap, to have no choice or voice of your own, to be told what's good for you, to be denied a decent education, to be kicked out of your job, thrown out of your house, to see your family starving, to watch them die because you can't afford medical care. The wealth of this country *is* generated by its workers and at long last we have founded our party and when we have power we shall have a basic minimum wage for everybody, a first-class health service, a first-class education system, and decent houses. . . .' He waved his left arm down across the valley. 'How can you expect people to lift their eyes unto the hills,' the arm swept over the moors towards Netherstone Edge, 'when they live in disgusting hovels from the day they're born and they're starved of beauty just as much as bread?'

Sarah nudged her. 'Don't mind him. He goes on like this all the time.' There was deep pride in her voice and, as far as Kessie was concerned, he could go on like this for ever, the deep resonant voice thrilling her ears and exalting her spirit.

They had reached the elevated boxing ring where a line of men stood waiting to part with their pennies to test their strength against the professionals, hoping to win the purse of two shining gold sovereigns. The little boys urged Tom to have a go but Sarah said, 'He'll do no such thing. All you lads can think on is bashing each other to pulp.'

The barkers were out-barking each other, promising wonders beyond belief inside the booths. 'Such sights as you have never seen, ladies and gentlemen. Only an 'apenny to come in and a farthing for the littl'uns.' A strong man in a leopard skin tunic was flexing his muscles, an enormously fat lady was standing immobile like a gargantuan basilisk, by her side a midget was poking a monkey chained to a pole to make it run up and down, a young girl in a pink ballet skirt was holding a sad-looking brown bear on a chain, and a fire-eater was taking an occasional gulp from the flames. But it was the faces and the clothes of the watching crowds that Kessie noticed, that Tom had made her notice, so many of them thin and pinched, and their garments so shabby and threadbare.

As they walked beyond the booths, the blacksmiths there were hammering the hot metal, the farriers shoeing the patient horses, the tinkers banging away mending pots and pans and kettles, and a diddicoy girl pushed a tray of cheap trinkets towards Tom. 'Buy something for your lady friends. You'll not regret it.'

He asked Sarah what she would like, she said, nothing,

and the diddicoy girl's ear-rings rattled with anger. Tom said, 'Oh, come on, Sal,' and the girl fluttered her eyelashes at him. After a great deal of protest, Sarah accepted a brooch. Then he said, 'May I buy you a memento of the occasion, Miss Thorpe?'

Kessie knew she was blushing hideously and her voice emerged in its poshest tones. 'Oh, how nice of you, Mr Whitworth. Thank you.'

Still confused, she chose a thin gilt necklace hung with bits of red glass shaped into horseshoes, not because she would ever wear it in public, but because it could be worn under her dresses.

'Come on,' said Sarah. 'We've work to do.'

They had. But Kessie wished the afternoon could have lasted for ever, just as it was, wandering around with Tom, and Sarah, of course.

The WSPU lorry was a stout wooden cart, drawn up not far from the black-stone wall that bounded the moorland. Christabel and the others were nailing the Women's Social and Political Union posters to its front, handing out leaflets, telling people to be here at three o'clock sharp.

Kessie asked, 'Any news of our American visitors?'

'No. Mother only said she *might* bring them up, if they wanted to see us in action. They hadn't arrived when I left Nelson Street.'

When everything was ready, Kessie held up her tortoise-shell hand-mirror for Christabel to check her appearance; Sarah, who scorned such personal preparations, climbed briskly up into the lorry; while her brother and other ILP male stalwarts stationed themselves round it in case of trouble. On the dot of three o'clock Christabel started to speak to the gratifyingly large crowd that had assembled.

'My name is Christabel Pankhurst and I am studying to be a lawyer. Did I hear somebody shout "Why?" Why not? The university thinks I will be a good lawyer. Yes, they do. And so do I.' The crowd laughed at her pleasantly playful assurance. 'This is my friend Sarah Whitworth who is a teacher and whom some of you already know.' There were murmurs of recognition. 'And this is my friend Kessie

Thorpe whom some of you also know.' There was a surprised murmur and heads craned to obtain a better view of Charles Thorpe's pretty young daughter. 'What none of us can be at the moment, nor any of you ladies, is a voter. Why not, if we can work in the mills and teach and be lawyers? We want to tell you why we claim the franchise. . . .'

From the lane beyond the wall came a meshing, grinding noise that exploded into a loud bang as thick white steam billowed above the piled black stones. The children were the first to move, scampering excitedly towards the entrance gap in the wall, and the crowd surged after them. As her audience disappeared, Christabel stood for a moment in injured astonishment, her finger still upraised, before she and her friends climbed from the lorry and jostled their way to the front of the crowd.

In the lane there was a large bottle-green motor car, with clouds of steam pouring from its bonnet. A man, presumably the chauffeur, had clambered from the driving seat and was holding out his hand through the swirling vapour to three women sitting in the back. In his thick leather coat, cap and goggles, he looked like a creature from a Jules Verne novel. One of the women was Mrs Pankhurst who, despite the situation, retained her gracious composure, but the lady by her side was anything but composed. In her voluminous flapping motoring coat she had the appearance of a disintegrating barrel and she was complaining in a curious nasal whine, 'Oh my, oh Mrs Pankhurst, my goodness, is this the place? Oh my. . . .'

The third lady was young and as unruffled as Mrs Pankhurst. Taller and slimmer than Kessie, her gloved hands were brushing specks from her golden silk-gaberdine motoring coat, when from the far side of the field the Salvation Army band went into their version of 'Marching Through Georgia'—'Shout aloud salvation and we'll have another song. . . .' The young lady lifted up her head and her laughter pealed out. 'Oh, Frankie, just listen to that! Isn't that just the cutest thing?'

Kessie turned to Sarah: 'I think our American friends have arrived!'

The excitement spread like the vapour trail from the Lanchester's bonnet. Children clustered round the motor car and when the crowd realised why they had come—'All the way from Amurrica to hear them girls speak'—far more of them than before gathered in front of the wspu lorry.

Christabel's eyes sparkled. 'To our posts, Mrs Pankhurst's missionaries. Let's get at 'em before they retreat!' She, Sarah and Kessie climbed hastily back into the waggon and her clear voice stilled the murmurs, 'Welcome to our American friends who like you are *longing* to know why we claim the franchise!'

The speeches were brisk, emphasising the basic theme that the vote was wanted to help all women, but particularly working women who were the most exploited and therefore the most in need of its protection. Christabel delighted her audience when a persistent male heckler called out, 'Don't you wish you was a man?', and without hesitation she called back, 'No. Do you?'

It was Kessie's turn and she was horribly nervous. Why had she, the least experienced, the least witty speaker, been left to provide the final flourish? She mustn't let Christabel down, she mustn't let her sex down, particularly not in front of their American visitors. She took a deep breath, her husky voice hesitated, then rang out melodiously and she knew she was carrying the audience with her.

Out of the corner of her eye she saw an elderly man in an old-fashioned stovepipe hat and black coat buttoned high into his neck. She had noticed him as they walked round the fair, the Ancient Mariner among the lay preachers. Now he was pushing his way to the front and his powerful voice shrieked at her like the winter wind over the moors.

'I suffer not a woman to teach, nor to usurp authority over the man, but to be in silence. They have begun to wax wanton against Christ. And withal they learn to be idle, wandering about from house to house, and not only idle, but tattlers also, and busybodies, speaking things which they ought not. I will therefore that the younger women marry, bear children, guide the house. For some are already turned to Satan. So said St Paul.'

52

Kessie was so angry she could have leapt from the waggon and hit him. How dare he quote St Paul at her in the year 1905?

'Speaking things I ought not? On the contrary, sir.' Her voice deepened with passionate fury. 'I am speaking of things which have been deliberately left unspoken for untold centuries. . . .'

But his words had roused a section of the crowd and youths were surging forward. 'Ay, that's what you want, luv, soom bairns. They'd soon shut you up.' 'What's a slip of a lass standing up theer for, telling uzz what *she* wants?' 'What she wants is a man!' 'Give uzz a kiss, luv!'

The ILP male stalwarts were struggling to hold back the roughnecks and Kessie heard Tom shout, 'Get to the back of the lorry, Miss Thorpe.' He had called to her, she realised, not to Sarah or Christabel. But how ugly the men's faces below her were, twisted with rage, venom spitting from their lips. How terrifyingly suddenly the mood had changed. And all this, Kessie thought with astounded horror, merely because women were asking for the vote?

The preacher's voice rose above the tumult: 'The man is the image and glory of God, but the woman is the glory of man. For man is not of the woman, but the woman of the man. Neither was man created for woman; but the woman for the man.'

In the mêlée, Kessie saw Miss Hartley lam out at him with her parasol and in astonishment he stepped back. But as she hit out, she lost her footing and fell heavily to the ground where she lay, quite still, her golden coat spreading around her. Abruptly, the mood changed again, to a resentful, disgusted shame, and people stared down uneasily at the inert body. Kessie jumped from the lorry, with Sarah and Christabel behind her, and they ran towards Miss Hartley, but her mother was there before them, sinking on her knees in the trampled grass. 'Oh my God! Oh, my Alice! You've killed her! You murdering barbarians! You've killed my daughter!'

Her daughter lifted a face smeared with mud. 'Nobody's killed me, Momma. I've twisted my ankle or something.'

53

The chauffeur pushed his way through the crowd and scooped her up into his arms. In an icy American-accented voice, he said, 'That was the most disgraceful scene it has been my misfortune to witness.' He strode away across the grass and Kessie heard Tom Whitworth muttering, 'What a sheltered life you've led.'

She ran after the Hartleys and their rather peculiar chauffeur. Introducing herself, she said, 'My aunt lives just down the lane. Would you care to come there until we can organise things?'

Summoned by her niece's frantic knocking, Aunt Ada stood on the back doorstep of Milnrow, watching the approaching procession. In her black bombasine dress, with her grey hair scraped into a bun, her pince-nez clipped to her nose, she looked formidable, but after listening to Kessie's voluble explanation, she rose calmly to the occasion.

'They'd best come in and make themselves comfortable.'

One by one, Mr Adams (whose true identity had now been revealed), Miss Hartley, her mother, the Pankhursts and the Whitworths came in through her back gate, past her prize arum lilies, and were introduced.

In the back room Mr Adams gently lowered Miss Hartley on to the sofa. Sarah examined the ankle, briskly giving her opinion that it was only a slight sprain which would be as right as rain within a few days, before wrapping it in a dampened bandage. Tom Whitworth disappeared with Mr Adams and they returned to say a telegram had been sent to the Duke and Duchess of Derbyshire, three rooms had been booked for the night at the Mellor Arms, and the motor car was being repaired. Excited that Tom was here, determined to prove to their American friends that not all Lancastrians were barbarians, Kessie went into the kitchen—a novel experience for her—to help Aunt Ada prepare the tea.

Despite the throb in her ankle, Alice was enjoying herself. Her fury over Momma's pigheaded insistence on her company at the fair and Franklin's surprising capitulation had vanished the minute they had arrived in that ridiculous fashion to the strains of 'Marching Through Georgia'.

Deepest Lancashire was a foreign land, with most of its inhabitants speaking a foreign language, but it had a vitality she hadn't met before in England and all in all she was having a most exciting afternoon. While Franklin had a wash, Mr Whitworth offered to carry her into the front parlour of this cute little house, an offer she accepted because he was a fascinating young man. Very tall and dark, almost black eyes, dreadful clothes and the peculiar local accent, but he had a style of his own, no doubt about that.

High tea—that was what old Miss Thorpe called it—was charmingly laid in the front parlour, on a round table spread with an exquisitely crocheted cloth. As usual Alice was hungry, so she sampled all the potted meats and chutneys, the scones, the teacakes and griddle cakes, the jams and crab-apple jelly. Old Miss Thorpe (she must be in her late fifties) kept asking Kessie to pass this and that to their guests and eventually Alice said, 'Where did you get the name "Kessie"? It's very pretty, but unusual, surely?'

Young Miss Thorpe paused at the directness of the question, but she had style too: nice bosom, slim waist, willowy height, shining eyes, well-cut shantung suit in a delicate shade of apricot that cleverly complemented her glossy chestnut hair, and a pleasant openness.

'Ah, thereby hangs a tale! A few hours before my birth my father was here in Mellordale. It was a beautiful New Year's day, so he decided to have a walk on the moors. Well, he happened to see a kestrel hovering in the sky and on his way back through the graveyard he also noticed a head-stone that a grieving husband had just had erected to his beloved wife Kessie. Then I arrived that very afternoon and his wild kestrel Kessie I had to be.'

'What a nice story!' Alice laughed delightedly.

A brief, polite smile cracked Franklin's lips. Sitting ramrod straight in one of the polished oak chairs—the house might be ridiculously small, but the furniture was good—clearly he was itching to leave. Serve him right for bending to Momma's wishes, Alice thought, and she per-sonally had no desire to go yet, so he could just wait.

The unexpectedly delicious meal finished, Mrs Pankhurst

and Momma's voices started to rise in polite disputation. '. . . among *our* colonies, the women of New Zealand and Australia have won their right to vote. A few of your far-flung, mid-western states may have been equally sensible, but how many of your eastern states have? It is surely in the *east* of your country that the centres of population and power lie?'

Mrs Hartley frowned because that was true and none of the eastern states had given women the vote. 'I was only pointing out that women's suffrage can be won without our descending to aggressive masculine behaviour. And just wondering if your tactics might not be questionable. . . .'

'Really?' Mrs Pankhurst paced towards the small bay window where she swung round. 'I had understood you were a supporter of women's rights, Mrs Hartley.'

'I most surely am but . . .'

Alice hid her amusement. It *was* fun to see Momma on the defensive for once, trapped in her have-it-both-ways position—for in the gospel according to Momma and her friends, women were to have the same rights as men, yet they were to continue to behave and be treated like ladies and to make advantageous marriages to dukes and such-like.

'We have been polite and persuasive for years and years and years, Mrs Hartley.' Kessie Thorpe was speaking now, with passionate conviction. 'So deeds, not words, is now our motto.'

'Deeds, not words,' Alice clapped her hands, 'I like that!'

With surprise and slight alarm, Franklin regarded her. Surely she hadn't become a convert to this militant women's movement? Then he dismissed the idea. Like a flower to the sun, she responded to temporary excitement and he truly could not see Alice, who enjoyed the good things of life, and, if truth be told, was a spoiled young lady who wanted her bottom spanking occasionally, standing in a cart or mixing with louts like the Whitworth fellow. Having never been so close to a society lady in his life, the lout was eyeing Alice with an ill-concealed, ill-bred admiration, and the sooner they left this house and these people, the better.

Alice herself could not say she had become a convert, but as Momma's enthusiasm for the Pankhursts and their tactics was diminishing, by golly, hers was rising. She was impressed by these women, especially the crystalline Christabel who said little but had a magnetism all her own. Not forgetting Tom who was saying, 'They don't meet Bible fundamentalists every day of the week, Mrs Hartley, thank the Lord. Still, St Paul does have one heck of a lot to answer for.'

He smiled at Alice, acknowledging her righteous anger at the preacher's ludicrous attitude. He *was* attractive, disturbingly, differently so, flaunting his masculinity before her in a way that none of her New York beaux had dared.

Kessie watched Tom Whitworth smiling and chatting to Alice Hartley, and jealousy stabbed her. Miss Hartley was not only a most glorious creature, and one who wore her superb clothes as if she had been poured into them, but she also had a casual confidence, a naturalness of manner, that outmatched even Christabel's. But maybe Tom was only being polite, and what claim had she on him anyway, just because he had bought her a cheap necklace and cared enough to order her to the back of the lorry?

Mrs Pankhurst and Mrs Hartley were still sitting arguing when suddenly Christabel's voice stopped them. 'We shall not rest until an Act of Parliament is on the statute book giving women the vote. And if we have to take further action that you may consider unladylike, Mrs Hartley, we shall do so!'

5

Suffering rattlesnakes! Alice's new Lancashire friends had taken the further action Momma would consider unladylike, and how!

From the moment Alice had met them, she'd had a feeling in her bones that the Manchester group was one to watch—which was perhaps why, before they left that little house in Mellordale, she'd given Kessie Thorpe her visiting card.

Fascinating and faithful a correspondent as Kessie had become, she had not said one single word about *this* escapade, so Alice devoured the morning newspapers before sending off a congratulatory telegram which also demanded to know the inside story.

Two days later the letter with the Manchester postmark and Kessie's stylish round handwriting arrived. Frensham Manor by then was in an uproar, maids whirling around like autumn leaves, even the butler looking agitated, because Mr and Mrs Asquith had finally accepted her sister's frequently extended invitations to visit, and Verena was in one of her states. Alice escaped into the comparative peace of her brother-in-law Lionel's study, where she slit open the envelope and read through the letter.

> The Laurels,
> Whalley Range,
> Manchester.
> 17th October, 1905

Dearest Alice,

Bless you for your telegram which Christabel will see as soon as she comes out of prison. How extraordinarily that reads! Herewith, as requested, the inside report from your special correspondent.

Some time ago, we decided we must take drastic action to focus attention on the question of 'votes for women'. We settled on making our stand during 'Liberal Week' at the Free Trade Hall, because the big-wig politicians would be there, and the Liberals are certain to form the Government after the next General Election.

Incidentally, are you impressed by our new clarion cry, 'Votes for Women'? We dreamed it up almost by accident, in the back garden of the Pankhursts' house of all un-dramatic places, when we were trying to decide what to paint on the banner Christabel and Annie Kenney were taking with them to the Free Trade Hall. 'Women's Suffrage' makes our opponents say 'Go on suffering' and stupid things like that, 'Women's Enfranchisement' sounds pompous, and we were talking about votes and women and, hey presto, we'd found our slogan.

Votes for women! Its inspired simplicity (if I say so myself) has already caught on.

Anyway, on the great night I just had to sit quiet because Christabel said it would be better to have one middle-class girl (herself) and one working-class girl (Annie Kenney) going into action, rather than two middle-class girls (her and me), to show that we represent *all* women. She thinks about political things like that which, I must admit, never enter my head. Merely being an onlooker, however, was almost as nerve-racking as actually standing up and inter-rupting the famous Sir Edward Grey in full flow.

I cannot describe the sensation it produced, Alice, two young women daring to stand up at a public meeting, to interrupt an important politician and to keep on asking the question the Liberals on the platform refused to answer—will they give women the vote once they are back in power?

After Christabel and Annie had been dragged from the arena, the police said they could go home, so do you know what Christabel did to turn words into deeds? She actually *spat* at the police inspector. It was the gentlest spray, like the froth of the cuckoo spit flower, but can *you* imagine spitting at a policeman, Alice?

59

In court the next morning, after the magistrate had sentenced Christabel and Annie, Mrs Pankhurst became rather weepy and said they had done enough and she would pay their fines. In case you don't know—to be honest, I didn't until the other day—if you're sentenced in a police court, you have the choice either to pay your fine and promise to be bound over to keep the peace, or to go to prison. Christabel said if her mother paid her fine, she would never speak to her again, and so off to prison she and Annie went. What wonderful, courageous souls they are!

Mark my words, as my father is fond of saying, 13th October, 1905, will go down in the annals of British history as the day the female sex finally stood on its hind legs to demand its rights. There can be no going back to the slave state now. It's onwards all the way!

I must dash, Alice, because we are rushing around like mad things, organising protest meetings, etcetera.

Fondest love,

Your exhausted but exhilarated friend,

Kessie.

Alice was feeling quite exhilarated herself, though she still failed to understand why the vote was so important. She was just telling herself that modern-day girls had no need to mark their crosses on a ballot paper to prove their emancipation when there was a knock on the study door and one of the maids said, 'Please excuse me, Miss Hartley, but Mr Adams has arrived.'

With her golden smile, Alice greeted Franklin, firmly closing the door on the domestic turmoil outside. 'It's all your fault, you know, all this fuss, for introducing Verena to the Asquiths. My poor dear sister imagines that she'll be able to persuade Mr Asquith into giving Lionel a job in the next Liberal Government. She *is* an optimist.'

Why her sister had married Sir Lionel Mainwaring, Alice could not now think. Apart from his title and his undoubted devotion to her and the children, he was an absolute ninny and, as a Liberal Member of Parliament, doomed to remain for ever on the back benches. Why Mr and Mrs Asquith had accepted the invitation, however, Alice *could* think. Noisy, outrageous Margot liked her American spunk and clever old Herbert Henry liked her, period. The glances his sleepy eyes gave her reminded Alice of some of her father's friends back home, when they chucked her chin or patted her behind.

Ignoring her comments on Verena—he was frightfully well-bred—Franklin said, 'After luncheon, why do we not go for a ride?'

Alice accepted the invitation for it was the most glorious afternoon, the sky the brightest blue, the sun butter bright, the air clean as new-washed linen. As they galloped across the Downs, Alice felt a pang of home-sickness, a longing for the Fall days on the Hudson River or in Connecticut, because it was American weather, not the hazy light that usually enveloped England, even on its better days. On the ridge above the manor house, Franklin reined in his mare and Alice brought her horse to a gentle trot. Below them the sea was a blue mill-pond in the bright light, the sun gleaming on the chalk cliffs, while inland the toy-town village of Frensham nestled in the fold of hedged fields and copses.

'It's a pretty little country, isn't it? I like England.'

They halted. Franklin dismounted and tethered his mare, then he came towards Alice, lifted her from her horse and went down on one knee. She looked at him, trying not to laugh. 'What *are* you doing, Frankie?'

'I am asking you to marry me, my dearest Alice. Will you say yes, and may I speak to your father on my return home?'

His voice was pleasant but it had a complacent tone as if he considered her answer a foregone conclusion.

She smiled at him. 'Do get up, dear Frankie. It's sweet of you, but I don't want to marry yet.'

Very slowly, Franklin rose to his feet and stood looking down at Alice, or as far down as he could manage because he was only an inch taller than she. His long, well-bred face was rigid, as if carved in stone and Alice thought, oh poor lamb, he is positively astounded and I don't suppose it entered his sleek head that anybody would refuse a scion of the Boston Adams. Then emotion began to break the petri-fied stare. Clearly Frankie was angry, so she thought she

61

had better explain that her refusal had nothing to do with him personally.

'I'm sure I will marry you one day, Frankie, but just at the moment I want to be free, I want to live my life to the full.' His face was growing longer, astonishment mixing with the anger. 'If we were married, you wouldn't want me to go off by myself, doing what I wanted, now would you?' He shook his head and Alice said triumphantly, 'There you are then.'

Franklin failed to see what on earth a virginal girl could mean by living her life to the full. He was extremely angry. How dare the daughter of a *tradesman* refuse his offer of marriage? Did she not appreciate the honour he was bestowing, the world he would lead her into *permanently*? Did she not, for God's sake, realise how furious his family would be, how greatly he would need to twist his mother's arm to persuade her to accept a *tradesman's* daughter?

She was smiling at him, that bewitching golden smile. 'We're wintering in Egypt, Frankie, and Poppa's joining us there, so I will mention your proposal to him.' *Mention* it to him! Such condescension. Franklin could have throttled that beautiful slender neck. 'We shall be back in England in the early summer because Verena's *enceinte* again, you know, and the baby's due then. Will you be over here in the summer? I'm twenty-one in July and I'd love you to be at my coming-of-age-ball. I might think about our engagement when I'm twenty-one.'

That charming, imperious, innocent, thoughtless manner was what he loved about Alice and breaking her in truly would be exciting. He smiled his agreement to their engagement next July.

In her study in the turret of The Laurels, with the gas-fire a purring orange glow, Kessie refilled her gold-plated fountain pen, a Waterman Papa had brought back from a business trip to the United States. Even here the fog was infiltrating, slipping through the window joints, lying in still wreaths around the lamp on her desk. The lamp was electric, Papa having had the gas mantles ripped out and miles of wiring installed, with lights that responded to the flick of a switch.

Signing her latest letter to Alice, addressing the envelope to the Poste Restante in Cairo, on a clean white sheet of paper, Kessie wrote: *Women's Social and Political Union* and underneath that *Why Working-Women Claim the Vote*. With a ruler she neatly underlined both headings. On another sheet of paper she tried various signatures, 'Kessie Whitworth', 'Mrs Tom Whitworth', 'Mrs E. T. F. Whitworth'. His Christian names were Ernest Thomas Feargus, chosen by his father in honour of three noted Chartist leaders, Ernest Jones, Thomas Cooper and Feargus O'Connor, and they'd agreed it was a good job his mother had settled for 'Tom'. He had gipsy blood in him which accounted for the dark skin and hair and was so romantic. His maternal grandmother, a full-blooded gipsy, had run off with a *gauja*, which Tom said meant non-gipsy, though his descriptions of the disastrous union were less romantic.

In the New Year he was going to London, to work for the Labour Representation Committee in the General Election, which was a wonderful step up the ladder. She didn't know how she would live without him, however, for over the last few months she had been spending an increasing amount of time in his company. Although she had kept this from her father, since the fearful row after Christabel's heroic, historic interruption in the Free Trade Hall, she had made it quite clear to him that she was no longer a child.

'We have put votes for women on the map. Hundreds of people are flocking to our banner. I have no intention of giving up my work for the great cause. If you want me to leave The Laurels, I shall.'

Papa had roared, 'Don't you speak to me like that, miss,' but after another outburst he had subsided and he did not now demand to know where she was going or with whom.

Meeting Sarah had opened her eyes to the true nature of the world around her, but in Tom's company her every emotion was heightened, her awareness, her sensitivity, her understanding. It wasn't that he was more intelligent, articulate, caring or compassionate than his sister or Christabel or Mrs Pankhurst or any of her new friends. It wasn't because he was a man . . . of course it was because he was a man, the most exciting man she had ever met, with an incredible confidence in himself and the future. *And* he had a sense of humour, an apparently rare attribute among Socialists who mostly seemed to believe that you could not possibly be serious-minded, yet still find life funny.

Since those moments in Sarah's room, nothing like *that* had happened—they were rarely alone, of course, and never in private—but occasionally she saw Tom looking at her with that same expression on his face and she knew he loved her. Staring out of the window at the thickening brown mass of the fog, Kessie ran her hands over her breasts, touching her nipples through the fine serge of her afternoon dress. What would it be like to feel his long fingers on her breasts?

She had been reading or re-reading several novels such as *Madame Bovary* and *Anna Karenina*, and surreptitiously she had borrowed one of the housemaid Doris's copies of *Dainty Novels* and *My Pocket Novels*. It was clear from Flaubert and Tolstoy that both men and women had passionate physical desires, if in Doris's novels the women merely swooned with love, though they were nice because they always had happy endings which Tolstoy and company did not. But not even proper literature explained what sort of feelings women had *inside* them, nor what men and women actually did together. Kessie was desperate to know whether her strong desire for Tom was natural and what precisely would happen if . . . when . . . but there was nobody she could talk to about that sort of thing. Not even Sarah. After all, she was Tom's sister.

Whatever Papa or her relations might say or do she wanted to marry him, she wanted to be his wife, his love, his comrade-in-arms, fighting for the splendid new Jerusalem until death did them part. He had no money, but soon, when she was twenty-one, she would be quite a rich young woman. So there was nothing to prevent them getting married. Except that Tom had to ask her. But first she had to ask him to her twenty-first birthday party and to make sure he accepted the invitation. A trembling bank of fog was lying above the electric lamp, it reminded Kessie of the smoke from Tom's perpetual, hand-rolled cigarettes, and there and then she decided she would have her party at The Laurels, not at the Midland Hotel as Papa had suggested, because Tom would be more likely to attend an informal gathering in her home.

The day before her twenty-first birthday, Kessie was convinced she had made a fearful mistake. Hotels were much better at these things. The house was in chaos, carpenters noisily constructing a dais for the orchestra, furniture being dragged around, caterers and florists toing and froing and arguing with Papa, the fearful noise of the British Vacuum Cleaner that he had insisted on buying for Sheba reverberating across the hall. Nothing would be ready in time. The beastly fog, as thick and damp as the wettest blanket, had been around since Christmas, and Tom Whitworth had not definitely accepted her invitation.

Everything *was* ready in time. The fog lifted and stars were bright in the night sky as the carriages jingled round the driveway, and one or two motor cars delivered their occupants, and Kessie and Papa stood at the door to receive their guests. Eventually she saw Sarah's small figure coming round the bend, on foot naturally, with Tom behind her, and Kessie's heart thudded with happiness. Not merely because he had come but because he looked so stunningly handsome in the full evening dress suit, white shirt, starched white bib, white bow-tie, black waistcoat, black tails and shiny black leather shoes that Sarah had promised, if he came, to bully him into renting.

Kessie's fears that her two sets of friends, the confident articulate 'new women' and the more conventional ones, might not mix were unfounded. Several of her relations had known Mrs Pankhurst when she was Emmeline Goulden and they were soon discussing the old days.

Her efforts to persuade Tom to dance were not so successful, however. Boldly, she swept into a curtsey.

'I claim the hostess's privilege. Will you have the next dance with me?' When he said he didn't know how to, she laughed.

'But I thought all gipsies danced!'

'In the dew-wet grass, round the camp-fire, with gold rings in their ears?'

He turned away. Kessie could have wept at her tactlessness. Somehow during the course of the evening she had to speak to him alone, if only to thank him for his astounding birthday present. Unobtrusively she followed his movements and, oh joy, later she saw him walking, by himself, out into the hall. Slipping after him, Kessie took a very deep breath because she knew she was behaving outrageously, and managed to waylay him outside Papa's study.

Forgoing the cigarette he'd had in mind, Tom allowed himself to be drawn into the study. The curtains were open and moonlight silvered the walls hung with mahogany-framed glass cases, in which rows of butterflies were neatly pinned. Once inside Kessie backed awkwardly away from him and crossed to the desk, switching on the lamp. Laughing breathlessly, she said, 'I just wanted to thank you for your absolutely wonderful present. It's, well, you couldn't have given me anything I'd treasure more.'

'I know you like Shelley and *The Masque of Anarchy* seemed particularly appropriate.'

'Oh, it's absolutely appropriate. "Rise like lions after slumber, In unvanquishable number!" If you substitute "lionesses", that's us!' Lovingly fingering the binding of the privately printed 1819 edition of the poem—where had Tom found it?—Kessie knew that was why he had chosen it.

He was standing very still, his face half hidden in the shadows, so she couldn't see his expression clearly. She laughed again, nervously, because he was moving slowly towards her, the glow from the lamp caught his eyes and they were very bright. Did he think she had invited him into the room to . . . had she? His fingers coiled round a strand of hair that had strayed from her elaborate coiffure down her neck. Shivering from the touch, she gazed at the black hairs on his wrist.

Tom gazed at her. In an off-the-shoulder ball gown of some silky pale green colour that brought out the green in her

66

hazel eyes she was ravishingly beautiful. Was she forward, bringing him in here like this, or was she simply an innocent? He reminded himself that she had a ferocious father, and that he must do nothing to jeopardise his new career prospects.

The words were tumbling from her: 'Christabel says Manchester isn't the centre of the world, even if we think it is. Mrs Pankhurst says we may have to carry the torch to London. Annie Kenney's volunteered to go to London as our torch-bearer, to sound the ground. And I'm mixing my metaphors and . . .'

'Kessie, stop talking.' Desire was rising hard in Tom. He slipped his arms around her waist and felt the stiffness of her corsets, he moved his mouth across hers and felt the softness of her lips.

Panic filled Kessie. This was the moment she had dreamed of. She was in Tom's arms, his lips were on hers, but she did not know what to do and she was still clutching *The Masque of Anarchy* in her right hand. The pressure of his lips was growing, his grip on her body was tightening, he was bending back her head with the force of his mouth, her body was arching against his and his was incredibly hard and strong.

The Masque of Anarchy fell to the floor with a thud.

Tom's tongue was between her lips, she could barely breathe, she felt as if she were on top of a volcano and the lava was pouring all over her. His hands were moving up and down her back, touching her bare flesh, he was holding her even more tightly, their bodies were swaying together and the focus of the ecstasy moved to that place between her legs.

'Kess, darling Kess, oh God Kess, I want you. . . .'

'Who is in there?'

It was Papa's voice, the door handle was turning, and they jumped apart. To hide her confusion, Kessie bent down to the floor to pick up *The Masque of Anarchy*. By the door, Charles Thorpe clicked the electric light switch. There was no need to ask what his daughter had been doing; the flushed faces, the panting breath and the glittering eyes told

67

him. Kessie was an innocent young fool and Whitworth was a damned scoundrel. He controlled his rage, it was after all partly his fault for allowing her to invite the bounder and he did not want to spoil her evening. 'Humph! Everybody's been wondering where you were.'

'Oh, Papa, I was just thanking Tom, Mr Whitworth, for his present.' She ran towards her father, 'Do see what he's given me.'

Charles Thorpe examined the book and his eyebrows shot up. 'Jumping Jehosephat! Where did you get this?'

'I didn't steal it,' Tom said laconically, though in a way he had. Whenever he had a spare minute, he enjoyed browsing through second-hand bookshops and he'd found the copy of *The Masque of Anarchy* at the back of a shelf in a seedy shop in Bradford. When he'd asked the bookseller how much he wanted for it, the old man had sniffed, looked at the book and at Tom, and had said hopefully, 'Five bob?' For a few seconds Tom had wrestled with his Socialist conscience. It was quite as much as he could afford; justice demanded he tell the man the book was worth a great deal more; Kessie would adore it. He had paid the requested five shillings.

Papa could be unforgivably rude, Kessie thought. How dared he suggest Tom had *stolen* her birthday present, even if he did suspect they had been making love. And why not? They loved each other.

Papa was saying brusquely, 'Isn't it time you returned to your guests, miss?'

The remainder of the party Kessie floated through in an ecstatic daze. Just before midnight everybody gathered in the morning-room, the waiters popped the champagne corks, the glasses were filled, Papa took out his gold watch and raised his hand.

'Now!'

The orchestra struck a chord, everybody held up their glasses to toast the New Year of 1906, downed them and joined hands to sing 'Auld Lang Syne'. Then the glasses were refilled and Papa held up his again.

'A second toast—to my dearest daughter Kessie.

Twenty-one today, and may her life be filled with love and happiness!'

There were tears in Papa's eyes as he kissed her. People were shouting, 'Speech, speech! Come on, Kessie! Let's be having you. You're used to getting up on your soap-box these days.'

Lifted on to a chair, Kessie made her speech which she finished by saying, 'Pray raise your glasses in another toast to 1906, the year in which women will get the vote!'

The party continued into the early hours and a couple of times Kessie caught Tom's eye, he smiled at her, and the absolute, perfect happiness flooded through her. Then people were leaving and at the front door Sarah said, 'It's been grand. Thanks for inviting us, Kessie.'

'Yes, thank you.' Tom fingered the black satin revere of his dress suit, 'Nobody but you could have got me into *this*.'

'You look gorgeous in it.' Kessie was astonished by her boldness (it must have been the champagne). But Papa had seen that she was with the Whitworths and was bearing down on them.

'When do you leave for London, Mr Whitworth?'

'Tomorrow, sir,' Tom's tone was extremely polite and it was very rare for him to say 'sir'.

'Good.' Papa's tone was extremely rude. Kessie blushed with embarrassment, Sarah frowned, but Tom's face remained impassive.

As the Whitworths went through the double-fronted doorway, Charles Thorpe almost jammed Tom against the hinges. Quietly but venomously, he said, 'If you go near my daughter again, I'll break every bone in your body.'

Neither of the girls heard the remark but they saw Tom's head go up sharply and his dark skin flush. Kessie wondered what Papa had said to anger Tom so.

When Sarah and Tom were walking through the fields round The Laurels, past the large detached houses and into the streets of Moss Side, Sarah asked why Mr Thorpe had suddenly been so rude? Tom glared. He said he had no idea, except men like him considered it part of their business to be rude. Sarah nodded and started to talk excitedly about the wspu's future plans. Although Tom kept his attention fixed on his sister, he was only listening to her key-words, a useful technique he had developed which enabled him to interject the odd intelligent comment, while concentrating on his own thoughts. He should not have accepted the invitation, and neither should he have allowed his desire to overcome him. Blast Kessie Thorpe! Tomorrow, thank God, he was away to London and she would be out of his life.

Everybody was finally gone from The Laurels and debris strewed the rooms, plates of half-eaten food, wilting flowers, a dropped sheet of music, empty chairs at forlorn angles. In the morning-room Kessie drew back the curtains and stood by the french window. The pale light was rolling back the night and she felt exultant. She wanted to cry out—I'm in love with the most wonderful man in the world, and he loves me as much as I love him! Soon he will ask me to marry him and then, oh then, together we shall transform the world for men *and* women!

Papa came up behind her and for several minutes they stayed silent. Then gruffly he said, 'That Whitworth lad. From what I've heard he has a reputation.'

'He is making his mark in the world.'

'That is not exactly what I mean,' Papa cleared his throat, 'A reputation . . . with women.'

Of course women liked Tom, but he loved her.

Kessie turned round, her hazel eyes shining, and her father regarded her with an anxious love. What a beautiful young woman she had turned into, but how little she knew of the ways of the world, of men in particular. One day she would fly the nest, but until that day arrived it was his paternal duty to protect her. In a couple of weeks he was due to sail for Calcutta on business and the thought of leaving Kessie to her own devices, even though Whitworth was taking off for London, worried him.

He put a hand on her shoulder. 'Why don't you accompany me to India? I'll pay your passage. Needn't touch your own money. Get away from all this. Women will have the vote in time. It's inevitable. If the Pankhursts and Sarah want to give the process a shove, let them. But you're made of different stuff, finer stuff.'

To go to India? Oh, that would be a fabulous experience! When she was little and Papa had disappeared abroad, he'd always said that one day he would take her with him to a far-flung part of the Empire. But then her excitement faded. Tom Whitworth, as Papa was well aware, would not be in India, and left to itself the inevitable could be a long time a'coming.

PART TWO

6

Whatever fervent Mancunians like Papa said, London was the greatest city in the world, the heart of the mighty British Empire, the hub of the universe, and how Kessie loved being here.

Waterloo Bridge was her favourite place in the capital, and to be standing on it, particularly on a clear October night like this—with the trams speeding along the Embankment like glow-worms, up river the lights of the Houses of Parliament reflecting in the Thames, down river the arms of the cranes from the docks hanging darkly against the sky and the dome of St Paul's Cathedral fringed by stars—to be standing here with Tom's arm round her shoulder, was perfect bliss.

Well, almost perfect.

From the moment she'd made up her mind, dug her feet in and regretfully refused to go to India with Papa—'You're as stubborn as a mule and as stupid as a jackass', 'Well, everybody says I take after you'—life had been hectic; travelling to London, settling into the WSPU's office in Clement's Inn in the Strand, learning how to use a type-writing machine, spreading the message far and wide. Today had seen the crowning of their six months of effort with their first ever Annual General Meeting. How grand that sounded! It had been a splendid meeting, the office crammed to bursting point with women who had come, not just from Manchester and London, but from the branches that were springing up all over the British Isles. After the AGM Tom had met her and a whole gang of them had gone to Lockhart's where they'd consumed mountains of crumpets and fancy cakes and drunk pots of tea and talked and laughed and argued.

'Some folks have to work for their livings and I have to be up at six o'clock. What was it you wanted to talk to me about *in particular, in private*, Miss Thorpe?' Tom's tone was teasing but it had a slightly irritated edge and he was not a great one for standing around doing nothing in particular.

Kessie had rehearsed what she wanted to say several times, and she knew she must stick to the salient points: she had known him for eighteen months and, though her relationship with him had blossomed, it had not actually borne fruit, and they had to get it sorted out because Papa would be back from India soon.

In the event, the words rushed out abruptly changed from those she had rehearsed. 'Tom, why can't we get married?'

'You know why not, Kess, because I haven't any money.'

'You can have mine.'

'I'm not living on your money, and that's flat.'

'We can live on what you earn then.'

'You don't know what you're talking about, luv. All the Labour Party can afford to pay me is thirty-five shillings a week, which is five shillings less than your Papa gives you as an allowance. We'd be screaming at each other within the year. When I wed you I want to be able to buy you things, Kess.'

At least he had said 'when'.

Kessie watched him, puzzled, as he ran his left hand through his hair. Tom was naturally left-handed and, as she had learned, despite childhood beatings, had stubbornly refused to use his right hand. She did not see why, in the new emancipated era, he had to be stubborn about her money. What was also baffling in this new era of the equality of the sexes was why, if the money business upset him, he hadn't suggested they have a liaison. Almost unbelievably, since those moments in Papa's study, he had only kissed her once, on a hot summer's day when they'd borrowed a tandem and bicycled out into Kent, singing 'Daisy, Daisy, Give me your answer, do,' as they pedalled along. In the afternoon they'd wandered through the meadows where the eruption within them both had been as volcanic as in Papa's study. Suddenly, Tom had wrenched her from his arms and walked

76

back to the tandem. She had lacked the courage to ask why, but she had to take it in both hands now.

'If we can't get married until you have made your fortune, why can't we just live together to begin with?'

The blood was roaring through Kessie's veins while she waited for his answer, but he went on staring down into the dark waters of the River Thames, as if he hadn't heard her. As it was she who had made the proposal, he simply had to agree, and what Papa would say, she could not imagine. Well, yes, she could, which was why she had to rent an apartment and the whole thing had to be a *fait accompli* before her father landed at Tilbury. Tom was speaking and his Lancashire accent was strong which meant his emotions were aroused.

'I don't want us to live together.'

Through blurred eyes Kessie stared at the lamplighter at the foot of the bridge. He was stretching the long pole to ignite the gas; with a sudden flare it caught and the final link in the chain along the Embankment was lit, but she felt as if in herself the light had been extinguished. She had debased herself, shamed herself, because she loved Tom so much and he had rejected her.

He put his hand on her arm but she shied away.

'Kess, you know I love you.'

'Do I?' The shame was swelling into anger, 'Do I?'

'Yes, you do. I love you too much to want to live with you except as my wife. Give me time to get myself established, Kess.'

In the glow of the lamp standard on the parapet his dark eyes were tender, nobody else called her 'Kess', and her anger ebbed. She was leaning against him and the tears were snuffling in her nose. 'You must think I'm a shameless hussy. . . .'

'No I don't. Come on, blow on this. But I wouldn't make a habit of asking men to live with you.' Through her tears Kessie took the handkerchief and smiled up at him. He touched the tip of her nose with his forefinger. 'It's getting parky. Shall I take you home?'

On the Embankment Tom hailed a cab and she sat with

his arm around her, warm and secure. He was talking about the Labour Party, but Kessie's mind wandered and it occurred to her that he didn't mind taking small sums of money from her, she would have to pay for the cab, so why did he object to larger amounts? Then he said something which gained her full attention.

'Whatever your gang's planning for the opening of the next session of Parliament, and I have no doubt you've summat in mind, you won't do anything daft, will you? You know what you promised your father?'

'Yes, I do. And no, I won't do anything *daft*.' She imitated Tom's flat 'a' sound.

Before he departed for India, her father had made her promise two things: to restrain her WSPU activities during his absence and to have no contact whatsoever with Tom Whitworth. She had told Tom about the first promise, but not the second. (And for his part he had not told her about her father's threat to break every bone in his body.)

Now he was coiling his fingers round those strands of hair that would stray past her ears, however firmly she pinned up her tresses. 'I worry about you, Kess. Promise me you won't do anything stupid?'

He sounded just like Papa. Suddenly, she was very angry. Tom was unashamedly ambitious, saying he wanted power, because without it he could do nothing for his weaker brethren. One of his favourite phrases was 'the need for positive action'. Surely that applied to personal as much as political matters, and if he really loved her the way she loved him, he would stop treating her like a child and take *positive action*.

'I don't see why you should worry about me.' Kessie pulled her head sharply away from the caressing fingers. 'I am quite capable of looking after myself.'

'Look after yourself then! I've wasted hours running round after you today. You and your dratted AGM.'

'You needn't waste any more of your precious time on me!' Kessie banged hard on the roof of the cab, the driver pulled on the horses and his head appeared upside down at the window. 'Yes, what was it you wanted, sir?'

It wasn't 'sir' who wanted anything. 'Sir' was getting out and she informed the driver of this fact. Tom stared at her. She stared back. She wasn't certain that she wanted him to go but after a few seconds he flung open the door, jumped down and slammed it shut. Kessie called out, 'Drive on, please.'

They were close to the Houses of Parliament. On the pavement by the statue of Boadicea in her chariot, Tom watched as the cab rounded Parliament Square, waiting for it to come back. It did not. He looked up at Boadicea, who had been another bloody-minded woman.

Blast Kessie Thorpe, he *did* worry about her: the world could be a nasty, brutish place, especially for boldly innocent young ladies. And Kessie was an innocent, however grown-up she considered herself to be, asking him to live with her! The proposal had slightly shocked him, though he realised it was her love for him that had prompted it, and if she thought he didn't want her . . .! Then she had no idea how easily men were roused, nor how Herculean his self-control had been. He respected Kessie and he was neither going to ruin her reputation by living with her in sin, nor have a furtive affair with her. That sort of thing was fine enough with his landlady's 'advanced' daughter, sneaking into her bed, writhing under the bedclothes and sneaking out again, but it wouldn't do for Kessie. And he wasn't ruining his career, either. It was all right for randy sods like Lloyd George, but a scandal would finish him in the Puritanical Labour movement, and there were several buggers who would be delighted to see him get his come-uppance. He wanted Kessie as his wife, the mother of his children. But only when the time was right. And meanwhile he was not putting up with her spoilt tantrums.

Tom stared at the Houses of Parliament. He was going to enter that building as an MP, soon, and nobody was going to divert him. Not Kessie Thorpe, nor anybody.

Three days later Kessie herself walked across Parliament Square. She hadn't heard a word from Tom, and she certainly wasn't going to contact him. The recent fine weather had vanished, the autumn air was drizzlingly damp and the Union Jack announcing that Parliament was once more in session hung limply from the Victoria Tower. In Old Palace Yard several scores of women were already assembling and as Kessie joined them her nerve-ends started to tingle: without a doubt this was the most important demonstration they had yet organised. She drew courage from Mrs Pankhurst whose face was composed, her hand casually adjusting the long chiffon scarf round her neck, and from Aunt Ada who was calmly folding her umbrella.

The day after their invasion of Milnrow, Aunt Ada had joined the Women's Social and Political Union, since when she had undergone the most extraordinary transformation. Gone were her severe black dresses, the grey hair scraped into a bun, the reserved manner. Her hair was now looped into more flattering 'earphones', she wore coloured skirts and natty jackets like the ones she was sporting today, and she aired her opinions with a fervid enthusiasm. The conviction that Mrs Pankhurst and her daughter Christabel had been sent by God (or the Virgin Mary?) to free womankind from the chains of male domination had given her a new lease of life.

As the inimitable, slightly cracked tones of Big Ben boomed three times, Mrs Pankhurst held up her hand. 'Onward!' Her head high, the chiffon scarf fluttering behind, she marched a few yards towards St Stephen's entrance to the House of Commons. Everybody followed. Among the crowd watching them interestedly Kessie saw a man's dark unruly hair, her heart leapt frantically, but he turned his head. It wasn't Tom, and the disappointment flooded through her.

Only twenty of them were actually allowed inside the sacred male precincts, but Kessie was among them. To her left dark rafters spanned the ancient stone walls of Westminster Hall, while in front a long passage stretched towards an arched doorway leading into the central lobby. As they traversed the mosaic floor, Kessie looked up at the glimmering chandeliers and the marble statues of dead British statesmen. In the central lobby they waited patiently and while Kessie was examining the statues there, among them the older Mr Gladstone's, Tess Billington came over. She and Tess, whose actual given name was Teresa, had arrived in London together, and Kessie liked her and admired her cool intelligence almost as much as Christabel's.

Tess's gaze travelled round the statues. After the inspection her stately head inclined thoughtfully, and under the sensible felt hat her coronet of plaits shook slightly as she said, 'It won't be long now before we have some women among this lot.'

Kessie giggled and felt her nerves settling. Policemen hovered nearby, but it was ages before anybody came to them, apart from Mr Keir Hardie who greeted Mrs Pankhurst warmly and smiled at Kessie. He was a wonderful man, like an Old Testament prophet with his white beard and piercing eyes, and she had met him with Tom about whom she was not going to think.

Eventually the Liberal Chief Whip appeared and in her most gracious tones Mrs Pankhurst said, 'We wish to know whether it is the Government's intention to introduce a Women's Suffrage Bill in the near future?'

'The Prime Minister regrets he can give no assurances. It is not a matter on which the country at large has strong feelings.'

'Has it not?' Aunt Ada snorted. 'We have strong feelings, sir!'

For several seconds after the Chief Whip had disappeared, they stood hesitantly in the central lobby, uncertain what to do next, until Mrs Pankhurst said, 'We have a constitutional right to air our grievances. Air them we shall!'

Fired by her ringing words, everybody went into action, unfurling their 'Votes for Women' banners, and loudly shouting their slogan. Then a police inspector called out, 'Now then, ladies, we can't have this. Will you kindly leave immediately.' Above the cries of 'No!', Kessie heard his voice bellowing, 'Clear the lobby!'

Everything then happened so quickly, and with such sudden belligerence, that Kessie was only half-conscious of what she was doing. It was as if she were in the middle of a scene at one of those cinematographic theatres to which Tom had taken her, the pace too fast for reality, the actions blurred and jerky, except that on the flickering screen all was silent, whereas here the noise was terrible, with policemen bawling, women shrieking, and Members of Parliament cheering and clapping as if they were Romans watching the Christians being thrown to the lions.

Somehow Kessie found herself clinging to Mr Gladstone's statue, her arms tightly wrapped round the cold white waist, shouting at the top of her voice, 'We are not asking for the moon. We are asking for our democratic rights as citizens of this country. . . .'

Hands were pulling at her legs, she was struggling, being half-dragged, half-carried over the mosaic floor towards the exit. She yelled, 'Let me go! Votes for Women! Take your hands off me! Votes for Women!'

Down the hall she saw Aunt Ada belabouring a policeman with her umbrella and Tess kicking out for all she was worth, but despite their resistance the three of them were bundled into Old Palace Yard. Pausing only to put her hat on straight, Tess shouted, 'Come on, we'll hold our meeting here. Votes for Women! We have just been flung out. . . .'

Two policemen were arresting her. What for? Exercising the right of any freeborn British citizen, the right of free speech? Furiously, Kessie shouted, 'Votes for Women! We demand that . . .'

A hand came down on her shoulder.

'You're under arrest, miss.'

Under arrest? Calmly, Kessie allowed herself to be marched across Parliament Square and when a cabby called out, 'What you been up to, ducks?', cheerfully she called back, 'We want the vote, that's all.'

It was only as they turned into Cannon Row that the enormity of what had happened struck her and the panic started. *She was under arrest*, she was being led under the high entrance arch to Cannon Row police station and across the cobbled yard, like *a common criminal*. In the stables a police horse neighed loudly, the noise made Kessie jump and she wanted to run away. She felt sick and what was Papa going to say when he landed in England to find his daughter under arrest and charged with . . . what? What would they do to her?

Inside the dark hallway of the police station, apart from Tess there were eight other of her friends, and in their defiant company her panic subsided. Being charged was a wearisome process. When it came to Kessie's turn, she was hauled into a room where a sergeant sat behind a high desk. Laboriously he wrote down the answers to his questions, while the clock in the corner ticked loudly. Then he sat back, stretching his arms.

'Kessie. That's a nice name. Haven't come across it before. Do you appreciate the trouble you're causing us, Miss Kessie Thorpe? Why a well-brought-up young lady like you should get herself arrested, I cannot for the life of me think.'

Chattily he went on and Kessie thought, you're not taking us seriously, are you? We're a joke, well-brought-up young, and not so young, ladies like us demonstrating in public. Well, we're no joke, I can tell you.

'I beg your pardon, miss, I never said you was.'

Kessie realised she must have uttered the last words aloud and blushed slightly. The sergeant handed her a printed sheet of paper in the blank spaces of which he had written her personal charge details.

Metropolitan Police   A Division
                                  Cannon Row Station

Take notice that you *Kessie Martha Thorpe* are bound in the sum of *two* pounds to appear at *Westminster* Police Court situated at *Rochester Row* at *10* o'clock AM on the *24th* day of October 1906 to answer to the charge of *using threatening and abusive words and behaviour with intent to provoke a breach of the peace* at the *Houses of Parliament 23.10.06* and unless you appear there further proceedings will be taken.

7

For twenty-four hours, from the moment the cab drove her from Cannon Row police station to deposit her, on bail, outside the house that Aunt Ada had leased in Thurloe Square, Kessie existed in a state of euphoric excitement, uplifted by the sense of divine mission, of being in the vanguard of women's march from bondage to freedom.

In the morning, giggling, she read the newspaper reports: 'Screeching, scratching women in Parliamentary lobby,' 'Turbulent ten in court today'. 'Turbulent ten' indeed! When she reached Rochester Row police court, with Aunt Ada who was simply furious that she had not been arrested, a large crowd of well-wishers cheered them to the echo, but of Tom there was no sign. Where was he? He must have heard the news by now. She had believed that he loved her, she truly had, but she had been warned about men and Tom had turned out to be like the rest, not to be trusted.

Briefly, desolation choked Kessie's throat, but it was forgotten in the momentous excitement of deciding that if they were found guilty as charged, they would refuse to recognise a male court implementing man-made laws, refuse to pay their fines and to be bound over to keep the peace, and instead would opt to go to prison.

The sentences, however, came as a shock. *Two* months in the *second* division of Holloway Gaol, whereas they had been told to expect a couple of weeks at most in the *first* division, which was where they should rightly be as political prisoners. After the magistrate had handed out the sentences, they were hustled from the courtroom, down dark steps to the passages below, to await their removal to Holloway. They had a long wait, briefly enlivened when friends and relations were allowed to see them, but eventually a man's voice bawled, 'Come on, you lot, get moving.'

Outside the court-house the Black Maria prison van was waiting and one by one they climbed inside, WSPU members and criminals all together. Along both sides of the vehicle were little cattle stalls, with half-gates, into which they were bundled. Kessie found that the stalls were neither high enough to stand up, nor wide enough to sit down, and from her crouching position she stuck her head over the top of the half-gate. All her friends had their heads sticking out like those caricature cardboard cut-outs you saw at the seaside, and she started to giggle.

'You'll stop laughing in a minute,' said Tess, who had already spent a brief spell in prison for creating a disturbance outside Mr and Mrs Asquith's house in Cavendish Square. 'These things are updated versions of the medieval rack.'

The rear door slammed shut, there were no lights inside the Black Maria, and Kessie had a moment's suffocating panic as the horses pulled and the vehicle lurched forward. Now she knew exactly what Tess had meant. There wasn't a spring in the entire diabolical contraption, and every movement of the Black Maria wrenched her body as it jolted, bucked, halted and flung itself into motion again. The experience was made more nightmarish because of the utter darkness from which disembodied voices, male and female, shouted and shrieked, cursed and moaned. Again she heard that word 'fuck' which several men had whispered in her ear when she was handing out leaflets on street corners. What exactly did it mean?

The last half-hour, after the van had stopped to let the men prisoners off at Pentonville, while the horses laboured up the hill to Holloway, was the worst, but the WSPU members started to sing, everything from 'Onward Christian Soldiers', to 'All through the Night', to Marie Lloyd's song, 'My old man says follow the van, and don't dilly-dally on the way'. The other prisoners joined in and the defiant noise drowned the rattle of the Black Maria's wheels.

Eventually, the vehicle jerked to a standstill, the rear door was flung open, and it was by now dark outside, so that the high turreted towers of Holloway loomed as ominous shadows. With aching limbs Kessie stumbled into the prison and by her side Emmeline Pethick Lawrence breathed, 'Oh dear Lord, give me strength.'

Kessie squeezed her hand and the older woman smiled back gratefully. Dear Mrs Pethick Lawrence who, with her husband Fred, had become a tower of strength to the movement, providing not only a unique organisational ability, but also money (they were rich Socialists) and premises for the WSPU (their London apartment was at the top of the Clement's Inn building).

Inside the prison they were ordered into line and marched up a broad staircase to a reception hall which was a huge place with iron tiers of cell gangways rising to a huge skylight. All the wardresses had painfully loud voices which reverberated round the cavernous hall.

'Right, you next.' Kessie followed the direction of an outstretched finger to where another wardress bellowed, 'Full name.'

'Kessie Martha Thorpe.'

'Age.'

'Twenty-one.'

'Birthplace.'

'Manchester.'

'Present address.'

'Thurloe Square, South Kensington, S.W.'

'Religion.'

'Unitarian.'

'Sentence.'

'Two months for disturbing the peace.'

'Colour of hair.'

'Chestnut.'

The wardress looked up at her, 'Red. Colour of eyes.'

'Hazel.'

The wardress looked up again, 'Brown. And you call us "ma'am". Can you read?'

'Yes, *ma'am*.'

'Write.'

86

'Yes, *ma'am*.'

What extraordinary questions!

'You know how to sew, of course.'

'No, ma'am.'

'What! A well-bred young lady like you?'

Kessie stared blankly at the wardress, refusing to accept the jocularity after the barked questions. She hated sewing and throughout her childhood she had mulishly refused to acquire this feminine skill.

'You can learn while you're in 'ere. Give us your coat and hat and bag.' These were labelled and shoved on to a shelf. 'Over there. Get weighed and measured.'

Kessie stood on the scales and another wardress bellowed, 'One hundred and sixteen pounds.' She adjusted the height rest. 'Five feet five inches.' She nodded. 'Get in line and no talking.'

It seemed to go on all night, being assembled into lines and bawled at by voices loud enough to fill the Free Trade Hall: 'Open your chests', 'Lift your arms', 'Bend your heads'. The inspection of their chests and hair was performed in the most perfunctory manner by a bored doctor, male of course. Kessie suddenly felt desperately tired and wanted to curl up in a ball and go to sleep. Then they were ordered into one of the side rooms where they were told to undress. Mrs Pethick Lawrence looked as if she were about to burst into tears.

'I can't. Not in front of everybody. I can't.'

Kessie herself was deeply embarrassed. She had never stood naked in front of anybody, except Sheba when she was a child. The sight of other prisoners throwing off their shabby clothes, revealing wrinkled stomachs and drooping breasts did not lessen the embarrassment (though many of the others were clasping thin arms around their naked parts). But Mrs Pethick Lawrence's agony was greater than hers, and Kessie sought to reassure her.

'I'll stand in front of you.'

Each of them was handed a coarse cotton chemise.

'Through there. Wait your turn and get your bath.'

The baths were in cubicles resembling the cattle-stalls in

the Black Maria, with half-gates, and they were disgusting, ringed with scum. They were expected to step into some-body else's—how many somebody else's?—dirty water. Mrs Pethick Lawrence had a note of hysteria in her voice. 'I am not getting in there. I am *not*!'

'Neither am I,' Kessie said firmly to a wardress, 'We require some clean water, please.'

Eventually, they were given some fresh tepid water, though the baths themselves remained nauseatingly unclean and the wardresses kept peering over the tops of the half-gates as they washed. Next they were marched into a room which contained hampers filled with clothes and boots. It was like being at a mad jumble sale, Kessie thought, with women rummaging frantically to find something to fit them. All the time the wardresses were shouting, 'Come on, make haste, you women.'

You women! As she struggled into the regulation second-division dark-green prison dress stamped with the broad black convict arrows, a dress that was too tight in the bosom, too wide in the waist and miles too long—did they cater for peculiarly shaped midgets and giantesses in Holloway?—Kessie remembered the little Jewish man's shop near Sarah's room and her horror at the thought of wearing second-hand clothes. The ghost of a giggle escaped her and looking at her friends, all struggling into similarly ill-fitting garbs, the giggles threatened to convulse her.

A wardress clanked over, the keys at her waist rattling. 'What's that round your neck?' It was the horseshoe necklace Tom had bought at the Wakes Week fair. Even if he no longer cared for her, even if he never had, she wanted to keep it. 'You should have given that up. No personal items allowed.'

'Please. It's very precious to me.'

'Take it off.' Kessie stared defiantly. 'Take it off before I tear it off.' Kessie went on staring and the wardress's voice softened, 'Come on, dear, I don't make the rules and regu-lations. We don't want a scene and you'll lose it in the end. I'll see it's kept safe.'

With trembling fingers Kessie unclasped the necklace and she wanted to howl with fury, but the wardresses were shouting at them to form into another line. They were marched to an office where they were issued with their prison numbers—Kessie's was 13,665—then they were ordered to quick march again, which was difficult as they were all trying to stop their garterless stockings from wrinkling down their legs. No garters were issued in Holloway, nor were corsets, and it was the most extraordinary sensation not to have encasing whalebone round your waist. Kessie no longer felt like giggling because the humiliation and denials of decency were shocking, but looking at her friends again—Mrs Pethick Lawrence had just tripped over her skirt—Kessie had to admit that she had rarely seen a more ludicrous spectacle than 'the turbulent ten' now presented.

Up an echoing iron staircase they tramped to an iron gantry lined by cells. One by one the doors were unlocked until it was Kessie's turn to be pushed inside. Behind her the door slammed shut and she gazed round the small, cold cell. There was a barred window high in the stone wall, a plank bed, a wooden stool, a bucket in one corner, and a caged light flickering dimly in the ceiling. The pervading odour of police cells, Black Marias and prison cells, a rancid mixture of stale urine and sick, hit her nostrils and she started to retch. All day she had been with her friends, sustained by their fears as much as their courage.

Now she was alone.

In front of the blazing fire in his room at the Home Office in Whitehall, Herbert Gladstone was warming his backside. He was thinking about his revered father, the late great Mr Gladstone, and wondering what he would have done about these women, now into their second week in prison, when his private secretary knocked and entered.

'Good morning, sir. I'm afraid I have dozens more requests to visit the suffragettes in Holloway before the rules allow.'

The Home Secretary sighed. *Suffragettes*, indeed. It was the *Daily Mail* that had christened the militant ladies *suffragettes*. What emotions they aroused! All these letters to *The Times* and these protest meetings. . . .

'Also, sir, Mr Keir Hardie has given notice of the question he intends to raise in the House, and I understand that Tom Whitworth is . . .'

'Who exactly is this *Tom* Whitworth?' Why did the fellow use a truncated version of his Christian name publicly?

Dropping the tail of his frock-coat, Mr Gladstone moved away from the fire and towards his desk, as his secretary replied, 'Whitworth is a protégé of Keir Hardie, an assistant secretary to the self-styled Labour Party. From my own contact with him in the last week, I would assess him as an extremely ambitious young man, using the suffragettes, notably this Miss Thorpe, to make political capital and further his own career.'

'Well, he's a dashed nuisance.' Herbert Gladstone sat down at his desk. 'Is there no way we can transfer these women to the first division?'

The secretary piously reminded his Minister that the 1898 Prison Act had separated the prisoners into three divisions. While he agreed that in theory the suffragettes should be receiving first-division treatment, that they should be allowed to wear their own clothes, to send out for food, to have writing and reading material, and to receive visitors, in practice such treatment was reserved for those found guilty of contempt of court, seditious libel and, oh yes, offences against the Vaccination Act. Refusing to pay one's fine and to be bound over to keep the peace, as the women had, was a second-division offence, entailing much harsher treatment. Still, at least by virtue of the 1898 Act they were kept apart from the worst types of criminals who were put into the third division.

'Yes, yes, yes,' Mr Gladstone said irritably, because he knew all that.

'Of course, sir, you personally may order their transfer to the first division.'

The Home Secretary looked even more irritated because he knew that, too. What he wanted was a way out of the dilemma without exerting his authority and over-riding the decision of the court. 'What about the infirmary? Cannot we transfer the suffragettes there?'

'Not unless they are sick, sir. That decision is up to the prison doctor.'

Herbert Gladstone frowned. 'Up to'. How he disliked Americanisms! Seeing his Minister's mood was far from happy, the private secretary decided he would impart his one piece of good news. 'Another suffragette prisoner is being released today, sir.' Mrs Pethick Lawrence had already been released, unable to endure the conditions in Holloway. 'She has given similar assurances to keep the peace for six months.'

With a note of hope in his voice, Herbert Gladstone said, 'Perhaps they'll all give their assurances and be released.'

'Unfortunately, sir, the second released prisoner, a Mrs Montefiore, found lice in her hair. With the WSPU's capacity for advertising their grievances, I do not think it would be a good idea to allow other ladies to be released because their heads are crawling with lice.'

Being in prison was infinitely worse than Kessie had imagined. She could not endure two months of this. She could not.

Throughout the night there was barely a moment's silence. Doors banged, feet clattered, keys rasped and during any pause she would lie rigidly on her plank bed, clutching the evil-smelling blanket around her, simply waiting for the next outburst. As the grey morning light crept through the barred window, there was the prison dawn chorus of bells, rattling trolleys, and the angry shouts of wardresses, a cacophony which mounted to a deafening, nerve-shattering crescendo.

Throughout the day women screamed and hammered in their cells. They must be from the second division and in some ways their lot was worse than that of the third-division prisoners. Admittedly they littered the stone corridors like mats, endlessly scrubbing, but at least they were together; whereas the second-division prisoners were confined to their solitary cells twenty-three hours out of twenty-four.

91

Previously Kessie had thought of herself as a self-sufficient person, she liked her own company, she enjoyed solitude, but sometimes the isolation became terrifying, the feeling of being totally shut off from the world, and, since no visitors were allowed yet, of not knowing what was happening, nor whether anybody cared about you any more.

Her cell was twelve paces by five—she walked it endlessly—the atmosphere was foul since there was no apparent ventilation, yet it was freezing cold because there was no heating either. Apart from the plank bed, the furnishings consisted of the wooden stool, the ledge on which sat the disgusting wooden bowl she had to eat out of, and in the corner the nauseating slop bucket.

Hard as Kessie tried, her bladder would let her down and sometimes even her bowels, because they were allowed to go to the revolting toilets only twice in twenty-four hours. Having to use the slop bucket in her cell, standing in line, holding the stinking pail, waiting to empty it, were the most horrible, shame-making things that had ever happened to Kessie.

To make the situation worse, on the very first morning as she tried to wash herself with cold brackish water and a sliver of hard yellow soap that gave no lather, to dry herself with the threadbare rag that passed for a towel, and to tidy her waist-length hair with a comb that would have been an admirable addition to her doll's house at home, she felt the familiar stickiness between her legs. It couldn't be, her period wasn't due for ten days and she was regular as clockwork.

The cell door opened and the wardress said, 'Come on, D13, you'll have to jump to. Time for chapel.'

The colour rushed into Kessie's cheeks but her voice emerged clearly, 'Please, my period's started. May I have a sanitary towel?'

'You'll have to wait.'

The wardress did eventually produce a sanitary towel which had been washed and rewashed and bore the brownish stains of previous wearers. Kessie regarded it with horror, holding it at arm's length. 'I can't use *that*.'

'You use that or nothing.'

The wardresses were rough, unsympathetic women, bawling and shouting, and the need to beg from them a fifth-hand sanitary towel to staunch the flow of blood nobody ever mentioned—least of all the male sex, though it was the natural process, Kessie thought, if she wasn't sure, that produced the babies men said were women's natural province—enraged her beyond measure.

Every day there was *something* that infuriated her and that at least helped to keep her going. Having to clean out her cell, down on her hands and knees with a scrubbing brush, put her in a rage for at least an hour. Sitting on the stool, stabbing a needle into the pile of *men's* shirts she was given to mend, angered her further, while the piteous crying of babies sent her into a positive fury.

When they were taken down to the exercise yard for their twice-weekly half-hour of fresh air, she whispered to Tess, 'Who are those babies who keep crying?'

Tess whispered back, 'They lock them in the cells while their mothers are working, the third-division mothers.'

The wardress shouted, 'No talking, you women.'

After supper, when the prisoners were free to do what they wanted until the lights were turned out at eight o'clock for the long clamorous night, was the best time. Kessie spent a good deal of it standing on her stool, peering down into the yard, pacing up and down for exercise, or reading in the dim light that strained her eyes.

As the most ironic joke of all, they had been issued with *A Healthy Home and How to Keep It*, a book full of patronisingly written pages about fresh air, personal hygiene and well-balanced diets. What splendid training the prisoners received in Holloway! One hour of fresh air per week, one tiny jug of cold water per day, and the dreadful stodgy food. But there was also the King James Authorised Version of the Bible, and the beauty of its language, the inevitability of human pain, and the human capacity to endure, brought tears to Kessie's eyes.

At the end of the first week, from a cell somewhere near hers, she heard moaning noises that grew louder and turned into agonised, animal-like screams. When the wardress came

93

in with her supper at four-thirty, Kessie broke the rules and spoke. 'What is that noise? It's unbearable. What is happening? It sounds as if somebody's being tortured.'

'Haven't you never heard a woman in labour before?'

'In labour? Do you mean she's having a baby? In her cell?'

'They'll take her to the infirmary when her time comes. Sounds as if she's having it hard, though.'

'Isn't anybody with her?'

'It's not our job to sit holding prisoners' hands.'

Kessie's self-control snapped and the words poured out of her. '. . . and how you can work here, treating women, members of your own sex, like this . . .?'

'I have a crippled sister to support and jobs is hard to come by. There's some things go on in 'ere that I don't approve of, but it ain't my business to say so.' Kessie started to cry. 'Come on, D13, pull yourself together. There, there, Miss Thorpe, don't cry.' The wardress was patting her shoulder. 'Where's that silly hanky of yours?' Kessie blew her nose on the bit of blue cloth that also served as a duster. 'What you're doing in 'ere is beyond me. This place ain't for the likes of you. And I haven't spoken a word to you. Understand?'

The likes of her. No, people like her didn't normally see the insides of prisons, certainly not in the second division. Kessie thought of her father's barrister, all those months ago, who had not wanted her to visit little Lily Harrison in Strangeways Gaol because it might upset her tender susceptibilities, and gave an ironic laugh. She looked up at the already darkening early winter sky, and she thought of Doris drawing the damask curtains in her bedroom at The Laurels, lifting nuggets of coal from the scuttle with polished metal tongs, poking the fire to make it blaze. She gazed at the plank bed and the coarse grey blanket and she thought of climbing on to her feather mattress, feeling the warm weight of fleecy blankets and eiderdown, smelling the lavender-scented sheets. She gazed at the hunk of stale bread on the wooden plate and the stewed tea in the tin mug and she thought of supper at The Laurels, five courses served from delicate Worcester china.

94

If she so wanted she could, of course, obtain her release by agreeing to pay her fine and keep the peace. No, no, never, never. She had to endure.

All the time, but particularly at night, the thoughts circled in Kessie's head. Tom had been right when he said the world was an unjust place in which the weak were trampled upon. When she emerged from this prison, from this needless degradation whatever one's crime, by heaven, she would shout about the conditions in here from the rooftops. She would fight and fight and fight until her sex took its rightful place in the world.

Tom. Where was Tom? What was he doing? Why had he deserted her?

8

Tom was standing at a bus-stop in the Strand, with an excited Alice Hartley by his side.

If Alice had to put her finger on *the* moment of decision, it must have come when she had briefly seen Kessie in that ghastly police court at Rochester Row, waiting to be carted off to Holloway. The fury had rushed through her body; to win the vote for women *was* the greatest challenge of the age, which required the strength of a militant organisation like the WSPU. She had suddenly seen that clearly. There and then she had decided that she was not going home with Momma; she was staying in England until the vote was won.

Naturally, Momma had gnashed her teeth and rent her hair—'Going to prison is not the way to go about things'—but Alice had found an unexpected ally in her sister, Verena, who was still fearfully depressed about her still-born baby, poor darling. With Poppa wanting Momma home, Verena wanting Alice to stay, her own mind made up, she had

95

remained in London. Franklin had not been pleased by her decision, but she hadn't been pleased with him, either. Naturally, he'd had the decency not to propose in the middle of the crisis over Verena, but when they'd gone on a cruise to Norway to cheer her sister up—some hope, as it had rained all the time—he'd proposed again and had become quite fierce when Alice had said she couldn't think about her engagement just at that moment. In the end he'd sailed for New York almost without a word, but she'd known he was only sulking and, sure enough, a ship-to-shore wireless message had arrived a few hours later, saying how much he adored her and asking when she would say 'Yes'.

Alice was certain she had made the right decision. London had become the centre of the women's rebellion. Visiting the WSPU at Clement's Inn had become a must on the European itinerary of any politically aware American woman, and scores of them, like Alice herself, were staying in England to join the Pankhursts.

The day she had reported for duty at Clement's Inn, Alice had found the actual offices depressing, a warren of rambling corridors and dark rooms in a big old office block across from St Clement Danes Church in the Strand. But my, what a hive of activity they were, typewriting machines clattering, telephone bells shrilling, eager recruits being interviewed, envelopes being addressed, donations being counted! After she had located Christabel's office, which was lined with law books, piled high with papers, and they'd had a cup of tea, Alice had said, 'What do you want me to do?'

Thoughtfully, Christabel had regarded her. 'You've heard about Emmeline Pethick Lawrence?' Alice had nodded. 'Fred's packed her off to Italy to recover from her *traumatic* experiences in Holloway,' Christabel's tone had been sarcastic. The other courageous souls, she had implied, were sticking it out, apart from Dora Montefiore and her lice. 'Well, she was our press liaison officer. The value of publicity cannot be overestimated, Alice. Would you care to take over?'

Alice had thought for a moment. She knew nothing about

publicity, but she could always learn. She had accepted the offer.

Conveniently, Fleet Street was only a few blocks away, and Alice found she got on like a house on fire with the reporters and photographers. They flirted with her outrageously, but as it made them even more willing to accept newsworthy stories, she didn't mind. She soon discovered that one of the distinct advantages of being the press liaison officer was that she worked with Tom Whitworth, who was raising Cain about the imprisonments, always dropping in to Clement's Inn. Alice had gone to a protest meeting at Caxton Hall to listen to him, and boy, could he speak!

This afternoon she had been leaving early, because she was going to a ball in the evening, when she had bumped into him in the dingy hallway. 'Hello, there.'

It transpired that he was on his way to the House of Commons, to try to see old Herbert Gladstone's Parliamentary Private Secretary. Alice had been intending to get a cab, but it was much more fun walking down the Strand with him to a bus-stop. Now, surveying the variegated colours of the London omnibuses, she said, 'Which colour do we want?'

'A green one.'

They waited in line for some minutes, then Alice announced, 'Oh, look, there's a green bus coming.'

She couldn't think why Tom's shoulders shook slightly as he replied, 'It's the wrong number, luv. It's not the colour that matters, it's where the bus is going.'

'I see. You'll have to teach me about these things.'

The dark eyes flickered over her body and he was surely insolent—calling her 'luv'—but he made a change from well-bred idiots like Algy Hereford, or even Franklin. Tom was a go-getter in the best Yankee tradition, and, spruced up, given some decent clothes, he could be a very interesting proposition, particularly in New York where his Lancashire accent, which seemed to bother the English but which Alice thought was cute, wouldn't matter a fig. Even in this mundane situation, waiting for a bus that didn't look as if

97

it were coming, the words were pouring out of him with an amazing, confident fluency.

'Imprisoning them in the second division is the best thing the Liberals ever did for women's suffrage. They never learn, the old-style politicians. Gladstone will have to transfer them to the first division, the uproar's too great to be ignored, and then he'll have to release them.'

'Absolutely. We'll go on squeezing old Herbert until his pips squeak.'

Tom grinned at her. She was a sassy miss, stunningly beautiful, and didn't she know it? It was a pity he hadn't met her before he met Kessie. Not that he'd committed himself to Kessie exactly, but . . . the thought of himself with an upper-class piece like Alice was a bit ridiculous. With her cornflower-blue eyes wide, Alice was looking from the approaching green bus to him, and he nodded.

'Yes, this is ours.'

The bus drew into the kerb, the waiting crowd allowed the vision that was Alice to climb in first, she lifted her skirt—very trim ankles in sheerest silk stockings—Tom held out his hand to assist her on to the platform and she said, 'May we go on the top deck?'

'Follow me.' The wardress came into Kessie's new cell, to which she had been transferred on the orders of the Home Secretary. 'You have a visitor.'

Her heart pounding with excitement, Kessie followed the wardress down the stairs, along the corridors to the solicitor's room on the ground floor. The sun was shining through the windows and she thought she could hear the birds singing. She'd written to Aunt Ada, and now at last she had been allowed to visit her. Dear Aunt Ada!

It was not Aunt Ada who swung round as she entered the bare white-washed room. It was Tom. Unbelievingly, Kessie stared at him. He was wearing his only decent suit, the dark blue one, his hair was brushed, his wide mouth broke into a grin, his dark eyes smiled into hers, and she loved him so much she thought her heart would burst. The wardress gestured for them to sit down on the chairs on either side of the table, while she herself sat in the corner.

For several seconds they gazed at each other, then Tom put out his hand to touch hers as it lay on the table, and she watched the black hairs on his wrist rise and flatten beneath the cuffs. The wardress coughed and Tom withdrew his hand. He went on gazing at her. Her hair was tucked up under the ridiculous regulation Dutch bonnet and as she turned her head he saw that her slender white neck had a dirty mark on it. Her delicate hands were red and chapped, her cheeks pale and there were dark circles under her eyes, but even so, even wearing the ill-fitting prison dress with broad convict arrows stamped all over it, she was adorable. He leaned towards her. 'Are they treating you better now?'

Kessie nodded. She could not trust herself to speak. His face was so close and filled with such tenderness, it brought the tears to her eyes.

He indicated the parcel on the table. 'I've brought in the things you asked for and Aunt Ada's put in some extras.' He lowered his voice. 'I was in Liverpool when you were arrested. I didn't realise you were one of the "turbulent ten" until too late. When I got back, Kess, you were already in Holloway. Do you know how I got to see you?' She didn't know anything at that moment, except he was with her. 'I said your father was abroad, your mother was dead and I was your fiancé.'

Tom had used this ploy because it was the only one Mr Gladstone's pompous secretary would accept. When he'd arrived in Holloway he'd had no intention whatsoever of informing Kessie how he had managed to obtain a visitor's pass, but now, seeing her in this dreary room in this foul building, the tears glistening in her eyes, her lips trembling, he suddenly knew he wanted her more than anything in the world. He wanted to protect her, to cherish her, and to hell with his lack of money and the problems of marrying across the English class barriers.

Ignoring the wardress, he took her hands in his. 'Kess, darling Kess, I love you. Miss Thorpe, will you do me the honour of becoming engaged to me and being my wife?'

99

For Kessie, the grim walls of Holloway underwent a glittering transformation and were Xanadu. 'Oh yes, Tom. Oh, yes. I love you. Oh yes, yes, yes.'

Within a fortnight of Tom's proposal, Kessie was sitting in the depths of an armchair in front of the blazing fire in the drawing-room of Aunt Ada's house in Thurloe Square, which were some of life's previously accepted comforts she would never again take for granted. She was still feeling stunned by the speed of events: the sudden announcement that the remaining eight suffragette prisoners were to be released forthwith on Mr Gladstone's orders; the fantastic 'welcome out' as they emerged from Holloway, a brass band playing 'See the Conquering Hero Comes', bouquets by the dozen, a huge crowd cheering and waving their Votes for Women banners, photographers snap-shotting away like mad things; the party at Clement's Inn; the dinner in honour of 'the turbulent ten' at the Savoy Hotel; feeling like royalty, but suffering from the bad cold she'd caught in her cell. Then meeting Papa as he landed at Tilbury.

Papa was sitting on the other side of the fireplace, still grumbling that she looked pale and drawn. Then he broke off to say that she was coming home with him to The Laurels this weekend and he would brook no argument. Dear Papa, whose reaction to her imprisonment had been so blessedly unexpected—he had exploded with anger, not against her, but against the Liberal Government, *his* party, which had so far taken leave of its senses as to imprison *his* daughter, merely for asking for the vote to which she was entitled.

Consumed by his fury with the idiot politicians, Papa had accepted Tom's presence at her side without comment. How he would take the news of their engagement was another matter but she had made Tom promise to keep it a secret until she, not he, had told her father, and it was about time she did. Kessie took a deep breath, preparing for the explosion to follow. 'Tom asked me to marry him when he came to see me in Holloway.'

Papa did not explode, but said, 'Did he, by gad? What did you say, miss?'

'Yes.'

Kessie watched him slice the end from his cigar, light it and inhale on the tobacco. He had always smoked in her presence, as even before her imprisonment they had both agreed that women's sensibilities were not the tender things some men imagined, and normally she liked the aroma. At the moment she thought it would choke her, but then Papa gazed at her through the cloud of smoke. 'If you said "Yes", there's not much point my saying "No". Is there?'

'Oh, Papa!' Kessie ran across to his armchair and flung herself into his arms.

'But you'll have a decent engagement,' he said gruffly. 'At least twelve months, and *this* time you'll keep your promise, miss.'

Kessie promised faithfully that this time she would. Charles Thorpe looked down at his beloved daughter. All he wanted was her happiness. On closer acquaintance, Whitworth was an intelligent, highly ambitious, if penniless lad, but had not his own father once been that? He had stood by Kessie in her hour of trial, his intentions had been honourable, and he was not after her money. Of that Charles Thorpe was now certain. How deeply Whitworth cared for her, how roving his eye was, how capable of being the loving husband she deserved, and how the two of them would fare in a class-conscious society coming from such different backgrounds, he was far from certain. But if he thwarted Kessie she was likely to rush straight into marriage, while if he gave her her head her ardour might diminish.

If Papa's reaction was unexpected, so were those of Kessie's nearest and dearest.

Aunt Ada said, 'I hope you know what you're doing. Women with babies cannot be in the vanguard of the movement, and those who are in the vaguard should not have babies.'

Blushing, she left the room. Kessie had not thought about having a baby, but she did so now because the memory of those agonised screams in Holloway filled her with terror. It was a subject she would have to discuss with Tom, but it

101

was fearfully embarrassing, so she would leave it until nearer their wedding day.

The next morning Kessie went in to Clement's Inn, partly to discuss the itinerary of the speaking tour Christabel had asked her to undertake as soon as she'd rested in Manchester, but mainly to give everybody the wonderful news of her engagement. While her friends congratulated her, nobody seemed actually delighted by the news, and everybody mentioned the difficulties of marrying Tom in a world not yet purged by the suffragettes.

Christabel, in particular, looked anything but pleased and said stiffly, 'Well, I hope you'll be very happy, of course, but marriage is a very difficult compact for a woman in any circumstances and . . .'

'But we're entering a new era of equality! You're leading us there! Tom and I will prove that a man and a woman who love each other can transcend all problems and forge a true partnership. And nothing and nobody will ever interfere with my work for the cause. Or come between *our* friendship.'

Lightly, she kissed Christabel on the cheek and was somewhat surprised by the fervour with which Christabel kissed her back. When she spoke again her voice was unusually breathy. 'I was worried that you might desert us, Kessie, and the movement can ill-afford to lose people like you. And I, well, if you did leave us, I should miss you personally.'

Kessie smiled and felt flattered because Christabel kept her personal emotions on a tight rein and she could not think of many people Miss Pankhurst would miss. Then they turned their attention to business matters, discussing which suffragette families Kessie would stay with while she toured the country speaking about her experiences in Holloway and the absolute need for women to have the vote forthwith.

Of a set of less than heartening reactions, Kessie found Alice's the most peculiar. She had been away visiting some baronial hall and they bumped into each other as they rounded one of the Clement's Inn corridors. Without so much as a 'Hello', she said, 'Is it true? That you and Tom Whitworth are engaged?'

'Yes,' Kessie laughed, and showed Alice her ring, two simple bands of gold entwined round a circlet of tiny seed pearls enclosing a rich red garnet.

For several seconds Alice stood as if turned to stone, and Kessie wondered if Americans were snobbier than she had imagined. Then the golden smile lit her friend's face, she kissed her affectionately and Kessie decided that, like everybody else, Alice had been taken by surprise.

In truth, Alice had scarcely been able to believe her ears when she'd heard the news of the engagement, and it had nearly killed her to congratulate Kessie. Had Tom gone mad? Kessie was the nicest person, with plenty of spirit at staff-officer level, but she had not the metal to match his. In any case, he was *hers*, even though she had not yet decided what to do with him. Had she seriously considered him as a husband? She wasn't sure but she had made plain her interest, to which he had clearly responded, so how dared he become engaged to Kessie? It was the first time in her life that Alice had been denied anything she wanted, or thought she might want, and she was furious. The only thing to do was to keep her feelings to herself, treat Tom with indifference, and see what happened, because he couldn't really want to marry Kessie.

A few days later Alice learned about *the letter*, and she had to admit that Kessie possessed considerable spirit. When Kessie came down to Clement's Inn, a few days before Christmas, to report on her speaking tour (which, according to the press reports, had been a huge success), Alice rushed into Kessie's office, unable to contain her curiosity.

'What exactly did you say in your letter to Mr Gladstone?'

'How do you know about that?' Kessie blushed, which made her look vulnerable. Was that what Tom found attractive?

'Ah, I have my spies. *Ectually*,' Alice mimicked her brother-in-law's precious pronunciation, 'Lionel told Verena and she told me, because *neturally* he would not dream of mentioning the unmentionable of the many unmentionables to *me*. I'm surprised he mentioned it to Verena, but he did.

Come on, Kessie Thorpe, tell us what you wrote about *sanitary towels*.'

'Well, I drew Mr Gladstone's attention to the fact that women in British prisons have practically to go down on their knees to obtain them. I said I thought this was disgraceful and I suggested that he, as the Home Secretary, did something to rectify the situation. And he is, Alice. I had a letter from him saying he's issued an urgent memorandum on the question of sanitary towels in women's prisons.'

Unlike Kessie, Alice was not a giggler, but as they looked at each other they were both consumed with hysterical laughter at the thought of the Victorian Mr Gladstone issuing such a memorandum. When they had sobered down, they agreed it was not a laughing matter. Then Kessie started to talk lovingly of Tom, who was spending Christmas at The Laurels, whereupon Alice's admiration of her spunk evaporated. Kessie, however, was aglow with the festive spirit and she took a bottle of sherry from the bottom drawer of her desk.

'Don't tell Christabel or I'll be drummed out of the regiment. *E*ctually, somebody left it here ages ago.' She quarter-filled two teacups. 'A very happy Christmas, dearest Alice, and as I shan't see you until the New Year here's to 1907, the year in which we *shall* have the vote.'

9

Kessie sat in her cell in Holloway, unscrewed the cap of her fountain pen and started to write her diary.

14th February, 1907. Here I am again! This time we've been put in the first division which shows we're winning and the Government must soon bow to our righteous determination and give us the vote!

Yesterday, we held our own Women's Parlt. in the Caxton Hall which was a brilliant idea, I think. When the news came through that in his speech opening the men's Parlt. the King had made no mention whatsoever of a Women's Suffrage Bill, Mrs P. was superb. She didn't go on at emotional length. She simply said, 'Rise up women.'

Up we rose!

We marched to the House of Commons to make our protest. I went with Christabel, Alice and Sylvia Pankhurst (with whom I do *not* have the same rapport as with C. Not sure why, as she's just as keen on votes for women and she's a more ardent Socialist than her sister). It was a bright, cold day and all the way down Victoria Street we sang fit to burst, but as we wheeled into Parlt. Square they were waiting for us. To my dying day, I shall never forget the sight of those mounted policemen ranged across the square, the sun shining on the horses' accoutrements, their breath rising like steam from a kettle. Several of the animals were pawing the ground and there was something *ominous* about the movements. A police inspector cantered up and said we could proceed no further, but Christabel said it was a legal demonstration and to that he had no answer, except to say he had his orders.

The struggle started, us trying to break through, them trying to stop us. Alice said you had to admire the skill of their horsemanship! Tom heard what was happening and came to look for me, and somehow in the middle of the scrummage he found me. He said I must return to Thurloe Square immediately because women were not made to be battered and bruised in pitched battles with 'Cossacks', though I think he was only being protective. Eventually, of course, he came with me and he's certainly a bonny fighter is 'our Tom'—he borrowed my hatpin and jabbed away with it at the horses' legs. I thought that was a bit cruel, but it worked and Tom and I actually made it to St Stephen's entrance. As we raced towards the central lobby, I heard Big Ben booming eight o'clock. I could hardly believe my ears because it was mid-afternoon when we marched out of the Caxton Hall, which meant we'd been struggling for close on five hours.

Alice was already in the lobby. She got through by pretending to be an innocent American visitor on her way to meet her brother-in-law in the H. of C., a policeman fell for her story and actually *escorted* her there! Several other suffragettes had made it, too, and while the policemen started to arrest them, I saw Alice whip a 'Votes for Women' banner from under her coat (a sumptuous fur one, of course). Calmly, she wrapped the banner round Mr Gladstone's statue!

Tom was simply stupendous when a policeman grabbed at me and said, 'You're under arrest, miss', he shouted, 'Take your hands off her, you swine!' It took *three* policemen to arrest him. Oh, I wonder how he's faring in Wormwood Scrubs? Knowing Tom, I imagine he will either convert the inmates *and* staff to Socialism, or organise a riot!

Over fifty of us were arrested, including Christabel and Sylvia, plus Tom and a couple of other men supporters, and this morning we were duly sentenced. The Black Maria hasn't changed for the better since last year, but climbing into it with Christabel, having her in the adjoining cattle-stall, somehow uplifted my spirits.

A wardress came into the cell with the meal Kessie had paid to have sent in: soup, lobster thermidor, lemon sorbet, cheese and biscuits. After she had eaten it she felt slightly sick, but it was a distinct improvement on the prison fare. Free association was allowed for first-division prisoners at certain times of the day, so she spent an hour with Christabel and Sylvia, after which she returned to her own cell, refilled her fountain pen from the bottle of ink she had packed in her suitcase and, her diary up-to-date, settled down to write to Sarah before the lights were turned out for the night.

A couple of days later, in Manchester, Sarah finished reading the last lines of Kessie's letter: 'See you soon, keep up the good work in our absence, fondest love, Kessie.'

She had every intention of keeping up the good work. Temporarily, the focus might be on London, but all over the country, fired by the suffragette exploits and the Government's dastardly response, women were flocking to enrol, women who a short while ago would not have said 'boo' to a goose, and as one of the paid organisers of the WSPU's north-west area, Sarah had plenty to occupy her.

After her release from prison Kessie came home for a rest and Sarah went to visit her. On her arrival at The Laurels, the maid left her standing in the hall. Eventually Sheba appeared. 'If you've coom to see Miss Thorpe, she's been having her breakfast in bed. She's fair whacked out and ah'm not disturbing her.'

'Would you tell her I'm here. It is important.'

Sheba held open the sitting-room door. 'Ah'm not hurrying her, mind.'

Crossing to the fireplace, Sarah warmed her hands in front of the blazing fire. What an opulent room it was, leather armchairs and satinwood sofas, embroidered antimacassars and cushions, huge paintings on the walls, maidenhair fern trailing from real china plant-pots. One day soon, everybody would live in similar comfort, and women like Sheba would not grow up to treat people like her and Tom as if they were 'nowt a pound'. Sheba was, of course, upset at the thought of her Kessie marrying beneath her. But Sarah herself couldn't say she was exactly delighted by the news. In the first place, why hadn't Tom told her about the engagement? They'd never had any secrets—for as long as she could recall it had been she and Tom together battling against the world. Fond as she was of the lass, Kessie came from an entirely different world from Tom and she couldn't see how a rich middle-class girl like her could help him in his great task of spreading Socialism throughout the nation.

When Kessie came into the room she was wearing a smart plaid dress and looking far from 'whacked out'. After their fond greeting—Sarah disliked what she called sloppy behaviour, so they didn't actually kiss—Sarah came briskly to the point of her visit.

'You know there's a big Liberal rally at Belle Vue tonight.

107

Mr Churchill and Mr Lloyd George are both speaking. I'm desperately short on experienced hecklers, and we want to make an impact. I don't expect you to get yourself arrested again, but if you could make the point with your usual aplomb and let yourself be thrown out without a fuss . . .?'

Kessie sighed. She had been looking forward to a rest, but glancing at Sarah's face she nodded her assent.

In the evening Kessie sat in her ten-shilling seat near the front of the Belle Vue arena. Behind her in the five-shilling seats, Sarah was holding her handkerchief to her face as if she had a bad cold, hunched under one of Kessie's larger hats which, on her small head, looked like a lampshade. Kessie herself was wearing a hat that shaded her face and had a veil. Such precautions were necessary because Liberal stewards had been ordered to refuse admittance to any female suspected of being a suffragette.

Sarah had agreed that Kessie should be the first person to heckle Mr Lloyd George, so should the audience lose its patience at the interruptions—Sarah had finally organised ten hecklers—and the going get rough, she would be safely away.

The two speakers came on to the platform. The first girl was inexperienced, interrupting Winston Churchill before he had got going, which was a mistake—better to throw him off-balance once he was into his stride—but she managed to hold aloft her 'Votes for Women' banner and to shout, 'When will you give us the vote?' He stabbed a finger towards the banner, 'You're holding it upside down.'

Kessie peered along the rows. She was. Guffaws rocked the arena and she was hard put not to laugh herself. As the girl was bundled out, Mr Churchill said, 'Gently, my friends. The ladies come here asking us to treat them like men. That is what I particularly want to avoid. We must observe chivalry towards the weaker sex, which is dependent on us.'

That opening was seized upon by Sarah who stood up and shouted, 'We do not want to be dependent on you, Mr Churchill, we want the vote.'

Naturally, Sarah refused to go quietly, and it was several

minutes before she was dragged, shouting and kicking, from the arena. During the rest of Mr Churchill's speech there were two further interruptions, one by Adela Pankhurst swamped by her mother's best rose-adorned hat, one by an ILP male stalwart.

The man next to Kessie, a well-dressed, middle-aged, middle-class man, said, 'Disgraceful behaviour. Country's going to the dogs. All the fault of these viragos and their tame poodles of men. Ruining the lives of decent women. What?'

Kessie smiled at him. Mr Lloyd George stood up and she started to breathe slowly and deeply, an action she had found calmed her nerves. Listening to his voice trumpeting the achievements of the Liberals' first year in office, soaring with passion as he described what they intended to achieve in the future, she experienced a pang of regret that she had to interrupt him. It was no more than a pang. His arm swept the air, he paused for dramatic effect, the audience held its breath.

Kessie jumped up, threw her veil back from her face, and her husky tones sliced the silence: 'Votes for Women! We shan't give up until we get them, Mr Lloyd George. So why doesn't the Liberal Government save itself and us . . .'

A tidal wave of noise drowned her. She stood limply, the gesture made, ready now to let herself be thrown out, and since she was near the end of the row there would be no problem. But as the stewards rushed down the aisle, the well-dressed man by her side shoved at her viciously. Unprepared for his attack, Kessie lost her balance and fell to her knees. He started to kick her with his brightly polished shoes, and his actions unleashed a fury among some of the other 'gentlemen' in the expensive ten-shilling seats. Bodies were on top of her, fingers were feeling her breasts and they were *his*, she knew they were, *his* lips were slobbering in her ear, and that word 'fuck' buzzed insistently. It was hideous, terrifying. Then she heard Mr Lloyd George's voice shout, 'Bring her up here.'

The stewards were fighting her assailants. She was lifted on to the platform and hustled across to a door at the rear.

109

The waves of abuse crashed around the arena, and a few cries of 'Shame' pierced them.

For several shaken minutes, Kessie sat in an ante-room with her head in her hands. Brusqueness disguising the kindness of the gesture, one of the stewards thrust a glass of whisky into her hand. 'Tha'd best drink this, lass.'

She thanked him and gulped it down. The spirit went to her head. Through the mist she heard distant roars at the further interruptions and storming applause as Mr Lloyd George finally finished his speech. Then he was standing in front of her. 'Well, Miss Thorpe, here's a nice how-d'you-do. Are you hungry?' She nodded. 'Why don't you tidy yourself up and join us for a bite of supper? We can have a *quiet* discussion.'

Somehow 'us' turned into Mr Lloyd George and herself alone. The stress and the whisky had made Kessie sleepy and she was not entirely clear how she came to be sitting in his suite at the Midland Hotel, across a supper table a waiter had just wheeled in. Part of her mind told her she had absolutely no business to be here but at least there were people about— the waiters, a secretary or somebody in the interconnecting room—and such an opportunity of presenting the suffragette case to him personally was not to be missed.

He was a fascinating companion. Throughout the meal his eyes danced, the magical voice leapt and lilted as he talked about his youth in Caernarvonshire and made far from discreet comments about his Cabinet colleagues and the members of His Majesty's Opposition. He had the same ability as Tom had to focus his attention on you, to make you feel clever, while putting you absolutely at ease. From time to time, he called out to 'Albert' who would instantly pop his head round the connecting door. That made her feel even more at ease.

'You'll have a brandy, *cariad*.' Firmly she shook her head. 'Just a little one before you go home.'

The brandies arrived and Kessie said, 'We haven't discussed votes for women.'

'No more we have. Why don't we sit on the sofa? Serious discussion benefits from comfortable surroundings.'

110

Gingerly, Kessie sat on the edge of the sofa. He was leaning back, his legs sprawled in front of him, the watch-chain tightly stretched across his slight paunch, with one arm on the back of the sofa, the other holding his brandy glass to the light.

She said, 'It's absolutely ludicrous that in advanced, civilised, twentieth-century England, women are denied the vote.'

'Of course, it is, *cariad*. It's even more ludicrous that in advanced, *rich*, twentieth-century England—and Wales and Scotland and Ireland—children go without shoes, their backsides stick through their threadbare trousers, they cry with hunger, and after a lifetime of toil their grandparents are herded into the workhouse.'

His voice soared, effortlessly tearing at the emotions, but what *was* his hand doing? Twisting a strand of her hair, stroking her neck. She pretended it wasn't. Must he call her *cariad*? She had little Welsh but she knew what that meant: *dearest*, or even *darling*.

'You won't get anywhere by bullying us, you know. Men don't like being bullied.' There was a chuckle in his voice and she swung round to face him.

'I wish you'd stop treating us as if we're bright, amusing, but naughty children. The Liberal Government came to power in a landslide victory and has a massive majority in Parliament. The Liberal Government says it's in favour of votes for women. The Liberal Government could pass a Women's Suffrage Bill tomorrow if it wanted. Yet the Liberal Government is literally riding roughshod over us, making the police do its dirty work, and throwing us into prison. Why?'

Her eyes shining, her colour high, her mind less sleepy, she stared straight at him. He pulled himself into a more upright position. Good. She had his attention and he'd stopped that embarrassing nonsense with his hand. He shrugged. 'You're being a nuisance. Governments have to stamp on nuisances, otherwise there'd be anarchy.'

'But if we don't agitate, nothing happens. And if we do, we're irresponsible nuisances to be stamped on.'

Impishly he smiled, acknowledging the circular nature of the impasse. Then he stabbed a finger at her. 'I'll tell you why we cannot pass your Bill, snap, as you imagine. Most women don't want the vote.'

'That's a favourite argument and I dispute it. But if I accept it, neither did most men want any change that's ever been made in our history. Reform is initially the work of an enlightened minority.'

'There's an élitist remark.'

'It's true.'

'If I accept its truth, you as the enlightened minority have to persuade the ignorant majority of your sex to support your righteous views. Until you've done that, most men won't shift.'

'They're going to have to,' Kessie cried passionately. 'Can't you see? Can't you understand what it's like being a woman? A second-class citizen in everything? Petted, patronised, told to be good little girls? Can't you see the frustration and resentment that have built up, even if some women don't know why? Can't you see the waste, when half the population is forbidden to use its talents? Can't you see why the vote is so important to us? It's the actuality and the symbol of our emancipation. Can't you see that we can help to make England—and Wales and Scotland and Ireland—better places for everybody to live in?'

'There's an innocent, idealistic child you are. And beautiful when you're angry, *ferch fach del*.'

Kessie had no need to understand Welsh to appreciate the nature of the last caressing words. He was leaning towards her, his hand was on her cheek, '*Mor anwyl wyt ti, mor anwyl i mi*.' The liquid sounds were softer and his lips were approaching hers. '*F'anwylyd*'.

She stared at his moustache like a hypnotised rabbit. He pressed on her lips, his arms grasped her body, and the use of her limbs returned. She pushed at him hard and leapt up.

'Mr Lloyd George! I am engaged to be married!'

As he scrambled into a sitting position, she held out her left hand and waved Tom's ring at him. Yet what difference to his outrageous behaviour did her status make? Spinster, engaged, married or widowed? What should she do? Scream? Make a dash for the door? Where were her hat and coat?

Smoothing down his rumpled jacket, he said, 'So you are. To young Tom Whitworth. There's a lucky lad. Why don't you persuade him to join us in the Liberal Party? He's wasting his time with that ragbag of Socialists, Marxians, trades unionists and God knows what else that calls itself the Labour Party.'

'It was Mr Keir Hardie of that *ragbag* who first suggested old age pensions.' What *were* they talking about? 'I want to go home.'

'So you shall, *cariad*, come and sit down.' He patted the sofa, slowly, solemnly, moving himself to the far end. She nearly laughed but the situation was appalling. How had she got herself into it? And how was she to get herself out of it? She was still standing, waving her left hand at him, when there was one sharp knock on the door, almost simultaneously it swung wide open and Tom came into the room.

Kessie stared at him and said the first thing that came into her head. 'I was just showing Mr Lloyd George my engagement ring.'

'Were you?' Tom walked across and glared at Lloyd George who rose slowly to his feet. 'You'll excuse the interruption, *sir*, but I've been searching for my fiancée. I was told she was manhandled at your meeting and that you had rescued her.'

Mr Lloyd George's voice had an edgy note but his words were smooth. 'I saw that she was rescued. She was shocked. And hungry. I was just about to put her in a cab and see she got safely home.'

Kessie had never seen Tom quite so angry. Nor quite so attractive. Anger always darkened his skin and being dishevelled suited his personality. He was very dishevelled, the collar of his shabby raincoat turned up, his black hair flopping wildly, and she wondered how he'd managed to get himself into the Midland Hotel, but oh, was she glad to see him. The two men were gazing at each other like boxers

113

measuring up for a fight. Kessie moved nervously, Tom grabbed her arm so tightly that it hurt and his body was rigid.

Albert appeared. Her coat and hat were produced. Words were spoken but they had no connection with the way the two men were looking at each other. Tom started to march her to the door but Mr Lloyd George took her hand in his and kissed it.

'Be happy. Be clever about the way you move your cause up the line of measures demanding Government attention. You have my full support. And if you ever want another discussion about votes for women, you know where to find me.'

She thought Tom was going to hit him.

All the way down Oxford Road and as the cab turned by All Saints Church, with the horses' hooves echoing in the silent streets, Tom raged at her. What the devil had she been thinking of, going with Lloyd George to his suite? Didn't she know his reputation? And even if she didn't, what was she doing any road? Compromising herself, behaving no better than a common street-walker. She was his fiancée and he expected her to show some sense and decency. Was she aware that while she had been dallying *tête-à-tête* with the Great God Pan, Sarah and several other women had been arrested?

Silently, not fully grasping everything he said, Kessie huddled in the corner of the cab. She was bemused, hurt, ashamed, and so exhausted she thought her head would float away. It had been a hideous evening, the scene at Belle Vue, the scene at the Midland Hotel, and now Tom storming at her. Nobody had *ever* spoken to her like that before. Finally, the anger stirred and she interrupted his diatribe.

'If you're so worried about my reputation, why are you alone with me now? We're not married yet. We're only engaged. If you think I'm so immoral, we can break off the engagement here and now.'

Weeping copiously, she tugged at her engagement ring, but she couldn't get it off her finger. Oh why did women cry so much more easily than men? She hated herself for

114

being childish and she hated Tom. He put his arm round her shoulder, the broad brim of her hat was in the way, he took out the hatpins, lifting it from her head and stroking her hair. 'Kess, Kess, don't cry. I shouldn't have shouted at you. It's because I love you. He didn't touch you, did he?'

She shook her head and then, worried by the instinctive lie, she looked up at him. 'I think he might have done if you hadn't arrived.'

Tom laughed sardonically.

'You are an innocent child, aren't you?' She just stopped herself from saying that Mr Lloyd George had made a similar remark.

The tears were staining her face, her lower lip was trembling, her body was soft against his and, Tom thought, you couldn't blame the bugger for wanting her and the idea of Lloyd George wanting her excited him more. God, it was time he married her, particularly now. 'You haven't asked me why I'm in Manchester.'

'Why are you in Manchester?'

'I dashed up to tell you Havers dropped dead of a heart attack this afternoon.' She started to giggle and he was annoyed, though it must have sounded a bit ridiculous, put baldly like that. 'Havers, Sir John Havers. The MP for The Dales. There'll have to be a by-election. The Dales is Labour country. And that's why I'm here. We can win the seat from the Liberals. *I* can win it. Kess, let's get married and we can fight the by-election as man and wife.'

10

Six hectic weeks later, Tom and Kessie walked hand-in-hand up the lane towards the graveyard that clung to the hillside above Mellordale.

Tom had been selected as the Labour candidate for The

Dales. Papa had bellowed a great deal about the shortened engagement, but fortunately he had grown fond of Tom—they both enjoyed a good argument—and even more fortunately Kessie's relations had stormed up to The Laurels, shouting that if Charles allowed his daughter to marry a Socialist agitator, none of the Thorpe family would ever be able to hold their heads up in public again. That did it. Papa not only gave his blessing to their marriage, but he agreed to help out with Tom's election expenses, seeing the Labour Party was such an impecunious organisation—though Kessie thought his still-seething fury with the Liberals for twice imprisoning his daughter might have had something to do with that gesture.

For *her* sake, Christabel had agreed that the WSPU would back Tom's election campaign. And that even though the majority of the Labour Party had refused to support votes for women *now*—despite Mr Keir Hardie's and Tom's passionate efforts—and the WSPU was therefore cutting its previous close links with the ILP and the Socialist movement as a whole.

And now only a week remained until their marriage.

Climbing up the lane, Kessie said, 'Isn't it a shame that Alice won't be at the wedding? Still, being invited to stay at Chadburn Hall while the King is there, obviously she could not refuse that invitation.'

'Who are we compared to him? We're only her friends.' Tom felt obscurely annoyed that Alice was not coming to the wedding.

Kessie said, 'Don't start that, Tom. You know I don't agree with you about the King.'

They walked on in silence, and he said, 'Have you reached a decision about our married name?'

'Mm. I agree that double-barrelled names sound pompous, even if emancipated men and women link them from the highest motives.'

'So do I take it that you have no objection to being . . .'

'Mrs Ernest Thomas Feargus Whitworth. No, I haven't.' At times Tom was not certain about her sense of humour—the way she had rolled out his full name had made that

116

sound pompous too. She was taking a deep breath, so he braced himself, knowing that something important was about to emerge.

'I've had my talk with Mr Statham and he will conduct the marriage service and allow me to omit the word "obey", because he doesn't see why women should obey men, either. That is one of the advantages of being a Unitarian. We've always believed that women are entitled to some equality on earth, rather than waiting until they reach heaven. But it will raise the dust, Tom, if I refuse to obey you, you do realise that, don't you?'

'Yes, me luv, I do, so hush up and obey me.' He put his hand over her lips and she kissed it.

They reached the graveyard where Tom placed the posy of flowers in the jam-jar on his mother's grave, while Kessie made a note to buy a decent flower holder. Then he said, 'I received your letter, me luv.'

Kessie let out a long, sighing breath. Hard as she tried, much as she felt she should be boldly direct, she had found it impossible to raise the subject of babies with Tom in person. Why he should choose to discuss such a delicate matter now, standing staring at his mother's grave, she was unclear.

Tom had been touched and amused, if somewhat surprised, by Kessie's letter in which she had explained that she did not wish to have a baby right away. Was it a question of God's will, or was there something that could be done, some element of choice? If there was a choice, did he mind if they waited before starting a family? Tom was quite clear why he had brought her to Mam's grave and slowly he started to explain. 'Our Mam was married when she was eighteen. She had ten kids in as many years, but she was a strong healthy lass and they all survived. Then she had several miscarriages before I was born, followed by Sarah a year later. Apart from working in the mill, she looked after Dad and twelve of us, and she kept our house like a new pin. You could see your reflection in the black-lead on our kitchen range. Our front doorstep and our window ledges always had their clean beige coats on because Mam was always donkey-stoning them. She was proud, you see.

117

She'd show 'em a half-gipsy girl was as good as any of 'em.

'Late one afternoon, we'd both just come in from the mill. Mam was putting the kettle on, I was getting my books together for evening class, and I heard her say, "Oh Tom, I'm feeling poorly." I turned round and she was sliding to the floor and it was like a leaf falling from a tree. It was minutes before I grasped the fact that she was dead.'

The memory still cut like a knife. Tom could see his young self in the kitchen of that house, down there in the valley by the Mellor stream, running to Mam's side, cradling her in his arms. He could hear himself crying at her to wake up and the great howl that rent his body when he realised that she never would.

'Mam was forty-six when she died. I was fourteen. Dad was at a union meeting. Organising the millennium for men, as Sarah's fond of saying. When I understood more about things like that, I came up here and I swore on Mam's grave that I would never give a woman a child unless she wanted my child.'

Leaning forward, his long fingers traced the words on the headstone, "Here lieth the mortal remains of Edie Whitworth, dearly beloved wife of Amos Whitworth, God gaveth and God taketh away.'

He said, 'It wasn't God. It was Dad killed her.'

Tom's inflection was hard and Kessie shivered. But then he straightened up, turned towards her, and smiling tenderly ran a finger down her cheek.

'So don't you fret yourself, my beautiful Kess. You don't have to have a baby unless you want to, and I shan't give you one until you do.'

Lightly, gently, he kissed her. She clung to him, her body was trembling and Tom, who passionately wanted a child, had not the slightest doubt she would soon want to bear his.

Her gloved hand resting lightly on Franklin's arm, Alice entered the banqueting hall at Chadburn Hall. King Edward VII's visit was informal, a gesture to honour the tenth wedding anniversary of his friends, the Duke and Duchess of Derbyshire, squeezed in at the end of the London season before he departed for Cowes regatta week on the Isle of Wight and to take the waters at Marienbad. His Majesty had, however, agreed to grace with his presence the public firework display later in the evening. Alice gathered there were thousands of people already waiting for admittance to the grounds. She thought how strangely coincidental it was that the Derbyshires' wedding anniversary should be the same day as Tom and Kessie's marriage.

Because of the firework display they were dining early, and for the first time in her life Alice was not feeling hungry. Food had never stopped appearing since her arrival at Chadburn Hall, she had never seen anybody consume such gargantuan quantities as King Edward, whose idea of a *snack* was a huge lobster salad or an enormous lamb cutlet or a piled plateful of quails. His Majesty's favourite dish at a fourteen-course dinner made Alice quail; the culinary equivalent of those Russian dolls that fitted inside each other in descending size, a turkey stuffed with a chicken stuffed with a pheasant stuffed with a woodcock.

For the first time in her life Alice was also feeling a mite overawed, and she wondered what a formal visit by His Majesty would entail. The chandeliers in the banqueting hall were not yet lit, only the candles on the table, for the golden evening light of a perfect English summer's day was enfolding the room, glowing on the magnificently panelled walls, glancing across the Van Dyck, Raeburn and Romney portraits of Derbyshire ancestors. The sunlight glinted on the silver gilt cutlery, the crystal goblets and glasses set the length of the huge dining-table, across the flowers floating in their Wedgwood bowls, over the smilax trailing its feathery way between the damask table napkins folded into the designs of the rose and star, the mitre, the cockscomb, the boar's head and, of course, the royal fleur-de-lys.

As soon as they were seated, Alice on the King's right hand, His Majesty waved a thick finger towards the decorations in her hair. She held her breath, wondering if she had overdone things, and was about to receive a blast of royal disapproval. But he said, 'Enchanting, *ma petite*. Where did you find them and how do they work?' His accent was slightly, gutturally German, the 'w's emerging almost as 'v's, though he scattered his conversation with French phrases, *à la mode*.

Alice informed His Majesty that she had spied 'the pea lamps' that adorned her hair in a shop in Bond Street and could not resist them. The tiny electric bulbs of pink and crimson (which matched the soft pink of her gown embroidered with a crimson *motif*) worked on some sort of wired battery thing.

'I thought I'd be attuned to the illuminations later on, sir.'

The King roared with laughter, Alice smiled, and he tilted his head to one side. This was a slightly alarming process, owing to the shortness and thickness of his neck, and she hoped it didn't hurt him.

'I have been hearing things about you, Miss Alice Hartley. They tell me you are a suffragette. Can this be true?' She admitted that it was. 'A beautiful young lady like you who can obtain anything she wants in the world, anything she wants from a man, merely by lifting a little finger? Why, tell me why?'

Alice smiled again because she didn't think he actually wanted to know. He didn't. He went straight on. 'My dearest Mama observed that women are not made for governing. As in so many things, my dearest Mama was shrewd in her judgement. That is not what women are made for. Mama considered that ladies demanding the vote were downright wicked creatures. So they are.'

It was all right for your Mama, Alice thought, she was the Queen of the greatest Empire the world has ever known. The King peered solicitously at her. 'You are not taking this *de mauvaise part, ma petite*?'

Suffering rattlesnakes, was she looking as cross as she felt? Because she must not offend the King of England who was a sweet, kindly old Teddy bear, if a grossly overstuffed one. 'No, sir. Only I don't agree with you or the late lamented Queen, if I may respectfully say so, sir.'

Laughter shook his frame and the table appeared to shake with it. 'American women are full of spirit. Beauty and spirit.' With everyone gazing at them, he said, 'I am about

120

to tell *la petite Américaine, la petite Alice*, that she must go back to her *suffragette* friends,' disapproval sounded round the table, 'and tell them—enough is enough. It is time they married and gave their attention to looking after their husbands and instructing their children, *not* my Government, how to behave.'

Now murmurs of approval ran round the table. The King lifted her hand and kissed it. 'The man who marries you will be fortunate indeed, *ma chère Alice*. Beauty and spirit.'

His tone was kindly, jocular, but Alice was sure he had meant every odious word he'd just uttered. *Hélas!*

Tom had suggested they retire early and blushingly Kessie had agreed. As part of his wedding present her father was paying for their honeymoon at this posh hotel in Cheshire. Not that they were having much of a honeymoon, two days only, because the campaigning for The Dales' election was about to start.

Sitting in the dressing-room of their suite, alternately brushing her hair and adjusting the straps of her nightdress, Kessie stared at her reflection in the gilded mirror, while images of what had been the most wonderful, perfect day of her life—as all wedding days should be—interposed themselves like the views through a camera lens.

The shafts of sunshine gleaming through the windows of Cross Street Chapel, Papa extraordinarily nervous, setting off down the aisle like a bullet, Christabel and Sarah lovely in their pale pink bridesmaids' dresses, but knowing from the expression in Tom's eyes that on this day, her day, she was the fairest of them all. The gasp that went through the congregation when she promised only to love and cherish Tom. The crowds and the pressmen, making her realise that they were of interest to the great British public, she the new woman, he the herald of the new Socialism. The journalists crowding round them, demanding to know what Tom (not she) felt about her refusal to obey him and why he had permitted this breach of the Christian marriage service? Tom holding forth about the centuries of women's slavery drawing to an end and obviously enjoying himself. Mrs

Pankhurst showering them with confetti, the tears in her eyes, as they drove away from the reception at the Midland Hotel, the tin cans, old boots and horseshoes, the 'Just Married', 'Votes for Women' and 'Vote Labour' streamers clattering, banging and waving behind them.

She heard Tom's voice calling. Emerging from the dressing-room, Kessie glanced at, then nervously averted her eyes from, the huge double bed, its sheet turned back invitingly wide. Her nightdress was of finest silk, a delicate shade of eau-de-nil, sleeveless, with two slender lace straps and a lace bodice over silk folds. To her astonishment, Aunt Ada had presented her with it, and another in pale blue, privately, a few days before the wedding. Brusquely, she'd said she had once been told that marriages were made, or unmade, in the bedroom, and she wanted her niece to look her best. Then she'd blushed a bright beetroot colour and left the room.

Her husband—Kessie loved that word—was dressed in a plain flannel nightshirt. He was coming towards her, his eyes were coal black, and he was smiling the slightly crooked smile that excited her so much. He put his hands round her neck and she shivered with delicious anticipation. But all he did was unclasp the gilt necklace with the red glass horseshoes.

'You don't want this old thing on, do you?'

'I've worn it ever since you bought it for me. Except in prison, when they wouldn't let me.'

He had bought it for her? Not by a flicker did Tom betray his surprise. He searched his memory and the incident came back to him, that day at the Wakes Week fair and that girl selling her tawdry junk. He was astounded and flattered that Kessie should have kept the necklace. Dropping it on to the table, he said, 'We don't want to get it broken, do we?' He lifted her face towards his and she was trembling like a leaf. God, he must be gentle with her, or as gentle as he could be.

'Relax, my lovely Kess, and let it happen.'

Oh, yes, yes, she was longing for it to happen. Tom was kissing her as never before, his tongue was opening her lips, licking, probing, twisting round hers, it was breathlessly exciting but it was the place between her legs that was throbbing and would Tom's body rub hers as she had rubbed herself? He was holding her tighter, crushing her against him, through the silk of her nightdress she felt something soft with a rigid jutting thing, and he was pressing those against that place and she moaned, 'Oh Tom.'

Picking her up in his arms, almost throwing her under the sheets, he turned off the bedside lamp and in the darkness his body was hot and strong against hers. She was gasping, he was gasping even more, his mouth was on hers again, his fingers, those long fingers, were inside her lace bodice, running over her breasts, pressing her nipples and oh, the sensation was a thousand times more exquisite, painfully exquisite, than she had imagined. He was saying things she didn't understand, one hand was rubbing that place, the other was pushing up her nightdress, and she cried out with the passionate excitement. He said hoarsely, 'Kess, darling Kess, I'll try not to hurt you.'

What did he mean? Hurt her? Then everything happened in a blur of shock and pain. He had that rigid jutting thing between her legs and he was trying to get it *right inside her*—and, she thought wildly—it won't go. Suddenly, he rammed into her and she screamed. He was on top of her, smothering her, grabbing her hair, biting her shoulder, thrusting himself faster and faster, harder and harder into her, he sounded like a grampus, except he was saying he loved her, and it was worse than being in the Black Maria, she thought hysterically, hauling up the hill to Holloway. As suddenly as he had entered her body he pulled himself out, there was a sticky mess on her stomach and it smelled disgustingly. After he had lain gasping for several seconds he did wipe the mess off, he was trying to hold her in his arms, to stroke her hair which he'd nearly pulled out by the roots, to kiss away the tears he had produced.

'I'm sorry, Kess, I'm sorry I hurt you. But you were very tight, my darling, and that excites a man.' Did it? Well, it hadn't excited her and if marriages were made in the bedroom then hers was an absolute, utter and total disaster.

'It'll be all right next time, Kessie mine. I promise you.'

Next time! She pulled away from him and buried her face

123

in the pillow. It was awful. It was hideous. It was as distant from her dreaming anticipation as a cesspit from a rose, as a Mellordale mill-worker from the King of England. How could it be like that? How could Tom have done that to her?

The Japanese lanterns were lit the mile length of the drive-way from the huge wrought-iron gates to the forecourt of Chadburn Hall, the multi-coloured fairy lights twined through the rose gardens, the spot-lamps shone in the shrubbery, and the pea-lamps in Alice's hair glimmered from the shadows of the terrace. A fountain of silver and platinum fireworks spewed into the dark blue of the night sky, upwards towards the glittering stars, illuminating the bowl of hills and the thousands of wide-eyed upturned faces, before falling like phosphorescent rain into the waters of the lake.

Alice's face was lit by the glow and Franklin said, 'His Majesty was right. You look enchanting, Miss Hartley. Shall I drive you back to London on Saturday? Or do you wish to go straight to Sussex?'

'I may be going to Mellordale to campaign in Tom's by-election. I haven't made up my mind.' Part of Alice wanted to go because it was bound to be exciting. But she was still furious with Tom and Kessie, too, and they would be on their honeymoon, their first night, more or less about now, but she wouldn't think about that.

Frankie was staring at her, his mouth half-open. He snapped it shut, opened it again and the words shot out. 'You cannot campaign for a *Socialist!*'

He made it sound like a leper and Alice said, 'Tom is not standing as a Socialist, but as a women's candidate.'

'You may think he's standing as a women's candidate, but does he? Now look here, Alice . . .'

'Don't you "look here" me!'

The cries of wonderment were sweeping round the grounds and firmly Alice returned her attention to the fireworks. Hundreds of catherine wheels were whirling on the framework of the final set-piece, igniting a border of tudor roses and fleur-de-lys. The heads of the Duke and

Duchess of Derbyshire fizzed on to the frame, glittering for several seconds before they were consumed into the larger crowned heads of King Edward VII and Queen Alexandra. From the bandstand the strains of the national anthem slowly swelled. Everybody on the terrace rose to their feet, bowing their heads towards his seated Majesty. Above them on the hill the words 'God Save the King' blazed into golden light, the crowds stood to attention, and the band switched to *fortissimo*. Thousands of voices sang, 'God save our Gracious King, Long live our noble King . . .', their voices rising with patriotic fervour as the cymbals clashed and the trumpets blared, 'Send him victorious, Happy and glorious, Long to reign over us . . .' Alice made up her mind. Or rather, Frankie's dictatorial attitude had made it up for her. She would go to Mellordale . . . 'God save the King!'

11

Kessie was waiting on the platform as the train steamed into Mellordale's grimy station and, like a sunburst, Alice appeared. The porter whose services she had secured, because Miss Hartley was bound to have dozens of bags, blouse cases and hat boxes, was appreciative. 'By gow! She's a good looker!'

His opinion proved to be shared by the majority of the citizens of The Dales, and Alice's clothes created a sensation. Each day she appeared in a different outfit, each evening another, cream shantung suits, tussore silk and Chantilly lace coats, chiffon, voile, ninon, lawn, muslin, finest cotton and broderie anglaise blouses, skirts and gowns. If it was chilly, they were slung with fox or sable or mink furs, if wet covered by sleek Bengali raincoats. All the garbs were topped by huge hats—straw hats, silk velour hats, hats smothered in feathers or decorated with half of Kew Gardens and Belle

Vue Zoo—and Alice had a penchant for translucent enamel animal heads on buckles and clasps.

'Aren't you overdoing it, luv?' Tom said. 'Half the women in The Dales have barely a rag to their backs.'

'They like seeing nice clothes. It cheers them up.' Kessie thought Alice was probably right, because everywhere she went she was surrounded by gawping men, women and children, and there was no animosity in their faces.

The night Tom took them to a fish-and-chip shop Alice almost caused a riot, and the police had to be called out to control the crowds who were watching Miss Hartley as she watched the potatoes bubbling and bouncing in the boiling fat, before eating her portions of chips, crispy battered hake and green peas from the normal newspaper wrapping. When Alice exclaimed, 'Just think, this time last week I was having dinner with the King at Chadburn Hall, but this is much more fun,' the clapping and cheering echoed through the mean streets, right up to Netherstone Edge.

That was the extraordinary thing about Alice, Kessie reflected, her ability to move from world to world without turning one glorious golden hair. Was it an American characteristic? Or was it just Alice?

The first few days of the campaign were fun, but then the Liberal candidate, Ralph Treadgold, woke up to two facts. Tom Whitworth was much loved in The Dales and the WSPU ladies were no joke. Henceforward, in all his speeches, Mr Treadgold mentioned that Tom Whitworth had gipsy blood in him, that he had been to prison, that he was surrounded by women, and that he had been unable to get his own wife to obey him. Which obviously made him untrustworthy, irresponsible, and not much of a man. The Treadgold claques appeared at Tom's meetings, or when the suffragettes were speaking, armed with bags of flour, pea-shooters, rotten eggs and squelchy tomatoes. There were scuffles and brawls in the streets and Alice said, 'Isn't it exciting? It's like the Wild West,' not that Alice had ever been near the Wild West. 'Nobody will ever again tell me how polite and well-behaved the English are!'

Actually, Kessie did not enjoy the rowdiness, but it was like facing the police horses in Parliament Square, or going to prison, something you had to do for the sake of the cause, whether it be votes for women or getting Tom elected as a Labour MP.

A few days before polling day the weather was glorious and after they had spent the morning canvassing, Kessie said, 'It's a simply heavenly afternoon, Tom. Let's go up to Netherstone Edge, please. We are entitled to a couple of hours off on our honeymoon, aren't we?'

Tom seemed none too sure that they were, but eventually he agreed and they left the airless, treeless streets of Mellordale behind, climbing steadily up towards the Edge. The sheep baaed at them, scampering into bleating circles, the ground grew steeper and stonier, and Tom held out his hand to help Kessie up. They were on the black rocks of the Edge that sheered up towards the heavens, below them the open moorlands rolled down to the stone-piled walls that ran across the landscape like black snakes, and way down in the valley the smoke lay in thick piles above the mills.

Up here the air was clear; up here the wind always blew.

In a cleft between the rocks they stretched out together, and Tom said, 'This is the grandest view in the world, I reckon. I used to come up here when I was a kid, sometimes with little Sarah tagging along, more often by myself, and I'd practise the speeches I was going to make one day.'

Grinning, he turned towards Kessie and the cleft in his chin stretched. Oh, how she loved him! What an extraordinary topsy-turvy business life was. On that first night, she had sobbed herself to sleep in shocked disbelieving anguish. In the early morning Tom had taken her relaxed sleepy body in his arms, sliding inside her not only without pain but with a sensation of mounting, rapturous ecstasy that she would remember to her dying day. Each time now the wonderment grew, she wanted to be with Tom all the time, with nothing to do but touch him, talk with him, walk with him, lie with him, oh that, oh yes . . . the sun was warm on Kessie's face, high in the sky a lark was singing, and the heat and the sweet sounds lulled her senses.

127

'Do you think you and Christabel could canvass some of the outlying farms for me tomorrow? You both say you like walking!'

Tom looked down at his wife, but she was asleep. Gently he kissed her soft hair, smiling at the suppleness of her body—since being in Holloway and denied corsets, she had decided they were a symbol of restriction. Except when she was dressed up for formal occasions, she had announced, she would no longer wear them. Bless her and her theories! She was nestling closer to him, and God he wanted her, here on Netherstone Edge, as he had once had Ella Warburton. . . . Tom pushed that memory to the recesses of his mind.

Virtually everybody except the suffragettes had told him he could not possibly hope to be elected at his age, at the first attempt, but this was his country, these were his people, and with Kessie by his side, nothing was impossible.

On the morning before polling day, Tom pulled the bed-clothes from his wife's somnolent body.

'Come on, Kess, it's six o'clock. Do you know where my razor is?'

Bleary-eyed, Kessie sat up. Why on earth should she know where his razor was? Then she remembered that he had dropped it on the floor last night—they were staying at Aunt Ada's house in Milnrow where Sheba's niece, Maggie, was looking after them. Having told her husband where his razor might be, she went back to sleep.

'Kess, get up, you lazy little madam. I can't find my collar stud.'

He never could. Tom was appallingly untidy and Kessie wished he had inherited his mother's proud neatness. This morning she told him so, which was a mistake, because his 'Mam' was sacrosanct. Pulling the bedclothes from her again, he started to shout. Didn't he realise how tired she was? Didn't he realise some people needed their sleep? What had the Rolls-Royce to do with his collar stud? He was bawling about that now, the beautiful 'Silver Ghost' model designed by Papa's friend, Mr Royce, which was his main wedding present, delivered to Milnrow last night.

'I know you're one of the few women in the world who can drive a motor car, but I can't afford to run a Rolls-Royce. I don't want a Rolls-Royce. You had no business accepting a present like that without consulting me. I . . .'

Kessie jumped out of bed, the chestnut hair streaming down her back. 'I . . . me . . . that's all I hear. You're a selfish, inconsiderate . . .'

'And you're a stuck-up madam who doesn't know how to make a cup of tea and . . .'

'We can't all have been born in a mill.'

It was a stupid remark and for one terrible moment she thought Tom was going to hit her. As she flinched, he spotted his collar stud on the floor, grabbed it and stormed from the room. She did not see him again until the evening.

As the sun set over the moors, it bathed Mellordale in an infernal glare, splitting into bands of crimson that deepened to indigo, slowly darkening to a deep velvety blue. The moon was a huge crystal ball and the stars were diamond bright.

It had been Alice's idea to have a torchlight procession and a final meeting on the moors—'You know that place where the fair was, where I first met you all.' Thousands of people had responded and were now making their way up to Mellordale moor. Some had brought their own home-made flares and torches, others had taken them from the boxes that Kessie had organised in the Market Square, and ignited them at the braziers. All over the hillside the lights were flickering, and it was as if human trains were chugging up the lanes, their carriage windows blazing. Tom and Mrs Pankhurst were standing in a lorry at the far end of the field, their faces illuminated by the glow of the flares, while the magnesium flashes of the photographers added to the theatricality.

Both the speakers had powerful voices, but Kessie doubted if half the audience could hear what they said. It didn't seem to matter. The beauty of the balmy night and the spectacle of the thousands of flaming torches were sufficient inspiration. Even the Treadgold claques were overwhelmed and had either disappeared or shut up. For those who could hear, Mrs Pankhurst's beautiful contralto and Tom's resonant baritone complemented each other, musically and politically, playing the theme of women's enfranchisement being not a side-issue but an essential for the forward march of a just civilised society. Which Tom Whitworth as the MP for The Dales would help bring into being.

Nobody seemed to want to leave but eventually people drifted away from the magic and hope the torchlight meeting had conjured back to their hard drab lives.

Tom kissed Alice's hand: 'Thank you for organising a truly memorable night.'

Demurely, Alice smiled her acknowledgment then watched him cross the field to join Kessie, who appeared not to be speaking to him. A rift already? By Alice's side a woman wrapped in a shawl said, 'Ee, he's an attractive young bugger. Don't they make a luvly picture? Just wed and all.'

Ee—an apparently obligatory noise before most people in The Dales spoke—he *was* attractive and all. It had taken Alice a full week to adjust to the word 'bugger'. Didn't it mean something, well, disgusting, if she wasn't sure what? In Lancashire, however, it was an all-purpose word—you lazy bugger, you nowty bugger, oh bugger it, I'll be buggered—if not all Lancastrians used it. Christabel didn't, nor did Kessie, though Tom did frequently, Sarah occasionally.

Walking down the steep lane back into town, the moon-light silvering Tom's dark hair (he'd be as handsome an older man as he was a young one), Alice could not make up her mind about him. Tom was far from 'daft' and Kessie was an enormous asset to him in the campaign, not only in the role of blushing bride, but because she had an articulate self-confidence when speaking which appealed to the bolder spirits, while her charming manners smoothed his rougher edges. Her father, the owner of one of the biggest cotton mills in The Dales, was a highly influential figure. Such thoughts must have crossed Tom's ambitious mind. But if that man hadn't dropped down dead to cause the by-election, would he ever have actually married Kessie?

It was a form of torture, Kessie decided, waiting for the votes to be counted in Mellordale Town Hall, and waiting for the recount was a greater agony. After what seemed like a century, the mayor called the candidates together, the recount was accepted by all three men and they went on to the Town Hall balcony.

Affecting his poshest voice, the mayor announced the result. 'I, Joshua Tattersall, the returning officer for The Dales constituency, declare that the total number of votes cast for each candidate was as follows: Marsham, C. W., three thousand, four hundred and twenty-one . . .', he was the Tory candidate who had never had a chance, 'Treadgold, R. H., six thousand, eight hundred and forty-four . . .', a tremor rustled through the crowds packed into the Market Square, 'Whitworth, E. T. F., six thousand, eight hundred and ninety-five. . . .'

The rest of his words, declaring that Whitworth, E. T. F., had been duly elected to serve as the Member of Parliament for The Dales, was lost in the roars, shouts and singing that rose to the tall mill chimneys. Tom had won. He was Tom Whitworth, MP. He had won by fifty-one votes, and Kessie had driven more than that number of his voters to the polling stations in the Rolls-Royce.

Within the fortnight Kessie was sitting in the Ladies' Gallery of the House of Commons. By her side was Sarah and they were both gazing down upon Tom who had, if not without considerable difficulty, managed to gain admittance for two such noted suffragettes as his wife and his sister to hear his 'maiden speech'. They were in agreement that it was just typical that a man's supposedly nervous oratorical début in a male preserve should be called a 'maiden' speech. Tom *was* nervous, Kessie could tell. Her secret knowledge that Tom was not always as supremely confident as he appeared only made her love him more. And in the charcoal grey lounge suit, which she had persuaded him to let her buy

131

when he refused to wear the normal House of Commons uniform of frock-coat and striped trousers, he looked as fine as any man present.

Tom glanced up at her and Sarah, she smiled reassuringly, Sarah waved and the lady sitting next to them said, 'Really!' Mr Lloyd George entered the Chamber, his eyes followed Tom's upward glance and when he saw Kessie he halted, bowed deeply and waved *his* hand. Heads on the Liberal, Tory, Unionist, Labour and Irish benches turned towards the object of the President of the Board of Trade's attention, the very attractive young lady leaning eagerly forward, a striking green and white hat on her chestnut hair. As the knowing smiles spread on the MPs' faces, hastily Kessie sat upright. Mr Lloyd George's behaviour was outrageous and she prayed he hadn't upset her husband.

When Tom rose to make his début as a parliamentarian, all at once Kessie couldn't look. She sat, eyes closed, rigid with tension.

'. . . and I was sent here by the electorate of three cotton towns, a male electorate, of course . . .' Baas of derision echoed round the Chamber, but they gave Tom confidence.

'From what I've heard so far, you need the facts of life as they're lived by most of the citizens of this country ramming home . . .' The baas turned to groans, but Tom proceeded to ram the facts home, and his information about specific conditions in the cotton trade was well marshalled. It was a brash, assertive speech, not *the* best Kessie had heard him make, but when Tom sat down he looked well enough pleased with himself.

She longed to run down, to kiss him, to tell him how proud she was of him, but they had to wait until the end of the debate. With half an ear she listened to the lethargic, boring speeches that followed, then Mr Lloyd George rose to his feet, nonchalantly surveying the House, his thumb tucked under the lapel of his frock-coat. He would liven things up, she thought, but he had only been speaking for a couple of minutes when Sarah's voice rang out:

'Votes for Women! That is the question this House should be debating. Votes for Women *now*! We demand . . .'

132

Kessie was as taken by surprise as anybody in the Chamber, and she was furious with Sarah. How *dare* she interrupt? Her sister-in-law was doing more than interrupting, she was unfurling a WSPU banner and flinging it over the rail of the Ladies' Gallery. As Sarah went on shouting, embarrassment flooded through Kessie, male protests rose to the high ceiling, MPs were on their feet, waving their order papers, and the lady next to them had retreated against the panelled wall and was squeaking, 'Really!'

The stewards appeared, pushing their way along the row towards Sarah, who now had her back to the grille that divided the Ladies' Gallery from the other public galleries. The banner floated to the floor of the Chamber where Mr Lloyd George picked it up. The stewards could not move Sarah and it was several seconds before Kessie realised what she had done. She had chained herself to the grille. Part of Kessie was still angry with her sister-in-law, but a larger part was filling with astonished admiration.

Still Sarah stood her ground, her hand chained to the grille, shouting, 'Votes for Women! Give us the vote and you'll have no more disturbances. Votes for Women now!'

On and on *and* on she went because there was no key, therefore no way the stewards could undo the padlock. The Sergeant-at-Arms was called, workmen were called, they tried to saw through the chain but Sarah would not keep still, and finally the Sergeant-at-Arms said the grille itself would have to be cut away. That took a long time and meanwhile the business of the Commons had to be suspended because Sarah continued to shout. Kessie sat watching the operation, the giggles bubbling inside her—it had been a superb idea—though she tried to look disapproving and Sarah studiously avoided her eye. What *was* Tom going to say?

Eventually, a triumphant Sarah was led from the Ladies' Gallery, a steward holding on to the section of ornate grille still attached to her wrist. In an ante-room she graciously permitted a workman to saw through the padlock, and then was escorted down to the lobby, with Kessie following

133

behind. Tom was waiting, shaking so much with rage he could barely speak. And before he could get into his stride, a message came down from somewhere on high that Miss Sarah Whitworth would not be prosecuted, but that she was never to be allowed inside the precincts of the Houses of Parliament again.

Mr Lloyd George walked up, a bundle of cloth over his arms. He bowed. 'Your banner, Miss Whitworth. Tut, tut, disrupting the business of this august House! Doesn't do it any harm, mind, occasionally.' Turning towards Kessie, softly the liquid Welsh voice said, 'You haven't been to see me to continue our discussion about votes for women. Why don't you have tea with me one day?'

His charm was as all-enveloping as Tom's. He knew she was a married lady now and he couldn't do anything very dreadful during *tea*, but Kessie did not feel her husband would be at all pleased if she accepted the invitation, so she just smiled politely.

Tom marched them down St Stephen's Hall and out into Old Palace Yard where the photographers and reporters were clustered. When they had finally disappeared, his fury blew like a newly tapped geyser. 'What the hell did you think you were playing at, Sal? I gave my solemn guarantees that you wouldn't interrupt. And you promised . . .'

'No, Kessie did. I didn't. You never asked me.'

Tom glanced at his sister before shouting about the way she had humiliated him, ruined his début as a parliamentarian, damaged his chances of pushing *her* cause in the immediate future. 'And I had planned to take you both for tea on the terrace. Well, there's no chance of that now, of course.'

'Oh dear, what a loss! But do you think you'd have passed up an opportunity like that? Not on your nelly you wouldn't. So why should I?'

Trying to keep their voices down in the public view of Old Palace Yard, they were quarrelling bitterly. Kessie attempted to defuse the heat, but the combatants swept her aside. 'Don't you tell me what to do and how to behave, Tom, I'm not your wife.'

134

'No, you're not, you're my sister. It's time you grew up and stopped thinking I belong to you. Because I don't.'

For a few seconds Sarah stared at him. Then she gathered up her skirt, dodged away through the traffic in Parliament Square and disappeared into the underground station. Kessie watched her go. Did Sarah really think that because she was Tom's wife, he could tell her what to do? How unexpectedly peculiar of her.

Sarah caught the first train back to Manchester.

Ignoring the whispers of her fellow travellers, who obviously recognised her from the photographs in the newspapers, she stared out of the window as the tranquil meadows and streams of the Midlands rushed by. She had no regrets about her action. The idea had come to her when she had seen a little girl chained to a park railing by her big brother (whom she'd given a smart clip round the earhole and ordered to release his sister). How Tom would react she had been unsure, but she had not expected injured masculine pride. She now knew what her brother thought about her, not to mince words she was a bloody nuisance. Well, he hadn't exactly leapt in her own esteem this afternoon. Henceforward she would lead her own life without any reference to him.

By the time they steamed into London Road Station in Manchester, Sarah had made up her mind what she was going to do. On the strength of her WSPU organiser's salary, two whole pounds a week, Sarah now lived in a flat in the Moss Side area. Nevertheless, suitcase in hand, she took the tram to Edward Dawson's lodgings. Edward had been around for some time, preaching his Marxian philosophy, urging her to live with him in a free relationship, unfettered by bourgeois family chains.

As soon as she was safely inside his room—for a bold Marxian he took a lot of precautions to ensure nobody saw her enter—without preamble Sarah said, 'Do you still want me as your mistress?'

She watched him stuttering his assent and saw the sweat beading his clean-shaven upper lip (moustaches were bourgeois, too). Despite his unconventional clothes, coloured shirts and velvet jackets—at least when he was not at his work as a draughtsman—he was a bit of a weed, thin-faced and lank-haired. But Sarah had always accepted without rancour that Tom had absorbed her share of Mam's looks and charm, and she was surprised that any man should show an interest in her.

Edward was accustomed to Sarah's frank manner but the offer he had longed to hear, couched in such bleak language—'mistress' was a deplorably bourgeois term—had caught him unprepared, and, besides, he was worried that his landlady might have seen her enter the room. Increasing his nervousness, Sarah was being extraordinarily brisk and practical. Tonight she would stay here but he needn't worry, early in the morning she would slip out unobserved, and in future they could use her flat.

Sarah herself was feeling nervous, but she had determined on her course of action, so she must see it through. Behind the screen in the corner of Edward's small cluttered room, she washed herself in the cracked hand-basin and donned her flannelette nightdress. While Edward in his turn went behind the screen she sat in his bed, letting her hair down, combing it and winding it into its night-time plait.

Eventually, Edward appeared in his nightshirt. Dousing the paraffin lamp, he climbed into bed beside her and the smell of the paraffin lingered in the darkness. His body was warm against hers but it was trembling. Fumblingly, he tried to kiss her just as a thought struck Sarah and she pulled her mouth away. 'You do know what to do, don't you? I don't want a baby or anything like that.'

Edward assured her that he did. (He was virginal as Sarah, but he had once had a conversation with one of his more experienced comrades.) For several seconds after that he lay by Sarah's side, breathing heavily. Finally she said, 'Shall we get on with it?'

Apart from exhaustion, she had no particular feelings. She didn't know whether she was supposed to, but she hadn't. Edward was panting, pressing against her, and then he was trying to climb on top of her. He didn't seem to be

136

getting anywhere and her head was swimming. 'Shall we leave it for tonight, luv? I'm dog-tired,' Lightly, she kissed him. 'Night.'

Sarah turned on to her side and within one second, it seemed to Edward, she was asleep, squashed against him in the single bed, breathing rhythmically. He had done his best, and briefly, as her small warm body lay under his, he had hopes he might get an erection. Sarah was such a strong character, he admired her so much, and he had failed her. How she must despise him and no wonder she had gone to sleep! Oh God—not God, he was an atheist—oh Karl Marx, make it come right next time!

12

Alice was bored.

After the excitement of Tom's election campaign, the summer holiday season seemed unbearably tedious. One afternoon, from sheer boredom, she called in to see if anything was happening at Clement's Inn. Nothing in particular was, but as she wandered across the hallway, a large lady appeared looking like a lost bloodhound.

'IIcllo, old thing, no need to tell me who you are. Seen your likeness in the jolly old newspapers, though you're much prettier in the flesh, if you don't mind my saying so.' Alice did not and smiled her golden smile. 'The name's Serena Abbott, but everybody calls me Stephen.' They shook hands. 'I ask you, do I look like a Serena?'

Alice agreed that she did not and wincingly withdrew her hand. 'May I help you?'

'Actually, old girl, I've come to join your gang, so if you'll point me in the right direction . . .'

'I'll tell you all there is to know. Come and have a cup of tea in my office.'

While they were drinking their tea, Stephen informed Alice that she was a doctor. 'So I have first-hand experience of being a woman in a man's world. Been meaning to join the WSPU since I first read about your deeds of derring-do, but you know how it is, the days whizz past. Then I read about your chum Sarah Whitworth chaining herself, and that did it. Had to come down to the Strand today, so in I popped and jolly glad I did.'

Alice had not been pleased by Sarah and Kessie's failure to give her—as the WSPU's press liaison officer—warning of the padlocking escapade. All the same, even without the extra publicity impetus she could have provided, she had to admit that Sarah's action had caught the public imagination as the perfect symbol of women's enchainment.

'I'm in general practice now. Surgery in Hampstead. Meet the problems of being a *lady* doctor, of course, but do my best to ignore 'em. Have a few men patients, though if I ask them to unbutton their shirts, some of them look as if I'm about to rape 'em. Dashed conceited of 'em!'

Stephen was almost a caricature of a certain type of English woman, booming as if through a megaphone, striding around, sitting with her legs apart, hair Eton-cropped, with only a monocle needed to complete the image. Yet how many of their sex had the gumption to fight through to become doctors? The conversation rattled along and from time to time the hearty manner disappeared, Stephen would become serious, and Alice found herself warming to this large, noisy lady, and even confiding to her how tiresome living with her sister and brother-in-law had become.

'Lionel is just plain stupid. Verena isn't, but she seems to think she has to take his side. And she never stops carping and criticising. That's the trouble with older sisters, I guess, but it's hard to live with.'

Stephen thought for a moment, then she said, 'I say, just had an idea. If you really are fed up with your relations, you could bunk with me. I've a house round the corner from my practice. 'T'isn't Park Lane or a mansion in Sussex, but it's comfy and you're very welcome to a half-share.'

138

'In Hampstead?' Alice frowned. 'Isn't that simply miles out of town?'

'It's ever so pleasant. Why not come out and have a shufti?'

Alice was a great believer that all problems are easily soluble and the solutions often appeared from the most unexpected quarters; she liked people who came to instant decisions, as Stephen had done. So the next day she ordered Lionel's chauffeur to drive her to Hampstead in their new Darracq automobile. It was indeed very pleasant, with cute shops clambering up the High Street, and cute little passageways, and Stephen told her there were acres of open land nearby known as Hampstead Heath, where she could ride.

The house was situated just off the High Street, a square building set in its own grounds, not big, only ten rooms and half of those could hardly be called rooms but were more like boxes. Stephen said she could have the upper floors and do them up as she liked. Within the month Alice had chosen her furniture and fittings, a good mix of the antique and the modern, and had moved in trunksful of her belongings, as well as her personal maid, Gertie.

Verena, of course, went into one of her states, though she calmed down when she learned that Stephen's father was Sir Humphrey Abbott, *Bart*—apparently baronet-style sirs were one up on plain ordinary sirs. Despite the cramped conditions, Alice was sure she had made the right decision: Stephen was the nicest person to share a house with, involved with her own busy life as a doctor, but always available if Alice needed her. Coincidentally, Kessie and Tom were thinking of buying a house in Highgate, which was just over the other side of Hampstead Heath, so she might have them as neighbours. That reminded Alice. Mrs Whitworth was sashaying around London in a Rolls-Royce automobile and it was high time she learned to drive herself.

Kessie had loved the house from the minute she'd first set eyes on it, while she was wandering round Highgate on a lovely summer's afternoon after giving a talk to a group of would-be suffragettes. The house was in a Georgian row at the top of South Grove, just off Highgate High Street, it wasn't swanky—after all it was in a *row*—with just two main floors, a basement and attics. At the front there was a small paved garden, at the back a lawn, flower beds and a kitchen garden, and the view from the rear windows was delightful, over the woods to the open expanse of Parliament Hill Fields. When the estate agent told her that Samuel Taylor Coleridge had lived a few doors away, that settled it, because he was not only one of her favourite poets, but he had written about 'the lovely lady Christabel'.

Persuading Tom to let her buy the house was, however, one of the more difficult tasks of Kessie's young life, but after days of argument which became heated at times, suddenly he capitulated. The next task was to persuade him that she needed staff to run the place. While they'd been in Mellordale, Maggie had begged for the job of cook-housekeeper once they set up their London home and Kessie could not think of anybody she would sooner have than dear Lancastrian Maggie. So she pointed out a fact of which Tom was well aware, the high unemployment rate in The Dales, and grudgingly he agreed to her employing Maggie.

Then, while she was supervising the redecorating, two young Cockney girls turned up on the doorstep, simply pleading for work. They introduced themselves as Ruby and Violet Mudge. Both were short and dumpy, both faces round, but while Violet's had an acquiescent bemused look, Ruby's was pertly animated. It was she who did all the talking, every so often turning to her slightly younger sister and saying, 'Isn't that so, Vi?' Vi nodded her agreement.

Excitedly, Kessie told Tom about the Mudges. 'They have fearful problems. Their father's out of work, their mother's sick, and there are seven younger Mudges to feed. Ruby and Vi are only seventeen and sixteen themselves. Do you know, where they're working at the moment the woman makes them sleep in the cellar and she weighs the food she gives them, so they're desperate to find decent jobs, and it was enterprising of them to call round, wasn't it? They're both keen supporters of votes for women. Actually, they were wearing those tin badges of Christabel and Mrs Pankhurst and me on their coats and . . .'

'That was *very* enterprising of them. You seem to think money is a piece of elastic, Kess, and what your father gave you when you were twenty-one will stretch for ever. It won't. At the rate you're spending, it'll snap any day now.'

'Do stop worrying about money, Tom.'

'There speaks somebody who has never known what it is to have not a crumb of bread in the house, not a piece of coal in the hearth . . .' Kessie listened patiently as Tom's voice swelled with oratorical fervour, until he said, 'I don't want to employ servants, and we can't afford three.'

'Four, actually. The gardener sort of goes with the property.'

'Like the cats? And what's the gardener's problem? Does he have a wooden leg?'

That remark made Kessie giggle helplessly, after a few seconds Tom also started to laugh, and the servant hurdle was overcome. Having engaged her staff, truly the minimum needed (she pointed out to Tom that she was not asking for a personal maid, but would dress herself and put her own hair up), Kessie still found being mistress of a house, even if it was less than half the size of The Laurels, almost as daunting as joining the WSPU. There were so many decisions to take, so many responsibilities on her shoulders, and Maggie had a disconcerting habit of sniffing, like her Aunt Sheba, if she disapproved of Kessie's actions. She, Ruby and Vi were embroiled in boring, north versus south warfare, while Peg-Leg Pete (after Tom's comment that seemed the obvious nickname for him) clearly believed that the garden was his own private property. When Kessie said she didn't like flowers in rows, she liked an organised disorder, and could she have more soft fruit next year, particularly loganberries which she adored, he just stared into the distance and whistled through his teeth.

Tom had made it clear that the running of the house was *her* preserve, so he wasn't helpful about her domestic

141

problems. Anyway, he was quite useless about the house. He couldn't even knock a nail in straight. His energies were concentrated on reading Sir Thomas Erskine May's *The Laws and Usage of Parliament*, an enormous volume which he said he needed to have at his finger tips, so that none of those clever buggers in the House of Commons could trip him up.

Neither of their neighbours was friendly, and one set wouldn't even say 'Good morning', which Kessie thought was beastly. Maggie said it wasn't *her* they objected to, even though she was a suffragette, it was Mr Whitworth, who if he was a Socialist, should be living somewhere in the East End. Kessie remembered the warnings about the difficulties of marrying Tom, but she was not going to let stupid snobberies upset her.

After Tom had healed his breach with Sarah, she came down to view the new house. But her attitude seemed to Kessie almost as bad as their neighbours', if in a different way. Silently, Sarah walked through the light, airy rooms, running her fingers over the pretty hand-printed wallpapers that Kessie had chosen, standing for ages in the bathroom, turning on the geyser, watching the boiling water gushing forth. Finally she said, 'Well, it's all a bit different from our house in Mellordale. And from Mr Keir Hardie's room.'

'I thought Socialism aimed to level up,' the anger flushed in Kessie, 'not down.'

'It does, Kessie, it does. But some of Tom's comrades are going to find the upward leap he's made hard to take.'

That had not occurred to Kessie, and she knew she had flown at her sister-in-law because of her general feeling of being overwhelmed. After Sarah had returned to Manchester, she asked Tom if his comrades would think he had gone all swanky? He said it didn't matter what they thought, what mattered was what he did; but after that Kessie noticed that she heard less from him about money and hardship.

It was the ginger cats, named Amber and Jasper, left by the previous owners who had gone abroad, that caused them to have the most tremendous row.

At The Laurels the cats had always had a free run of Kessie's bedroom, but Tom was not as fond of animals as he was of children, and one night as he came home late from the House of Commons, he fell over Jasper who was apparently stretched outside the bedroom. His cursing woke Kessie who switched on the bedside lamp and when he came into the room and saw Amber curled on the eiderdown, he picked her up and threw her on to the landing.

'Tom, how could you!' Kessie sat up indignantly. 'She's *expecting*, apart from anything else.'

'Look, I've told you, Kess, I'm not having those damned cats in the bedroom. I'm not having them upstairs at all. They're dirty . . .'

'They are not. They're very clean animals and . . .'

'Where I come from people don't keep animals as pets. They can't afford to. Whippets and racing pigeons, yes, they earn their keep, and some folks grow fond of 'em but . . .'

'I *can* afford to keep pets. I like cats and . . .'

It developed into another fearful argument about money, Tom swore at her and for two days Kessie refused to speak to him, which did not appear to upset him greatly. Then he announced that he was off to a Socialist conference in the Midlands until Thursday, which made her even more furious, but it also gave her time to think. Their differing backgrounds, which had bred different standards, were the cause of the problem and they would *both* have to learn to be tolerant, because clever as Tom was, infinitely more worldly-wise than she, he was not right about *everything*.

On Thursday, Kessie asked Maggie to prepare a special dinner. Kessie herself spent an hour arranging cut flowers, vases of roses, dahlias and gladioli, and a further hour choosing which gown to wear and putting her hair up. Normally, she just grabbed something from the wardrobe and rolled her hair into a wodge. For tonight she chose a sleeveless gown in sea-green chiffon with a tight waistband and a low-cut neckline that showed off her bosom, round her neck she placed her four-strand pearl choker and in her hair, which she had piled high, she wound a pearl headpiece with a drop emerald that nestled in her fringe.

When she heard Tom's voice in the hall, casually she called out from the sitting-room, 'I'm in here.'

Glancing briefly at her, he came in swearing about bloody-minded members of the Labour Party who had the vision of moles and the courage of field mice. '. . . and if you produce an *idea*, they dive for cover. Sometimes I think . . .'

He then did what in theatrical circles Kessie believed was known as 'a double-take'. Whistling loudly he walked towards her, while she tried not to giggle. After he had kissed her, a long passionate kiss that made her whole body tremble, he said, 'Are we expecting the King?'

'No, it's all for your benefit, sir,' Kessie curtsied and their reconciliation was complete.

The meal was delicious and afterwards they went upstairs to the bedroom, where they made love on the white fur rug that her father had brought back from India.

When they lay in sated content, Tom gazed up at the stuccoed Georgian ceiling. The reason he had offered only a token resistance to living here at The Grove in considerable style off Kessie's money was really very simple. He could not expect Kess to live, or to bring up their children, in some poky room in some dismal hovel. Mind you, he had to admit that her strength of will had taken him by surprise, as had the strength of her passion.

Within a very short while of their marriage, twisting her fingers round the hairs on his chest, one night she'd said, 'Tom-cat, do you have to come out of me like that? I don't want you to.' She didn't want him to! Tom had half-choked on his cigarette but he'd said, no, he could use summat but he couldn't abide the things and he'd give her a book to read. First thing the next morning she'd asked for the book and he'd handed over his copy of Richard Carlile's *Every Woman's Book or What is Love?*, the 1828 edition he'd found at the back of a second-hand bookshop.

Typically, once Kessie had got used to the idea, she'd gone one better than Richard Carlile's contraceptive sponge, returning from a visit to Manchester to tell him shyly that the Unitarian minister's wife had shown her a much better method, a sort of cap-thing which had been fearfully embarrassing to fit, but was quite simple to use now she'd got the hang of it.

Tom had to admit that from then on their love-making was half as good again, freed from the fear of 'an accident', but he wasn't altogether sure that he liked the control being with her. When would she decide to have the baby she frequently asked him to give her in the ecstasy of orgasm?

Sensuously, Kessie stretched herself on the white fur rug. For some time she had been thinking she ought to see *all* of Tom because he'd seen all of her, often, since the moment he'd slipped the eau-de-nil nightdress from her shoulders and she had stood, naked, blushing, but not ashamed, before him. She'd felt all of him, ah yes, and she'd caught glimpses below the dark hair on his belly, but she'd never had the chance to examine him properly. So suddenly she sat up, rolled Tom on to his back, and sinking on to her heels, stared down at him.

What a surprise he was.

Was that thing that looked like a limp sausage the part of him that grew thick and hard and strong and gave her such pleasure? Was that thing that looked like a collapsed haggis bag the part of him that fitted so snugly beneath her? Tom was putting his hands over his parts, as coyly as a virginal girl, and Kessie started to giggle helplessly. He leapt up, grabbed his dressing-gown, and stood over her, looking nine feet tall and terribly saturnine. He was hauling her up by her hair and Kessie stopped giggling. For a moment she was genuinely frightened, fearful of what he might do to her. Then the corner of his mouth twitched.

'Some men would have killed you for that.'

She sighed with relief, and felt pleased with her action, as if she had struck another blow for women's emancipation. 'You're not some man. You're my Tom-cat and I love you, I love you, I love you.'

'Mm.' He picked her up and carried her to the bed where they made love again.

Just before he fell asleep Tom remembered the lecture Charles Thorpe had given him the day before the wedding, about loving, honouring and cherishing his daughter in the full solemn meaning of those words. And one word of advice, the old boy had added, don't underestimate Kessie.

In future, Tom yawned, he would not.

PART THREE

13

Tom leaned back in his chair and rolled a cigarette.

'Do you realise, Kess, that in a couple of weeks we shall have been married *one whole year?*'

They were having tea on the terrace of the Houses of Parliament. It was a beautiful summer's day, and pleasurably Kessie watched a string of barges moving slowly down river like black water beetles, and the sun flashing on the windows of the trams rattling over Westminster Bridge. An occasional gust of warm wind blew across the river, fluttering the tablecloths, causing the lady guests to clutch their large floppy hats. Kessie was glad she was wearing a neat straw boater. Several Tory and Liberal MPs lifted their hats to her and nodded politely to Tom as they strolled past with their ladies, which was a good sign. He was beginning to make his mark, and the speech he had just delivered had been splendid. Provided her husband was in the House, a guarantor of her good behaviour (ha!), Kessie was allowed in to the Ladies' Gallery, though actually she had an ulterior motive for being here today.

'You're looking beautiful, Kessie mine. It's a treat to be able to look at you for more than five minutes at a time.'

Tom's tone was teasing but there was an underlying edge of truth in his words, and Kessie was feeling guilty about the amount of time she had been spending in Clement's Inn. To be honest, when Christabel had asked her to help plan a women's suffrage rally, saying that they wanted to make it the biggest and best demonstration ever seen in the British Isles, Kessie had not realised what she was letting herself in for. To an extent, she did now see why Christabel had been worried by her engagement, because being a militant suffragette and being married, even to her darling, understanding Tom, was difficult. In the last few weeks, while

Kessie had been negotiating with the railway companies which were to bring women from all over Britain to London for the demonstration, arranging time-tables, haggling over excursion fares and cut-price meals, he had been amazingly patient. 'It's like living in the middle of the booking office at Euston Station,' he'd joked. Even with Maggie's invaluable assistance—she, Ruby and Vi had turned into the best staff anybody could wish for—there were certain domestic problems that only Kessie could solve, and sometimes there did not seem to be enough hours in the day.

Tom was blowing a series of perfect smoke rings. The sun caught the dark hairs on his wrist, he saw her looking at them and his mouth stretched into that slightly crooked smile that excited her so much. She knew why he'd emphasised the fact that they'd been married *one whole year*, but somehow she couldn't tell him how the memory of that woman in labour in her cell in Holloway haunted her and how frightened she was of having a baby. It was a fear she had to overcome, that her love for him would help her overcome.

'May I interrupt the love-birds to say How do you do, Mrs Whitworth? You obviously do exceedingly well, more lovely than ever.' Mr Lloyd George drew up a chair and sat down, 'May I join you? Does your husband know what a lucky fellow he is?'

'Oh, I think so. You're always reminding him, aren't you?'

With half his mind Tom listened to Kessie adroitly change the subject, asking the Welshman what he intended to do about a Women's Bill, seeing he was supposed to be a supporter of women's suffrage? Tom smiled inwardly. Every time they met Lloyd George sniffed around her like a dog after a bitch on heat, and this was all he ever got for his pains. But you could hardly blame him, because in the last year Kessie had bloomed into a *very* desirable young lady, while retaining her eager enthusiasm and the touch of shyness which made her doubly attractive.

Tom leaned forward, stubbed out his cigarette. God how he wanted her to settle down and have a child. Not just to

150

silence the stupid jibes about the lack of lead in his pencil, but because to have a child of his own, their own, would be a wonderful thing. Tom knew he had lead in his pencil: when he had told Kessie that he had sworn on his mother's grave never to give a woman a child unless she wanted one, implying that the sole reason had been his beloved Mam's constant pregnancies, he had not been entirely truthful.

'You're a leading member of the Government, Mr Lloyd George. Saying you'll do your best for us is simply not good enough.'

'We have other problems on our platter apart from votes for women, Mrs Whitworth.'

'We have been hearing *that* excuse for a *very* long time.'

From the recesses of Tom's mind came the memory of Ella Warburton. For nearly two years, back in his late teens, he had known her as no more than a quiet, contained member of The Dales Rambling Club. But one day they had all been on a hearty walk across the moors, talking and arguing nineteen to the dozen as they strode along, and for the first time Tom had noticed that Ella was a pretty lass when she became animated. A sudden summer storm had broken across the moors, the clouds lowering, the rain pelting down. Ella and he had dropped behind the others and while they ran towards a shepherd's hut, he and she had sheltered beneath the rocks of Netherstone Edge. Their passion had been as unexpected as the storm and as overwhelming. Ella had been unmistakably a virgin, so when she had told him she was in the family way, he had promised to marry her.

It had happened in his early days as an ILP organiser, he was tied up in Preston the weekend he had said he would be in Mellordale to discuss their wedding plans, and the next thing he knew Ella was dead, from septic poisoning following a back-street abortion. Because they were mere acquaintances, nobody had suspected that he was the father of her aborted child, and Ella had died without saying a word. Tom had wept and cursed—even if his career had been ruined by the too-early responsibility of a wife and child, he would have married Ella. It had been then, too late, that he had sworn the oath on his mother's grave.

'Votes for Women!'

Looking up from his unhappy reverie, Tom saw a launch sailing past the Houses of Parliament, draped with WSPU banners in their distinctive new colours; white for purity, purple for dignity and self-respect, green for hope. Standing in the bows were the pugnacious figures of Aunt Ada and Flora Drummond, booming together through their megaphones. So that was one of the reasons Kessie had wanted to have tea on the terrace! She was smiling at him triumphantly and, my God, the WSPU didn't miss a trick.

'Votes for Women! Come to Hyde Park on Midsummer Day. Cabinet Ministers especially welcome. Votes for Women!'

Midsummer morn dawned with a pale blue sky and a warmly rising sun and by midday it was shining brightly from the pearly heavens. As the boom of Big Ben echoed twelve times up Whitehall, Kessie started the huge task of assembling her cohorts in Trafalgar Square, the largest of the assembly points throughout London.

'Would you like to climb in?'

She waved her hand towards the four-in-hand where several men, including George Bernard Shaw, were already seated, and Tom said, 'Why are the men riding and the women walking?'

'Because it's a women's demonstration.'

'And women are indubitably the stronger sex, aren't they, Kess*ee*?'

Mr Shaw's eyes were the brightest blue and the sun highlighted the white hairs in his red beard and moustache. He pointed his forefinger at her and he had long slender fingers like Tom's.

Kessie nodded happily. 'Indubitably, infinitely, immeasurably, inexorably, the stronger sex.'

'Your wife has a way with words.' The soft Irish voice paused. 'A luxuriant, lush, overgrown way she needs to prune.'

Kessie stuck out her tongue at him and he held up his hands, mocking her still.

152

'Kesseee!' He always called her Kessee, elongating the sound to express various emotions, usually amusement, occasionally disapproval.

Having sorted out the male support groups, Kessie turned her attention to the female front-line infantry. Soon after one o'clock she had them assembled in contingents all round Trafalgar Square, ten thousand women, massed twelve abreast, with flags fluttering above them in the gentlest breeze. Then they had to wait because the Portsmouth and Southampton contingents, two trainloads of them, had not arrived. Somebody shouted, 'We want women in charge of the railways!' and there was a gale of laughter, but Mrs Pankhurst said impatiently, 'If they don't turn up soon, you must give the order to march.'

While Kessie paced anxiously up and down the base of Nelson's column, watching for the missing contingents, the hokey-pokey merchants did a roaring trade, ladling cooling ice-cream from their brightly painted stalls. Tom climbed from the four-in-hand.

'Calm down,' he told her. 'They'll be here or they won't. You'll set off with or without them.'

Tom was finding his wife's panicky cries—'I can't do it, it's all gone wrong'—slightly irritating, because she only too obviously could and it seldom had. He could not be irritated with her today, though. She was looking lovely, her beautiful white dress emphasising her tall slender figure and full breasts, a perky white straw boater entwined with green and purple ribbon on her chestnut hair.

At half past one, there was a loud cheer as the Southampton and Portsmouth suffragettes finally arrived, flushed and perspiring, having walked at the double from Waterloo Station. Kessie joined Mrs Pankhurst at the head of the procession and gave the signal to the bugler to sound the advance. The bands struck up, the horses broke into a gentle trot, and the slither of shuffling feet deepened to a steady tramp as they wound their way through the crowded streets up into Park Lane, which was jammed solid with thousands more women and thousands more flags, patiently waiting for Mrs Pankhurst to lead them into Hyde Park.

153

The scene inside the park as the processions flowed in like the White Nile in full spate, breaking into tributaries as the marshals headed their groups towards the platforms that had been erected for the speakers, was breathtaking beyond expectation, hope or belief. How pretty the effect of the massed white dresses was. The numbers who had turned out to see and hear the suffragettes on this most beautiful of Midsummer Days were staggering, men, women, children, babes-in-arms, greybeards in bathchairs. Kessie took her place on her stand and, like the speakers from the other platforms, explained to her section of the crowd why women wanted the vote and why Mr Asquith had better listen to them. When some London Larrikins, their stiff collars and cuffs shining starchily in the brilliant sunshine, their straw boaters and black bowlers stuck at rakish angles, started the familiar chant, 'Sit Down, Sit Down', the crowds chanted back, 'You sit down. We want Kessie.'

In the middle of the afternoon, Kessie briefly left her platform in other capable hands. With Tom holding her arm firmly, they pushed their way through the dense throngs, past the hawkers shouting, 'Votes for Women. Get your Votes for Women favours here. You won't find them cheaper nowhere in London'; past the platform where Mrs Pankhurst was standing in front of an enormous picture of herself; past the platform where Christabel was sitting, in her Bachelor of Law mortar board, her gown draping a simple white Holland dress. As they had for Kessie, the crowds were chanting, 'We want Chrissie.'

They saw Aunt Ada in a white silk dress. Her aunt said, 'If I were to drop down dead tomorrow, I'd die happy. This shows what women can do, eh?'

They reached Sarah. Most of her lasses had not been able to afford fancy white outfits, but they'd done their best. There were lots of mill-girls among them whom Tom knew from the old days and he joked and chatted to them. There was no doubt women liked her husband, Kessie thought, but who could blame them?

'Hasn't Edward come with you, Sarah?'

'No.' Sarah's tone was abrupt, which Kessie now

154

appreciated meant she was upset. Kessie didn't particularly care for Mr Dawson, while Tom positively disliked him and had been very rude last time they'd met: 'Do you ever think for yourself? Have you read anything except *The Communist Manifesto?*' She wasn't sure how far Sarah had gone with Edward. Were they actually . . .?

Sarah realised she had sounded rude, and hastened to explain.

'I've let him get his feet under the table, if you know what I mean,' she laughed mirthlessly as she thought, and into my bed. After his initial problems, Edward had become enthusiastic about love-making. 'He keeps asking me to marry him. Him and his Marxian, free-love principles!'

'You're not talking about Edward Dawson, by any chance?' Tom put his arm round his sister, 'For God's sake, Sal, you're not going to marry *him*?'

'Of course I'm not.'

Sarah wrenched herself away angrily, jumped on to her platform, and raised her voice: 'Ladies and gentlemen . . . and ordinary folk.' The crowd laughed, delighted, and she was back on safe ground, telling them yet again why women wanted the vote.

Tom and Kessie continued on their way over the sun-dappled grass, or what could be seen of it for the crowds, and Kessie said, 'That was not very tactful of you.'

But Tom just smiled and tightened his arm around her. Oh, how she loved him, tactful or not! They met Alice, who was looking simply stunning in a pleated white linen skirt, a jacket piped with purple brocade, a pale purple jabot at her neck, and a huge white straw hat wound with green and purple ribbons on her golden hair. Several American girls were with her, but firmly planted on either side were Franklin Adams and Stephen Abbott. What an extraordinary contrast her escorts presented! Franklin elegant in a lounge suit with a cutaway jacket, straight tight trousers, short stiff collar, a trilby hat and swinging a gold-topped cane; Stephen in a green two-piece which made her look like a carnival dragon, a very small straw boater on her Eton-cropped hair.

Kessie liked Stephen immensely. For some reason she

could not quite put her finger on, she was not similarly fond of Franklin. Oh, he exuded Boston charm whenever they met, always frightfully polite and correct towards her. She had the impression, though, that he barely accepted Tom, and had they not met in suffragette circles, he would have been as patronising, dismissive or downright rude towards her husband as, alas, far too many people outside the movement were. Still, Franklin was undoubtedly a good catch, so why didn't Alice marry him? Fond as she was of the American girl, Kessie agreed with Sarah that for Alice votes for women was no more than a temporary lark.

After a light-hearted conversation they left Alice and her escorts and made their way towards the 'conning-tower' on top of the control pantechnicon that Emmeline and Fred Pethick Lawrence were manning with a rota of volunteers.

Viewed from above, the scene was even more breath-taking. From Marble Arch at the north to the Achilles statue at the south, from Park Lane on the east to Kensington Gardens on the west, the whole area was a sea of humanity. The splashes of white where suffragettes congregated round the platforms were like foam on the constantly swaying, surging grey-blue waves of the crowds, the noise was as if the waves were rushing towards the beach, swishing, breaking, ebbing, flowing again, and the voices of the speakers were crying like seagulls above the swell. The sun was high in the cloudless heavens, shining on the straw hats, the bonnets, the parasols, the banners and flags that bobbed like boats on the vast ocean of people.

Kessie clutched Tom's hand. 'It's beautiful, it's wonderful, it's fabulous, it's fantastic, it's miraculous, and I can't find the lush, overgrown language to describe it!'

'It's not miraculous, because it was you who organised it, Kess,' Tom lapsed into broad Lancashire, 'But, by 'eck, ah've never seen owt like it.'

After gazing at the incredible scene for several more minutes, they made their way back to Kessie's platform. Just before five o'clock, the bugle from the conning-tower sounded peremptorily. Simultaneously with twenty other well-trained female voices, Kessie read out their succinct

156

resolution, 'That this meeting calls upon the Government to give women the vote without delay.'

Thousands of hats were raised or thrown into the air, and it was as if a sudden storm had hit the oceans of people, whipping the waves into a brief fury. The speakers called out, 'Votes for Women!' and half a million voices shouted back, 'Votes for Women!' The noise was quite the most extraordinary, the most exciting, the most uplifting, the most heart-stopping Kessie had ever heard.

The Midsummer Day demonstration was over. It took ages to get out of Hyde Park, though the police had for once been helpful, dismantling the railings to allow the crowds to disperse. Eventually Kessie and the inner group of suffragettes made their way back to Clement's Inn. There in her office Christabel composed a letter to accompany the resolution that her sister Sylvia had hand-painted on an illuminated scroll, while they opened several bottles of champagne. Holding their glasses high, they toasted the resolution before it was despatched by special messenger to Mr Asquith at number ten Downing Street.

'You can tell Mr Asquith,' Alice called out to the messenger boy, 'that if he doesn't reply immediately, promising us a Bill first thing next session, Alice Hartley will personally camp on his doorstep until he does.'

They were opening more champagne, everybody was drinking toasts to everybody, and Kessie leant her head on Tom's chest. 'I think I'm squiffy. I do love you. We shall have the vote next session, shan't we? Perhaps I shall have a baby.'

Tom kissed her, a long lingering kiss, with their tongues entwined. When they drew apart, Kessie caught Christabel's eye. Her friend was definitely not pleased by such a public display of affection, but frankly, Kessie did not care.

They had organised the greatest assembly of people ever seen on British soil. There had not been an unpleasant incident or a single casualty. Everything had been as bright and warm and friendly as the smiling sun. The vote would soon be theirs. And next spring she would bear the child Tom was so eager to have.

157

14

The weather remained beautiful but it was about the only thing that did. When Mr Asquith's reply finally arrived at Clement's Inn, it was simply unbelievable. Kessie read his letter over Christabel's shoulder, scarcely crediting what her eyes were seeing. Curtly, the Prime Minister thanked Miss Pankhurst for her communications but had nothing to add to the statement he had recently made in the House of Commons.

Nothing to add, to a statement which had merely said that at some unspecified future date, the Prime Minister intended to introduce a Bill to give the vote to all British men, a Bill which *might* be capable of amendment to include women? Nothing to add, when they had organised the greatest demonstration ever seen on British soil and half a million people had voiced their feelings about votes for women?

Like wildfire, the news spread round Clement's Inn and people wept in disbelieving shock. Immediately, Alice decided, if not to camp on his doorstep, at least to accept Mr Asquith's oft-extended invitation to take the air with him in the park. Two days later she reported back, sitting on Christabel's desk.

'You will never in a million years guess what he started to talk about. A new book his younger children are reading called *The Willows in the Wind*, or is it *The Wind in the Willows*? Anyway, it's all about a toad, a rat and a mole which sounds a barrel-load of fun. I told him that in regard to women's suffrage he is the mole, Mr Lloyd George the rat and Mr Gladstone the toad. He found that amusing. Do you know what he said about our rally? That on such a beautiful summer's day half a million people would have turned out for anything, a public hanging or a football match, provided it had been well advertised, and passed by acclamation anything that was asked of them. He said his opposition to women's suffrage was based on reason and the balance of nature. In the animal kingdom, did not the male protect his mate, the female tend the nest? I could have puked. And had I seen Mr Barrie's latest play, *What Every Woman Knows*? I said, "I know what every woman knows, Mr Asquith. That we're men's pets, third-class citizens." He found that amusing, too.'

Alice inhaled deeply on her cigarette, exhaling a cloud of smoke which she regarded speculatively, as it swirled around her long ivory cigarette holder. 'I haven't seriously felt like murdering anybody before, but I could have killed him, sitting in that automobile, purring along East Carriage Drive under those trees that only a fortnight ago echoed to half a million voices shouting "Votes for Women". When I told him *that* he thought it was a huge joke, and said how much he admired spirit in a woman. He and the King, they both admire our spirit, so long as we don't do anything with it. Discussing our emancipation with him is like talking to a blancmange.'

Christabel got to her feet. 'The only thing to do with blancmanges is to eat them. Don't worry, we shall devour Mr Asquith.'

They went on talking, and Kessie's spirits were marginally uplifted by Christabel's determination, but she was so angry she even went off love-making, though for a few days after Midsummer Eve she had stopped using her 'thing' and she knew Tom hoped she was already pregnant. When they went up to The Dales she still wanted to kick every man in sight, including Tom, and she was not pregnant. Her period started on the dot and she told Tom she couldn't think about having a baby just at the moment. He flew into a rage and they had the most fearful row.

Eventually he calmed down. On a beautiful afternoon they walked up to Netherstone Edge, stretching out between the black rocks, and Kessie ran her finger along the cleft in his chin. 'You know how much I love you, Tom, but . . .'

159

'We won't talk about it any more, Kess, *but* I would like a child before I'm forty.'

'You shall have more than one before you're thirty, I promise.'

The day before they were due to return to London, Sarah turned up at Milnrow. In the evening Tom had a meeting with the local Labour Party stalwarts which, as she had not been invited, Kessie presumed meant the men were having a booze-up. She and Sarah sat in the front parlour of Aunt Ada's house and Kessie was in a reminiscent mood. Do you remember the afternoon of the Wakes Week fair when Alice sprained her ankle? Who'd have thought we'd all have been together, still fighting for votes for women three years on?

With a quarter of her mind Sarah listened to her sister-in-law's husky voice recalling the good old days. She'd thought she could keep the news to herself, but it was no good, she had to confide in somebody, and who better than dearest Kessie? Her words, however, emerged with unintentional brusqueness. 'I'm expecting.'

Kessie blinked and sat up in her chair, her mouth half open.

'Edward did it *deliberately* because I said I wouldn't marry him. It was after I came back from the Midsummer Day rally. I'd made up my mind I'd have to tell him we'd reached the parting of the ways, and I was only being kind to him . . .'

Sarah's voice trailed away and Kessie was unsure whether she was fighting back the tears or the anger. Feeling absolutely stunned, she said, 'You'll have to marry Edward now.'

Slowly Sarah walked towards the small bay window, staring out at the lone street lamp that had just been lit and was shedding a pool of greenish light on to the steep steps leading up to Milnrow.

'He's quite nice, really,' Kessie suggested doubtfully, 'and I'm sure he'll be a good husband and father and . . .'

'He's a weak-kneed shit.' Sarah swung round. 'And you know he is. I'm not marrying him. I'm not marrying anybody who does that to me.'

160

'Oh, Sarah, I know you're a terribly strong person but to have an illegitimate baby . . . you know what people are like. And the baby. Oh Sarah, think of the baby.'

'I am not having the baby.' There was a silence while Kessie stared at her, her forehead furrowed, a baffled expression on her face. 'I am going to get rid of it. I've been recommended to someone good.' There was another silence and when Sarah spoke again she could not quite control the tremor in her voice; she'd not had much sleep since she'd known for certain and it had taken her longer than she'd expected to make up her mind. 'Kessie, will you stay with me? Will you be there when I . . . when I come back?'

Kessie ran towards her, throwing her arms round Sarah, begging her not to do it, saying Edward really wasn't such a bad sort, she ought to tell him, and she didn't know about things like that but couldn't they be dangerous? Perhaps Tom . . . Sarah cut in sharply.

'No. I don't want Tom to know!'

It wasn't just that she was aware of how much her brother loved children, she remembered also the weekend when he'd come home after Ella Warburton's death. She'd gone into the bedroom and Tom had been lying on the bed *weeping* and he'd kept saying, 'She shouldn't have done it. No woman should do that.'

Sarah disengaged herself.

'If you'd rather not get involved, I'll understand.'

Kessie tried to persuade her sister-in-law not to do it, but eventually she said, 'If you've made up your mind, I'll stay.'

'And you won't tell Tom?'

'I shan't tell anybody.'

'But not Tom. Not ever. Promise.'

Kessie promised.

Tom was not pleased when she said she needed to go to Manchester for a few days. Why? he demanded to know. Kessie had to be evasive, invoking WSPU business, which did not go down well and they had another row. But he accepted it finally, and when he returned to London, Kessie travelled to Manchester with Sarah.

161

On the appointed night Sarah insisted on going to the woman's house by herself. It was a dismal evening and Kessie paced restlessly round her sister-in-law's flat in Moss Side, waiting for her to come back. She glanced out of the window, the rain was gusting up the street and Sarah would be drenched, so she put more coal on the fire and went into the kitchen—how neatly Sarah kept it, she had inherited her mother's proud neatness—where she lit a low light under the kettle, ready for tea on Sarah's return.

Anxiety and misery were racking Kessie. Even if her attendance at chapel had been less than assiduous since she had married Tom, she was still a Christian and to get rid of an unborn child was a mortal sin, not to mention a legal crime.

The door was opening, Kessie ran towards Sarah who was soaking wet, deathly pale, barely able to drag herself inside. As Kessie propelled her towards the fire she started to shiver violently, and as she helped Sarah out of her sopping clothes she kept gasping, 'Oh God, oh God!'

Kessie tried to persuade her to go to bed, but she insisted it would help if she kept walking. Every few seconds she doubled up with pain, clasping her hands to her stomach. Then she swayed and as Kessie half-carried her to bed, her face contorted with pain, Sarah panted, 'Will you get some towels and put them under me? They're in the chest. The woman said I might bleed a bit, and I am.' Kessie gave Sarah the towels and wiped her clammy face. 'Put something in my mouth, or I shall scream out loud.'

She gave Sarah another towel as a gag, and her hands were icy. Frantically, Kessie filled the stone hot water bottle, but as she lifted the bedclothes to slip it in, she saw that the towels were already bloody. Sarah's freezing hands were clutching hers, the crimson stain was widening, oh dear God, Sarah was bleeding to death and she must get her to hospital.

In hospital they would know precisely what she had done, Sarah would be charged, she would be charged, Tom's career would be wrecked, his wife and sister conspiring to commit a criminal abortion. And the WSPU would be

162

damned. It was to such wickedness that women's demand for freedom led. But she had to do something . . . because if she didn't, Sarah would die. What about the woman who had done this to her?

'Sarah, Sarah, where does the woman live? What's her address?'

Sarah's body was stretching, writhing, the towel had fallen from her mouth, and from time to time a short scream escaped from her gritted teeth. Kessie stared round wildly. Oh God, somebody will hear her. Oh God, what am I to do? There was one possibility.

'Sarah, can you hang on? I'm going to leave you for a few minutes. I must get help.'

'No,' Sarah shouted. 'Not Tom.'

Kessie assured her she was not going for her brother, who was miles away in London. Sarah rallied the last ounces of her courage and said she would hang on. Kessie ran down Raby Street towards Alexandra Road, the squalling rain hit her face, she lost her hat and almost slipped on the wet pavements, she splashed through the puddles and the hem of her skirt was sodden. As she ran, she made a pact with God. If He would let Sarah live, she would have a baby to replace the one Sarah had destroyed. She would have as many children as Tom wanted, he'd said he would like four, so she would have four and she would love them all dearly, if only He would let Sarah live. When she reached Doctor McPhee's house next to the herbalists in Alexandra Road, she hammered on the front door. She had known Doctor McPhee from her childhood, and he had nursed her poor mother. She banged the iron knocker until his housekeeper answered. 'Mercy me, who is it? Why, Mrs Whitworth, what in the world . . .?'

Pushing into the hall, Kessie called his name and he came down the stairs in his dressing-gown. 'Please, Doctor McPhee, you have to help me. You have to come. It's my sister-in-law. She's dreadfully ill. Please, please . . .'

He dressed and came, examined Sarah and said she should be in hospital. She cried out, 'No!' Mutely, pleadingly,

Kessie gazed at him. In a voice as flinty as the granite of his native Edinburgh, he said, 'If I can't stop the bleeding, she'll have to go to hospital.'

Taking off his jacket, he rolled up his sleeves and delved into his Gladstone bag, all the time issuing quiet firm commands, which Kessie obeyed as if she were a puppet. She dragged the sofa in front of the fire, Doctor McPhee carried Sarah on to it, Kessie filled kettles and humped coal to keep the fire blazing. It was like a furnace in the small room, the sweat was beading Doctor McPhee's forehead, rolling down Kessie's cheeks, but Sarah ceased shivering.

After, oh Kessie had no idea how long it was, he said, 'The bleeding's stopped.'

'Oh, Doctor McPhee, thank you, thank you.'

'We're not out of the woods yet, lassie.' At least the agonising bouts of pain were no longer racking Sarah's small body. Doctor McPhee told Kessie to heat some milk which he made Sarah drink. Her head sank exhaustedly on to the cushions on the sofa, after a while it turned sideways, her eyelids closed and Doctor McPhee said, 'She should sleep now. I've given her a sedative.'

He told Kessie to remake the bed, she put the crimson sheets to soak in the kitchen sink, and he carried Sarah back. They sat by her bedside. Kessie was so tired she could hardly think, and as the pale dawn light filtered through the curtains, Doctor McPhee said they could leave her for a wee while and he could do with a cup of tea. Kessie went into the kitchen where the dark red water stared at her accusingly from the sink and there was no milk left. She heard the sound of the horse's feet, the rattle of the cart's iron wheels, the cry of 'Milk-o'. Wearily, she went down the stairs with the jug; it had stopped raining but it was a dank grey morning and cold.

After she had made the tea she and the doctor sat in front of the fire drinking it, and the ash was piled high under the grate.

'Will she be all right?'

'There's a question, Kessie. She should live. And I should report this.'

'Sarah did it because she's not married.' Which was not the whole truth.

While Kessie gazed at him pleadingly, Doctor McPhee humphed, gulped his tea and asked for another cup. He couldn't report it, not now. 'I brought you into this world, Kessie Thorpe. The wee-est scrap you were and the nurse said you'd never live. But you did, my little lassie, and you've always been a bonny fighter. If I get struck off the register at my age, it won't matter. I shall retire to the Highlands.' The tears of gratitude trickled down Kessie's face and gruffly he said, 'I'm doing it for you. Not her.'

When Kessie telephoned Tom to say she could not return to The Grove for a few days yet because Sarah was ill, he was obviously concerned and asked what was the matter with her? Kessie shouted, 'She's had a sort of breakdown.'

'*Sarah?*' He said something more, lost in crackling on the line.

'I can't hear you.'

'I said bring her to London. She can rest here. We'll look after her.'

Yes, that would have been an excellent suggestion, except that Sarah's mind was as bruised as her body, as Doctor McPhee had said it might be. She was adamant that she did not want to see Tom until she was in full control of herself again, so Kessie shouted into the telephone mouthpiece.

'I'm taking her up to Mellordale for a few days to pump some moorland air into her lungs.'

'I can come up to see you both . . . '

'No! I mean, well, I'll be back any day now and aren't you busy in London?'

'Very. I'm missing you, Kess.'

'I'm missing you, Tom. I love you. I'll see you very soon in just a few days.'

The few days turned into a week and then another week, because Sarah haemorrhaged, Doctor McPhee dashed up to Mellordale and though the bleeding stopped, more than ever Kessie could not leave her sister-in-law. If only she could tell Tom the truth.

She *was* missing him dreadfully and she was also missing

165

being in the thick of their autumn campaign. She had to content herself with reading about Christabel and Mrs Pankhurst's arrests for conduct likely to cause a breach of the peace (which meant organising a demonstration in Trafalgar Square), and Christabel's spirited handling of her own defence. She was the first woman lawyer ever to do so in a British court, though even if the newspapers said she had out-rivalled Portia, it didn't prevent her or her mother being sent to Holloway.

Slowly Sarah grew stronger. Well wrapped against the increasingly chill autumnal winds they walked on the moors, talking of the future, of the world that would be once women had the vote, anything rather than Sarah's recent experience. Kessie found her refusal to see Edward, who kept writing to *her* asking what was the matter with Sarah and why she wouldn't see him, a little hard to accept. After all, it was his child she had destroyed, without his knowledge. But it was Sarah who had been through the terrible experience, not him, and Kessie knew where her loyalties lay.

Sarah's mind, in fact, was not as bruised as Kessie imagined. It was her physical weakness that was making her so dependent on Kessie. She now saw very clearly that she had lain with Edward simply because she had been angry with Tom, which was the worst possible reason. And, of course, as the child-bearers, women were hideously vulnerable. Never again would she, Sarah Amelia Whitworth, allow herself to be in that appalling position. She was through with men, whom she neither wanted nor needed in a close relationship. The physical side of things left her stone cold, any road.

One evening towards the end of October, a woman called Matty Hargreaves, who had worked in Charles Thorpe's mill for several years and knew Kessie well, came up to Milnrow, asking timidly to speak to her. For a couple of hours, Kessie was closeted in the front parlour with Matty, and during the next week a steady trickle of women arrived at Milnrow, to go into the front parlour with Kessie. Several times Sarah thought she was about to tell her what

166

they were up to, but Kessie didn't. She noticed, however, that when Kessie emerged from the sessions she was wearing her particularly pleased, helpful expression.

15

It was now six weeks since Kessie had said she was staying in Manchester for a few days. From what Tom had heard Sarah was looking pale but showing no signs of 'a sort of breakdown'. What the hell the two of them were up to in Mellordale he had been unable to fathom, until this morning when he'd seen his election agent who was down in London and he had told him what his wife was doing.

'She's *what*?'

'I've had half a dozen folks to see me. Three of them were that vague I didn't catch what they were on about. T'other three were clear enough. Kessie's instructing women how not to have babies. Votes for women is one thing. This is another kettle of fish altogether. In a God-fearing Non-conformist area like The Dales, it stinks. Not to mention what it does to your Irish Catholic voters. You'd best stop her, lad, and sharp.''

To cool his anger Tom walked back through gathering fog from central London to the Highgate house. Had Kessie gone mad? Was she so enraptured by the idea of women's emancipation she thought she could change the world over-night? How dare she start changing it in The Dales without saying a word to him? He had been returned by a margin of fifty-one votes. He'd done well since, he was writing articles for the newspapers now, but was she determined to ensure his defeat at the next General Election? He had given Kessie endless rope but, by heck, this time she had hanged herself. The moment for a showdown was overdue.

When he reached The Grove, Alice was in the hall with Maggie. She had called several times recently, ostensibly to

167

find out what was happening to Kessie who, with Christabel and her mother still in Holloway, was badly needed at Clement's Inn. He was going to put a stop to Clement's Inn, too. It was all right for Alice, she was unmarried.

'Hello there, Thomas. Any news from up North? Has Kessie said when she's coming back?'

'No. Can I have tea, Maggie? Do you want to join me?'

Alice's cornflower blue eyes opened wide. She was attractive, and by God she knew it. 'I'd love to.'

'Ask Ruby to bring it into the study. You don't mind if we go in there? I have to check an article.'

When Alice said she didn't in the least mind, Maggie sniffed, though she had not, Tom reflected sardonically, yet achieved a sniff of disapproval to rival her Aunt Sheba's. They went into the study, Ruby brought in the tea, they consumed it while Tom read through his article, swore under his breath, crossed out several sentences and scrawled in the amendments.

'We are not in a good temper today, are we, Thomas?'

'No. Nothing to do with you, luv.'

Alice perched on the end of the desk. She just adored the way Tom said that Lancashire 'luv'. Looking down on his untidy black hair shining in the lamplight—it was a dreary afternoon, the fog was thickening, so Ruby had drawn the curtains and lit the lamp—her fingers tingled to smooth it into place. He smiled up at her, that slightly crooked smile. Why had he married Kessie? As he half stood up to lean across for an envelope, Alice moved forwards, their faces touched, he stopped, staring straight into her eyes. If he touched her again she would not be able to resist. It would be Kessie's stupid fault for staying away so long and if Sarah was suffering from such a prolonged breakdown she should be in a nursing home.

Alice lowered her eyelids but did not move away.

Tom gazed at her. The signals were favourable, the demurely lowered eyes, the tense stillness of her slim body, the flush in her cheeks that was not caused by the fire. He put his hands round Alice's neck, lifted her beautiful face towards his and kissed her. Her lips were open within a

168

trice, her tongue was caressing his, her fingers digging into his neck. She had to be a virgin, an upper-class girl like her, but nobody would need to teach her. As he pulled her hard against him she shuddered in his arms.

'Tom, Tom darling, I want you. Take me.'

It was an invitation no man could refuse. She was unloosening her hair. He buried his face in the golden cascade. It hadn't the same sweet smell as Kessie's. Sod Kessie. He wrenched off his jacket, collar and tie, and as he undid the buttons down the front of her blouse, her fingers were undoing his shirt buttons, pulling it over his head. God almighty, she was one of the randiest women he had met, at least at this stage of her initiation. Her clothes were strewn around the desk, she was beautiful, standing naked in front of him, the shameless hussy, thrusting her breasts towards him, rotating her head in its golden glory. Her breasts were smaller than Kessie's. Bugger Kessie. He was as thick as a python, as hard as an iron pipe, and she was moaning with excitement, clinging, writhing, gasping in his arms. He half-carried her to the sofa, she gave one sharp scream as he rammed inside her and she was nowhere as tight as Kessie had been. The hell with Kessie.

Kessie paid off the hackney cab. She'd just made it in time—the fog was going to be a 'London particular', which was the peer of a 'Manchester special'. She let herself into The Grove with her key, the cabby carried her bags into the hall, and Tom's overcoat was on the hallstand. How lovely! She'd expected him to be at the House of Commons. Maggie came down the stairs, 'Mrs Whitworth, it's nice to see you! Why didn't you let us know you were coming?'

'My sister-in-law is much better and said she didn't need me any longer so I hopped on a train. It's nice to be back, Maggie. My husband's in?'

'Yes. He's in the study.' Without taking her coat off, Kessie ran towards the short corridor leading to the study. 'Miss Hartley's been having tea with him.'

'Alice? Well, it'll be nice to see her.' She ran on, flinging open the study door. 'Tom, it's me. I'm back, darling . . .'

169

The words died on her lips.

Tom was standing in the middle of the room. His chest was bare. Kessie saw the silky black hairs and the smooth brown skin of his shoulders. As she came through the door, he was buttoning up his trousers.

And Alice, oh Alice, was lying on the sofa and she had a lovely body, small firm uptilted breasts with rose-pink nipples in velvety brown rings. Tom liked breasts—oh Kess, you have the most beautiful breasts in the world. Alice's skin had a sated sheen, and her pubic hair was a browny gold, not the corn gold of the hair on her head. The study was Tom and Kessie's special room where they worked and discussed, they had made love on that sofa. . . .

It was Alice who moved first, clutching her arms across her naked breasts. At the movement Kessie spun on her heels, speeding like a top down the corridor, into the hall where Maggie was picking up one of her cases. Kessie spun past her, snatching at the case, and, as she slammed the door behind her, Maggie's startled cries, 'Mrs Whitworth, Mrs Whitworth', mingled with Tom's frantic shouts, 'Kess, Kess, come back.'

The fog faced her. It had not yet settled but was still swirling in huge ochre gusts, wreathing and snaking in brown layers, it choked her nostrils and throat as she ran and ran, hauling her heavy case. She was grateful for its noxious enveloping arms because it shielded her from them, from that, from . . . oh, dear God, she prayed, let me die now, this minute. Then wavering yellow headlights were in front of her, she heard the pig-squeal of the brakes and the driver shouting, 'For gawd's sake, miss, you can't dash around like that in a pea-souper like this. You orlright?'

The car was one of the new motorised taximeter cabs. The driver was calling it a day, but as he lived in Southwark he agreed to take her to the Savoy Hotel. The Savoy was the only hotel she could think of; in the lost days of innocence she had stayed there with Papa. With her eyes shut, her hands to her ears, she sat in the back of the taxi, but she could hear Tom's voice calling, 'Kess, Kess', and she could not shut off her mind.

The fog lasted for three days and for three days Kessie existed in a disembodied state, sitting in her room at the Savoy, wandering through the fog-transfigured city, walking backwards and forwards across Waterloo Bridge, through the thick curtain that had turned to a ghastly green. The mournful hoots of sirens drifted up river making her shiver with a desolate, uncomprehending despair. She thought of throwing herself into the Thames, of being mercifully swallowed in its icy invisible depths, escaping from this nether world into which no light penetrated; in which the darkness, the denseness, the stillness of the choking, blanketing particles merely lessened during the day to thicken at night; in which figures loomed from and were swallowed back into the filthy silence; in which the few sounds were muffled, emerging as the coughs, the groans, the shouts of creatures doomed for eternity; in which the largest, richest city in the world lay in the shades of hell; in which she, Kessie Thorpe Whitworth, was the most lost of lost souls.

Sheba had often said, 'It don't do to think too much, Kessie,' but how could you stop thinking? The fearful, terrible irony was that she had run into the study to tell Tom what a wonderful, emancipated marriage she now realised they had. Those halting, tangential conversations with the women in the front parlour in Milnrow had revealed to her an astonishing world of marital silence, rectitude and shame. And those were the women who had the gumption to seek her advice.

Sitting in the fog-wreathed room at the Savoy Hotel, she heard Matty Hargreaves' voice stalking around the reason for her initial visit like an animal around its prey, until finally the words had tumbled out. Was it by accident or design that Mr Tom and Mrs Whitworth had not yet had a bairn, and if by design what did they do?

Later she had said—the words were burnt into Kessie's memory—'My first 'usband was ever so good, you know, he didn't bother me much, you know. With Mr Hargreaves it's different, you know. You see, until I wed him I didn't realise I was allowed to move, you know.'

171

Not *allowed* to move. Why did the inarticulate keep saying 'you know'? Because they hoped you did? As Matty had stumbled on with her explanations—she and Mr Hargreaves had four bairns and they didn't want any more, couldn't afford any more—Kessie had thought of Tom, of being allowed to move, of that other time in a fog-blanketed London. They had finally persuaded a cabby to take them home to Highgate; as the cab moved gingerly through the swirling vapour, desire had overwhelmed them, but Kessie had said, 'We can't, not here,' to which Tom had replied, 'We can you know.' In the back of the cab, an oasis of passion, they had and oh, the *movements* when the horse had pulled hard or stopped, jolting Tom deeper inside her.

Moreover, from what some of the other women had said in the front parlour at Milnrow, women who had been married for years and had dozens of children, Kessie inferred that none of them had ever seen their husband's bodies, nor the husbands theirs.

Unlike unmarried Alice. And had unmarried Alice known she was *allowed to move*?

Oh, how could Alice have done that to her, Alice who had been not only her dearest friend, but a sister-in-arms? How could Alice have betrayed her with Tom? And Tom, oh, dearest God, how could Tom, whom she had loved, adored, trusted, have betrayed her with Alice? How long had it been going on? Before they were married? Since their marriage? How many times had Tom and Alice . . .? Had she been completely blind? The deceived wife who was the last to know of her husband's infidelity? Did everybody else know?

On the fourth morning, as the chambermaid drew back the curtains in the hotel room, Kessie saw that the fog had lifted. The Embankment Gardens, the arches of Waterloo Bridge, the grey sweep of the Thames were visible. There was a watery sun in the pale blue heavens. The wound Tom and Alice had inflicted was still bleeding profusely, but it was not mortal, there was nothing to be gained by continuing to lick it with self-pity.

172

After she had called at Clement's Inn, Kessie returned to The Grove where Maggie took her hand. 'Mrs Whitworth, are you all right? I've been that worried about you.' When she asked if her husband was in, Maggie's face became guarded. He was still in bed. Her voice conveyed the information that if Mrs Whitworth intended to leave him, she would pack her own bags immediately. It was only too obvious that Maggie had not the slightest doubt what Tom and Alice had been up to . . . the anguish and shame refilled Kessie.

Tom was lying on his back in *their* bed, there was a dark stubble on his chin, his mouth was open and he was snoring. He did not normally snore. As she leant over to shake him, his breath smelled sour with whisky. 'Tom, wake up.'

Rolling on to his side, he clutched at the bedclothes and groaned. He did not normally drink much. He had once told Kessie about an uncle who had been a drunkard, how one of his boyhood tasks had been to drag him from the Ainsworth Arms, and how he'd sworn never to be like him. Tom had sworn a lot of things. They did not apparently include obeying the seventh commandment.

'Tom, can you hear me?' He groaned his assent. 'I wanted to talk to you but obviously you're in no fit state. So I'll just tell you what I've decided to do. Before Christabel was imprisoned she wrote to ask if I would undertake another speaking tour for the WSPU. Because I wanted to be with you, I told her I couldn't. In the circumstances, I consider it an excellent idea. I've seen Mrs Pethick Lawrence and I'm catching the train for Glasgow. I shall be away for a week or two, which will give us time to consider how we can repair our marriage. Or whether we want to.'

Tom struggled to sit up, to focus his bleary eyes. 'Christ, Kess, you can't go like this.' She wished he wouldn't blaspheme.

'I don't think you are in any position, literally or otherwise, to tell me what I should or should not do.'

While Kessie was travelling to Glasgow, in front of a blazing fire in Stephen's sitting-room, Alice was unburdening her

173

heart. As she related the sorry story, Alice rested her head against Stephen's knees and her therapeutic fingers were at work as they had been so many times in the past, massaging Alice's neck and shoulders, stroking her hair, soothing her scalp. Only this time, while Stephen lambasted Tom for being a dastardly seducer, a filthy betrayer, a brute and a beast which all men were at heart, Alice could only think of *his* long fingers caressing her.

'I say, old girl, you're not likely to be in trouble, are you?' Alice shook her head. Stephen said they should be grateful for small mercies. 'And what about poor Kessie?'

Ah yes, poor Kessie. They had met briefly at Clement's Inn. Kessie had been looking pale but composed, Alice had put out her hand, but in her iciest voice Kessie had said, 'We don't want anybody here to know what has happened, do we? So here we try to behave as if nothing has happened. I suggest you keep out of my way as much as possible.'

With that she had spun on her heel and walked swiftly away. It dawned on Alice that Kessie was not as soft-centred as she had imagined.

After she had described the encounter, Stephen ran her hand through her own cropped hair and her nostrils twitched; 'If you take my advice, old thing, you'll give Kessie time to recover from the shock. And the best thing you can do, meanwhile, is to keep your mind occupied. Moping around never did anybody any good. How about helping out in the evenings in my sixpenny surgeries?'

The sixpenny surgeries—Stephen had special ones for her poor patients, charging only sixpence for a consultation *and* medicines—were a bit depressing, with snuffling lines of people sitting meekly on the wooden benches in the waiting-room, but Alice enjoyed donning a white coat and handing out the brightly coloured medicines. One of the cheekier Cockney men patients said, 'Cor, chase me Aunt Fanny, where did you fly in from, miss? You're a tonic in itself.'

Wonderful a friend as Stephen was, she seemed to take it for granted that Alice had hated every minute of her experience with Tom, so there were certain things she had to keep

174

locked within herself. In fact, Alice had been astonished by the force of her passion, and also by his. *Why* had Tom married Kessie when his love for herself was clearly as demanding as hers for him? Still he *had* married Kessie and now she supposed he was consumed by guilt: Alice had telephoned him three times, and she had left a note for him at the House of Commons and he had not answered.

So be it.

She had lost her virginity, which was a highly prized possession, and she must protect herself. Her mother had always said, 'Marry a man you like, not one you love.' There was somebody she liked, if not loved, and Frankie was in London.

When they met at the Arundels' ball and Alice asked him if he would care to see the flowers in the conservatory— they had the most glorious Christmas roses already in flower—Franklin was not unduly surprised. He had ceased to be surprised by anything Alice did. And this evening there was an extra sparkle in her blue eyes, an extra glow in her cheeks, an extra gloss on her golden hair. When she said, almost shyly, that she had been thinking about their engagement, he immediately went down on one knee in front of the Christmas roses, and she told him she gladly accepted his offer of marriage.

She held out her hands, he stood up, taking her gently in his arms. The passion with which she clung to him, however, *did* surprise him. As she raised her beautiful face towards his he almost thought she was asking him to kiss her properly which, naturally, no gentleman would do with his newly affianced, though it was the devil of a temptation. Hastily, he detached her from his arms, suggesting that, as he had first proposed over three years ago, they might not require an overlong engagement.

'Verena knew Lionel for four years before they became engaged, and even then they had a two-year engagement. I think we should wait at least a year, don't you? It is the proper thing, isn't it?'

Alice's interest in doing the proper thing was new, but she was being *truly* demure this evening. So that when she

175

said she hoped he wouldn't mind if she continued her work for the suffragettes a while longer, even though Franklin had imagined she would immediately abandon her militant nonsense, in his triumphant mood he smiled his assent. After all, he approved of votes for women, in principle.

Franklin was not, however, prepared for what Alice proceeded to do next.

The idea came to her at the Arundels' ball, because that was where she met the eccentric Mr Garner. Needing something to give maximum publicity to the fact that Christabel, Mrs Pankhurst and dozens of other suffragettes were still languishing in prison, she put the proposal to Mr Garner, and he was game.

A week later, not a bad morning for the foggy month of December, with a pale blue sky and a watery sun, Alice hired a taxi to take her to the Welsh Harp public house at Hendon, in the country north of London, which was where Mr Garner had told her to rendezvous.

After he had made all the preparations he shouted, 'Ropes away, boys,' and the huge gas-filled balloon lifted from the ground. Slowly it gained height, its 'Votes for Women' banner streaming behind. The crowds on the ground waved and cheered, and it was a fantastic feeling, drifting in space, suspended in time, the second most fabulous sensation of Alice's life.

Wrapped in a heavy overcoat and deerstalker cap with earflaps, Mr Garner said, 'I shall be busy, my dear. You just enjoy yourself.' Alice did, feeling like a Lady Gulliver surveying the Lilliputians beneath her. She turned to speak to Mr Garner but he had disappeared. Had he fallen out? What was she to do? She had no idea how to steer a balloon. Presumably, it would eventually land of its own accord, but where? How long would it take? He could not have fallen out. Could he? Peering over the side her heart fluttered because he was clinging to the basket like a fly to a wall, fiddling with ropes and bags of sand. She *was* glad when he climbed back inside and she favoured him with her golden smile.

They were over central London, swathes of smoke drifted beneath them from thousands of chimney pots, the bends of the Thames were visible, crammed with boats. Mr Garner's timing was exquisite, his steering perfection, for below them was the Mall. Alice saw the royal coach with its escort of Household Cavalry, their breastplates catching the sun's pale rays. Mr Garner said, 'Here, let me give you a hand.'

Like an early snowfall, they threw hundreds of 'Votes for Women' and 'Release the Imprisoned Suffragettes' leaflets from the balloon. Alice felt intoxicated, leaning over the side, bowing her head and rotating her wrist as Their Majesties did. As they floated over Admiralty Arch the balloon swung sharply, and they were blown miles across the rooftops of London, out into the open country, over birch woods and sandy heathlands, ending up in the branches of a copper beech tree on the edge of a ploughed field. Getting down was difficult but they were assisted by a group of wide-eyed, open-mouthed farm labourers who had been working in the field. Alice brushed her plaid suit and adjusted the scarf round her hat. 'Where are we?'

'Near Dorking, miss.'

Dorking. That rang a bell. Of course, the Pethick Lawrences' country house was near Dorking. A passing carriage gave them a lift to The Holmwood where neither Emmeline nor Fred was at home, but their housekeeper entertained them royally. Eventually, Mr Garner left to rescue his balloon, while Alice returned to London.

Stephen greeted her with an enormous bear-hug. 'Congratters, Alice. You've done it this time, old girl. Your picture's in all the newspapers. Lots of lovely publicity for the WSPU.'

The next morning Verena telephoned. The gist of her conversation was that Alice had indeed done it this time. The King was absolutely furious, not only had she insulted him, she had been guilty of behaviour that struck at the majesty, the dignity, the awe of monarchy, at the very heart of the British constitution.

'I guess in the old days I'd have had my head chopped off

on Tower Hill. Who cares, sister dear?' Verena made it clear that she did, along with millions of loyal subjects. Alice said, 'I am not a citizen of the United Kingdom. And I have a greater loyalty. To womankind.'

Franklin was even more furious. In fact he became quite nasty, claiming that now she was his fiancée she must control herself, and all that rubbish. Alice just smiled demurely, until finally he kissed her on the forehead. He was sweet really.

The day before the official announcement of their engagement, Alice told Stephen the good news and for the rest of the week her friend behaved most peculiarly: shutting herself into her sitting-room, sniffing her way past Alice in the hall. Had she been crying? Surely not Stephen. Then, gruffly, she clasped Alice to her broad flat bosom. 'Hope you'll be ever so happy, old girl. Don't leave us just yet, eh?'

Alice decided it must be her age. Older women sometimes became all emotional at the thought of young things marrying. In herself she felt better, her inner equilibrium was returning, and she only dreamed of having Tom every other night now.

By no means all loyal citizens were upset by her escapade. For days people recognised her in the streets and called out, 'Where's your balloon, ducks, gorn and lorst it?'

16

Kessie read about Alice's balloon exploit and her engagement while she was in York. Oh well, Franklin was in for a surprise on his wedding night, though she was sure Alice would find some explanation for her ruptured hymen.

When she left the platform after her meeting, Tom was waiting in the ante-room. His hair was brushed, he was wearing his best suit, she knew she still loved him, but Tess

Billington had been right. Many moons ago, way back in the Manchester days, she had said Kessie was in for a tough time because she was a romantic. 'Except at rare moments, Kessie, it is not a romantic world.'

Her father had started her romantic ideas with his 'wild kestrel Kessie' notion, encouraging her to believe the world was a lovely place in which she would marry Sir Galahad and live happily ever after. Where did she think her Sir Galahad had acquired his sexual experience and learned to express himself so pithily—'God made the consummation process difficult because He made men quick and women slow'? From second-hand bookshops? She had put Tom on a pedestal, her knight in shining armour who would change the slightly less than lovely world. In fact, if he was anybody romantic, he was Sir Lancelot, who had committed adultery with his best friend's wife.

Did he love Alice? His presence here in York would suggest not. But having fallen from his pedestal, with such a spectacular crash, he was not going to pick up the pieces simply by smiling at her tenderly, and keeping his eyes studiously on her while the ladies of York fluttered around him. But she agreed that he could take her out to supper.

That idea was scuppered by the management of the nearby hotel which required that a gentleman be attired in evening dress. Tom created a scene and Kessie watched in detached embarrassment. It was not the first time he had embarrassed her in public, by lashing out against conformity. His Lancashire accent, she had observed, always thickened during the scenes. After a while she had had enough.

'I'm not hungry, actually. But I am tired. May we leave?'

They stood in the narrow street where the cold clear moon was silvering the white of the medieval timbers and the towers of York Minster. Tom asked where she was staying. 'Oh, miles out, with a suffragette family. But I can get a cab. When do you have to be back in London?'

'Tomorrow.'

'Why don't we go to the station buffet? They won't throw you out of there.'

Tom had not expected it would be easy, but it was going

179

to be one hell of a sight more difficult than he had imagined. Kessie had him boxed in a corner. It was not a position he cared for, he cared even less for lengthy explanations and apologies, but Kessie liked explanations, God knew he owed her an apology, and he badly wanted her back.

The station buffet was crowded, smoke-filled, and now she said she was hungry. The tired sandwiches, the bright saffron seed-cake and the dehydrated Madeira cake sat in glass-domed rows along the counter. 'They embalm them under those,' he said. 'They learned the trick from the ancient Egyptians.'

Kessie giggled, he smiled at her and she stopped giggling. They found a table by the window. 'Kess, I'm sorry, I'm sorry. It was an aberration, the one and only time.'

'With Alice, I presume you mean?' Kessie's voice, like the moon, was at its coldest and clearest. God, she was angry with him.

Deepening the intensity of his voice, Tom carried on. 'Alice is a beautiful girl and she was on offer. I reckon I was taking my revenge on you, on her, on women if you like. Can you understand? I was missing you. I was angry with you because I didn't know what you and Sarah were up to in Mellordale. I still don't know, but I'm willing to bet she didn't have any nervous breakdown.'

His dark eyes looked at her searchingly, but Kessie went on drinking her tea. Several times she had nearly written to him and now it was on the tip of her tongue to tell him the truth, to say: I was seeing your sister through the after-effects of a criminal abortion. But she couldn't. In this question of loyalties, hers had to lie with Sarah. And what did it matter what she had been doing? Tom had still vilely betrayed her.

'Then I heard about your "clinics". Why didn't you ask me, Kess?'

'It never entered my head that you would disapprove. I thought I was helping those women. But don't worry, I shan't ever go near any of your constituents again.'

Why did even the most intelligent women have this tendency to swing to extremes? 'You were helping them.

180

But you weren't helping your cause. Or me. Politics is like standing on a hill. You can see the panorama and you know how you want to change it. You keep the landscape in front of you but you can only follow one path at a time. Christabel appreciates that.'

'You and Christabel have much in common,' Kessie paused, 'politically.'

'You must get the vote first, Kess, then . . .'

'Yes, I do understand your point, thank you.'

'Can you understand how it happened?'

'No.'

A train roared past the window, leaving a wodge of smoke in the night air. It was a ridiculous place to be having a soul-searching discussion with your wife and typical of Kessie at her stroppiest to have suggested it. His voice at its deepest, he said, 'Kess, I want us to have a child. You keep putting it off. Can you understand how I feel about that?'

'Actually, I came back to tell you I wanted to have a baby.' Tom put his face in his hands and when he looked up his eyes were at their darkest. 'I realise now that I took our marriage for granted but you destroyed my *trust*, Tom, and I think trust is the basis of all human relationships. If you need other women, though I thought our love was special . . .'

'It was. It is.'

'Then why Alice? And in our own house?'

'I've tried to explain.'

'Are you being honest with me? Or with yourself? Several people warned me not to marry you. My father once told me you had a "reputation". I didn't understand what he meant.'

'I don't think your father is in any position to throw stones.' The minute he'd said it Tom knew he'd made a blunder, that Kessie would insist he explain his remark and that when he did the revelation would cut even more ground from beneath her. He had no option, nevertheless, but to tell her that her father had a mistress in Mellordale. To soften the blow he said, 'It's a steady liaison. It's been going on for twenty-odd years.'

181

'More or less since I was born. I presume everybody else in Mellordale has known for years? At least I now know where my father went every Tuesday and Friday.'

'Don't think badly of him. Your mother was an invalid for a long time before she died.'

'If you have a *steady* liaison with Alice, will that be all right?'

'If we weren't in this damned place, I'd go down on my knees. I have sinned. *Mea culpa.* If it'd help I'd cut off my left hand.'

'I don't think that's what wants cutting off.'

'Oh Kess, you wouldn't like me without it.'

He smiled at her, she did not smile back. She stood up.

'I suggest you do some serious thinking, Tom, about yourself, about me, and whether what *you* want is all that matters in life.'

Kessie found a cab which took her to her friend's house, which was not miles out of York, but quite near the Minster. Most of the night she lay awake. Her body wanted Tom, but her mind did not. He could not simply turn up and turn on the charm. Had he really expected her to bring him back here and say, impregnate me now, this minute? It was going to be a long time before she could reassemble the pieces he had shattered.

Without Kessie, The Grove seemed empty and Tom hated sleeping alone, though he missed her as much out of the bedroom as in it. He had never quite accustomed himself to having servants, and pert Ruby's subdued behaviour, Vi staring at him with saucer eyes, and Maggie's coldly correct manner did not improve his temper. When he was asked if he would go up to Manchester as a replacement speaker for Ramsay MacDonald, who was ill, Tom accepted with alacrity.

His speech was one of the best he had ever made. He had felt the invisible cord that binds an audience to an orator tautening until he released it, and the applause had thundered round the Free Trade Hall; not the main hall, but he would fill that one day soon. He had taken as his theme the division

182

of the haves and have-nots, the iron law that had been in force for centuries but which would be changed by Socialism, namely to those who have shall be given, from those who have not shall be taken. How he wished Kessie had been there, instead of her father, though the old man took him out to supper afterwards.

Throughout the meal they enjoyed themselves arguing about politics.

'Liberalism is a creed of *realistic* reform. The trouble with yours, Tom, is you base it on *equality*. There'll never be equality because folks are born with different talents. Nature herself deals out the inequality. You can't get round that.'

'All right, I'll give you that. Equality is a myth, but equity isn't.'

When they were having their brandy and cigars the old man started humphing and grunting.

'Your wife was in a hoity-toity mood when she honoured us with a visit on Wednesday.' He paused but Tom made no comment. 'I'd like a grandchild, you know. Isn't it time Kessie had a babe?'

Past time, Tom thought savagely, but he could hardly tell the old boy why his daughter had been in a hoity-toity mood: Actually, Dad, she caught me shagging Alice Hartley and, by the way, I blew the gaff on your little arrangement over in Mellordale.

On his return to London, Kessie was back at The Grove, but Tom's delight was soured on hearing the reason she had cut short her speaking tour. It was because Aunt Ada, emerging from a stint in Holloway, had collapsed, and it was an urgent telegram from Christabel that had recalled Kessie. Stephen, who was called in, said it was only a slight heart attack, Aunt Ada herself said everybody was making a ridiculous fuss and she had her girls to look after her—with Tom and Kessie's departure from Thurloe Square, she had turned it into a suffragette lodging house—but she was obviously delighted to have her niece by her side and Tom could not object.

On New Year's Eve they were invited to a party. When they returned to The Grove in the early hours of New

183

Year's Day, Kessie made straight for the stairs but Tom caught her hand: 'I have your birthday present, me luv. It's in the sitting-room.'

In the sitting-room he handed her a small package, wishing her a happy twenty-fourth birthday. Kessie unwrapped the parcel, looked at a gold Victorian locket on a chain and thanked him politely.

'I noticed you no longer wear that old horseshoe necklace,' he told her.

No, she had taken it off in the Savoy Hotel and it was now at the back of a drawer, alongside *The Masque of Anarchy*. But she did not tell him that. Tom put his hands on her shoulders, he was slipping off her velvet evening cloak, running his fingers over her bare skin and up to her cheeks, fingers that had touched Alice (and how many other women?) as tenderly. Passionately, he told her how much he loved her, but Kessie broke away. 'I'm sorry, but I can't forgive you just like that. You hurt me too much. I need time to think.'

'I can't go on grovelling,' Tom's voice was rising. 'Would you like me to move out while you *think*? This is your house, kept up by your money.'

'Do you have somewhere you want to go?'

'No.'

'Stay then.'

'For God's sake, Kess, stop behaving like a girl in a penny romance. Grow up!'

They were both breathing heavily. Tom saw the oak cigarette box on the occasional table. Picking it up he threw it with the full force of his bowler's arm towards the fireplace. As it hurtled through the air, the lid flew open and cigarettes scattered across the carpet like snowdrops. Where it hit the fireplace several chips of marble dropped to the tiled base.

Both their eyes followed the trajectory, swivelling back to stare at each other. Tom moved towards Kessie, she took a step backwards, he pulled her hard against him and he was kissing her passionately. For a few seconds Kessie struggled, she had *not* forgiven him, but then she was responding with every fibre in her being because it had been such a long time, she loved him so much and she wanted him desperately.

Over breakfast, as Ruby bustled in and out, chirpy as ever—'Posty's late this morning. He says he has a bad leg but Vi and I think he's on the booze'—they were both quiet. Occasionally, and this was one of the occasions, Kessie found Ruby's early morning cheerfulness difficult to take. She and Tom ate in silence.

Their mutual passion last night had, to begin with, been extraordinarily fierce, as if they were in physical combat. Their clothes had been half off before they reached the bedroom, where Tom had jammed her against the wall. When she was excited, standing up was one of the positions Kessie enjoyed, remembering the evening she had first met Tom, and the couple in the alleyway near All Saints Church. They had made love half the night, the fierce straining had flowed into the wildest sweetness, Kessie's mind had passed beyond thought and there had been nothing in the world but the ecstasy of being with Tom. She had felt as if her whole body was opening, a wide rushing channel, drawing him further and further inside. He was throbbing and enormous, she wanted his child and she cried out for him to give her one, he cried back that he would, she had wanted to stay like that for ever and ever but she had reached her climax and she had felt Tom pouring himself into her again.

Ruby trotted in with the belated post, Kessie sorted the letters into hers and Tom's. She had not used her 'thing'. Usually, she or he said, I haven't—have you? got it in, but last night neither of them had said a word. Absent-mindedly, she opened her letters. The contents of one of them were astonishing.

A firm of solicitors on the Isle of Wight wished to inform her that she was a beneficiary under the terms of Mrs Gertrude Ashworth's will. Aunt Gertrude had been Papa's eldest sister, but Kessie had hardly known her because she had married a Manchester biscuit manufacturer (dog-biscuits, Papa called them) who had made his fortune and retired early to the distant, fashionable Isle of Wight. Shortly after his early retirement, Uncle Hubert and Papa had had

185

the most colossal row, so that neither family had spoken for years. Last summer, after Uncle Hubert's death, out of the blue Aunt Gertrude had written to her sister Ada suggesting they meet for old time's sake. Aunt Ada had taken Kessie with her to Claridge's Hotel, where her sister was staying while she was in London, and Kessie had liked this virtually unknown aunt. Later, she had invited them both to the theatre and they'd had a sumptuous dinner before she returned to the Isle of Wight. It had all been very pleasant. Aunt Gertrude had listened with interest to their talk of women's emancipation but had made little comment and Kessie's only further contact with her had been a few polite letters.

Now there was this extraordinary news from the solicitors. Inside the letter there was a sealed envelope—'To be sent to my niece, Mrs E. T. F. Whitworth of The Grove, Highgate, London N, after my death'. Kessie slit open the envelope and read through its contents:

> Willow Bank House,
> St Lawrence,
> Isle of Wight.

Dear Kessie,
 I cannot tell you how much I enjoyed meeting you in London. During these last months of solitude, I have thought a great deal. I wish I had possessed your courage when I was young. I had so many dreams. I wished to do so many things. I have lived for nigh on seventy years, and I have done none of them.
 I am leaving you a moderate sum because money gives you independence; not overmuch because in excess it can be destructive. I am also leaving you Willow Bank Cottage, which is quite cut off from the main house. (I doubt you will have much in common with your Uncle Hubert's relations to whom, I shall, being childless, leave the bulk of the estate, as is fit and proper.)
 The cottage will provide you with a haven in times of stress, and perhaps a happy summer house to which you may bring your children. Think of me occasionally as

you use the money. Fulfil yourself. Make the world a better place for women, as your noble Mrs Pankhurst said.

Yours sincerely,
Your Aunt Gertrude.

Why, oh why, had she said nothing like this while she was alive? Because too many emotions had been suppressed for too many years and she had become one of life's onlookers? Poor Aunt Gertrude, what friends they might have been, if only she could have spoken from her heart.

Kessie handed the two letters to Tom, 'To those who have shall be given.' (His Manchester speech had caused quite a stir.) While he read them through, she came to a decision. Last night had not really settled anything. The bedroom was important but you didn't spend your entire life there. She still needed time to think; probably, if she was being honest, she still wanted to punish Tom.

'I think it would be a good idea if I went to the Isle of Wight, as the solicitors suggest, don't you?'

After last night, when he thought he was home and dry, not to mention that she could, hopefully, be pregnant? Tom opened his mouth to say he thought it was a bloody awful idea, but Kessie shot the protests from his lips. 'I'll take Aunt Ada with me, to recuperate. The air around Ventnor is noted for its beneficial mildness.'

It was over two months from the day that Kessie and Aunt Ada left London before Tom saw his wife again. He was damned if he was dashing over to the Isle of Wight as he had dashed up to York; he had grovelled enough and he intended to win this particular battle of wills. So he concentrated his energies on the Labour Party, on the new session of Parliament which promised to be a stormy one, and on travelling to The Dales for his political surgeries.

The post-cards and letters arrived in shoals from Kessie saying she had been thinking a great deal about their marriage, and suggesting that he come over to Willow Bank Cottage where they could discuss things calmly. The topic she did not mention was when she and Aunt Ada were returning to the mainland. Tom had never expected her rejection of him to continue so long. One thing had, alas, become obvious. Kessie was not pregnant, so that fond hope, which would have ended the battle between them, was dashed.

Then Tom had a speaking engagement in Manchester, which Sarah attended. Within a few days of that encounter he was standing on the deck of the ss *Brighton Queen*, watching the coastline of the Isle of Wight grow large and clear.

When the steamship docked at Ventnor pier and Tom saw the steep narrow streets and the villas clambering up the wooded cliffs, he liked the town. The drive to St Lawrence in an omnibus that stopped frequently to deliver letters, parcels and magazines, as well as picking up and putting down passengers, was delightful; it wound through a profusion of trees and exotic undergrowth, thick even in the dying winter days, with the foliage-draped rockface sheering up on one side, and glimpses of the sea on the other.

When he finally found Willow Bank *Cottage*, halfway down a track overhung with trees that led from the main St Lawrence road, he stopped short, amazed. Solidly built in grey stone, it had huge bay windows and soaring gables. The Whitworth house in Mellordale would fit comfortably into its downstairs; and as for the garden, with its rolling lawns and fine stone-walled terraces . . .! Tom was reminded, not for the first time, that by marrying Kessie he had moved into another world, though that was not why he had married her.

A plump housekeeper answered the front door bell, informing him that neither Mrs Whitworth nor Miss Thorpe was at home, and would he care to leave his card? On a silver plate by the hallstand, Tom saw the buff envelope of a telegram, which he picked up and opened. The woman was scandalised, 'That is addressed to Mrs Whitworth. What do you think you're doing?'

'I'm Mr Whitworth and I sent it.' Fortunately, it was his delayed telegram.

The housekeeper thawed immediately, showed him into a sun-filled sitting-room and introduced herself as Mrs Dobell, saying she had worked for his wife's late lamented aunt and what a nice lady Mrs Whitworth was, despite her interest in this women's suffrage business. After Mrs Dobell had brought in tea and home-made shortbreads and he had consumed them, Tom stood in the bay window, thoughtfully looking out across the steeply sloping garden.

On his visit to Manchester he had given another first-class speech that Kessie had not heard. But Sarah had and he had gone back with her to her flat in Moss Side. No mention had been made of Edward Dawson, but Sarah had been fidgety and clearly ill at ease. Eventually, she said, 'I gather you were furious with Kessie because of her clinics, and because she stayed so long with me. Is that why you're up here in Manchester and she's down there on the Isle of Wight?' Tom shrugged awkwardly and Sarah leaned towards him. 'Shall I tell you *why* she stayed so long with me?'

When she had told him, for several seconds Tom stared at her. His first emotion was fury. How could Sarah have done such a thing? How could she have involved Kessie? And how could Kessie not have told him? Then the fury had ebbed away, to be replaced by a kind of admiration. Kessie had not breathed a word to him because she had given Sarah her solemn promise. He thought of the two of them, alone in this flat, and Sarah so sick, and my God, Kessie had not panicked. Bless her and bless Doctor McPhee because without them both Sarah could have died, as Ella Warburton had died.

Her head defiantly to one side, Sarah said, 'I don't regret what I did, Tom. It won't happen again, I can tell you. But if I'm responsible for you and Kessie falling out, then I'm sorry. Please, for my sake, if no one else's, make it up.'

Tom turned away. 'I've hurt Kessie badly.'

Sarah frowned.

'I can guess how, and I don't want to know who with. Look, if you can't persuade the woman you love that you do love her, you're slipping, Tom Whitworth.'

Now he leaned his forehead against the window pane.

Was that what Kessie wanted to hear? It wouldn't hurt him to retell her that.

He saw her coming through the wicket gate, climbing up the steep path. She was wearing a rust-coloured woollen two-piece, she had a tartan scarf round her neck, a matching tam-o'-shanter on her chestnut hair. The fresh air had brought the colour to her cheeks, a sparkle to her eyes. Clearly she hadn't pined in his absence, because she was slightly plumper. She looked incredibly young and, oh yes, trusting.

Kessie glanced up towards the house and saw him in the window. For a moment she stood still, then she started to run, and they met at the bottom of the steps. He held her tightly in his arms and she looked up at him.

'I have news for you. I'm expecting.' Tom frowned slightly, she saw the frown and giggled. 'It's yours. I've missed two periods and I've started to be sick in the mornings which is horrid. . . .'

'Why the hell haven't you told me?'

'Because . . . I'm telling you now.'

'Kess, my darling Kess.' He swung her round in his arms, putting her down very gently. 'Shouldn't you be resting?'

'Tom, don't be silly, it isn't due for ages—not until 1st October.'

17

Stifling a yawn, Tom leant against the green leather benches in the House of Commons. They had been sitting virtually nonstop since February, night and day, battling over 'the People's Budget'. It was now early September and yet another Tory backwoodsman was on his feet bleating at Lloyd George. Tom was about to leap to his feet when the usher came in with the message. Would he telephone Miss

Walmsley urgently. For a moment, he had to think who Miss Walmsley was.

Maggie!

When he got through to The Grove, she started to shout as if he were at the North Pole, but Maggie regarded the telephone as the devil's device, so he tried to control the temper fuelled by his anxiety.

'I know you wouldn't have troubled me unless it was important, Maggie, just tell me what's happened . . . After I left this afternoon? Yes, of course you did right to let me know. The nurse is there? Right, tell Mrs Whitworth I'm on my way home.'

In Mellordale Tom had grown up with childbirth—'Our mam says can your mam come round, she's started'—but now that it was happening to his own wife everything was different. Reaching The Grove, racing up the stairs, the sight of Stephen's large frame emerging from their bedroom only increased his fears. A doctor present so early in the proceedings? Oh, Christ. Stephen barred his path. Yes, she said, there could be problems because the baby was premature but, all right, he could see Kessie for a couple of ticks.

As he went in to the bedroom Kessie was having a contraction. She held his hand tightly, gasping for breath, her body rigid with the pain. The spasm passed and she smiled bravely.

'It'll be all right, I know it will.' She was still clasping his hand. 'I wish you could stay with me, Tom.'

'So do I, luv.' With his free hand, gently he stroked her hair, but a few minutes later Stephen ordered him out of the room.

On the landing she said, 'You might as well go back to the House of Commons. You've done your bit.'

Tom glared at her, but he knew she did not like him— probably Alice had told her what had happened—and fighting Stephen was a battle he did not need. But he did not return to the House. Nobody was remotely interested in him or his feelings, and he sat alone in the study. At some point Ruby shoved a tray of food at him. The night wore on and Tom was dozing in an armchair when he heard Kessie

191

screaming, long protracted screams that cut the air like rending cloth. The traffic up and down the stairs increased, steaming kettles in hands, and Kessie's screams mounted to a hideous crescendo.

Oh God, it had to be a male creator that had dreamed this up for women.

Tom was staring out of the window watching the dawn pink of another fine day touch the treetops, listening to the chirruping of the birds. It was several seconds before he realised why he could hear them so clearly. The screams had stopped. Muffled, as if on a distant echo, he heard the baby's cries, and he leapt up the stairs four at a time. On the landing, the smiles spreading across their faces, were Maggie, Ruby and Vi, and it was Vi who said, 'Oh, Mr Whitworth, isn't that the loveliest sound?'

The nurse showed him his daughter, the tiniest little scrap that made Tom catch his breath, and she said he was lucky to have her, with the difficulties of the premature birth it had been touch-and-go, but Doctor Abbott was a wonderful doctor. Stephen said Kessie was exhausted and must rest, so that it was not until the afternoon that he was finally allowed into the bedroom. Her chestnut hair was spread across the pillow, the babe was in her arms, wrapped in the shawl that Aunt Ada had crocheted.

Tom leaned over to kiss them both. 'Thank you, my darling.'

Kessie said, 'It was hideous, you've no idea how hideous. And she's not exactly beautiful, is she?'

To Tom she was. The picture of Kessie and their baby daughter was the most beautiful sight he had ever seen, and he could have wept.

'I think we'll call her Anne, don't you?'

'I love you, Kess, you're incomparable.' Tom pushed back the shawl and ran his finger over the puckered red face. 'Hello, Anne Whitworth, welcome to the world.'

It was at a heroic moment in the history of her sex that Anne Whitworth entered the world. Her mother's friends, as their latest gesture in protest against imprisonment and the

192

continuing denial of citizenship, had *hunger-struck. For six whole days* they had gone without food in Holloway. Secretly, Kessie was not sorry that she had been pregnant, so that her bravery had not been put to the test. After six days, the Government had finally admitted defeat and released the hunger-striking suffragettes.

'They'll have to give us the vote now, won't they?' she said excitedly to Stephen who nodded, before wagging a finger at her.

'You are not to get worked up, Kessie. You had a bad time, you're not strong yet, and the watchword is easy-does-it.'

Being made to take things easily, to have plenty of rest, was frustrating in one sense, as Kessie longed to go into Clement's Inn, but in another it gave her time to get to know her daughter. Although she was being determinedly off-hand about her motherhood—not for her the cooing wonderment of maternity—actually she found Anne quite enchanting, so tiny, so vulnerable, so dependent, feeling the air with miniature hands that were the same shape as Tom's, turning towards Kessie's breasts with pursed, sucking mouth.

Not that she was breast-feeding. Stephen said, 'Good grief, old thing, you don't want to do *that*, ties you down no end,' and although she suspected that Tom would have liked her to have fed Anne herself, she agreed to put her daughter on the bottle. Then Ruby asked if her sister could possibly look after the baby, once the nurse had left, and having watched Vi with Anne, Kessie agreed to that, too. She couldn't say she had *enjoyed* being pregnant, though it had been an interesting experience. The birth *had* been as awful as those screams in Holloway had led her to fear, but Tom's absolute delight made it all worthwhile, and she was feeling pleased with herself and darling little Anne.

Finally, after three weeks, the longed-for day came when Stephen said she could return to normal, though slowly did it, and visitors other than the family arrived. (Papa had been almost as peacock proud as Tom.) Among the early arrivals

193

was Christabel, whom she immediately took upstairs to the nursery.

Having peered into the bassinet Christabel said, 'Oh, what a shame—she's asleep.'

'Yes, and please don't waken her. She's a powerful pair of lungs, I can tell you.'

'With you two as parents, that's no surprise.' Christabel laughed.

They had tea in the conservatory that Kessie had had built on to the back of the house, and Tom joined them before he left for the House of Commons. Munching a neat stack of Maggie's wafer-thin salmon and cucumber sandwiches—like Sarah he tended to speak with his mouth full—he said, 'Nobody can ever again say women lack initiative or sheer guts.'

'No, Tom, they cannot.' Triumph glowed in Christabel's eyes. 'With the hunger-strike, the women of Britain have at last found the weapon to beat the Liberals' obduracy.'

'Makes me ashamed to be a man, the whole disgusting episode. They can't let women go on hunger-striking. They'll have to frame a Women's Suffrage Bill soon.'

Christabel looked surprised at his admission of masculine guilt, but as a reward she gave him one of her upturned smiles.

While they had their tea, Kessie gazed round the conservatory. The subtle shades of pink, red and cream of her geraniums, fuchsias and begonias nodded in the gentle breeze, through the open glass door the sweet scent of the new mown grass and the headier perfume of the last of the roses wafted. In a pile of grass cuttings that Peg-Leg Pete had left on the path, idiotic Jasper was licking elegant Amber and the cats' orange fur was bright against the soft green. It was all so civilised that it seemed doubly incredible that women had needed to be imprisoned, to hunger-strike, simply to make civilised Liberal politicians concede their right to citizenship.

From upstairs, Kessie heard her daughter's cries, and she jumped up. 'Do excuse me, won't you? I'll bring her down for you to see, Christabel.'

Later in the afternoon, deep in the corridors of the House

of Commons, Herbert Gladstone passed Tom and nodded politely. He had never warmed to the uncouth fellow, but his recent obvious delight over his daughter's birth was touching. Mrs Whitworth he had always considered one of the nicest of the suffragettes and he was glad to hear she had withdrawn from the fray by having a child.

Why, oh why, had the women's revolt erupted during his tenure as Home Secretary?

When he was ushered into the Prime Minister's suite, Mr Asquith was sitting in an armchair looking particularly benign, his heavy chin resting comfortably on his wing collar, his receding silver hair brushed into a quiff.

'Ah Herbert, do sit down.' Apprehensively, Mr Gladstone lowered himself on to one of the straight-backed chairs: because the PM in a benign mood always worried him. But he came straight to the point as usual, which was one thing to be said in his favour.

'These hunger-striking women in Winson Green prison in Birmingham, Herbert. Do you intend to release *them* at the end of the week?' The Prime Minister's interest in these particular women was understandable, because two of them had somehow managed to climb on to a roof, to loosen the slates and to hurl them at Mr Asquith as he emerged from a nearby rally. 'Or do we implement His Majesty's suggestion?'

From Marienbad, where he had been taking the waters, among his other activities—for a man of his advanced years, his virility was astounding—the King had written 'suggesting' that the existing officially authorised methods for dealing with prisoners who refused to eat be implemented in regard to the increasing number of suffragette hunger-strikers. Mr Gladstone had been doing his best to ignore the suggestion, but since his return home the King had been growing increasingly apoplectic about the suffragettes, demanding that action be taken.

The Prime Minister sighed. 'Our options are limited. We keep releasing the hunger-strikers so that they may continue to commit mayhem. Or we allow them to starve themselves to death and have dozens of martyrettes on our hands. That

195

is hardly an option. Or you issue the orders for them to be mechanically fed to save their lives.'

The justice of the women's claim was, in Herbert Gladstone's private opinion, beyond doubt or argument, and to forcibly feed women because they wanted the vote was outrageous. And yet, in a civilised, law-abiding country, lawlessness could not be allowed to continue. . . .

'They can't be forcibly feeding them. They just can't. It isn't possible. It's monstrous. It's obscene, it's . . .'

'Calm down, Kess.'

'What are you going to do?'

Tom proceeded to make a passionate speech in the House of Commons, denouncing forcible feeding as a form of barbarism that would not be tolerated in Czarist Russia. But less than half the House supported him, the majority agreeing with the Home Secretary that it was the only option open to the Government.

'What else are you going to do?' Kessie demanded.

'Keep hammering away. What else can I do?'

'You can resign in protest.'

'What good would that do? The buggers'd be only too glad to see the back of me.'

The urge to do something herself was raging through Kessie. But how could she, with a newly born baby?

During the brief October break an exhausted House of Commons was allowing itself, Tom was asked if he would attend a Socialist conference in Vienna because Mr Keir Hardie was unwell again. His interest in foreign parts was not high, and he told Kessie that he didn't want to leave her or Anne at that moment. Kessie urged him to go. He would enjoy himself once he was there, she said, all those arguments in smoke-filled rooms about whither goest international Socialism.

After seeing him off at Victoria Station, Kessie called in at Clement's Inn where she found Christabel in a state of excitement.

'They've over-reached themselves this time. Look at those letters and telegrams.' She waved at the pile on her desk.

'Many are from people who say they've not supported women's suffrage before, but this outrage has converted them. Our heroic members will not have long to endure, and they will not have endured in vain.'

Kessie listened to her friend at her most volatile. Then Christabel said she was going to Newcastle where dozens of women were converging because Lloyd George was making an important speech about his wretched Budget, and the House of Lords . . .

Kessie interrupted her.

'When are you going?'

'Tomorrow.'

'I'm coming with you.'

'Are you fit enough?' Kessie did not reply, and Christabel kissed her. 'Oh, soul of fire and iron! What friends I am blessed with!'

Kessie had no clear idea what she would do in Newcastle, but she could not sit at The Grove doing nothing. When she got back home she burst into tears—she was alarmingly tearful at the moment—because Tom had left a package. Inside was a pair of mother-of-pearl earrings and a note:

My darling Kess,
    Robert Herrick said it infinitely better than I can—

> Thou art my life, my love, my heart,
> The very eyes of me:
> And hast command of every part
> To live and die for thee.

Look after yourself, my darling, and our little girl, Tom.

The tears still welling in her eyes, Kessie went upstairs to the nursery where she leant over the bassinet with its pink muslin frills. Anne had just woken, her little legs were treadling under the exquisite day-gown Aunt Ada had embroidered, and she was cooing gently. When she saw her mother, she chuckled with delight. Kessie took her in her arms, nestling her chin on the down of soft hair, and the tears ran down her cheeks. She didn't want to leave her daughter, she ought not to. Should she telephone Christabel to say she had changed her mind about going to Newcastle? No. Anne would be safe in Vi's adoring hands and she would only be away for twenty-four hours.

18

'Nervous?'

'Very.'

'So am I.' Lady Constance Lytton tucked her arm into Kessie's as they walked slowly down the hill in Newcastle. Con was not only a prestigious new recruit, but one of the nicest people Kessie had met. They were comrades-in-arms, solidarity and shared sufferings their strength.

They were nearing the Palace Theatre where Mr Lloyd George was due to speak and they slowed their pace. Round the theatre the crowds were thick, the police ranks thicker, the barricades feet high, and a posse of guards was checking and rechecking everybody's credentials before they were allowed inside. While Kessie and Con Lytton were wondering what their next move should be, they heard shouts and saw the distant figure of Jane Brailsford. Jane had approached the barricade carrying a small axe concealed in a bunch of chrysanthemums. Now she had thrown away the flowers and was chopping at the barricade with her axe, and on the wind they heard her voice calling out defiantly, 'Mr Lloyd George talks about the new society his "People's Budget" will usher in. Nothing will be ushered in until women have the vote. . . .'

Two policemen had her by the arms and were dragging her away. Kessie turned to Lady Constance. 'Lloyd George hasn't arrived yet. I've just heard those people saying he hasn't. If we keep on walking and we're lucky, we should meet his car.'

Slowly they continued down the hill but people had recognised them and they were being followed by a growing crowd and a photographer was running up, almost falling over his heavy camera in his excitement. A lad yelled, 'Are you going to plant a bomb, missus?'

If they were going to do something, they had better do it quickly, because the police could hardly claim not to know they were here with militant intent, when half the population of Newcastle appeared to do so. A large motor car was coming towards them, purposefully Con moved into the roadway, walking down the tramlines, her head in the tricorne hat held high. She lifted her arm, Kessie saw it was not Lloyd George inside the car and shouted, 'No!', but she was too late and Con had thrown her stone.

Taking a deep breath, Kessie threw hers. It bounced harmlessly against the long curving mudguard. A broad Geordie voice said, 'Bravo, hinnie.' Two policemen were running towards her. Bravo, hinnie.

The police cells in Newcastle were quite the most disgusting Kessie had been in. Cannon Row was Buckingham Palace by comparison. There was a men's urinal outside her window and, apart from the stench, the conversations were . . . she was too exhausted to find the words to describe them. She could only trust that Newcastle prison would be less revolting. Stripping the filthy mattress and blanket from the bed, she lay on the plank board. The cell door was opening. What did they want now? Why couldn't they leave her alone?

'Merciful heavens, I can't talk to her in there. It's like a sewer. Bring her out. We'll use the inspector's office.'

Merciful heavens, it was David Lloyd George's voice.

Kessie sat in the inspector's office while Lloyd George prowled around her. 'I've come to pay your fine, Kessie. You can't stay in this place. And you're not being forcibly fed.'

'I haven't been sentenced yet. I don't know how much my fine will be.'

Lloyd George waved his hands in the air, as if that was a matter of supreme unimportance which, with the Chancellor of the Exchequer come personally to obtain her release, it probably was. She had to stop him. 'When I am released, do I accompany you to your hotel room to repay you for services rendered?'

The question stopped him in his tracks. 'No. I will take you back to *your* hotel room, Mrs Whitworth, and what you do there will be *your* business.' He was very angry with her and it had been a palpable hit. 'Where's your husband?'

'In Vienna.'

'Where's he staying?'

'I don't know.'

'For goodness sake, Kessie, I can find out.'

'Find out then.'

'If you're determined to be a martyr, so be it. You won't get the vote this way.'

'You tell me how we will get the vote then?'

'Very well, go on hunger-strike!' He walked angrily towards the door. 'Let them forcibly feed you!'

'*Them?*' Kessie stood up and she was shaking with anger, '*Them*? Don't you mean *you*? No prison governor in this country can forcibly feed anyone without the consent of the Home Secretary, the Home Secretary of a Liberal Government of which you are the second most important and powerful member, some would say the first. So please don't talk to me about *them*.'

Flinging open the door, David Lloyd George called out to the waiting police constable, 'Take Mrs Whitworth back to her cell.'

The Governor of Newcastle prison looked at the telegram in his hand. It was the authorisation from the Home Secretary to feed those suffragette prisoners refusing to take nourishment, unless there were medical reasons for not doing so. Personally, the Governor was in favour of votes for women and he wished to heaven these determined ladies had had themselves arrested and hunger-struck elsewhere. Also, he disliked his chief medical officer, but you tended to get the dregs of the medical profession in the prison service; he had said only one of them needed to be released on medical grounds, Lady Constance Lytton, who undoubtedly had a defective heart, and that was that.

Mrs Brailsford, too, would have to be released, even if she was, in the doctor's words, as strong as an ox, because her husband was a famous journalist who could raise Cain if his wife was forcibly fed. But as for the others? Mrs Whitworth, a nice woman, was married to that young MP, but he was only a Labour MP, and Miss Pethick, another nice woman, was the sister of Mrs Pethick Lawrence, and . . . but he couldn't release them all, or he'd be in trouble. Where did he draw the line?

'Constance Lytton and Jane Brailsford have been released.'

Christabel put the telephone receiver in her office back on its hook and Alice said, 'And the others? Kessie?'

'They'll be forcibly fed as from today. Kessie wants to do it. We cannot go against her free will and choice. It will not last long, Alice, it cannot last long. The uproar is already too great. Tom will be back from Vienna soon and I have no doubt *he* will get Kessie out.'

After she left Clement's Inn, Alice held up the traffic in the Strand to cross to St Clement Danes Church. Religion was something she seldom thought about, going to church was partly to pay your respects to Him, partly a social occasion, but with its high-backed wooden pews and the gallery running round three sides, she liked this church which reminded her of the ones back home. Kessie liked its cool peace, too, and in the past they had sometimes sat here together, escaping from the hurly-burly of the office.

Kessie was now sitting in Newcastle prison, waiting to be forcibly fed.

Alice hated people who kept up quarrels and Kessie had rebuffed all her conciliatory efforts, even the genuine American teddy bear she had brought back from New York for her baby. (Alice had been home for the summer, mainly to meet Franklin's family, and while she had found the Senator a nice enough old guy, she foresaw battles ahead with her future mother-in-law, that iron-willed Daughter of the Revolution, Mrs Clementine Adams.) Yet she still

201

could not bear the thought of Kessie being forcibly fed and she determined to do something about it.

Alice stood up, inclined her head towards the altar, went outside and hailed a cab. At the Labour Party's dingy office, she explained why she urgently needed Tom Whitworth's address in Vienna. She then telegraphed him: 'Kessie being forcibly fed Newcastle Gaol Stop Come home soonest Stop Alice Hartley.'

She then took another cab back to Hampstead, where Stephen waved sheets of paper at her. 'Bagged our hundred and twenty-first signature, and three more big guns have agreed to sign.' Stephen was organising a doctors' petition to Mr Asquith, begging him to stop forcible feeding forthwith, on medical, if not moral, grounds. 'Any doctor worth their salt knows that with forcible feeding food can get into the lungs, or the heart can be permanently damaged. Ye gods! That I should be speaking of such things in twentieth-century England!'

From the silver salver in the hall, Alice collected the mail that had arrived by the fourth post and went up to her sitting-room to read it. Among the letters was a belated reply, not from His Majesty to whom she had written pleading for his personal intervention the minute she heard about the forcible feeding in Winson Green prison, but from Sir Arthur Ponsonby, his Private Secretary.

Dear Miss Hartley,

His Majesty has requested me to thank you for your letter and to inform you that he is fully cognizant of the decision taken by his Secretary of State for Home Affairs in regard to the feeding of Suffragette prisoners who insist on starving themselves to death. It is a decision which His Majesty endorses.

Yours truly,
Arthur Ponsonby.

Having read the odious letter, Alice went into her bedroom. The diamond and ruby encrusted case for eau-de-cologne pads which the King had given her as a present (for valour at the bridge table, Alice considered, as he was the world's worst bridge player), was sitting on a lace mat on her dressing table. She wrapped the case into a parcel, in which she enclosed a brief letter.

Sir,
    It was an honor to receive this gift from Your Majesty. While English women are being tortured in English prisons, I cannot use it with honor.
Yours very truly,
Alice Hartley.

Alice addressed the parcel to His Majesty King Edward VII at Buckingham Palace.

With great regret, the Governor informed Kessie that unless she agreed to take nourishment she would be mechanically fed. He begged her not to subject herself to this unpleasantness. Lying on the bed in the cell, Kessie shook her head.

Going without food had been as hideous as she had anticipated. Her stomach felt as if it were filled with gnawing rats, her tongue had a thick fur coat, there was the most peculiar taste of lime in her mouth, she was like a running tap, constantly crouched over the slop-bucket, and her head was whirling. But they were only allowing the suffragettes to hunger-strike for forty-eight hours and now she had to screw up her courage.

An hour later she heard the clatter of a trolley in the stone corridor. It stopped outside her cell, the door opened, two doctors in white aprons, and six wardresses came in, their caps and collars stiffly starched. The older doctor she already knew to be a brute, though the younger one wasn't so bad. Kessie struggled to sit up as the wardresses dragged her bed into the middle of the cell, and she didn't know which was hammering the most, her head or her heart.

Suddenly, all six wardresses grabbed at her, two of them went for her legs, two for her arms, one put a hefty arm across her waist, another round her neck. They dragged her head up and propped it against some pillows, before tying a towel round her neck. The younger doctor was behind her, half kneeling on the bed and he jammed his left knee on to her shoulder so that her face was turned towards the other doctor who was standing in front of her. The younger doctor took her nose in one hand, her jaw in the other and now he was trying to force open her mouth.

'Don't struggle, Mrs Whitworth, it makes it worse for yourself if you do.'

Kessie could not help struggling as her mouth was slowly forced open. The wardresses were holding her even more tightly by the arms, the hips and the ankles. She was pinioned in a human vice. The brutal doctor was moving closer, a long rubber tube in his hand. He was inserting it into her wide open mouth. She tried to wrench her head, but the young doctor jammed his knee harder on her shoulder, tightening his grip on her nose and jaw.

The tube was being pushed down her throat.

The first brief sensation was a tickling one, then she could not breathe, she was choking to death, she felt as if she had been hit on the head with a sledge-hammer, her lungs were bursting, her chest was being branded with hot irons. She wanted to scream, 'Stop it, stop it', but she couldn't.

The brute was sticking a Fergusson's gag between her teeth, it dug into her gums, and there was a slight smile playing round his lips. Oh God, dear God, he was enjoying himself. From behind, the knee pressed harder on to her shoulder, in front the brute placed a funnel on to the end of the tube, picked up a jug and poured in the liquid. From the smell Kessie knew it was Benger's food which Sheba had given her when she was ill as a child.

The funnel had a glass section and Kessie watched as, agonisingly slowly, the oatmeal coloured mess dripped through. She had to stay like this, her jaw stuck open, the gag piercing her gums, the red hot irons branding her chest, her lungs about to explode, a knee dislocating her shoulder, pinioned by six wardresses, until the Benger's food had slid through the long tube into her stomach. The liquid wasn't moving, it had stuck, she could swear it had stuck, she was choking to death, it was impossible to breathe, her lungs would burst like an overblown balloon. The younger doctor was feeling her pulse.

'It's nearly over, Mrs Whitworth.'

One of the wardresses put a bowl of water under her chin. The brute started to pull out the tube, it was a live electric eel, a razor-sharp sword being drawn through her flesh, the most excruciating pain Kessie had known, worse than what she'd just been through, worse than any of the agonies of bearing Anne. It was out, her throat and chest were minced, mangled meat, the wardress was dipping the tube into the bowl and globs of mucus and green and yellow phlegm floated on the water. The sight made Kessie retch, she was spitting and the pain was unendurable. More phlegm and mucus and drips of Benger's food sprayed the towel, making her heave more violently. She was shivering uncontrollably, everything was swirling around her, the most brilliant colours she had ever seen coalescing before her eyes. She kept on spitting, retching, coughing and she *had* to stop herself because she could not endure the pain. The wardresses were wrapping blankets around her, splashing her with eau-de-cologne, but she went on shivering in helpless jerking movements and the scent could not overcome the stench.

'My dear Alice, may we drop the subject over dinner? Your friends have brought the mechanical feeding on themselves. They may secure their immediate release simply by agreeing to keep the peace.'

Across the Prime Minister's dinner-table Frankie was silently begging Alice not to push the subject any further, when from the far end of the table Margot Asquith's extraordinary voice reached them.

'I disagree entirely. The ruby in her navel is entirely tasteful. The whole routine is tasteful. Next time she is in London, I shall invite Miss Allan to perform here.'

Behind Margot a servant was carving the calf's head into the thinnest slices and its tongue stuck out towards the guests in jellied defiance. For the first time in her life, the sight of food made Alice feel sick. How could they sit here in the dining-room of number ten Downing Street, the heart of the mighty British Empire, these allegedly civilised English men and women, stuffing themselves with food, discussing Maud Allan's 'Dance of the Seven Veils', while Kessie and dozens of other women were having food brutally forced into them in cold prison cells?

How could they?

After her fourth forcible feeding, Kessie wondered how long she could endure. The thing that was keeping her going was her hatred of the older doctor who, as the food dripped through the glass funnel, bared his teeth at her. 'Taste nice?'

She could not in fact *taste* anything. There was no sensation of food going into her stomach. The agony was concentrated on her jaw, her gums, her throat, and most fearfully on her chest. During her third feed she had choked *while* she was being fed, they'd had to pull out the tube, momentarily she had passed out and she had only been semi-conscious as the tube was forced down her throat again. Her gums were so lacerated from the Fergusson's gag that they started to bleed the moment it was jammed into her mouth and the doctor had to swab the blood to stop it trickling down her throat. Just now, after this last feed, she had sicked up half the Benger's food, some of it over the brutal doctor which, despite the pain, had given her a certain satisfaction. He had sworn at her, pushing her back on to the pillow, the vomit had run down the towel, and the younger doctor had said, 'I say, sir, steady on, sir.' Then she had started to shudder so violently that they had wrapped extra blankets round her and brought in a hot water bottle.

'Give it up, Mrs Whitworth.' A wardress had stayed behind and was patting her hand. 'Nothing's worth what you're going through. You're suffering much worse than the others, you know. Do you think we enjoy it?' Kessie wanted to say *he* certainly does, I can see his face, I *make* myself watch him because I will not let him defeat me, but her throat was so lacerated she found it difficult to talk. 'You have a baby daughter, haven't you? Go home to her. You'll get the vote eventually, pet. Do you think anybody will remember you went through this to get it? Of course they won't. It's just not worth it. . . .'

206

'Please, please leave me alone.' Kessie managed to get the words out, though her voice sounded a long way away and like a bullfrog's. Her vision was blurred but she sensed the wardress's huffiness as she left the cell.

Why *am* I lying here three hundred miles away from my baby? Kessie thought. *Is* it in the hope of being remembered by the generations to come? No, I am doing it for Anne and for Anne's daughters, because the vote is the key to unlock the door to freedom. I've been thinking a lot about *my* mother. I always had the feeling she wasn't as ill as she pretended to be. Yet she died quite young. Did she simply give up on life? Was that why Papa took a mistress? Did she escape into being an invalid? From what? From marriage? From having more children? I shall never know because she never talked to me but I shall talk to Anne, to all my children.

If only I could breathe the fresh air, if only I could be warm again. What's Tom going to say? Will he forgive me for going behind his back and deserting Anne? Will he understand that I had to make my gesture, to pit my strength against this obscenity? Pain is like an advancing medieval army, storming and raping. I don't know how long I can endure it, or the sound of the rattling trolley, the clattering announcement of the torture. But women endure childbirth. And this is only like going into the last stage of labour twice a day . . . despite herself, Kessie started to giggle, the pain was like broken pieces of glass being crunched into her flesh . . . oh Anne . . . oh Tom. . . .

19

In Vienna Tom, as Kessie had predicted, had been enjoying himself in noisy debates, arguing long into the night in smoke-wreathed cafés. He had not bothered with the newspapers and his Socialist comrades, mostly men, were not over-interested in women's emancipation, which they believed would come with the millennium. One Belgian chap, though, had said that only a country like England that lived and breathed by the law could have introduced forcible feeding, which Tom considered a discerning remark. Still, he was surprised not to have heard from Kess, the inveterate letter and post-card sender, but maybe she was busy with Anne, bless them both.

Tom did not see either telegram—there was one from Maggie as well as Alice—until he returned to his cheap lodging-house at three o'clock in the morning. When he read them an icy fury filled him, first and foremost against the Liberals, then against Kessie herself, but he retched at the thought of her being forcibly fed and, as soon as the Post Office opened, he despatched a telegram to the Governor of Newcastle Gaol: 'Riquest immediate releese Kessie Whitworth Stop Will pay fine Stop Tom Whitworth.' He had written 'demmand' but had crossed it out and put 'riquest' (the spelling, which was not Tom's forte, became more mangled *en route*). He then caught the Paris express, to connect with the London boat train.

Before his telegram arrived, Kessie had been released.

First of all her father had stormed into the Governor's office. Charles Thorpe had been in mental agony since hearing of his daughter's arrest, but he knew it was a point of honour among the suffragettes' relations *not* to pay their fines. Then Sarah turned up at The Laurels, saying she was the last person to suggest paying anybody's fine, but from what she had heard forcible feeding was truly dreadful, and since Kessie was not fully recovered from Anne's birth, she felt that . . . Charles Thorpe set off for Newcastle within the hour.

While Mr Thorpe roared about paid lackeys who did other people's dirty work and the test of a man was for him to be able *not* to obey orders, a telegram was brought into the Governor's office. It came from the Home Secretary, ordering Mrs Whitworth's release on medical grounds, namely her recent confinement. Why had that not been taken into account in the first place? (Herbert Gladstone had been only too happy to order Mrs Whitworth's release, though it was Lloyd George who had shown him how it could be managed. She couldn't have been one of his endless women, could she? Not a nice girl like her.)

When Tom reached The Grove, Kessie was in bed. Her father and Stephen were both there and Stephen collared him.

'I've sedated Kessie but when she comes round, you be gentle with her. She's in a shocking and shocked state. Kessie's a highly strung girl and she was not fully recovered from her confinement. By George, I could strangle those brutes with my bare hands. Call themselves doctors? Forcible feeding has never before been used in England except on lunatics *in extremis*.'

When Tom went into the bedroom and saw Kessie, the last remnants of his fury against her evaporated. She was sleeping, her head on one side, the chestnut hair falling across her shoulder, her lovely skin was a yellowy-grey, her face so thin that the cheekbones and jawline were jutting. One of her arms was on the eiderdown and it was black and blue from the bruising where the wardresses had gripped her.

For a long time Tom sat by the bedside. Despite the sedation Kessie kept twisting her head, shivering and moaning. He could kill them all, the entire Government, the prison staff, the doctors. The thought that hammered in his head, stoking his rage, was that Jane Brailsford had been released. To Lady Constance Lytton's release he had no objection, because she had a weak heart, but Jane Brailsford was a healthy woman. She had been released because her husband was a famous journalist. *His* wife had been forcibly fed.

Although Parliament had reassembled after its brief recess, Tom stayed with Kessie for a couple of days. She clutched Anne in her arms, she clung to him, weeping and saying, 'I'm sorry, Tom, no I'm not. I think I reached the limits of my endurance, but I had to do it, you do understand, don't you?' He said, yes, but he wanted her to promise never to be

209

forcibly fed again. 'I'm not *asking* you, Kess, I'm *begging* you. Don't push yourself past your limits. I can't bear it. We'll end it for everyone soon but, please, in the meantime, promise me that.'

Kessie wept and promised, and he wanted to take her in his arms, to carry her to the House of Commons, to shout, 'Look at her, you bastards, this is what forcible feeding does to a woman.'

When he returned to the Commons, at Prime Minister's Question Time, Tom was surprised at his own calmness as he asked how long the Government intended to torture women, to drag their country's name through the mire? In reply, Asquith was at his most blandly bored. When he sat down, an arm draped across the green leather front bench, his legs sprawled in front of him, Tom stared at him.

He was growing fat and slovenly, the double chin hanging over the thick folds of his neck, and recently he had been drunk in the House. The one-time pride of Balliol! The cynosure of Liberal reason! This slob who had no idea how half the citizens of England existed, this coward who had approved of Jane Brailsford's release but had allowed Kessie's body to be assaulted.

Slowly, Tom rose to his feet, slowly he came down the gangway. As he reached Asquith his passion was so fierce that momentarily it subdued the Chamber. 'You say, "The women can walk out this afternoon." So long as they abandon their principles. Can we expect you to abandon yours at the behest of bullies? You say, "There is no option." Women must be imprisoned, women must be tortured, their bodies assaulted, their minds tormented, because *they* have left *you* no option. There is a very simple option. Women want the vote. They have been asking for fifty years. Give them the vote and your problem is solved.'

Mr Asquith pulled himself into an upright position, retreating against the green leather bench, but Tom grabbed him by the lapels of his frock-coat, hauled him to his feet, and shook him like a rattle. He saw the fear in Asquith's eyes, he smelled it on him, and the bugger was right to be frightened because he wanted to batter him to pulp. The murderous impulse drained away, he was being dragged off, the Speaker was ordering him out of the House, but he shook off the restraining hands. 'I shall be happy to be suspended. At times, this place makes me vomit.'

After he had emerged from the Houses of Parliament, Tom walked off his fury by striding along the Embankment, up into the new Kingsway, past Euston Station, on into Camden Town where he bought Kessie a bunch of deep yellow chrysanthemums from a flower seller, and up the long haul of Highgate West Hill. When he finally got home, she was sitting by the fire surrounded by the evening newspapers and she threw herself into his arms.

'Oh, Tom, you shouldn't have done it. It won't do your reputation any good, assaulting the Prime Minister, but I do love you!'

As Kessie was arranging Tom's flowers her eye was caught by Alice's bouquet, one of the many she had received on her release from prison. Momentarily she paused. She was going to have to do something about Alice Hartley.

Kessie went to bed early, for she tired very easily and her heart would keep thumping. When Tom came up, bringing her cocoa with him, while she drank it he lay by her side smoking and reading. Did he enjoy those weedy cigarettes he still insisted on hand-rolling? Was it his conservatism that made him reject proper cigarettes, or was it to prove to his envious colleagues that he remained one of them? She had decided what to do about Alice.

'I shall invite her to tea.'

'Who?'

'Alice. You will be here, won't you?'

'No. I shall be in the House.'

'You don't know which day she'll come.'

'I shall still be in the House.'

'Oh, Tom.'

'There are several things in my life I am not proud of. Alice Hartley is one of them.'

'What are the others?'

'I'll tell you one day.' But he doubted he would tell even Kess about Ella Warburton.

'Alice is going home soon, you know. Permanently. Her wedding date is fixed.' Tom shifted his position in the bed, deliberately, and silently Kessie agreed that Alice's imminent departure was a reason for the invitation.

When she heard those familiar New York tones in the hall, Kessie's heart started to thump loudly, and she clutched Anne to her bosom. She felt absurdly nervous. With arms outstretched, Alice swept into the room, a vision in a pale tan walking costume, with a huge cream hat covering her neck and shoulders. Behind her Ruby was laden down with flowers, a box of chocolates, a large flaxen-haired doll and the teddy bear Kessie had previously refused to accept for her daughter. She kissed Kessie as if nothing untoward had ever happened, and flashed her golden smile at Anne, whose little face lit up, not because of the visitor's attention, but because her Daddy had come into the room. Tom took his daughter in his arms, holding her high in the air, 'Who's my beautiful girl?' Kicking her chubby legs, Anne chuckled and gurgled with delight.

After he had handed Anne back to Kessie, he turned towards Alice and Kessie watched while they chatted. Alice, as usual, was flirting with Tom—an instinctive reaction to any attractive man, or did she still want him? Tom's face wore its especially attentive expression, which meant his mind was really miles away. Good.

'I have to go now, Alice. I wish you every happiness in your marriage. Come and see us when you're visiting London as a married lady.'

'Oh, I shall.'

As he went, Anne's face crumpled but Kessie soothed her, kissing the down of fine hair that was growing into a beautiful copper colour, an amalgam of her mother's chestnut and her father's black locks.

Alice hoped Kessie was not intending to keep the baby in the room, because babies would cry and interrupt the conversation. Tom's adoration of his daughter was a surprise—who'd have imagined him as a doting Papa?—and Kessie had certainly known what she was doing when she became

212

enceinte. Considering what she had been through, she was looking well, thinner, but women tended to grow fat after child-bearing, so her terrible experience in Newcastle had been helpful in that way. Alice had just known Tom would wait to see her before he took off for the House of Commons.

Ruby came in with the tea and carried the baby back to the nursery, which was a relief. Inevitably they talked about forcible feeding and how long the Liberals would dare continue with it, and Alice said, 'It must have been a ghastly experience.'

'It was.'

Despite the blazing fire, the simplicity of Kessie's response made Alice shiver. Impulsively she put out her hands and they were hugging each other. 'Kessie, I am so sorry. Please, please, forgive me.'

But even as Kessie said yes, Alice knew she was not really sorry. She was filled with regret that she had betrayed her friend, but not that she had experienced those rapturous minutes in Tom's arms. Hastily she changed the subject, and soon she and Kessie were talking just like the old days. Kessie could always make her laugh. Was that one of the reasons Tom had married her? Because she made *him* laugh and laughter was a precious thing?

'I made my poor effort for the cause the other day. I was invited to one of Margot Asquith's theatrical luncheons and Lillah McCarthy was the star attraction. After the show was over, Lillah and I crept into the Cabinet Room and we daubed "Votes for Women" and "Stop Forcible Feeding" all over the lovely clean blotters round the Cabinet table. We used her stage make-up, carmine number two it was, so it showed up beautifully!'

'Alice, you didn't! What a superb idea.'

'Wasn't it?' Alice almost purred with satisfaction.

While Alice lit a cigarette, Kessie leant back in her chair. Their reconciliation had been easier than she had anticipated, but perhaps that was only to be expected. Alice had always believed that the past was the past, today was what mattered, and the future lay in dazzling wait. She was a golden lass, as perfect as the doll she had brought for Anne, enhancing any

213

company she entered. If people were hurt or fell by the wayside as she swept on her way, Alice would not understand that it might be her fault. Perhaps that was the price you paid for golden lasses; and lads, like Tom.

'Mr Asquith telephoned me yesterday.' Alice blew out a cloud of smoke. 'He asked if I was one of the naughty ladies who had desecrated the Cabinet Room? Actually, he did have a chuckle in his voice. He said he would be in Hampstead tomorrow and why did we not have a drive on the Heath before I depart for my homeland? I accepted the invitation and I shall do my very best to make him understand what an abomination forcible feeding is.'

The following day was mistily autumnal, the sun flickering, the leaves drifting from the trees, piling in gold and auburn ridges along the edge of the carriageway. Alice had chosen her attire carefully: she was aware that she was looking delightful in a hand-pleated, dove-grey costume, with the new-style long jacket and fantail, and one of the very latest cloche hats that hugged her head. Mr Asquith was looking sloppy. Why didn't Margot smarten him up? When he started to chatter about Henry James—who said men *talked*, but women *chattered*?—she interrupted him.

'Mr Asquith, please stop forcible feeding.'

'How little you young ladies understand about the process of government, if you will forgive me saying so. The matter is outside my control. May I point out that by using the violence of the hunger-strike, your friends have forced us to use what you call the violence of forcible feeding.'

Alice could have hit him and she understood exactly why Tom had assaulted him, but she controlled the impulse. 'It is your Government's unspeakable behaviour that has forced us to hunger-strike. If you have no control over your Government, you have no right to be Prime Minister.'

The sleepy eyes blinked slightly. She had been rude but she didn't care, and her rudeness was not preventing him from patting her hand. '*Us*, Alice? Why should you worry your beautiful head about the demands of a minority of unruly women in a country that is not your own?'

214

'Because I am a woman, Mr Asquith.' That remark made him pat her hand with greater vigour, and he was a disgustingly hopeless proposition. No, nothing was hopeless.

When they returned to Stephen's house, she asked if he would care to take tea? He told his chauffeur to come back in an hour, and after they'd had tea in Stephen's downstairs sitting-room—inviting him *upstairs* to her quarters might seem forward—they sat sedately on the sofa. He rested his hand on its curving back, then slowly his fingers ran along her shoulder and tickled her neck.

So be it. He had made the first move. She turned her face towards his, and his receding cupid's bow lips pursed themselves into a moue and made a smacking sound against hers. 'My dear, you are so young, so beautiful, so vital.' Alice stood up, so he did too, 'My dear child, I have not offended you?'

Slowly, Alice took off her fantail jacket, placing it on an armchair, while the heavy lidded eyes watched her. Turning her back towards him, she said, 'Will you undo my blouse?' She felt him jump away and she swung round, 'That is what you want, isn't it?'

His face sagged and he stood looking like an untidy sack of potatoes, but his eyes were saying Yes. 'You can have me, if you promise to stop forcible feeding. In writing.'

He put his face into his hands and Alice thought perhaps she should not have added 'in writing'. After he had stumbled from the room, she watched him walk through the narrow passage into the High Street. What was he going to do until his chauffeur returned? The thought of having him on top of her, or anywhere near her, that fat flabby body, was disgusting, but she would have been prepared to suffer Mr Asquith's making love to her. It couldn't have been worse than being forcibly fed, and it would have had a certain curiosity value.

Alice decided that she would make one more stab at Mr Asquith. Before she sailed for home with Franklin—and Mrs Pankhurst, who was off on an American lecture tour, partly to rally American public opinion in favour of the suffragettes, but mainly to earn money to cure her son

Harry who had been stricken with infantile paralysis—the opportunity arose for her to show her public contempt for the British Prime Minister. She and Franklin were invited to a reception at the Foreign Office.

As soon as they arrived, Lord Algernon Hereford bore down upon them.

'Miss Hartley, I haven't spied you in the park recently. Not given up the old gee-gees, surely? Lookin' more ravishingly beautiful than ever, what? I say, you're a lucky chap, Mr Adams.'

They endured the conversation with him until Alice spied the Asquiths. Then she abruptly disengaged, leaving old Algy in mid-sentence. Innocently, Franklin escorted her across the room towards the Prime Minister and his wife. For once, Alice's voice overtopped Margot's.

'In God's name, Mr Asquith, I beg you to stop forcible feeding.'

Like the dying wail of the bagpipes the chatter faded away, every eye turned on the American girl. She was looking ravishing, a circlet of diamonds and rubies on her upswept golden hair, a matching ruby and diamond bracelet over her long white gloves, a full skirted, deep ruby-red gown flowing around her tall slender body.

'You cannot be aware, Mr Asquith, of the horror in which you are regarded throughout the civilised world . . .'

Margot slapped her face.

Alice flinched but held her head high and the mark on her face was momentarily as red as her gown.

Franklin offered her his arm—bless him, because she had not been sure what he would do—and said, quietly but clearly, 'I share my fiancée's views, sir. Have I your permission to escort her from the room?'

Mr Asquith nodded.

The walk to the door was one of the longest Alice had known, with everybody staring at them, and she was grateful for Frankie's arm beneath hers. She was proud of him, too, in a way she had not been before. He had backbone. Maybe being his wife would be fun.

20

The *Oceanic* sailed through the Narrows into New York harbour, the bright winter sunshine glinted on the crown and upheld torch, and Alice thought that no matter how many times you saw the Statue of Liberty, the guardian angel of the New World, she really was a magnificent, inspiring sight. Momentarily the ghost of the girl who had sailed out of New York harbour close on five years ago fluttered past Alice, but she was a woman now and soon she would be Frankie's wife. As they berthed at the North River pier the quayside was lined with women waiting to greet Mrs Pankhurst, waving and cheering, holding up their banners with the English slogan, 'Votes for Women', and Alice's heart leapt with pride.

In the next few days Alice attended several receptions with Mrs Pankhurst. Then Franklin entertained her and a family party to luncheon at Delmonico's. As Alice lit a cigarette to have with her coffee, the head waiter politely requested her to extinguish it, because the New York city fathers had banned the smoking of cigarettes by women in public.

She laughed. 'I don't believe it.' Frankie, however, said it was not a decree to which he objected. Smoking in public was scarcely the action of a lady, now was it? Her mother agreed with him and Alice said, 'Suffering rattlesnakes! You give me one good reason why men should smoke in public and women shouldn't.'

'Where did you acquire that extraordinary expression?' Momma was dodging the real question, so Alice ignored hers. In fact she had learned the expression many years ago, from Jonesey, their head coachman, who recently, if reluctantly, had learned to drive Poppa's splendid Model F Buick automobile.

217

'Let me tell you something, Momma, something I've learned from going around with Mrs Pankhurst here. The fact that the city fathers can issue such a ban and get away with it is symptomatic of our women's movement. You will never get the vote by being polite. Politicians are the same the world over, only the degree of their odiousness varies. President Taft has no more intention of giving us the vote than Mr Asquith has, and it will take for ever to win over the states one by one.'

'I have always supported our beloved leader, Susan B. Anthony, in the contention that we must have an amendment to the constitution,' Momma said indignantly.

'All right, so you have. But you will only amend the constitution by well-organised militancy. I was speaking to Alice Paul and Lucy Burns before I left England and they're thinking of coming home soon. What we three haven't learned about building up a fighting organisation, isn't worth knowing. I reckon that between us we should be able to knock American suffragists into shape.'

With a cold expression on his face, Frankie was examining his well-manicured hands. When he looked up, Alice gave him her most golden smile, to which he responded with a fleeting one. He wouldn't want her to have a baby straight off, now would he, so she could work with her country women who were eager enough, goodness knew, to have the vote and merely wanted a good kick in the right direction.

The next few weeks positively shot by, consumed by dress fittings, conferences with the chefs and *maître d'hôtel* at the Brunswick, where they were to have the wedding breakfast, and rehearsals. Frankie considered that Alice should never have returned to London last time, but should have concentrated on the arrangements for their marriage, and maybe he had a point. Then it was the great day, a glorious winter's day, the sky blue, the sun shining, the air tingling fresh, as Alice had just known it would be.

Floating down the aisle of St Thomas's Church on Poppa's arm, with the organ thundering 'Here Comes the Bride', Alice heard the gasps of admiration. Truly, she felt as if she were walking on air, barely feeling the weight of her long

218

satin train held by two tiny page-boys, the coronet of exquisitely waxed orange blossoms securing her billowing Chantilly lace veil. She could not recall much of the actual ceremony, but she enjoyed nodding her head to the guests packed either side of the aisle, her veil swept back now, as she returned on Frankie's arm.

Alice had asked everybody to come in coaches, not automobiles, and now she and Frankie led the bridal parade the short distance along Fifth Avenue from St Thomas's Church to the Brunswick Hotel. The police had agreed to halt the traffic, Fifth Avenue was thick with gawping crowds, and it was like the greatest days of the New York Coaching Club parades, the spanking whites and creams and clarets of the coaches, the clatter of the horses' hooves, the cheers of the crowd, the post-horns sounding triumphantly.

'Oh Frankie, isn't it exciting?' Alice clutched her husband's hand and smiled up at him. He was at his most elegant, a beautiful pale grey waistcoat beneath his frock-coat, a perfectly folded silk cravat adorned with a simple diamond tie-pin. Everything had worked out for the best and she was glad she had married him.

The Brunswick had outdone its own reputation for eye-catching displays of mouth-watering food, the wedding breakfast was superb, and even Frankie's mother looked faintly impressed. When it was time for them to leave, almost graciously she pecked Alice on the cheek. 'I am sure you will make my son a good wife.'

They were honeymooning in Palm Beach—Frankie had hired a whole Pullman car for the journey—and for her going-away outfit Alice had chosen a deep strawberry-coloured silk-velvet costume, with a large velvet hat adorned with ostrich feathers, a sable fur, and a matching muff decorated with a tiny sable head in translucent enamel. While the train rattled through the gathering darkness, Gertie assisted Alice with her night-time toilette (she had grown fond of Gertie, who had only too willingly accepted the invitation to continue as her personal maid. Having an English maid was chic.)

'Oh, Miss Hartley, I mean Mrs Adams, you look

beautiful. Mr Adams will be . . .' Gertie put her hand to her mouth and blushed.

In the sleeping compartment, relaxed in a silk dressing-gown, Frankie poured out two glasses of champagne and handed her one. 'To you, my dearest wife, and to long, blessed years of happiness.'

When they had drunk the champagne, politely he suggested she retire to bed first. Demurely, Alice did, arranging her hair on the pillow. Turning off the light, Frankie climbed in beside her and, apart from a perfunctory kiss and murmuring, 'My dearest Alice, how much I love you,' he surely did not waste time. She was feeling excited, because it had been such a very long time since . . . She heard the intake of breath as he went inside her comparatively easily, the fantastic sensation was as mind-stunning as she remembered, her body was responding, but she had barely started before he had finished. For several minutes afterwards, he lay breathing heavily by her side, but he didn't say a word. Alice, feeling both surprised and frustrated, nestled against him, slipping her hands under his pyjama jacket.

'Frankie, darling . . .'

Sharply, still without saying a word, he pulled away from her, climbed out of the bed and turned up the light. Sitting on the side of the bed he looked down at her, and like an upturned pot of red paint spilling across the floor, the colour suffused his cheeks. Then he gripped her by the shoulders, and hauling her upright, he ripped the nightdress from her shoulders and stared at her breasts. Alice tried to cover them with her hands, but he grabbed her wrists and held them hard, all the time staring at her breasts, insolently, dirtily. Alice felt degraded and just a teeny bit frightened.

'Who was it? How many times? You strumpet, you filthy Jezebel, you Scarlet Woman!'

'Frankie, please, don't, you're hurting me. And I don't know what you mean. Frankie, I love you.'

'Love me! I loved you, you little whore! Do you think I would have stomached all that nonsense in England if I hadn't?' His hand slapped her cheek. Alice fell with her face into the silk pillow and she was truly frightened, crying as

220

she had never cried before. What should she do? Brazen it out? Ask him again what he meant? Make him explain, so that she could explain that it must be due to her being such a bold horse-woman? She had never expected him to behave like this, to be so certain that she was not a virgin.

'It was Tom Whitworth, wasn't it? Wasn't it, you damned slut? Answer me!' His voice was venomous and he was hauling her up again. 'Did you think it escaped my notice, your ogling that low-bred, Socialist skunk? Is he good? Is that why a nice girl like Kessie married him? Does he serve all you emancipated whores?'

'Frankie.' The tears were running down Alice's cheeks and she tried to bury her face on his chest. 'I am sorry, truly I am. It was a moment of madness. It was only once, I swear it was, and before we became engaged.'

'Only once! Before we became engaged! You harlot! You jade! You hussy! You cyprian! You bawd! You wanton! You lascivious, depraved quean!' He was holding great lumps of her hair and as each phrase spat out, he banged her head against the carriage wall. Alice closed her eyes, feeling like a water-rat she had once seen being shaken by a dog. Eventually, his rage worked itself out, his furious breathing grew calmer, Alice opened her eyes and he said, 'How many other people know?'

'Only Kessie.' Alice did not think mentioning Stephen would go down well, on the contrary it might provoke another outbreak of uncontrolled fury.

'Kessie won't talk.' Franklin looked at her, coldly, calculatingly. 'Second-hand, tarnished goods. But you *are* my wife, you cheating, deceiving, dissembling whore. You now bear one of the proudest names in this whole goddamned country, Mrs Franklin Adams, and don't you *ever* forget it. Don't you *ever* disgrace that great name. If you do, Alice, I'll kill you.'

Throwing back the bedclothes, he tore the nightdress from her. This time he left the light on and as the train swayed wildly on the tracks, Alice just lay there. It would not last long, and it did not.

When they arrived in Palm Beach, Frankie was his usual

221

courteous, charming self and Alice decided he would soon recover from his shock, be himself, and their marriage would smooth itself out. By the end of the week, she no longer knew what Franklin's self was, and she had stopped thinking of him as 'Frankie'.

By day they breakfasted on the balcony of the bridal suite, they rode along the palm-fringed sands, she wore the stunning outfits of her trousseau, and Franklin was the proud, delighted, justifiably possessive husband, basking in the admiration of his beautiful bride. But at night, oh that was a living nightmare. Very soon she would waken up and everything would be different, real, because what was happening was not.

At the end of the second week, Franklin drank overmuch at dinner and when they were in their suite, by themselves, after he had torn her most beautiful gown from her shoulders, he threw her on to the floor face downwards. Hauling her into a crouching position, he mounted her like a dog mounting a bitch, and he spat the words he had spat every evening, 'Did you do *this* with him?'

Afterwards Alice lay awake while he snored by her side. Eventually, she got up and went on to the balcony, staring out at the slowly lightening sky. In the first days she had tried to talk to Franklin, saying she now appreciated that what she had done to him was, by his standards, unforgivable, but who had set those standards? Why was it acceptable for him to have had mistresses (with those tricks he must have had dozens, though she did not voice this assumption), but not for her to have sinned once? He had looked at her coldly and said he had no wish to discuss the matter, though he would have thought the answer was obvious.

The sun was flushing on the horizon and the answer he considered obvious was not so to Alice. However lethal a blow she had struck at his pride, his behaviour was beyond belief, excuse or forgiveness. That cruel vicious streak must always have been there and she had simply never noticed it. But Alice was not interested in why people behaved the way they did, only in what they did, and what Franklin was doing to her was at worst sadistic, at best degrading.

222

Alice knew that she would have enjoyed doing *all* those things with Tom. Or had Franklin shown any tenderness, any gentleness, made any attempt to give her satisfaction, to bring her to that rapturous climax, as Tom had done, then she would have enjoyed doing them with him. The sun was tipping the horizon, setting the sea aglow with gold and pink light, and she could not live through one more day of Franklin being the perfect Boston gentleman, nor one more night of him treating her like a whore.

In New York, tomorrow evening, Mrs Pankhurst was speaking at the Carnegie Hall, the most important date of her lecture tour. Silently, Alice went back into the bedroom and through to her dressing-room, where she performed her own toilette, donning the simplest outfit from her trousseau, a fine cream wool costume with a cream and brown velour hat. Apart from her travelling bag containing her jewels and toiletries, and one of her furs—for it would be cold in New York—she took nothing else. Silently, she shut the door while Franklin was still snoring. Without undue surprise—for obviously she had seen the torn gowns and the bruises on Alice's body—Gertie packed a bag for herself and the two of them left the early morning hush of the hotel, observed only by the desk clerk and the hall porter, taking a hire-carriage to the railroad station.

For most of the long journey from Palm Beach to New York, Alice's mind was a blank. She had no idea what she was going to do, and the only thing she really noticed, as they whooshed through Virginia, was a beautiful chestnut foal galloping through a meadow, because it was the colour of Kessie's hair. Dear Lord, how she wished she could talk to Kessie.

In New York they checked into a hotel, Alice tried to sleep but couldn't, so she drank cups of coffee until it was time to leave for Mrs Pankhurst's meeting.

When she and Gertie arrived at the Carnegie Hall, hundreds of people were milling around under the marble colonnades trying to gain admission, but the manager immediately recognised Alice. 'Mrs Adams, this is an honour. Surely, we have two seats for you and Mr Adams.'

Mr Adams, needless to say, did not arrive to claim his seat, so Gertie took it.

When Mrs Pankhurst's slight, well-groomed figure walked gracefully on to the stage, the tears stung Alice's eyes and she willed their leader to take New York by storm, as she had anti-suffrage Boston, but the initial applause was only moderate. New Yorkers' curiosity had brought them to listen, but they had yet to be impressed. Mrs Pankhurst let the clapping die away before holding out her arms in the gesture Alice knew so well.

'I am what you call a hooligan.'

It was the most superb opening to a speech that Alice had ever heard and despite her exhausted, dazed state, she was on her feet with the rest of the audience, laughing, cheering, stamping. For one and a half hours Mrs Pankhurst spoke at her simple, compelling best, but when the last questions had been answered and the eager American suffragists flocked towards the ante-room where she was holding court, Alice hesitated. How greatly she wanted to see Mrs Pankhurst, yet what reason could she give for being here by herself in the middle of her honeymoon?

'Alice!' Momma's shriek rose above the hubbub and the crowd parted before her like the Red Sea before Moses. 'What in the world are you doing here? What's happened? Where's Franklin? Why didn't you let us know you were coming? What . . .'

'Momma, please hush up,' Alice struggled to control the quiver in her voice, 'and just let me come home with you.'

For once her mother didn't argue. She took Alice's arm and propelled her towards an exit, where Poppa was waiting in the back of the Model F Buick. When he saw his daughter, he would have exclaimed, but his wife caught his eye. She shook her head slightly, he recovered, held out his hand and Alice climbed into the back with her parents, while Gertie got into the front beside Jonesey. As the engine fired, the long gulping sobs shook Alice's body.

'There, there, my little chickadee.' Poppa put his arms round her shaking shoulders.

'I am not going back to him, Poppa.'

224

'Brides often feel this way.' Momma patted her hand. 'It's nothing to fret about. You'll feel better after a good sleep.'

Momma was convinced that her little Alice was suffering from a *crise de larmes* (she was studying French at the moment), as young brides often did. Firmly she told her daughter she must wipe away her tears, they'd telegraph poor Franklin who must be out of his mind with worry, such a nice gentleman, and—

'Momma, Franklin is not a gentleman,' Alice sobbed. 'I can't tell you what he did to me, but I can tell you he is not a gentleman.'

For twenty-four hours Alice slept soundly in her own bed in her own bedroom in the brownstone residence on Fifth Avenue that was home. When she awoke she felt immensely refreshed. It had started to snow, so she stayed snug in her sitting-room, reading, smoking and thinking as little as possible.

Neither Momma nor Poppa said a word about Franklin, though telegrams kept arriving and Alice presumed they were from him because Momma whisked them from the silver salver as soon as the maid had placed them there.

The snow stopped falling, briefly lying deep and crisp and even, before the traffic churned it up, and Poppa suggested he and his chickadee went for a ride. Jonesey drove them into Central Park which was a glittering fairyland, the trees slung with snow, the lake smooth with ice, though the skaters were already cutting its smoothness into looping patterns.

'Oh Poppa, do you remember when I used to skate? Do you remember that white fur hat and coat and muff you bought me and you said I was your Snow Princess?'

'You still are my Snow Princess,' Poppa took her gloved hands tightly in his and they sat in the back of the Buick, warmed by the thick travelling rugs and the depth of their love. Tactful as her parents had been in regard to Franklin, much as she knew her father adored her, Alice was not certain how he or Momma would react to the decision she had made. Leaving one's husband after a fortnight,

225

particularly a Bostonian Adams, was not a gesture that would go down well in the upper reaches of New York society.

Alice turned her head and looked her father straight in the eyes. 'Poppa, I am not going back to him. Among many other things, he called me a tradesman's daughter.'

Hallelujah, that had been the right remark! She saw the fury spark in her father's steely blue eyes and he was trembling with rage. 'Alice, there are certain things that cannot be uttered, and you have been in a state of shock these last few days. Momma and I have both known that. We shall say no more, but if you cannot be that man's wife, you shall not. If he tries anything, I'll drag the precious name Adams through the mud, God help me, so I will.'

'Oh, Poppa,' Alice was genuinely crying.

The Buick slithered on an icy patch of roadway, her father put his arm protectively around her, and was it just over two weeks since Franklin's arm had been around her as their carriage had pranced up Fifth Avenue? Alice wiped away the tears and with her head on her father's chest, silently they drove past the Bethesda Fountain which was hung with icicles like diamonds on a necklace. While he was still in this mood, Alice decided she might as well put her next proposition to him, though she was equally uncertain how he would react.

'I'd like to go back to England, Poppa. Not that I want to leave you and Momma, but plunging back into the fray there, if only temporarily, of course, will keep my mind occupied. What do you think?'

'I shall miss my little chickadee but I guess that just at this moment, for you to be three thousand miles away, would be a sound idea.'

Back at the house, without any weeping or wailing or gnashing of teeth, Momma agreed, and Alice loved both her parents dearly for their understanding and concern for her. Before she sailed, there were those awful moments when Franklin hammered on the front door, demanding to be let in, and from her sitting-room Alice could hear his upraised voice. 'She is *my wife*.'

226

After an eternity, Poppa came up to the sitting-room, where Alice was smoking furiously. 'There won't be any more trouble,' he told her. 'You just leave everything to your old Poppa.'

Alice recrossed the Atlantic with Mrs Pankhurst, whose only comment on her unexpected return was, 'In general, though my own marriage was blessed, I would not advise women to marry.'

Passionate as she was in public, in regard to personal matters Mrs Pankhurst was a true Victorian lady, almost obsessively reticent, which made it the more astonishing when, on the third night out from New York, she came to Alice's state-room and almost broke down. Suddenly, Alice realised not only that she was desperately worried about her sick son Harry, but that she was a lonely, middle-aged woman. It had not occurred to her before that one could be personally bereft in the middle of so much activity and adulation.

By herself, Alice spent hours pacing the upper, first-class deck. The Lord had been merciful, she was not *enceinte*. Standing on the deck, with the wind rising, the grey Atlantic waves mounting higher and higher, she turned her face towards England. Henceforward, like Mrs Pankhurst, she would dedicate her life to the cause; like Christabel she would be a Young Siegfried, a maiden-warrior. Until women had the vote.

21

'Harry's funeral was unutterably sad. Oh poor Harry, just twenty-one, all his life before him. To see Mrs Pankhurst at the graveside was heartrending. She looked like an old, old woman, Sarah, but afterwards she said to me, "I shall fight on, Kessie. There is nothing else left for me to do. Harry would have wished it."'

Kessie looked at her sister-in-law and for a moment they were both silent. Then Kessie said, 'Alice was at the funeral.'

'What's she got to say for herself?' Usually gossip did not interest Sarah, but that madam's reappearance after *two whole weeks* of marriage was something special.

'Well, she came back to The Grove for a meal and it seems that Franklin was an *absolute brute*. I can't say I'm altogether surprised. There was something about him I never did like.' While Alice had been explaining about Franklin's brutishness, the thought had crossed Kessie's mind that it might have had some connection with his bride not being *virgo intacta*. It was not a matter she had felt able to raise with Alice, and it was certainly not one she could mention to Sarah, so she said, 'She just upped and left him. Wasn't that spirited of her?'

'Mm. Very. Though it's a lucky old Alice to be able to *afford* to leave her husband.'

Kessie absorbed this observation. Unlike Sarah, neither she nor Alice had ever known what it was like to be without money.

'Anyway, she's getting a divorce, and wants to be known as Alice Hartley, as if she had never been married. She says it's lovely to be back in England and Stephen has been simply wonderful. She's become a super-dedicated suffragette.'

'Until she meets the next man she fancies.'

'Don't be horrid, Sarah. I think Alice really went through the mill with Franklin and it's affected her whole attitude to life.'

'Your halo's bright tonight.'

Kessie giggled and sat back in the armchair. The flames were leaping in the grate, the shutters bolted, the screen in place around the door to shield them from the winter draughts. Here at The Laurels, life continued with the solid reassurance of Kessie's childhood. Yet in prison cells throughout the land, women were still being pushed to the limits of their endurance. Kessie felt furiously impotent. Oh well, tomorrow she was travelling to The Dales to help Tom in the General Election the Liberals had called, hoping to obtain a mandate for 'the People's Budget'. When Tom was returned to Parliament—no if about it—they would fight on for women's suffrage.

It was while they were campaigning in The Dales that the story of Lady Constance Lytton's imprisonment in Walton Gaol in Liverpool broke. Kessie found out everything she could about it and in the evening she retired to bed early. Sitting propped up by pillows in the double bed in Milnrow, with a fire blazing in the grate, she picked up her fountain pen, opened her diary, and started to write:

24th January, 1910 What has been happening to darling Con Lytton is quite beyond belief. Apparently, she's been brooding ever since she and Jane Brailsford were released from Newcastle, while we others were forcibly fed. She became convinced that she had been released solely because of her aristocratic lineage, not because of her weak heart. When she heard about the forcible feeding now going on in Liverpool, she decided to disguise herself as a working-class woman and have herself arrested for creating a disturbance outside Walton Gaol. She chose the name Jane Warton.

As the unimportant Jane Warton, her heart was *not* tested and when she hunger-struck, they forcibly fed her. On Saturday night, somebody leaked the story of her imprisonment to the Press Association. They immediately contacted Lady Emily Lutyens to find out if her sister really was being forcibly fed in Walton. Lady Emily didn't know, but rushed up to Liverpool on the overnight train to find out. When she arrived in Walton Gaol, Jane Warton had just been forcibly fed for the eighth time. But then, a few hours later, Lady Constance Lytton was released on medical grounds, i.e., the same state of collapse as Jane Warton had been in. What price equality under the law of England? I think the whole episode is—

Tom came into the bedroom carrying a bowl of hot water and his shaving tackle. 'God, I don't know why Aunt Ada bothered having it put in; it'd freeze your balls off in that bathroom.'

'We don't want that to happen, do we?' Kessie blotted the page she had just written and shut her diary.

Tom grinned at her and started to lather his face. His dark skin acquired a shadow in a trice and he was obsessive about shaving night and morning. While he was making swathes in the lather with his cut-throat razor, they discussed the topic of the hour and Tom echoed his wife's thoughts. 'By God, she's got guts has Lady Constance Lytton. And she's proved her point about English class-consciousness. Pity her timing wasn't better, though. Making her stand in the middle of a General Election wasn't the brightest of ideas.'

Kessie had to admit he had a point. Tom was wiping his face with the towel, running his long fingers over the smoothness of his chin, and as she watched him Kessie thought of her own problem.

Should she tell Tom, or should she not?

The day before they'd left London she'd gone to see Stephen for a medical check-up. After examining her, Stephen had said, 'You've recovered well from your ordeal, Kessie, but I don't believe in withholding the truth from intelligent women. Forcible feeding has left you with a distinct heart murmur.'

Kessie had stared at her. Was that why she still felt so tired? 'Will it affect my future life? What about having more children?'

Stephen had replied, 'If you're sensible, you should be right as rain, but I wouldn't rush into having another baby. A labour like last time and you could be in the soup.'

There had been a robin preening its red breast on the plane tree outside the surgery window and Kessie had watched it as she'd said, 'You won't tell Tom, will you?'

Stephen's nostrils had twitched, and she'd patted Kessie's shoulder. 'I've told you, old thing; what you tell your husband is your business.'

Now Tom was buttoning up his pyjama jacket and climbing into bed beside her. 'I don't reckon I'm going to have any problem being re-elected, do you?'

'No.' Kessie snuggled against him and decided she would not tell him about her heart because it wasn't really serious and Tom would only worry. Besides, there was plenty of time. Sooner or later she'd have more babies. She'd promised God.

The minute Tom was re-elected as the Member of Parliament for The Dales, with a majority that had leapt to fourteen hundred, and they were back in London, Kessie went to Clement's Inn to see Christabel.

'Did *you* know Con was in Walton and what she intended to do?'

'Yes.'

'How could you let her do it? I mean, knowing that . . .'

Christabel bridled. 'How could I stop her? She's a grown woman. Why should I interfere with a conscious act of her courageous spirit?'

'Because you know she has a weak heart, Christabel, and you know what forcible feeding can do to its victims. Look what it did to . . .'

Kessie just stopped herself from saying me. Nobody was to know what it had done to her, except Stephen.

Christabel leaned forward. 'If Constance's revelations do not put an end to the abomination of forcible feeding and bring us the vote, I cannot think what will.'

Kessie decided not to push the matter further, for superb as Christabel's public composure had been in the days following Harry Pankhurst's death, she knew how deeply her friend was grieving for her dead brother.

'And I want you to be the first to know, Kessie, that in view of Constance's heroic action, which *must* have its effect even on this Government, we have decided to call a truce, to give the Liberals time to frame a Women's Suffrage Bill.'

'I am glad.' Kessie hugged Christabel. 'I'm sure it's a wise decision.'

'One thing we are demanding, however, is that Mr Churchill sets up an immediate, rigorous public enquiry into Constance's treatment as Jane Warton and the many disturbing issues it has raised.'

Winston Churchill was the new Home Secretary. In a Cabinet reshuffle, Herbert Gladstone had been packed off to South Africa as the first Governor-General of the newest Dominion of the British Empire. They were all hopeful that the new Home Secretary would prove more sensible in his approach to the suffragettes.

When his reaction to the Constance Lytton affair became known, Kessie said furiously to Tom, 'A flat refusal to hold any sort of enquiry. Ha! And I quite liked Mr Churchill. I thought class solidarity would make him act in Con's case, if not for us lower types. Didn't you?'

'No. He's an ambitious bugger, Kess. In a choice between having the Liberals indicted in a public enquiry, and supporting his own kind over the treatment of a suffragette . . .' Tom waved his left hand in a gesture indicating the choice had never been in doubt.

'Well, Victor Lytton's going to be as outraged as any of us, I can tell you.'

The Earl of Lytton, Lady Constance's brother, *was* outraged and his fury led him to set up an all-party committee to frame a Women's Suffrage Bill. Tom was one of the most active members of the committee, and with her husband so involved Kessie was soon back in the thick of things, though in view of her heart condition she tried not to overdo it. Tom, she knew, thought she was spending less time than of yore at Clement's Inn because of Anne, and she did not disillusion him. Sometimes she took her baby daughter with her to the offices, where everybody made a terrific fuss, saying what a bright child she was, just like her mother.

In the middle of all the activity—what a relief it was to be working without the pressure of demonstrations, imprisonment, hunger-striking and forcible feeding—there came the shock of Edward VII's sudden death. Kessie was asked to write an appreciation for the black-bordered edition of their weekly newspaper, *Votes for Women*.

'*Appreciation?*' Tom said, 'Of *him?*'

She took no notice, but when she delivered the article to Clement's Inn, Alice read it and said, 'Very good, but the King endorsed forcible feeding, you know.'

'He had no option,' said Christabel, 'but to endorse his Liberal Government's diabolical decision.'

Alice seemed none too sure about that, but Kessie agreed with Christabel, certain that the late King had no hand in the decision.

Tom refused to go to the King's funeral, but Kessie took Anne to watch the awe-inspiring procession. Not that she would remember it, but as an old lady she would at least be able to say that she had been there.

Not long afterwards, Kessie was in Christabel's office, discussing various points of their coming Bill when Christabel's secretary put her head round the door. 'There's a Miss Devonald come to join us. She's asking to see you and she's *very* insistent.'

'Show her in then,' Christabel laughed.

A tiny figure, even smaller than Sarah, bounded into the office like a rubber ball and started to talk in the clearest of clarinet voices. Her father, she announced, was Professor Devonald, the Egyptologist, and until recently she'd been in Egypt with him, which was why she hadn't joined the WSPU earlier. They lived in Cheltenham but they'd rented a house in London, Highgate actually, just down the hill from Mrs Whitworth—the pixie face and the bright brown eyes beamed at Kessie—because Daddy was writing the definitive book on the early Egyptian civilisations and needed to research at the British Museum. She was sorry she'd missed all the fun, but she presumed they still wanted recruits?

'We most certainly do.' Christabel smiled. 'Would you like to sit down . . . what is your Christian name?'

'Dorothy.' The girl sat down, gazing at Christabel with rapt adoration. 'But my friends call me Didi. Dorothy Devonald, D.D. You may if you wish. I have five brothers and they all want kicking hard, well, apart from Georgie, he's not bad, so I know all about being a downtrodden woman.'

Anything less downtrodden than Dorothy would be diffi-cult to imagine, and Kessie tried hard not to giggle. 'How old are you?' she asked.

233

Dorothy cleared her throat. 'Nearly eighteen, but Mummy knows Mrs Pethick Lawrence—they're both interested in reviving the working-class cultural heritage, folk songs and country dancing, you know—so Mummy's sure I'll be in safe hands and if anything goes wrong and I have to go to prison, like Mrs Pethick Lawrence and you two and everybody, she won't mind.'

'I'm sure that will not be necessary, Dorothy. Nothing will go wrong this time. Our Bill has passed its second reading by a large majority and by next summer the first women will be dropping their voting papers into a ballot box!'

After their rousing processions which were held in as perfect weather as the rally in Hyde Park two years ago, and were as huge a success, and before they crossed to the Isle of Wight for the holidays, Kessie threw a celebration party at The Grove, organising it as carefully as if it were a suffragette demonstration.

The dining-room looked lovely, masses of flowers, lit by candles and the standard lamp, the deep red velvet curtains drawn, the Cranberry Victorian glass set that Kessie had found in a shop in Covent Garden glinting on the white linen tablecloth. The meal was delicious, up to Maggie's very best standards, and most of the guests had two helpings of her walnut hedgehog. After Ruby had carefully served the wine, Tom stood up.

'My lord', Tom bowed towards the Earl of Lytton, 'ladies, gentlemen, and ordinary folk,' he grinned at Sarah, who put her head to one side. 'Pray raise your glasses. May I propose a toast to the lady without whose heroism it is doubtful any of us would be here tonight. Constance Lytton!'

'Constance Lytton!' Everybody sipped their wine, Con, who had recovered well from her ordeal, blushed, her brother Victor patted her hand, and Aunt Ada started to sing, 'For she's a jolly good fellow'. Everybody joined in and Con blushed even more.

'Now the second toast, if the ladies will, in the circumstances, forgive me for placing them second.' Tom inclined

234

his head toward Christabel and Mrs Pankhurst, who smiled their forgiveness, the black hair flopped forward, and he did look handsome in the evening dress suit Kessie had bullied him into wearing. 'Pray raise your glasses again to the two ladies without whose dedication, determination, vision and courage none of us would be here to . . .'

The cheers and the clapping rang round the table and Tom said, 'Let me finish. You're not supposed to interrupt the toast-master. Seeing you have—to you Mrs Pankhurst, and to you Christabel!'

When they had drunk that toast, Tom asked them to raise their glasses to his wife and everybody who had suffered for the cause, and finally to the Women's Suffrage Bill and its safe passage through both Houses of Parliament.

'You know neither mother nor I will obtain the vote as a result of this Bill,' Christabel said, 'because neither of us is a householder any longer, nor do we personally rent business premises.'

'Ah, but my wife is a householder.' When he had allowed Kessie to buy The Grove, Tom had insisted the property went in her name. 'Aren't you, me luv?'

'Now we know why you've been working so hard, Thomas!' Alice gave him her golden smile as Christabel held up her glass.

'Our troublous times are over. We have made the break-through. After that—the deluge!'

22

The Caxton Hall was packed for the ninth Women's Parliament with delegates who had come from all over the British Isles. Kessie, Alice and Sarah were all sitting on the platform, and the mood was noisily angry. For halfway through

November, the Westminster Parliament had only just re-assembled and all sorts of rumours were flying about what the Liberals intended to do now that the skirmishes over 'the People's Budget' had developed into a full-scale war with the House of Lords. All attempts to find a compromise had collapsed, and at this very moment Mr Asquith was making a speech in the House of Commons. At Caxton Hall they waited to hear what he had said, about their promised Bill in particular, before deciding what action to take.

Not far from Caxton Hall, the police commander was addressing the ranks of uniformed and plain clothes men lined in front of him.

'Now listen to me, you men, and listen hard. You will be dealing with gangs of screaming harpies, hundreds of them with one object in mind, to get inside the Houses of Parliament. They scratch, they bite, they kick and they run. Your job is to stop them. Be it clearly understood, the Home Secretary don't want them arrested. He wants Parliament Square clear of women, none of them in the House, but he don't want them cluttering up the police courts. Nor do we. How you stop them today is your business, but stop them you do. Good luck to you.'

Sergeant Brooks was an ambitious man and he had been pleased to be selected for the Special Branch, but being shunted into 'B' Division to watch over suffragettes was not what he had bargained for. They were a menace to society, but they were also a toffee-nosed lot with the sort of connections that shouted 'foul' before you even dribbled the ball.

Looking at two of the constables from the East End 'V' Division, he thought that the suffragettes might well get their come-uppance today, then he could return to his proper work. He said to one of them, a large man with a florid face, a barrel chest and powerful arms, 'How you stop 'em is your business, is it?'

'Don't you worry, mate,' Arthur Wilkins laughed. 'We'll stop 'em so's they won't bother you no more. We've organised a little 'elp from the lads down our way wot don't approve of this women's rubbish. We're used to dealing wiv slags of a Saturday night as they piles out of the gin palaces.

236

This lot can't have nuffink on them. We deal wiv them orlright, don't we, George?'

George was a big lad, too, and he agreed that they did.

In Caxton Hall, Mrs Pankhurst held out her hands and the noise subsided. 'My dear friends and sisters, I have just received the following information. Mr Asquith has announced his intention to dissolve Parliament and go to the country in another General Election, in order to obtain a further mandate in his battle against the House of Lords.' There was an astonished murmur. *Another* General Election within the year? And what had he said about *their* Bill? 'In an inordinately lengthy speech dealing with innumerable topics, Mr Asquith made no mention whatsoever about our Bill or its future prospects.'

Dismayed, angry shouts drowned her voice. When the uproar had died away, Mrs Pankhurst read out a protest resolution and called for volunteers to petition Parliament.

A bout of nerves was assailing Kessie, who had never expected to lead another deputation. Tom had not been keen about her attending the Women's Parliament, so she had promised that if the news was bad and it came to the crunch and, as usual, the police barred the way, she would either find one of the regulars from 'A' Division and have him escort her to the House of Commons as a dutiful wife, or return quietly to Caxton Hall.

Kessie's group moved towards the door. They were leaving in groups of twelve, to make sure they infringed none of the mouldy old statutes and forgotten Acts of Parliament that had been dug up to be used against suffragettes.

Into the drizzling rain of the murky November afternoon they stepped. Aunt Ada unfurled her umbrella, which had 'Votes for Women' embroidered in her immaculate green, white and purple stitching. Kessie and Sarah held up their banner and, with Dorothy Devonald bouncing behind them, her 'Women's Will Beats Asquith's Won't' flag flying, they wheeled into Victoria Street.

The pavements were more than usually thronged with

237

people, the traffic was dense, obviously grinding to a halt towards Parliament Square, and a cabby shouted at them 'Bleeding suffragettes!', but some people gave them a cheer as they tramped along, singing 'The March of the Women'. Nearing the square, Kessie took a deep breath, preparing herself for the rush against the police, but as they approached Sarah let out a loud whistle. All round the square the crowds were packed like sardines in a tin, with lines of policemen linking arms to hold them back.

Clearly, some people viewed the suffragette demonstrations as entertainment; better than the music hall and free into the bargain. The entertainment had already started. There was a cordon of police across the flower beds, drably empty of colour in the November gloom, women from the earlier groups were trying to dash between them, some had obviously succeeded because above and beyond the scrimmage, Kessie could see the cantering police horses. Beyond them was their objective, the Houses of Parliament, its lights already lit on this damp grey afternoon.

Kessie smiled, hoping her nerves were not apparent, 'Come on, the cordon's breaking.'

Hand-in-hand, she and Sarah dashed through a gap, then halted in their tracks, appalled. They were both by now accustomed to foot constables grabbing them in none too kindly a manner, even to the police horses, but what was happening today was something entirely different. Policemen had their truncheons out, upraised in terrifying manner. A girl was being dragged along by her hair by a policeman shouting, 'We'll find out which is the 'ardest, me fine lady, you or the cobblestones.'

In front of them a woman was thrown to the ground, a police horse was cantering up and a constable yelled, 'Ride over 'er, that'll teach 'er not to come 'ere no more.'

Immobilised with shock, Kessie watched the rider urging his horse towards the woman, but just as the hooves were about to trample her, Sarah leapt for the reins. The horse veered past the woman, its rider hit out at Sarah's clinging hands, the use of Kessie's limbs returned, she stretched out, trying to untangle Sarah from the reins, but she herself was trapped in a rush of bodies and buffeted towards Westminster Abbey. Her heart was pounding, she had to get out of this, to reach the House of Commons, to tell Tom what was happening.

Sarah managed to free herself and fell heavily to the cobblestones. For a few seconds she lay bruised and breathless, before struggling to her knees. By heck, if they wanted to fight dirty, so could she! Tom and she had learned the hard way how to stop the chants of 'gipsy brats' at school in Mellordale. A boot was coming towards her and a voice was bawling, 'We'll learn you to come 'ere again.'

Wriggling out of the way, Sarah bit the constable on the ankle. He hopped on one foot, howling, while she jumped up and ran as fast as her winded breath would allow towards the Houses of Parliament, weaving her way through the grappling bodies and rearing horses. Out of the gloom two more constables came at her, one of them went for her neck, the other for her legs. While one bent her head backwards until she thought her neck would snap, Sarah kicked and lashed out at the other with her feet.

'You're a little bleeder and no mistake.'

The constable let go of her head and shoved a finger up her nostril. The blood gushed on to his hand and down her chin like a newly tapped geyser and the pain was intense, but Sarah dug her teeth into his fingers. He screamed, pulling his finger from her nostril, causing another gush of blood. For a moment the pain was so fierce Sarah thought she would pass out. With the grip relaxed and the other constable's attention focused on his wounded comrade, she dodged away, spitting at both of them, 'You sodding buggers!'

Taking several deep breaths, she wiped the blood from her chin, rotated her neck to ease the pain, breathed deeply again, and plunged back into the mêlée, her eyes firmly set on her objective, the Houses of Parliament.

Dorothy was picked up by a huge policeman who was more like a gorilla than a man, proving beyond doubt Mr Darwin's thesis that *homo sapiens* had evolved from the ape. He flung

239

her towards a group of yahoos, East Enders by the sound of their nasal tones and mangled vowels, and she cursed her lack of weight. The beastly youths were forming into a circle, tossing her backwards and forwards like a football, and the policeman was laughing. Why wasn't she six feet tall and built like a gorilla herself? What was the crowd doing, standing watching? It was *not* feeding time at the zoo. Then Dorothy remembered a piece of advice her brother Georgie had once given her, and as she landed from the next buffet she kicked the youth in the crotch. His howl of anguish was highly satisfying, but now the circle was closing in on her, their faces ferocious.

Hallelujah!

Bursting through the crowd came a group from the Men's Union who piled into the East End louts, and it was like the most vicious rugby scrum. On her hands and knees Dorothy crawled through the legs towards the railings.

At least some of the crowd were being helpful, a woman produced a bottle of smelling salts, Dorothy sniffed at it and her head felt clearer. One of the young men from the Men's Union was bending over her, 'I'll kill them, Didi, I'll kill the whole lot of them.'

It was an old chum of one of her brothers, and she gasped, 'Leave some of them for me.'

'You're the spunkiest girl in the whole world, Didi, but don't you dare move an inch without me from now on.'

Dorothy looked up at him. He was considerably taller and stronger than she was and there was no point in turning down masculine help when it could be useful. She grinned, he helped her to her feet, and together they advanced through the murk towards the distant lights of the Houses of Parliament.

Back in Caxton Hall, Alice, a member of the last contingent, was still waiting patiently to set off. She hadn't intended to take part in any demonstration—her role was press liaison officer—but she was so furious with Mr Asquith that she decided to be part of the action at ground level. As they finally received the order to march, Alice retied her scarf securely round her hat and pulled her heavy dogskin motoring gloves up her arms. As they wheeled out of Caxton Hall, a young man from the Men's Union shouted, 'Take care! The gloves are off today and they're trying to drag young women into side streets.'

Alice shrugged, nobody was dragging her anywhere, but she heard the shouts and screams before she reached Parliament Square and as they turned round the corner, the scene was unbelievable. She was in the middle of a maelstrom and the police appeared to have gone insane. A constable lunged towards her, twisting the scarf round her neck, pawing at her breasts. 'Take your hands off me, you disgusting little man.'

'I can put my hands where I like today, miss.'

'Not on me, you can't.'

He was a young man, he turned up the collar of his cape to hide his number, and he looked ashamed. But as Alice put out her hand to uncover his number, another voice shouted, 'Oh no, you don't.' Something came down upon her hand and the pain was agonising. Alice had never fainted in her life, her dazed mind fought not to black out, but she felt herself falling, and a voice was saying, 'Here's a beauty for you, lads.'

Another voice, a resonant male voice, shouted, 'What the blazes do you think you're doing, officer? Inciting these yahoos to assault this lady?' The voice was close by Alice, 'Can you stand?' An arm, a body was supporting her, 'My God, your hand!'

Shaking her head to clear the fuzziness, Alice looked at her hand. The double leather dogskin glove was cut the whole length and the flesh was like raw meat, red and bloody. 'I'll take you to Thomas's Hospital. May I introduce myself? The name's Conway. Jonathon Conway.'

Through blurring eyes, Alice looked up at him. So he was. She had seen him in *Trelawney of the Wells* only the other week and an exciting performance it had been. 'I am Alice Hartley and I think I shall faint any minute.'

'Cabby!' Jonathon used full stage voice and a cab on the far side of Whitehall halted. As he half-carried her along he glared round Parliament Square, 'I see here more devils than vast hell can hold!'

Inside the building that the suffragettes were struggling so desperately to reach, Tom walked into the 'Aye' lobby. They had asked for an emergency debate to get a motion through the House that the Women's Bill be given its third and final reading *before* the dissolution of Parliament. They'd got the debate, though Asquith had disappeared like greased lightning. As the 'Ayes' were counted, only fifty-two Members were found to be in favour of the motion. The buggers, Tom thought. Tim Healy, the Irish MP, pushed his ageing leprechaun way towards him.

'It's mayhem out there. I've just rescued some Irish ladies, who are in a shocking state. Is your wife among the deputations? If she is, you'd better find her.'

Tom raced for the central lobby where Mrs Pankhurst was standing, the first deputation having been allowed inside. 'Is there not a man among you in this House? Cannot one of you ensure that our Bill will not fail while my girls are being beaten and degraded out there in the square?'

Mrs Pankhurst was given to over-emotionalism, and Tim Healy, like all Irishmen, to exaggeration, but as Tom reached St Stephen's entrance and gazed across the square, he saw that this time neither of them had exaggerated. Christ, he had to find Kessie.

Kessie had finally located two policemen who were *not* assaulting her friends and she ran towards them breathlessly. 'Please, I have to get to the House. To my husband. He's an MP. Tom Whitworth . . .'

'Go on, pull the other one, it's got bells on it, miss. You're not married to him, the Socialist bastard, though they say he's fond of the ladies, eh George?'

Kessie blinked. Actually, she had expected them to recognise her and say, 'Certainly, Mrs Whitworth,' and the impertinent tone made her tremble slightly, but in her iciest voice she said, 'Kindly escort me to the House of Commons.'

Arthur Wilkins looked at the wide hazel eyes, the smooth

242

fresh face, the slim quivering body. This was the best assignment he'd ever had, all these young women thrusting their bodies at him, twisting in his arms (his missus just lay there), and they smelled so good, too. This one in front of him had the sweetest scent, like a garden full of roses, and he turned to his mate. 'She's a real beauty, ain't she, George? But you shouldn't be here, should you, my little darling?'

Kessie stared at him and took a step backwards, but George had moved behind her. Suddenly, he pinioned her arms, his other hand was across her breasts, his fingers were kneading them and there was nothing furtive about the movements. 'Lovely and firm, they are, Arfur.'

As she kicked out, Arthur grabbed her legs and the two of them were carrying her towards a side street behind the Abbey. Kessie started to shout and George clamped a rough smelly hand over her mouth, and then they were in the street where she parked the Silver Ghost when she drove Tom to the House. Oh, Tom, help me, help me. Arthur dropped her legs and George turned round and she couldn't say a word, her throat was parched, her lips frozen. George was hauling her against his back like a sack of coal, her head tight against his shoulders, her arms pinioned round his neck, her feet off the ground. She had never in her life felt so helpless or terrified or disbelieving, because Arthur's red face was sweating, his mouth was half-open over tobacco stained teeth, he was panting with a sexual excitement, and he was moving closer, pulling off her hat. Frantically, Kessie tried to wrench her head away, but he held her chin tightly, unloosening the kirby grips, and her hair flowed around her shoulders.

'Anyfing we does today, me little red'aired beauty, is done in the performance of our duty, ain't it, George?' Kessie felt the back beneath her heaving with laughter. 'We're going to show you a fing or two, ain't we, George?'

Sticking his truncheon between his legs, Arthur moved closer. It was an obscene parody of the sexual act and Kessie closed her eyes. His body was pressing against her, the truncheon was wedged between her legs and with an enormous effort she opened her eyes. When she was being forcibly fed she'd made herself keep her eyes open, at least part of the time, to prove to the doctor she was not cowed. Perhaps she could shame this policeman. The attempt had no effect. His disgusting wet lips were coming down upon hers and she tried to kick out with her feet, but George heaved her further up his back, tightening the grip on her arms. Kessie bit the slobbering lips as hard as she could, she felt the blood trickling into her mouth as it had from her lacerated gums in Newcastle, and she wanted to vomit.

'Now that was a naughty girl, that was.'

Arthur dropped the truncheon on to the pavement. With one hand he wiped his mouth, his eyes were as red and angry as the blood smear on his lips, the other hand tore at Kessie's jacket, pulling off the buttons. She heard them bouncing on to the cobbles. With a rending sound her blouse split, she felt the calloused hands pulling out her breasts and above his head the pile of Westminster Abbey was black against the grey sky. Oh God, she wanted sanctuary in His house now.

'You've never seen anyfing like these, George.'

'For gawd's sake, 'urry up. I can't wait much longer.'

Arthur's hands wrinkled her skirt and underskirt up round her waist, his fingers slid across her thighs, into her sex, and he panted, 'Oh Christ, you're lovely.'

Desperately, Kessie tried to scream but no sound emerged. Desperately, she tried to move her legs but she was sandwiched between the police constables like a piece of ham between two pieces of bread. Arthur's hands were pulling down her knickers, fumbling with his fly buttons, oh God, oh God, please help me. She breathed as deeply as she knew how and her screams echoed in the dank air.

Sergeant Brooks saw the old woman with her arm round the young girl. His job like the other Special Branch and CID lads was to watch out for the known militants, though that was virtually impossible in this scrummage, and generally to stop the suffragettes getting near the Houses of Parliament. He had no objection to a bit of rough stuff, but some of the gangs were going too far and some of the police constables, especially those East Enders, were disgracing their uniforms.

He saw the constable stop the old woman and he heard him shout, 'What are you doing here, granny?'

'Asserting my rights as an English woman.' Doubling his fist, the constable hit the old woman in the chest, her knees buckled under her and she slid to the ground. He started banging her head up and down on the cobblestones, 'You rich women are all the same. It's time you was taught a lesson,' and the girl was screaming, 'Stop it, stop it, you'll kill her.'

By God, he would! Sergeant Brooks ran fast, hauling the constable off the old woman who had lost consciousness.

Not far away Tom raced towards a group of suffragettes, shouting, 'Have you seen Kessie Whitworth?' None of them had, not recently, and he stood in the middle of the square, his head turning like a weathercock in a gale, trying to see her tall slim figure.

Jesus wept! Where was Kessie?

The cab driver helped Kessie into The Grove and said to Maggie, 'Something shocking, what's been going on in Parliament Square today. She's done in, poor lady.'

Her jacket was slung across her shoulders and Kessie was clutching it tightly round her. Gently, Maggie disentangled her arms and for the first time in her life she blasphemed. 'Oh, my God, oh Mrs Whitworth.'

'Just run me a bath, Maggie, please. Please.'

Kessie lay in the bath, the hot water lapped her chin, soothing her body, but all the waters of all the oceans could not wash away the horror, the degradation, the defilement. The temptation to slip under the water assailed her. Somebody had once told her drowning was an easy death. How could they know? And she had a child, sleeping sweetly in her cot, her little hands stretched across the eiderdown, and children were so vulnerable in sleep.

Down in the hall she heard voices and they were coming up the stairs, Tom's, Sarah's, Maggie's. The water was cold and Kessie let it out, wrapping a bath towel round her, sitting huddled against the wall. They were outside the door and Tom was saying, 'Kess, it's me.' Yes, she knew his voice.

245

He was rattling the handle, 'Let me in, luv.' Kessie pulled the bath towel more tightly round her, shrinking into a smaller huddle. Now there was muttering outside the door. Maggie and Sarah were begging her to open the door but Tom seemed to have disappeared. Kessie stared at the rose-patterned wallpaper, at the matching rose design round the rim of the bath, and Stephen's voice was saying, 'Kessie, old girl, open the door. We want to help you. Can't sit there all night, can you?' The handle was rattling again, 'Kess, I don't want to, but if you won't let us in, I shall have to break the door down.' Sarah said, 'Come on, Kessie, don't let the buggers break *you*.'

That made her smile slightly, she clutched the towel tightly round her and opened the door. Tom tried to take her in his arms but she drew back and Stephen said sharply, 'Leave her, Tom. Come with me, old girl.'

Stephen examined her carefully, gently rubbing ointment on the bruises on her arms, thighs, neck and breasts, asking if she wanted to tell her what had happened? Kessie shook her head. Stephen's square face was set like a ferocious stone lion's, she gave Kessie a strong sedative which she drank because what she wanted was oblivion.

When she came swimming up through the waves of consciousness it was night-time, the curtains in the bedroom were drawn, she heard the gas-fire spluttering and Tom was sitting by the bed, holding her hand. She withdrew it from his grasp.

His eyes were black, his skin at its darkest, and his voice shook slightly as he said, 'I love you, Kess, I love you. I'll see to it that bloody Winston Churchill and whoever did this to you suffers for it, by God, I will.'

After a while, Kessie said, 'I suppose you want to know what happened?'

'Only if you want to tell me.'

Did she? She didn't know. But she would.

'Two policemen took me behind Westminster Abbey. One was called Arthur, the other George. Arthur stood in front of me and George slung me over his back. I could hear the chimes of Big Ben.'

Tom put his hands to his face but his eyes never left hers, 'Did they . . .?'

'If you mean did Arthur *quite* get himself inside me—no. A gang of louts came into the street, chasing several of my friends, and several lads from the Men's Union were chasing them. That put Arthur off his stroke which is the *mot juste*. There was a general curfuffle and George and Arthur slunk off and I . . . well, I slunk off, too. I understand now why wounded animals want to be by themselves. Eventually, I found a cab. George and Arthur definitely thought I was a . . . a . . . good *fuck*.' Kessie spat out the word and momentarily Tom closed his eyes. 'They were under the impression that was why I, why all of us, were in Parliament Square. Our presence there had nothing to do with votes for women. Nothing at all.'

Kessie's unnaturally contained voice broke, harsh sobs racked her body and she turned her face into the pillow. Tom tried to take her in his arms but she pulled fiercely away. 'Don't touch me, Tom. Please, don't touch me.'

23

Kessie felt as if there was an enormous gulf between her and the rest of the world. She saw and heard what everybody was doing and saying, she observed their emotions, yet they were distant, on the far side of an unbridgeable chasm. The dank, dripping November days and the swirling fogs formed a curtain over the distance. Obsessively, she wanted to wash herself, to lie in the bath, to cleanse her dirty, defiled, contaminated body. Her bruises were changing colour interestingly and her heart had stood up remarkably well, so Stephen informed her, though it might have been better if it had packed up altogether.

The only living things she could bear to touch, or have

touch her, were Stephen in her medical capacity, and Anne. Little Anne was now a walking, talking handful, but when she put her chubby arms round Kessie's neck, or nestled against her, the love was pure, innocent, trusting. Though Tom was seething with rage, he was at his gentlest and tenderest with her. But she could not talk to him any more, nor stop herself flinching as he came near.

Sarah talked non-stop.

'I went down to Rochester Row with my case packed, ready for a jolly stint in Holloway, but the magistrate just dismissed us, Kessie, every single one of us. Charges dropped, it was all a mistake so run along home, ladies. You know who issued those orders? Mr Winston Spencer Churchill. He knows he was responsible for what happened on Black Friday. He wasn't having any of us standing up in open court telling what really happened. We've christened it Black Friday. It's the right name, don't you think?'

Politely, Kessie nodded.

'Tom says he'll crucify Mr Churchill. After the General Election, of course. That's one of our problems. There isn't a Government to crucify at the moment. Did he tell you he extracted a statement from Mr Asquith? Not about Black Friday, needless to say, but a promise that if the Liberals get back to power, they'll allow another Women's Bill in the next Parliament?'

Again Kessie nodded politely.

'We're supposed to be thrilled about that. Well, Christabel seems to have fallen for it. She's extending the truce. I told her she's mad. The country's outraged by Black Friday, so now's the moment to press hard and mount a strong deter- mined General Election campaign. No! Christabel doesn't think so and if our Blessed Lady doesn't, who dares argue? I wish you'd talk to her, Kessie. She listens to you as much as she listens to anybody.'

Momentarily, Sarah paused, her head on one side, but Kessie just smiled politely. She could not rouse much interest in what was happening on the other side of the chasm.

'Alice was at Clement's Inn, her hand bandaged and in a sling, surrounded by journalists all telling her how courageous she is, and lapping it up. She was wearing a *fantastic* hat, a whole flower garden on the top. She had an actor in tow. You know he's an actor because he never stops quoting Shakespeare in mellifluous tones and holding his profile up to the light. Jonathon Conway. Have you heard of him? Apparently, he rescued Alice.

'And Dorothy Devonald was there saying she's going to shoot Mr Churchill and telling everybody what a good shot she is. Her brother Georgie taught her to use a pistol. She's a ferocious child, isn't she? Everything's black and white to her, no greys in her vision of life.'

Occasionally, Kessie did not think there were many greys in Sarah's vision either, and her speech rate had accelerated over the years. Most people spoke fast from nervousness, but not Sarah, neither she nor Tom lacked confidence. Perhaps it was because she had so much to get off her chest that she rattled along like an express train. Kessie was sure her sister-in-law was trying to help but she wished she would stop talking, though she was glad that Sarah went to visit Aunt Ada, who had been felled by a blow in Parliament Square and had had another heart attack. Sarah said she was looking a bit better and sent her love.

The next afternoon Sarah came marching into the drawing-room, waving the *Star*. 'By heck I was right about Didi! She's attacked Mr Churchill!' Momentarily, Kessie's interest was stirred. Oh dear Lord, Dorothy hadn't shot and killed him, had she? 'She thrashed him with her riding crop, shouting, "You brute, you swine, that's for all the women assaulted and maltreated on Black Friday." Look.'

Kessie looked at the black print on the grey-white paper. How spirited of Dorothy, she thought dispiritedly. She would be spending Christmas in Holloway, but with the truce still operative, at least she wouldn't have to hunger-strike. And when was Sarah returning to the centre of the universe, Manchester?

Sarah decided to go with Tom who was off to The Dales for the General Election campaign. Before she went, she knelt down on the carpet, taking both Kessie's hands in hers, and Kessie had to fight not to withdraw them.

249

'Come on, luv, spit it out. Shout, scream, yell, weep, but get it out of your system.'

But Kessie only turned away.

Stephen kept urging Kessie to spit it out, too. As Christabel had spat at the policeman outside the Free Trade Hall on that long ago evening? Nicely brought up young ladies did not spit.

After Sarah and Tom had left, however, Kessie knew she must make an effort to face the world again. For one thing, she must visit Aunt Ada, still at the nursing home in Pembridge Gardens.

Even walking the few feet from the front door to the Silver Ghost, which had been brought round from the garage by her devoted mechanic, was terrifying. Although the mechanic had offered to chauffeur her, free, because he thought what had happened to the ladies on Black Friday was a disgrace, a positive shame, Kessie had declined the offer, because she could not bear any man near her. Holding the driving wheel in her hands, she felt nervous, but safe, nobody could touch her here, high above the pavements, and slowly she set off.

The world had not changed.

The noise, the smells, the sights were the same. The thwack and jingle of harness and bells, the rattle of the trams, the snort of the motorised transport, the trundle of high-wheeled handcarts; the smell of dung and leather and petrol fumes; children in thick woollen sailor suits bowling their hoops; horses drinking eagerly from the water trough after the long haul up Highgate Hill. In a smoky pall London lay beneath her, the spires of the City churches smudgily grey against the sky, and it was from the top of Highgate Hill that, in legend, Dick Whittington had heard those City church bells telling him to turn back to London. Like him, she had to turn back to the real world, to stop remembering, remembering, those calloused hands, those slobbering lips, that erect . . .

Driving through Camden Town, Kessie saw a chimney sweep, his face as black as his battered top hat, and chimney sweeps were supposed to be lucky. Should she stop the car and complete the luck by touching the black top hat? She should do no such ridiculous thing. Her luck surrounded her—Tom, Anne, friends, money, intelligence—and it was her intelligence that would see her through. She was managing to drive the Silver Ghost, to manoeuvre it through the traffic, to avoid the tram-lines, to ignore the chants from small boys, 'Coo, look at 'er. Are you a suffering-ette, miss?'

Yes, actually, she was and the cheap twist to the word was accurate.

Eventually, she reached Pembridge Gardens, though there were damp patches under her arms which Kessie dabbed with her favourite rose scent, to kill the smell of fear. In a warm, bright room Aunt Ada was being splendidly cared for, but oh, how pale and shrunken she was, even her hair had thinned, and every day of her sixty years was only too apparent. The thought of taking out a civil warrant, charging the Metropolitan Police with causing grievous bodily harm to her aunt, recurred to Kessie. But Stephen had said that, much as he sympathised, Kessie would be on a hiding to nothing. Her aunt had suffered a minor heart attack two years ago which Stephen could not medically deny. The police defence counsel would claim that a woman of her age, with a history of heart trouble, had no business to take part in a demonstration, however legal, and she could have suffered another heart attack at any time. In this *bloody* world, Stephen was probably right.

If Aunt Ada's physical condition was distressing, her spirit was undimmed. No, she did not want to come to The Grove. Kessie had her own life to lead, and when Ada was fit enough she would return to Thurloe Square, where Hetty had volunteered to look after her. (Hetty was one of her suffragette lodgers and a trained nurse.)

'Don't you worry about me, Kessie. Just come to see me as often as you can and bring Anne with you. She's a little treasure is Anne. You and Tom should have more children.' Yes, Kessie thought bleakly, she had been intending to before . . . but Aunt Ada knew nothing about that. She had

251

problems enough of her own. 'It's been a grand fight,' Ada was saying. 'I don't regret a minute of it. I shall go on doing all I can until I fall off my perch and the Good Lord calls me home.'

'Oh, Aunt Ada.' Kessie took the wrinkled hand in hers. Her aunt was the first person she had willingly touched, Anne and Stephen apart, since . . . A tear trickled down her face. It was the first time she had cried since . . . A rush of anger swept through her. It was the first real emotion she had felt since . . .

Papa came down from Manchester to visit his sister and he had aged, too. Perhaps it was the shock of his nice Liberal world collapsing around him. Kessie decided to return to Manchester with him to help Tom in his campaigning. Her husband was delighted to see her, she sat by his side on the platforms, listening to his angry speeches, to the roars of applause, but they were sound and fury, signifying nothing. Afterwards the crowds pressed round them, Kessie felt her skin growing clammy and she found it difficult to breathe. In one particularly enthusiastic crush, a policeman came protectively towards them and the street lamp caught the truncheon lying peaceably by his side. Her heart started to pound, she was gasping, she turned to Tom who put his arm round her, and she could just bear the pressure of his long fingers on her shoulders.

They dashed down to The Grove to spend Christmas with Anne, travelling back to Mellordale immediately afterwards for polling day, when Tom was returned with a slightly increased majority. They stayed over for a New Year's Eve celebration party, walking back to Milnrow well after midnight. Tom produced a large parcel. 'For your twenty-sixth birthday, my darling.'

Oh yes, it was New Year's Day, her natal day.

Inside the parcel was a dark maroon leather Victorian photograph album with shining gold leaves and thick cardboard pages with slots for various sized photographs. Politely, Kessie thanked Tom who said, 'Push the clasp right back.'

252

Kessie did as she was told and the clasp released the tiny cylinder of the mechanical music, rotating it against an iron comb, hidden behind the false golden leaves. The tinkling fairy-like music filled the room and Kessie said, 'Oh Tom, it's lovely. Oh, thank you.'

For days he had thought what to buy her, tramping high and low to find a music box she would like. It looked as if the effort might have been worthwhile, though to surmount the hundred-feet-high barrier she had erected, he still needed to move *very* carefully; the barrier entangled with the barbed wire of her shock, for unlike him Kessie had been brought up to believe that British policemen were wonderful, a view that earlier demonstrations had only slightly dented.

In the morning they awoke to a dazzling white world, a platinum sun in an azure sky, the snow piled in drifts, glistening like tinsel on the branches of the lone rowan tree. Tom took his wife breakfast in bed and said he'd dug a path to the coal shed, so that there was a blazing fire in the front parlour. There would be, Kessie thought, he always had the fire halfway up the chimney, probably a reaction to the days when the Whitworths had shivered fuel-less through bitter winters. Why didn't they take advantage of the weather, Tom asked, and have a day to themselves? Kessie nodded her agreement.

They had three days to themselves for later more snow fell silently from the sky and the wind howled down from the moors, driving it into ten-feet drifts, trapping them in Milnrow.

Shut off from the world, Kessie felt herself relaxing. She caught up with a pile of back correspondence, laughing ironically at the contents of two particular envelopes. One was a New Year card of a ship setting forth into 1911, from Cannon Row police station, and the other was a letter from Winston Churchill, informing her that her sustained efforts on behalf of Miss Lily Harrison, convicted of infanticide in the year 1905, had borne fruit and that he was recommending to His Majesty King George v that Miss Harrison be granted a free pardon.

253

On the third evening, they were sitting either side of the fire, the parlour cosily lit by an oil lamp and the glow of the flames, and Kessie looked across at Tom who was reading. His collar and tie were off, the buttons of his shirt sleeves undone. When they were alone he always unloosened them. The black hairs at his throat were glinting in the firelight and she thought of their bodies interlocked in love and tried to recapture the ecstasy. It was the same desire that George and Arthur had shown. No, it was *not* the same, her and Tom's physical passion was the complement of their mental love, part of the whole. Suddenly, the words were pouring from her, Tom put down the book and was listening with real concentration, not the intensity that meant his mind was on other things.

'I've been thinking ever since Black Friday, Tom. Those two policemen showed an *atavistic* enmity, the same as I saw in the faces of those men at the Wakes Week fair, and heard in the voice of that preacher—do you remember him?—except I didn't recognise it then. I was their quarry, something to be trapped, squashed, stamped upon. Do you know what I think our standing up and asserting our rights has now led to? A *real* sex war, stemming from a deep-rooted, *atavistic* hostility, and it came to its head in Parliament Square on Black Friday.'

Her voice was at its huskiest, her face frowningly eager, as she leant towards him. 'I see now why men and women will never be equal in *every* way. There is the physical strength difference, and the fact that we are the child-bearers. Perhaps that's partly how chivalry came into being, a genuine desire for the man to protect his mate, though I think it's always had more to do with keeping us in our places, at least two steps behind you. But why is there this urge to dominate and degrade us? Why can't we be the complementary partners we were surely meant to be?'

Tom was thinking fast as the verbal cascade splashed around him. The barrier between them was breaking down, and he had to find the right response.

'"The female of the species is more deadly than the male",' he said. 'I'm serious, Kess. Kipling encapsulated *our*

254

fears. We're terrified of women taking over and submerging us. You frighten me at times.'

'*Me* frighten *you?*' She giggled slightly and it did Tom's heart good to hear the sound.

'Domination and degradation are difficult to separate. You think about it, Kess. I penetrate your body, not you mine. When we make love you often like me to dominate you, don't you? It's all too easy to carry a wanted sexual aggression into everyday life. And men have problems. We have to get ourselves up. You don't. Some men can't.'

Kessie blushed. 'I've never noticed you having problems.'

He inclined his head and the black hair flopped forward. 'And there's our fear of the insatiable female.'

'What do you mean, the insatiable female?'

'Kess. You did Greek mythology at your posh high school. Think about the gods who needed to adopt animal forms to shag the female mortals.'

Kessie blinked. When she had studied Greek mythology at Manchester High School, no such thoughts had entered her head.

They went on talking about the deep-rooted fears and antagonisms between men and women, which Tom agreed the suffragettes' movement had brought to the surface.

Then he said, 'Men treating their wives as chattels for so long, one law sexually for us, another for you, comes from another fear. We can never be certain a child is ours, least-ways not until it's born and maybe looks like us. Unless she's promiscuous, a woman can be sure who the father is.'

Jumping up, Kessie stood over him. 'Tom Whitworth, for someone who can, when he wants, be charm personified, at times you are as charmless as a basketful of rattlesnakes. And as tactful as a sledge-hammer.'

'Kess, I didn't mean you.'

'Whose child do you think Anne is, Lloyd George's? Winston Churchill's? He has been nice about Lily Harrison . . .'

'I was speaking in generalisations.'

'I should take a deep breath before you utter your next generalisation.'

255

Tom was not altogether sorry that he had uttered because Kessie had sailed at him like the *Fighting Téméraire* he knew and loved.

As they later went up the narrow stairs and reached the front bedroom, she shivered slightly. 'It's bitterly cold, isn't it?'

Tom had been sleeping in the back bedroom, as he had been miserably sleeping alone at The Grove, but was that an implicit invitation? When they were in the double bed that had been their honeymoon bed, he put his arm around her and she did not pull away. Her body was warm, soft, and God he wanted her, but as he tried to kiss her, she pulled away as if he'd hit her. So he stroked her soft hair instead and soon, from her regular breathing, he knew she was asleep.

He lay awake, smoking in the darkness.

She started to moan and toss in the bed.

'Don't touch me. Leave me alone. Don't touch me, don't touch me.'

Tom stubbed out his cigarette and took her in his arms. 'Kess, Kess, it's all right, there there, my darling, it's all right.'

After he had soothed her back to sleep and she lay peacefully at his side, Tom resolved that he would never forgive those two bastards. He'd see they got what was coming to them.

In the morning he decided it was time he dug a path through the snow and they returned to the world. Most of the barrier between them had tumbled down and it shouldn't be difficult to climb over the remaining bricks.

Winston Churchill did not doubt that the women had been roughly treated in Parliament Square, because somewhere along the line his instructions—that the police act swiftly to remove the women and prevent the previous scenes of wild disorder—had been twisted into the directive that it did not matter *how* they were removed. But he categorically refused to believe that British policemen had actually assaulted or raped women. The WSPU was a copious fountain of mendacity with a particular animus against the police force, while Tom Whitworth, who had been the noisiest of the parliamentary protesters, making the wildest accusations, was a destructive, envious young man who aimed to shatter the great and glorious structure that was the British Empire. If his wife had been badly treated, a fact Mr Churchill regretted as she was a nice young woman, it was partly Whitworth's fault for allowing her to take part in such demonstrations. The police commander had admittedly made a grave mistake in bringing in those East End Divisions, but Mr Churchill had conducted a strenuous internal enquiry to ensure a similar day did not recur, and that was as far as he was prepared to go.

On a bright March afternoon he told the House of Commons that on 18th November last the Metropolitan Police had behaved with the forebearance and humanity for which they were noted. Of that he was satisfied and there would, therefore, be no public enquiry into the day that had been termed, not by him, but by the suffragettes and their supporters, Black Friday.

After making a fierce but unavailing protest, Tom leaned his head against the green leather bench. They had closed ranks again and those two bastards were going to get away with what they'd done to Kessie, unless . . .

A few days later they were having breakfast at The Grove, Kess and he, companionably reading the morning papers, while Vi gave Anne her breakfast upstairs in the nursery. Suddenly Kessie exclaimed, 'Listen to this!' Tom had a fair idea of what she would read out. 'Last night, two policemen, A. Wilkins and G. Kedge, were found beaten up in an alleyway in Whitechapel. The dastardly assault on the officers of the law appears to have had connection with the events of last November. Hung around the constables' necks were placards bearing the legend, "Remember Black Friday".'

Kessie looked at her husband as he ate his finnan haddock. 'A' for Arthur, 'G' for George. Tom could not have done it personally because he had been in the House all last night; but then again, people slipped in and out of the Chamber and nobody took any notice. She caught Tom's eyes but they had their darkly non-committal expression and somehow she did not want to ask if he had been in the sacred precincts *all* night. She did not approve of people taking the law into their own hands, but a small part of her was not unhappy that last night certain people had.

Finishing his breakfast, Tom felt a real glow of satisfaction that he had avenged his wife's wrongs. What a vulnerable quality Kessie had, despite that inner core of steel, the quality that made sods like Kedge and Wilkins go for her and men like himself want to protect her. He thought of the innocent, middle-class miss who had leapt from the bed in Sarah's room as he entered, blushing furiously. My God, what she had been through since then in the battle for women's emancipation—imprisonment, hunger-striking, forcible feeding, virtual rape! It was almost unbelievable. While he'd always admired Kessie's spirit and her courage, women were *not* made for such violence, or at least not women like her. Even the clouds of Black Friday must have a marginally silver lining, because she must now realise that enough was enough, that she'd done more than her whack for the cause, and that her days as a militant suffragette were over.

PART FOUR

24

From the windows of the office block Alice gazed excitedly across the expanse of Trafalgar Square, every inch of pavement a solid mass of people, every lamp-post festooned with spectators. Poppa had paid a fortune to obtain this privileged view of the Coronation procession but boy, was it worth every cent!

Soon after half past ten the fairy-tale coach had gone down to Westminster Abbey for the solemn ritual of the crowning of Their Majesties King George v and Queen Mary. Now the strains of the National Anthem were swelling above the pealing bells, and the soldiers lining the route were presenting arms, as the full procession came back up Whitehall. Pulled by its eight gorgeous cream-coloured horses, flanked by the escort of the Household Cavalry, the plumes of their helmets tossing in the stiff breeze, the Coronation Coach was wheeling into the square, and the roar of the crowds almost drowned the bells and the bands.

'Oh my, Alice, just look at those crowns on their heads. Oh, I could just weep with joy.' Momma leaned from the windows, calling out loudly, 'God bless Your Majesties! There, Alice, did you see, King George looked up and Queen Mary waved to us, I know she did.'

Alice laughed, but there was a lump in her throat. When it came to pageantry, there was nobody to touch the English. Seemingly endlessly, the procession marched and rode past, phalanx after phalanx, column after column, and it surely made you realise how vast the British Empire was, how truly it encircled the globe: black, brown, yellow and white soldiers from Africa and the West Indies, from Malaya and Ceylon, from the Dominions of Australia, New Zealand, Canada and South Africa. The cavalrymen from India, the jewel of the Empire, resplendent in their bright tunics and turbans, the pennants fluttering above them, were truly superb. With typical English perversity, after weeks of stifling heat and sunshine, it was a cloudy, coolish day, but nothing could dim the brilliance of the occasion.

While the troops continued to march past, the bells to ring, the crowds to roar, the distant guns to boom, their food was served, a cold collation of Whitstable oysters, Scotch eggs, Russian salads, game pies, cold meats, delicacies in aspic, wafer ices, strawberries and cream, and bottles of champagne. As they chatted and ate, yet again Momma's eyes fixed accusingly on Alice's right hand.

'I had no idea what the monsters had done to you. You're scarred for life.' There was a battle scar running diagonally across Alice's right hand but she could use the hand, and the scar was something of which she was proud, not ashamed. 'Poppa and I only came over for the Coronation, you know, and you must return home with us. England is a once-great country sinking into the mud.' That hardly tied in with what they were witnessing, nor with Momma's raptures, but she added firmly, 'If England wasn't on the decline, she couldn't have treated her women the way she has.'

'Don't be silly, Momma. That isn't the reason and you know it isn't.'

These days Alice had curiously divided loyalties. When she was at home and people criticised Britishers, she defended them furiously, yet the same was true here when people attacked the Yankees.

Now Momma had turned her attention to another topic, Jonathon Conway. 'You cannot go around London with *an actor*. You should not be going around with any man. You are to all intents and purposes an unmarried lady.' Poppa had brought the news Alice wanted to hear, that her divorce would be through by the end of the year. 'Do you wish to turn your poor mother's hair grey? Tell me, Alice, truthfully, you are not considering marrying this . . . this . . . *actor*, now are you?'

'No, Momma, I am not. He saved me on Black Friday and he's become a good friend. If you want the truth, I'm not considering marrying anybody. Once was more than enough.'

That information did not cheer her mother up.

Later that evening, as she arrived at Hatchett's restaurant for Christabel's Coronation party, Alice looked speculatively at her escort. Johnny was attractive, with deep-set grey eyes, wavy brown hair, an interestingly hollowed face, not to mention his splendid profile. His Christian name was spelled 'Jonathon', with the final 'o' rather than 'a', because he said his parents couldn't spell. Like Tom. And rather like Tom being born in a mill, Johnny had been born in a dressing-room as his mother came off-stage after a performance as Ophelia, which must have given an interesting twist to the plot of *Hamlet*. His parents ran a fit-up company that toured the British Isles, but Johnny himself was more ambitious and wanted his own company, to be an actor/ manager to rival the late Sir Henry Irving. Alice liked ambitious people and he had a certain style, if it was a bit Johnny-come-lately. He was fun and he made her laugh but, no, she had no intention of marrying him.

'Now is the winter of our discontent made glorious summer by this daughter of Lancaster,' Johnny declaimed as he kissed Christabel's hand. She laughed, 'It wasn't your winter of discontent. It was ours.'

Their wintry days were over. Mr Asquith had just *put in writing* the assurances that his Cabinet had unanimously agreed 'to give effect, not only in the letter, but in the spirit' to the promise that their Bill would become the law of the land in the next Parliament. When that happened British women would finally have the vote they had struggled for, and what would Alice do then, poor thing? Think about it—and Johnny—later, and enjoy herself tonight.

The champagne flowed, the conversation flowed, Christabel was the sparkling jewel, and Emmeline Pethick Lawrence made a flowery speech in praise of her and her mother. Alice saw that Kessie was trying to smother her giggles, for Emmeline could be overblown at times, but what she said was absolutely true.

263

Nobody was certain what had happened to Kessie on Black Friday. There were rumours that some of the girls had been *raped*, though Verena said that could not be true of Kessie because nice girls did not allow themselves to be raped. Alice had thought of Franklin and what a dear innocent her elder sister was. She had tried to talk to Kessie, but she had admitted nothing; ditto Stephen, on the grounds that she never discussed her patients, which was suspicious, because she frequently discussed them in hilarious detail. Whatever had happened to Kessie, she had recovered, for she had recently confided to Alice that she was *enceinte* again.

'I saw an aeroplane while I was in Dover recently, quite the most extraordinary sight,' Mrs Pankhurst laughed. 'I do not see them catching on as a means of transport.'

'Oh, I don't know,' Alice said. 'Ballooning is fantastic, so going in an aeroplane must be fun. They're faster and you can steer them better.'

'I'd like to go up in an aeroplane,' Kessie said, but Tom shook his fist at her playfully. 'Not while you're my wife you don't!'

A superb raconteur, Johnny Conway entertained them with several of his stories, and only Stephen failed to join in the general laughter. Stephen was becoming a big bore. She had been wonderful when Alice first returned from New York and a sort of delayed shock hit her, and she had been splendid over nursing her hand, but she did not approve of Johnny whom she said was a bounder, not at all their kind of person, and she was behaving as if she was Alice's mother, or husband, or something, wanting to know where she was going and when she would be back and . . . she was leaning across the table, waving her champagne glass in Alice's face.

'Cheers, old thing. Here's to the golden days ahead, the days of freedom, of you and me, old girl, hand in hand as we tread life's path. . . .'

She maundered to a stop and Alice decided she was drunk. She had no intention of going anywhere hand in hand with Stephen and if she was called 'old girl' or 'old thing' once more, she would jump on the table and scream.

Turning towards Johnny, she gave him her golden smile and her fullest attention.

When the party finally broke up, Alice was feeling deliciously light-headed. In the foyer she watched Tom wrapping a silk evening cloak round Kessie, gently kissing her neck. Then Johnny's honeyed voice whispered in her ear. 'The evening is yet young, divinest Alice. Care to come back for a nightcap?'

This was an invitation and a half, but why shouldn't she accept?

'My automobile's parked round the corner in Swallow Street,' she whispered back. 'It's a dear little green Napier. You can't miss it. Shall I see you there in a few minutes?'

Johnny smiled, kissed her hand and loudly declaimed, 'Good night, sweet princess, and flights of angels sing thee to this night's rest.'

Having bade her farewells to everybody and quietly told Stephen she was spending the night with Kessie and Tom, Alice left the restaurant with the Whitworths, parting company from them as they climbed into a cab. In Swallow Street Johnny was waiting, the Napier fired at the first crank of the handle, and off they bowled with him calling out the directions. Johnny started to sing 'Ta-ra-ra-boom-de-ay' and Alice joined in. Round Piccadilly Circus they swung, past Leicester Square they roared, and when several cab drivers shouted at her she waved cheerfully back. Once or twice Johnny said, 'Steady the Buffs,' whatever that meant.

In the middle of Covent Garden, he said, 'Slow down, divinest one, we're here.'

Alice pulled hard on the hand-brake and they skidded to a halt by a pile of orange boxes. Porters were weaving along the pavements, the baskets on their heads making them look like leaning towers of Pisa, and they whistled and shouted as Johnny assisted her from the driving seat. What an extraordinary place to live, in the middle of a fruit and vegetable market, but Alice supposed it was handy for the theatres.

As they climbed the stairs to his apartment, Johnny said, 'You should take up racing driving.' Alice hiccoughed and

265

tripped on the step, he slipped an arm round her shoulder, and the sensation was decidedly pleasant.

His apartment was a mess, a dressing-gown thrown on an armchair, dirty plates and pot of jam on the table, which Johnny hastily removed, cursing his bone-idle manservant. Alice made herself comfortable on the ottoman, he produced a decanter of whisky and two glasses, and proceeded to regale her with stories about his touring days in the provinces. One was about some 'digs' which actually had a bath but you couldn't use it because the seals were ensconced there. Alice didn't understand it and what were 'digs'? When Johnny explained that 'digs' was a theatrical term for lodgings, where you dug yourself in for the week, and music hall artistes had to put their performing animals somewhere, she laughed uproariously.

After a while he moved on to the ottoman, his deeply mellifluous voice was breathing Shakespeare in her ear, while his hands caressed her bare shoulders. Alice wanted him, she wanted him badly, so she said, 'I have been married, you know Johnny, however briefly.'

At that remark he didn't waste any time and soon they were both undressed and in his bed. Thank the Lord, he was not like Franklin, he was more like Tom, his body hard and hungry if not as lean and with only a line of brown hairs on his chest, rather than the profusion of silky black ones, and he brought her to almost as lovely a climax as Tom had. Stretching her arms above her head Alice felt much, much better.

'Jonathon Conway, you have skills other than acting.'

Jonathon lay feeling wonderfully drained and slightly astonished. Why in God's name had Franklin Adams let go of her? Had she been too much for a well-bred Boston gentleman? For without any doubt, Alice was a goer and her dropping into his arms in Parliament Square had been a gift from the gods, because she was golden in person *and* purse. His theatrical star was in the ascendant, but if he was to finance his own company, he needed a backer. . . .

He leaned up on his elbow, looking down at her.

'Shall we celebrate our nuptials ere too long?'

266

'If that means you're asking me to marry you, Johnny, the answer is no. I have no desire to marry again. Matrimony is not for me. I doubt it will be for many women in the future.'

In amazement Jonathon stared at her. Every woman wanted to marry.

Arching her back, her beautiful breasts jutting towards him, she said, 'But I'm happy to carry on like this, if you are, Johnny.'

Yes, he was very happy to. Jonathon accepted life as it came. Even if she wouldn't marry him yet, she was still a gift-wrapped package. He drew her towards him. Alice laughed her golden laugh and wriggled her body sensuously.

The next few days were among the more peculiar of Alice's life. On the tenth day she decided she needed to speak to somebody and the obvious person was Kessie. Unfortunately, when she arrived at The Grove in her Napier, Kessie and Vi were about to take little Anne for a walk. The stifling heat had returned and Alice would have preferred to have sat in the garden, drinking Maggie's delicious homemade lemonade, but having arrived unannounced she could hardly upset Kessie's plans.

After several attempts to impart her extraordinary news, temporarily Alice gave up. First of all, Kessie explained at length how useful this new type of baby car she'd bought for Anne was, because it folded flat, so she could put it in the Silver Ghost or take it on a train. Next, half Highgate stopped to raise its hats or comment how fast Anne was growing—Kessie was obviously well-known and well-liked—and Anne would keep jumping out of the damned baby car and trying to push it herself.

Slowly they progressed through the woods up on to Parliament Hill Fields. Below them London shimmered in the heat. Vi took Anne to watch the boats sailing on the pond and from a distance, where you couldn't hear her constant chattering, she looked so sweet in a pale blue crocheted frock and matching slouch hat (her Great-Aunt Ada's handiwork, no doubt), white knee socks and little patent leather shoes with ankle straps. The two young

267

women sat down on a bench and, at last, Alice could make her announcement.

'Stephen's thrown me out.'

The effect had been worth waiting for. Kessie slewed her head round, her hazel eyes wide with astonishment. 'What do you mean? *Thrown you out?*'

'I have a confession to make. You know the night of Christabel's Coronation party? Well, I stayed with Johnny Conway, but I told Stephen I was staying with you and you must have let the cat out of the bag.'

Kessie looked confused. 'Yes, she telephoned me and asked to speak to you. Just after breakfast it was. I remember thinking it was a bit early in the day. . . .'

'The old sly-boots! Anyway, when I returned to Hampstead in the afternoon Stephen was, well, I don't know how to explain what she was like. Half the time she shouted at me, she called me a *whore* at one point, and I had quite enough of that from Franklin. . . .'

Ah, thought Kessie, listening to Alice describing her outrageous behaviour as if she were talking about the vicar's tea-party, so Franklin had known his bride was not *virgo intacta*.

'Then Stephen became all gruff and British, begging me to realise where my moral duty lay, as a harbinger of the new era. I ask you! Harbinger of the new era! I told her, and I did not mince my words, that what I did was absolutely no business of hers. And do you know what she did then, she went down on her knees in front of me, Kessie. It was *awful*. So I said, wouldn't it be better if I left? She jumped up and shouted, yes, and we haven't spoken all week, but yesterday she asked when I was going. I had intended to go in my own good time, but obviously I can't stay any longer. The atmosphere is simply *gruesome*.'

'What are you going to do? Are you moving in with Johnny?'

'Certainly not,' Alice fanned herself vigorously. 'What do you take me for?'

At the moment, Kessie thought, that would be hard to define. To have behaved the way she had with Tom, Alice must be a sensual lady, so physical abstinence must come hard and perhaps having an *affaire* with Johnny Conway would be good for her, though how Kessie wished she would marry him. Or anybody. *Affaires* were, well, difficult and immoral, but at least she and Johnny were well-suited. Each as self-absorbed as the other.

'Ectually, I'm in negotiation for an apartment in the Adelphi Chambers. Would you believe it, I have to have a *male* guarantor, though patently I have my own money. Oh, Kessie, we must get the vote, there's still so much to be done before we really do have equality.'

In the evening, when Tom came home Kessie poured out the astonishing story of Alice and Stephen. 'Isn't it extraordinary? I can hardly believe it. I mean, I thought Stephen adored Alice and would put up with *anything* she did.'

'In this case, maybe she adored her too much.'

'What do you mean?' Tom's inflections had been most peculiar.

'Nothing. You're not to get excited, me luv, particularly about our Alice.' Tom came up behind her and patted her stomach. Kessie pulled away from him. 'It's not Alice I'm worried about. It's poor old Stephen. Can you imagine the state she must have been in to have gone down on her knees in front of Alice? Do you think I should talk to her?'

'No.'

Kessie decided that Tom was probably right. She must not over-excite herself, she must think of the baby she was carrying. A slight panic fluttered through her at the knowledge that only she, and Stephen, possessed, the knowledge of her damaged heart.

25

Fortunately, Kessie's second child arrived in the world at top speed, like a circus clown bursting through a hoop, which was splendid because it meant her heart wasn't in the least bit strained. She was the sweetest little thing, with a down of orange-gold hair, cooing at the world she had been so eager to enter, and they called her Constance in honour of Constance Lytton. Poor Lady Constance had recently suffered a stroke which had left her paralysed down the right side, an affliction that her family and friends felt sure was the delayed result of her treatment in Walton Gaol. Tom was absolutely delighted with little Con, though a surprising number of people who should, in Kessie's opinion, have known better, said he must be a teeny bit disappointed to have another daughter. When the day finally came that nobody made any such comment, Kessie decided, then the equality of the sexes would have arrived.

Only a week after baby Con's birth, from what seemed clear skies, Mr Asquith dropped his thunderbolt, informing the House of Commons that his Government intended to introduce a Franchise Bill to give the vote to all British men. If Parliament and the country so desired, the Prime Minister said as an afterthought, the Franchise Bill might be capable of amendment to include women.

'Capable of amendment to include women!' Kessie shouted at Tom, 'He's doing it to scupper *our* Bill and he *promised* us we should have one, "not only in the letter, but in the spirit".'

A few days later David Lloyd George publicly stated that the Women's Bill had been scuppered, though the word he used was 'torpedoed'. Kessie wrote him a long furious letter to which he replied by return of post. He was delighted to know they were friends again, the previous Women's Bills had been highly unsatisfactory, amendments to the new Franchise Bill would give more women the vote, he promised to put his full weight behind them, and if anything went wrong this time he would resign in protest. When she was fully recovered from her daughter's birth, on which his heartiest congratulations, why didn't she take tea with him?

'Oh . . . oh . . . every time I have a baby something appalling happens.' Sharply, Tom said, 'Calm down, Kess. You *have* just borne a child. You are not to do anything wild. Apart from the invitation to tea, I agree with Lloyd George.'

Did he indeed? During the battles over the reform of the House of Lords, when Tom was horse-trading with Lloyd George about the Labour support, they had become surprisingly friendly, but how dared he support him over the women's amendments? And tell her to calm down?

Dorothy Devonald came rushing up to The Grove.

'This is it, isn't it, Kessie? Into battle we go again.' With slightly raised eyebrows Kessie looked at her as she tucked into a plate of Maggie's fairy cakes. What did Didi mean? Again? She had only been in one battle, if admittedly Black Friday had been a ferocious début, and she had no real idea what she was talking about. Having consumed her fourth cake, Didi said, 'Oily George and 'Erbert 'Enery have to be taught that we will not take their perfidious betrayal lying down. A deputation is marching on Parliament, but that's only a smokescreen for the real action. While there's the usual hullabaloo in Parliament Square, a select group of volunteers will be window-smashing. I've volunteered and I've been selected.'

In astonishment, Kessie stared at Dorothy. Organised window-smashing? Why had nobody told her about this drastic plan? She had been in the WSPU for six and a half years, longer than almost anybody now, and while she shared the furious anger, she felt sure that smashing windows was no way to influence Oily George or 'Erbert 'Enery Asquith, or public opinion. Forcibly she told Dorothy so, but the girl was adamant.

'Nonsense, Kessie. There's been a *two-year truce*, apart from Black Friday. They reneged on us like the dastardly politicians they are. What do you propose we do? Sit and wait for another two years?'

And she rushed off, back to Clement's Inn, before Kessie could properly answer.

Just before midnight Dorothy turned up at The Grove again. Hearing the commotion in the hall, Kessie came downstairs in her dressing-gown to find Didi in a state of euphoric excitement. Thank goodness, Tom had another

271

late sitting in the House, because he would have been furious at this intrusion.

'We did it, Kessie!' Her voice was like the wind scything through the reeds. 'It'll be in all the newspapers tomorrow morning, but I had to come up to tell you. I'm out on bail—*two hundred pounds*—what about that? Daddy said he had no idea he had such a valuable daughter! My target was Liberty's windows in Regent Street—Madge was just across the road—and we used hammers, not bricks. I worked it out scientifically and it's much more reliable with hammers —some of the girls are rotten shots with bricks—and if you swing low the hammer doesn't hook and the glass falls *inwards*, not on top of you. I smashed six windows before a stupid old policeman lumbered up to arrest me. Oh Kessie, it was just like playing hockey, sweeping towards goal, out-whacking your opponents and smashing straight through the net.' Dorothy paused and started to splutter with laughter, 'Except that it's *gaol*, not *goal*, that I shall score.'

'Except that you were not playing hockey.'

For a moment Dorothy stopped jumping up and down, her glittering eyes blinked uncomprehendingly, and with a cold sensation in her stomach Kessie realised that she had enjoyed the violence, just as those policemen had enjoyed themselves on Black Friday. No, that was not true. She was just a child caught up in the righteous fury of the minute. Kessie told her to go home and get some rest.

In the morning the newspapers were filled with the stories of the outrages that had occurred last night in central London, and later in the day Dorothy and her fellow window-smashers were remanded in custody to Holloway, to await trial.

Kessie was too involved with her new baby and Anne's reactions to her little sister to take an active part in WSPU affairs. Christmas came, and her own birthday, and it was into the New Year of 1912 before she had the time to go to Clement's Inn for serious discussions.

She found Christabel in martial mood.

'It is now all-out warfare which *they* declared, not *us*, but we shall take up the challenge unflinchingly.'

'Must we take it up violently? Can we not be unflinching, but calm? Tom thinks we should go all-out to lobby support for the women's amendments . . .'

Christabel's expression told Kessie she had made a bad mistake in mentioning Tom. In ringing tones she said, 'We have fought for a Women's Bill, for the recognition that we are citizens in our own right. After all these years, after all the suffering, should we settle for mere *amendments*, for simply being tacked on to a *man's* Bill?'

Which was precisely what Kessie had said to Tom.

Within the week, further thunderbolts fell. Clement's Inn was ransacked by Special Branch officers, Emmeline and Fred Pethick Lawrence were both arrested, Mrs Pankhurst didn't need to be arrested because she was already in Holloway, awaiting trial for leading a window-smashing raid on number ten Downing Street, and only Christabel had escaped the net, though there was a warrant out for her arrest.

The evening the news broke, Tom was rushing off to Northumberland to attend a miners' conference and Kessie could only have the hastiest of conversations with him as he charged into the study, grabbed some papers, and charged out again.

'They couldn't let you lot go on window-smashing, Kessie, they had to do something, and at least Christabel's got away . . . where's my blasted travelling bag?'

'You had it in your hand a minute ago.' Kessie had bought her husband a handsome leather gentleman's toilet case which he was always forgetting. 'You must have left it in the study.'

'I get it, Daddy, let me, let me.' Anne ran as fast as her legs would carry her into the study, staggering back with the leather case.

'There's a clever girl.' Tom took the case. 'Thank you, sweetheart. See you in a couple of days. Be good and do what Mummy tells you. 'Bye, Kess.'

After the flurry of his departure, while Kessie stood in the

273

hall, Anne, who had the sharpest ears, looked up at her. 'Where Aunty Kissy gone?'

'I don't know.' The approximation was the nearest Anne could get to Christabel. 'And it's time for your bath. Go on, up you go.'

It was Alice who answered that particular question, the next morning over the telephone because she was far too busy to come in person. Christabel had escaped to Paris, though Kessie was not to tell one single soul where she was, not even Tom, because the Special Branch bloodhounds were baying after her. If the Liberals thought they had smashed the movement by these arrests, they could think again, for Christabel was the wSPU incarnate and she was safe. The triumph in Alice's voice was unmistakable. Was it because she had been at the centre of things, while Kessie had known nothing? Why hadn't Christabel contacted her? The hurt that she had not done so ate into Kessie's soul like acid.

When Tom returned from Newcastle, she said, 'Do you think it was because I was critical?'

''Course, it was. "Power tends to corrupt; and absolute power corrupts absolutely."'

At least he had quoted Lord Acton correctly which most people did not, and Kessie said, 'How corrupt are you likely to become?'

'With you by my side,' he patted her behind, 'not in the least.'

These days Tom was not by her side very much. He was in the House of Commons, or dashing around the country, and when he was at The Grove he spent most of his time playing with the children. Everybody said what a wonderful father Tom was, and he was in his element crawling around being the big black bear, tossing Con up in the air, or reading a story to Anne, but it left precious little time to discuss the things Kessie wanted to talk about. While she agreed that the miners' strike was the biggest thing to have hit the working classes and they were on the move as a coherent body at last, what had hit women was just as important.

They hardly seemed to have time to make love, though Tom sometimes returned with a glint in his eye, slipping his arm around her waist and saying, 'Let's go to bed.' But they couldn't because Anne was jumping up and down squealing, 'Daddy, Daddy, you promised to take me to ve zoo.' She had difficulties with her 'th' sound and automatically Kessie corrected her, '*Th*, darling, *th*, with your tongue between your teeth.' Tom's grin said he'd like to get his tongue between *her* teeth.

Those moments when Tom went inside her were as ecstatic as ever, and he teased her because apparently she always said, 'Oh, Tom.' He said, 'Don't ever let it be, "Oh, Dick", or "Oh, Harry"!' Their bodies knew each other, fitting together like the pieces of the most perfect jigsaw puzzle, but they seldom had those post-coital conversations she enjoyed so much, because he was tired, or she was tired, it was late and they had to be up early in the morning.

Then Sarah's letter arrived and Kessie knew it was important because it was a fat one and brevity was normally her sister-in-law's suit. Like Tom's her handwriting was standard elementary-school style, but just as he had imposed his character on the cramped, sloped, looped letters by flourishes and twirls, Sarah's character had given her writing a distinctive neatness. As her eyes scanned the neatly regular opening lines Kessie was not surprised, she was shattered, but she read on.

15 Hulton Street,
Moss Side
M/c.
3rd March, 1912.

Dear Kessie,

I don't suppose you will be surprised to hear that I have resigned from the WSPU. It's not a sudden decision. In fact, I've been thinking long and hard ever since Black Friday because when I saw Christabel then, I suspected she thought she had become Lady God, or at the very least the possessor of Papal Infallibility. Now I'm sure. I know you believe that Black Friday revealed a basic sexual antagonism. Maybe it did, but if that's true, we shan't overcome it the latest Pankhurst way.

Violence is of itself evil, and I abhor it.

Superb as Mrs P. is as an orator, or marching at the head of a deputation, she's always bowed to Christabel as the strategist and tactician. The vision Christabel now has is of millions of blackguard men grinding down millions of shining women. The creed she is now preaching is of women as top bitches, instead of men as top dogs. I am simply not interested, because I want a better world for both sexes. That's what we all wanted in the early days, Christabel and Mrs P. included. I am convinced they have gone right off the rails and I am not prepared to follow them any longer.

Not that I'm abandoning votes for women. Not bloody likely! What I am doing is returning to my roots, to our movement's roots. One thing that struck me during my cogitations was that we are all *winners*, Kessie. I know we're not winning against the Government at the moment, but as women we're confident and articulate. I reckon we have to be, to be suffragettes. But the world is full of *losers*, Kessie. Do you know what I mean? Of course, you do. Your sensitive eyes and ears are wide open to the poverty, the disease, the injustice and the inequality that surround us. I reckon it's up to us, the people lucky enough to be born *winners*, to give the *losers* a helping hand. I want to re-set women's emancipation in its proper, wider context.

I've kept mum thus far on the basis of don't count your chickens before they're hatched, but one thing I did learn in my WSPU days was how to raise money. Well, I've raised several hundred pounds, I've dozens of volunteers who feel the way I do, we've rented an old warehouse in Hulme, we're in the process of doing it up, and we're opening it as a People's Centre.

Guess who says he'll lend a medical hand? Doctor McPhee! He's retired now, of course, and he keeps saying he's off to the Highlands to live out his days in peace, to escape from terrible wee lassies like me. Between you and

276

me and the gatepost, I reckon he'd be bored to tears talking to the sheep, shooting grouse, or stalking across the heather.

We're having the grand opening of the People's Centre on 15th April. You'll be there, won't you? You might ask my brother if he can spare the time to make a speech. Not only to prove that we believe in the equality of the sexes, but Tom's always been a king in these parts and his national reputation is growing fast, isn't it? You keep him in check and he might be Prime Minister one day. Fancy yourself at number ten Downing Street?

Lots of love and big kisses for Anne and Con,
Sarah.

The salvo was not quite finished and at the bottom of the last page Sarah had written a P.S. 'All great movements are about people, Kessie. The cause is the people, and the people are the cause. I don't reckon the Pankhursts were ever very good about people. If you decide to stay in the WSPU, you and the sensible lasses must take charge fast.'

Before Kessie had time to assemble her thoughts, a letter arrived from Christabel in Paris. She was sorry not to have contacted Kessie before she fled and not to have written sooner, but since she knew how involved with her family Kessie was, she hadn't wanted to burden her with further problems, and her own life had been hectic in the extreme. She understood Kessie's doubts, violence was anathema to women, but they were fighting *institutional* violence and she, Christabel Harriette Pankhurst, swore that theirs would be controlled. She hoped Kessie would understand and stay in the WSPU, because she valued her friendship, her courage, and her expert knowledge.

Kessie felt racked with indecision, veering first towards Sarah's certainty, then towards Christabel's. Tom always said that people who sat on fences, unable to make up their minds, ended up by doing themselves a nasty injury.

A month later they travelled to Manchester *en famille* for the opening of the People's Centre. On the morning of the

277

great day, a dank, grey morning, she decided that Anne needed a new hat and Papa said he would come with them into town. Each time she saw her father now, with a pang Kessie realised how quickly he was ageing, the erect back slightly stooped, the ginger hair and moustache quite grey, though he insisted he was in good health. The chauffeur deposited them outside Kendal Milne's, while Papa stayed in the Sunbeam. Inside the department store Anne threw a screaming, stamping tantrum because her mother refused to let her have the fur hat she wanted.

'It's quite ridiculous for the summer months. If you don't stop that, I shall smack you and Daddy will not take you out tomorrow.'

In the end Kessie did smack her daughter, not before time the shop assistant's expression said, and she had always sworn that she would not use physical force on her children, nor descend to the blackmail of 'If you don't . . . Daddy won't'.

But she let Anne watch the metal containers whizzing along the overhead wires to the central accounting booth where the cashier extracted the bill and the money, inserted the change and sent the container hurtling back to the counter. That put Anne in a better temper and when they emerged into Deansgate, Papa said, 'Who's a beautiful little lady?' Rolling the dark eyes that were so like Tom's up towards the hated hat, a straw bonnet garlanded with corn-flowers and daisies, Anne smiled smugly.

As Kessie climbed into the back of the Sunbeam, at the far end of Deansgate she saw a newspaper boy frantically waving a clutch of papers, though she could not hear what he was shouting. What happened next was the most extra-ordinary experience of her life, one she knew she would recall to the day she died. It was as if a glacier was slowly pushing its away along the busy thoroughfare, freezing trams and buses, carts and carriages, horses and pedestrians in its track. The frozen moment was followed by an equally extraordinary noise, a whisper that hissed towards them.

'The *Titanic*'s sunk.'

Although the traffic started to move again, people

clustered in stunned groups. Papa said authoritatively that it was a vicious rumour, undoubtedly spread by the envious Germans or French or Americans to smear the British genius. The *Titanic* was unsinkable and there was nothing more to be said.

Despite the devastating news about the *Titanic*, the thunderbolt to end all thunderbolts, or perhaps because of it, hundreds of people turned out for the opening of Sarah's People's Centre. The narrow cobbled street was packed, the newly whitewashed building gleamed like the Taj Mahal among the soot-blackened terraces, and the cheers rang to the leaden skies as Tom and his sister jointly declared the Centre open. Afterwards the crowds pressed around him more than her, and Sarah was right, in these mean streets he was the king. She was right about his growing reputation, too, because Tom's presence had brought dozens of reporters and photographers from the national dailies, not just the local newspapers. They posed as a family group, Kessie on one side of her husband with baby Con in her arms, Sarah on the other, Anne proudly clutching her Daddy's hand. After a while Kessie left him to hold court while she wandered round the teeming warehouse. How hard Sarah and her volunteers had worked to make it so spankingly clean, so comparatively inviting. Then Sarah came up and said, 'Let's do a bunk and have a cup of char. I'm dropping with exhaustion.'

In a dark little room that was her office, and showing no signs at all of exhaustion, Sarah bustled around making the tea. While Kessie drank hers, she talked about her doubts and indecisions. Sarah waited till she'd finished, then she said, 'You know your trouble?'

'Many moons ago Tess Billington told me that my trouble is that I'm a romantic.'

'So you are, and you take everything too much to heart. It's a tough old world. The only way to survive successfully is to stand on your hind legs, shout as loud as you can, and pick yourself up when you're knocked down.'

Fired by Sarah's positive approach, Kessie made up her mind. With Christabel still in hiding in Paris clear heads

279

were needed in London, so she would stay in the WSPU to try to pull it back on to a firm course.

When Mrs Pankhurst and Fred and Emmeline Pethick Lawrence were tried for conspiracy at the Old Bailey, Kessie attended every day of their trial, squashed between Alice and Sylvia Pankhurst in the public gallery packed with suffragettes. When the Attorney-General opened the proceedings for the Crown by telling the jury that votes for women had nothing to do with the trial, and that they were to return their verdict solely on the question of whether the accused had conspired to incite women to commit acts of violence, Kessie thought Alice was about to climb over the gallery rail in her furious indignation.

The jury were more or less forced to return verdicts of Guilty, but the foreman begged the judge to exercise his clemency in view of the undoubtedly pure motives that lay behind the accused's actions. Despite the plea, his lordship exercised it only to the extent of sentencing Mrs Pankhurst and Mr and Mrs Pethick Lawrence to nine months in the second division with hard labour, instead of the two years he said their crime merited. There was uproar in the courtroom. Afterwards the WSPU had a conference at Clement's Inn and agreed on a mass protest meeting in the Albert Hall at which Kessie should be the principal speaker.

When she returned to The Grove and Tom heard what had been arranged, he said, 'You haven't forgotten you have two small children, have you?'

'No, I have not. It may interest you to know, seeing you're not around very much, that I spend more time with Anne and Con than many of the allegedly maternal, conventional women who leave their children in the care of governesses and maids.'

'For God's sake, Kess, you don't have to react like a spitting cobra to a mild observation. What's the matter with you?'

But Tom went with her to the Albert Hall. To begin with Kessie was shaking with nerves because she had not spoken to such a large audience in ages, and this was a vital speech if ever she had made one. Her old confidence quickly returned, however, and by the time she reached her peroration she knew that seven thousand people were hanging on her every word.

'We are hereby giving the Government fair warning. Unless they transfer all the women still serving prison sentences for their *political* belief, that our sex is entitled to vote, to the first division as *political* prisoners, all the suffragette prisoners, including Mrs Pankhurst and Mr and Mrs Pethick Lawrence, will hunger-strike.'

As roars of applause crashed around her, Kessie prayed that their defiant, yet reasonable, gesture would work. The sympathy of the country at large was with them. Nobody, however, knew better than Kessie what was being asked of the imprisoned suffragettes, from the fifty-four-year-old Mrs Pankhurst to the nineteen-year-old Dorothy Devonald, should the Liberals not respond.

26

Soon after the Albert Hall rally, Kessie thought they had won through. With protest petitions from all over the world raining upon Mr Asquith like April showers, he agreed to transfer Mrs Pankhurst and the Pethick Lawrences to the first division.

Tom said, 'Don't get too elated just yet. Only if they were to transfer the likes of Dorothy to the first division, would they be admitting your political motivation. That would be the thin end of the wedge to giving you the vote.'

'Yes, I do understand the implications, Tom, I really do.' Kessie knew she had flared at him but she was tired and sometimes he treated her as if she were still the naïve little miss from Whalley Range.

Sadly, Tom was right. The Liberals refused first-division status to anybody else, so that from Holloway Mrs

Pankhurst gave the order for the hunger-strike, to be led by her and the Pethick Lawrences. Within a few days the feeding tubes were again being rammed down suffragette throats.

It was the wretched affair of Emily Wilding Davison in Holloway that convinced Kessie she must return more actively to the fray. Emily was one of the most dedicated and courageous of suffragettes, if her devout Christianity gave her what Kessie secretly regarded as a fanatical edge. She too suffered particularly badly from forcible feeding and, in what Kessie was certain was a spur-of-the-moment act of desperation, Emily leapt over the iron gantry, shouting 'No surrender' as she plummeted into the well of the prison. Thank the Lord, wire netting broke her fall. *But*, and this was the truly unbelievable part, the new Home Secretary, Reginald McKenna, ordered a specialist by the name of Crisp English to examine Emily, and he pronounced her bruised and battered body fit enough for the forcible feeding to continue.

Kessie attended an emergency meeting at Clement's Inn and when she next saw Tom, which was at breakfast because she'd been exhausted last night and fallen asleep before he came home, she said, 'We're stepping up the picket outside Mr Crisp English's house. Everybody thinks it will be a good idea if I do a speaking tour of the major cities to try to make people understand just what is going on. I can obviously speak from my own experience of forcible feeding.'

'I see.' Tom's voice was ominously flat. 'How long will you be away?'

'Oh . . . not more than a fortnight.'

'What are you going to do with Anne and Con?'

'Leave them with Vi, of course. They'll survive without me for a fortnight, honestly they will.'

For the minute she thought Tom was about to lose his temper—he had been behaving a bit like an old-fashioned husband recently—but he was as enraged as anybody about Emily's treatment and he briefly smiled his agreement. At the end of the week she bade her husband and her daughters a temporary farewell and set off on the road.

Kessie was in Edinburgh when she saw the newspaper headlines. She'd given a morning talk and an afternoon one, she had her major meeting at the Usher Hall that evening, and she was taking a breath of air in one of her favourite cities, walking along the Royal Mile towards the castle, when a newspaper boy clipped the latest news on to his board.

'Prime Minister Accused of Driving Women to Commit Suicide: Further Wild Scenes in House of Commons: Members of Parliament Suspended.'

The front page cartoon of Tom—with his flopping black hair, cleft chin, gangling height and outflung left arm he was a cartoonist's dream—told her who one of the MPs was. Immediately she tried to telephone The Grove and speak to him, but when the operator finally made the connection, Maggie said Mr Whitworth had gone to Bristol. Kessie felt desolate. What was Tom doing in Bristol? Apart from wanting to tell him how proud she was of him, she'd also wanted to ask if he would join her for the last week of her tour, since he'd been suspended from the House.

Not that she regretted her speaking tour, on the contrary it was proving infinitely worthwhile, but while the majority of her audiences were sympathetic, there were the organised claques. It wasn't the dead mice they threw at her that upset Kessie—she was accustomed to dead mice, laid in tribute at her feet by her cats, Amber and Jasper—it was the gangs waiting as she left the halls. Despite her female gymnast bodyguards, youths stretched out to feel her thighs and her breasts, as they hissed their sexual filth. In Bradford, she had retched in the gutter and last night for the first time in ages, the nightmare had returned. She was fleeing from hordes of men, she knew George and Arthur were at the head of the stampeding mob, their faces red, sweating, lustful, she kept on running and running and she had to find Tom . . . oh well, she would be home by the end of the week.

When Kessie returned to The Grove, Maggie was preparing a cold supper for Tom, who had apparently telephoned from Bristol, to say he would be back late in the evening. 'Leave it here,' she told Maggie. 'You know how

283

Mr Whitworth likes eating in the kitchen. You go to bed, I'll wait up for him.'

Kessie was half-asleep in Maggie's rocking chair when she heard the front door bang. Looking up at the kitchen clock, she saw it was well past midnight. She ran up the stairs from the basement to meet Tom in the hall, but his response to her embrace was cool. Was he cross with her for having gone on the tour? Well, she didn't want to be cross with him. Following her down into the kitchen, he washed his hands before slumping into the rocking chair.

Kessie gave him his supper: collared salmon with dressed beetroot and cucumber, rolls and butter, a slice of rice and apple cake, cheese and biscuits. While he ate the meal, she found the milk on the larder cold slab to make two cups of cocoa, congratulated him on his stand over Emily, and asked what he had been doing in Bristol.

'Helping the girls at Wills' cigarette factory,' he said shortly. 'They're trying to organise themselves into a union, you know.'

Oh yes, so they were. Kessie chattered about her tour and she knew she was chattering, but Tom was being singularly uncommunicative, until suddenly he said:

'Do you intend to go on rushing around the country?'

Carefully, Kessie poured the hot milk from the enamel pan into two cups. 'I intend to go on working for women's rights,' she stirred the cocoa and sugar and handed one of the cups to Tom. 'Why? Do you think I shouldn't?'

'I think it's about time we got a few things straight.' Tom sipped the cocoa, while Kessie stared at him. 'You are no longer a young girl, Kess, you're a twenty-seven-year-old woman with a husband and two children who all need you. Here. At home. I have no desire whatsoever for you to "sit and sew", to use one of your favourite derogatory expressions. You've never been daft, me luv, and you know full well that from where Christabel's broomstick has landed her in Paris, she is quite unable to control a gang of violently militant women, if indeed she wants to. Though you refuse to admit it, you know the WSPU is now on a stony road to nowhere. So while the children are young, while they really

284

need their mother—and you're a very good mother, Kess—
why don't you get your priorities straight, work with me
to . . .'

'My priorities? Are you sure you don't mean *your* priorities?' Kessie's astonishment was turning to fury. 'It's all
right for you, Tom, you're a man and your public life is
expected to take pride of place, but I'm struggling to find
the right balance. Isn't that what women's emancipation is
about? I don't want to be trapped.'

'What by, for God's sake? Me? The children? Are you
saying you refuse to accept that having children in any way
affects a woman's life?'

'No, I'm saying it does.'

'Children *you* chose to have when *you* wanted to have
them!'

'What about *your* responsibility towards the children?
Will you stop promising Anne you'll be home when you
know you won't, and you'll take her here, there and everywhere when you know you can't? That child adores you
and I have to deal with her endless disappointments.'

They were both on their feet, facing each other on either
side of the kitchen range, going at it hammer and tongs, and
the accumulated irritations shot to the surface. Kessie was
shouting about him slurping his soup and leaving soggy
cigarette ends in the bathroom and swearing all the time,
Tom was shouting at her about letting the cats into the
bedroom and leaving lights on and giggling like a silly
schoolgirl.

'I am not giggling now.'

They were bawling about money.

'If you weren't so bloody extravagant, I could keep you
these days.' Among the horse-trading over the support for
the Liberals, the Labour Party had extracted payment for
Members of Parliament.

Kessie yelled, 'I am not extravagant. You try running this
house.'

'Is that what you want? The role reversal Christabel's
veering towards? Me in a cap and apron?'

At the thought of Tom in a mob-cap and apron, Kessie

285

had to stifle a giggle. 'No, I do not. I want us to be partners, real partners. Is that what you want? To see me on my hands and knees scrubbing? I did that when I was in Holloway.'

Kessie felt her voice growing huskier, breathier, which it did, blast it, when she was really furious. She tried to keep it level, firm, because this was no ordinary row and if Tom truly wanted to get things straight, there were a few things she had to say.

'Do you know what you've always resented? The fact that your father couldn't keep your mother and she had to go out to work, instead of staying at home and being your mam.'

At the mention of his mother, Tom's skin darkened with fury, but Kessie hadn't finished. 'Has it ever occurred to you that your mam might have liked working and disliked bringing up you lot?'

'Shut up about my mother. You know nothing about her life, or what Dad did to her! Nothing.'

'Perhaps she loved him, despite everything. As I love you.'

'Shut up, Kessie.'

'You preach the equality of the sexes but now the actuality is upon you, oh, that's something different. I wonder if you've ever cared about votes for women, really thought about what sexual equality means and . . .'

'For once in your life, shut up about votes for women!'

Tom slapped her face, not hard, but the tears gushed into her eyes. For a few seconds they stared at each other in horrified amazement, before Kessie hurled herself at him, pummelling her clenched fists against his chest. He caught her wrists. 'Kess, I'm sorry, I didn't mean . . .'

He was trying to draw her into his arms but she screamed, 'Let me go. I hate you, I hate you.' They were struggling and shouting and Kessie lost her balance and fell to the floor.

Her hazel eyes wide, shocked, tear-stained, Kessie looked at him as he bent towards her. 'Kess, darling, I'm sorry.'

She spat at him. 'Don't touch me. You're just like *them*. Don't touch me.'

Scrambling to her feet, she ran from the kitchen.

Tom slumped into the rocking chair. Jesus Christ, what was the matter with Kessie? Sometimes he wished he had married one of those ILP girls in Manchester, one of the trot-off-and-make-the-tea brigade, as his sister called them. No, he did not. What Kess had given him, physically and morally, not to mention materially, none of them could have provided. But there *were* differences between the sexes, even Kess admitted that, so it followed they had different functions, particularly with children. He shouldn't have hit her, but he'd had one hell of a week. Still, however angry she had made him, he should not have hit a woman. Not just *a* woman; she was his wife.

Tom went upstairs, but the bedroom door was locked. Oh God, he was too tired to do further battle with her, or to grovel through the keyhole, so he slept in one of the spare bedrooms. In the morning they were both subdued, he apologised again, and she apologised, too, though her eyes were filled with accusation.

Violence was something Kessie had not thought about until it overwhelmed her on Black Friday. Recently, she had given it considerable thought, coming to the conclusion that it lurked in everyone, including herself. Because she had deliberately goaded Tom last night and she had wanted to batter him. Not that that excused his behaviour. How could he have hit her? No gentleman would do that, however great the provocation, and it was high time Tom learned to control his temper.

In the next few weeks they did not see a great deal of each other because, apart from anything else, the political scene was tense, with a battle going on for the Irish Home Rule Bill. At least the uproar over Emily Wilding Davison had had its effect and *all* the suffragette hunger-strikers were released. After a brief recuperation, Didi came bounding up to The Grove.

'Were you put in the punishment cells?' Kessie shook her head. 'Well, after I'd barricaded myself into my cell, they finally broke through and stuck me in a punishment cell. They're underground and they're just like coal-holes, except the walls are made of some sort of rubber stuff. Oh it *stank*,

Kessie, you know, with the hot weather, and I must say I felt like a pit-pony when they brought me up at the end of the week, all blinking and stumbling.'

Dorothy appeared to accept what had been done to her, and to Emily, as a normal part of suffragette life, and said she was off to Cheltenham for her 'hols'.

A horrified Kessie told her husband about the punishment cells and Tom said, 'God almighty! You needn't worry about the effect on Miss Devonald. She has neither your nervous system, nor your imagination.'

Which might, or might not, be true, but it sounded a little callous.

For their own holiday they crossed to the Isle of Wight, but Tom kept returning to the mainland, which put Anne in a fractious mood. Having two children certainly kept one occupied, but Vi had come with them, of course, so when Kessie's temper frayed she swam out into the cool green depths beyond the enfolding arms of the secluded beach below Willow Bank, or went for long walks across the grassy cliff-tops, or through the lush mysterious thickness of the Undercliff. As Aunt Gertrude had predicted it might be, Willow Bank Cottage *was* a haven in times of stress. Stress? All was not well between her and Tom, it was as if a curtain had descended between them, but she hoped they would soon sweep it away.

The summer over, back at The Grove, apart from helping to organise the women's freedom march from Edinburgh to London, Kessie was also involved in organising a suffragette Autumn Fayre, to raise funds and spread the message. The day she took Anne to enjoy a ride in the Black Maria on the children's merry-go-round, and the pleasure of hurling woollen balls at the cardboard cut-out figures of Herbert Henry Asquith, David Lloyd George, Reginald McKenna, Winston Churchill and all the well-known 'Antis', Lady Louise Claremont was there.

There was nothing surprising in this because Kessie had sent invitations to dozens of such socially prominent suffragette supporters, preferably titled, for people were snobby and their presence brought in the crowds. She and

288

Lady Louise met at a stall spread with Aunt Ada's delicate crochet work, and Kessie told her that though her aunt was a permanent invalid, confined to her bed as a result of Black Friday, she still had not stopped working for the cause. Proudly, Anne confirmed her mother's explanations.

'My Great-Aunty Ada made vose.'

'*Those*, darling.'

'Then I shall definitely buy a set of mats for my dressing table.' Lady Louise opened her reticule and smiled at Anne. 'She is so like you, Mrs Whitworth, but she has your husband's eyes, wouldn't you say?'

'Do you know my Daddy?'

Lady Louise nodded and laughed. There was something about the way she held her elegant head under its huge, osprey-feathered hat, something about her tinkling laughter—was it a note of triumph?—that set Kessie's brain ticking furiously. How did she know Tom? He hadn't met Lady Louise with her and he'd never said he knew her. He'd been singularly uncommunicative recently, his absences had been frequent, and why had he suddenly become interested in the Bristol cigarette girls? Claremont Hall was in Somerset, not far from Bristol. Kessie stared at Louise Claremont who was smiling graciously at a young newspaper reporter.

'My dear young man, the only thing a man should ever hold over a woman is an umbrella. To protect her from the rain.'

It all slotted into place. Oh yes, little Anne, Lady Louise *knows* your Daddy. In the Biblical meaning of the word. Had he been with her that night, the night of their terrible row? How could he, of all people, have taken up with her, of all people, one of Edward VII's later mistresses? The rich, sleek, arrogant, spoiled bitch, years older than Tom, though she wore well, fine-boned, thin-bodied, but then she could afford to.

In the weeks that followed Tom didn't look any different, or behave any differently. His affection for the children was undiminished, and he expected Kessie to appear in public with him as his loving wife. Occasionally, they still made love because she couldn't always resist him. One night he said, 'God Kess, that was beautiful,' and it had been, but how could he make such remarks when he was betraying her with Louise Claremont?

Did he think she didn't know?

The next morning Kessie announced that she was taking the children to Manchester but apart from saying, 'Don't stay away too long. Give my regards to your father,' Tom made no other comment. The children loved being at The Laurels, which Anne called 'grand-dad's castle', and if it didn't come into that category, Kessie now fully appreciated how privileged her upbringing had been.

Naturally she went to see Sarah at the People's Centre, which was a hive of activity, with classrooms and clinics and advisers and a soup-kitchen. Although she hadn't meant to, while they were having a cup of tea Kessie blurted out, 'Tom's having an *affaire* with Lady Louise Claremont.'

'The bugger!'

Kessie started to cry and Sarah comforted her. Then she said, 'I'll tell you something, Kessie. I wasn't best pleased when I first heard that you and Tom were engaged.' Wiping away the tears, Kessie looked up in surprise. 'I thought you weren't the right person for him, a bit too posh. You know! But you're the best thing that ever happened to my brother. You tell him straight—either he comes to his senses, or you'll leave him.'

Somehow Kessie couldn't bring herself to do that. Her pride would not let her. It was up to Tom to make the first move in regard to Louise Claremont. She considered methods of counter-attack other than staying in Manchester. She could have an *affaire* herself. How did you set about having one? She could not march up to David Lloyd George, or any of the other possibilities, and say: I'm willing now. Anyway, she was not willing. One thing Black Friday had done to her was to make the thought of any man except Tom touching her intimately an impossibility.

At the end of the month she decided to return to London with the children, and to re-immerse herself in WSPU activities. But what was happening within the suffragette ranks was not edifying, either. Kessie went to a mass rally in the Albert Hall, intended to welcome Mrs Pankhurst and Emmeline and Fred Pethick Lawrence back after their heroism during the Conspiracy Trial and the hunger-striking. To the stampede of applause it was Mrs Pankhurst alone who walked gracefully to the centre of the stage.

'Where's Pethums and old Fred?' Dorothy asked.

Where indeed?

Holding up her lorgnettes, Mrs Pankhurst read out a prepared statement to the effect that Mr and Mrs Pethick Lawrence found themselves unable to agree with the WSPU's latest militant policies and were therefore resigning. An astonished roar swept through the auditorium which Mrs Pankhurst silenced with an imperious gesture. Then she started to speak and it was a spine-tingling speech, which she finished with a superbly rousing challenge.

'And my last word to the Government is—I incite this meeting to rebellion!'

Virtually everybody in the vast auditorium was on their feet, or leaning from the loges and the distant balconies, shouting, clapping, stamping, cheering. The waves of sound beat against Kessie like the storm waves crashing against the cliffs below Willow Bank, but she sat quite still. The uproar went on and on, and it was a devastating experience, being here, listening to the applause from thousands of women, her sex, her comrades, and being utterly apart from it and them. Suddenly, Kessie could bear it no longer and pushing past Dorothy, she made for an exit.

Outside she leaned her head against the red brick of the Albert Hall. The fog was closing in rapidly and across the road the browny-yellow swathes were thickening around the Albert Memorial, which Tom called a 'neo-gothick rabbit hutch'. Kessie giggled, the fog caught at her throat and she was coughing and spluttering. A cab clopped by and on an impulse she called out:

'Will you take me to Clement's Inn in the Strand?'

The cabby agreed and the night-watchman there recognised her and let her in to the now-empty lower floors, for the WSPU had moved into antiseptic new offices in Lincoln's

Inn House. Kessie walked along the rambling corridors that had rung with laughter and echoed to the tread of purposeful feet, past the rooms in which so many plans had been made. With her head against the locked door of her old office, she watched the fog wreathing along the corridor and the tears were running down her face.

For over seven years, seven glorious, heroic, wonderful, terrifying, uplifting, agonising years, she had travelled willingly, lovingly, admiringly with Christabel. The memories were swirling with the fog. Once she had sworn that nothing and nobody would ever come between her friendship with Christabel.

'I do remember him at Clement's Inn.'

Falstaff's words came into her mind. Would they be remembered? Where had it all gone wrong? What was she to do now? The answer to her first questions Kessie did not know, but she knew what she had to do now because like the Pethick Lawrences she could not agree with the latest militant strategy. No further could she travel with Christabel. In her whole life Kessie had never felt more desolate, not even when Tom had first betrayed her with Alice. And her decision to resign had nothing to do with him.

Alice did not deliberately set out to make love with Tom a second time. It just happened when they bumped into each other, by accident, one snowy night just before Christmas and she invited him to her apartment in the Adelphi Chambers for a warming drink.

When she was astride his lean hard body, revolving her head, flexing her muscles, caressing her naked breasts, and he said, 'Go on, Alice, work me,' she just knew their coming together again had been ordained. After a while she leaned towards him, licking those silky hairs on his chest. He rolled her over and he was ramming into her, his sweat was dripping into her eyes and the slight smarting made her more excited. She was thrusting up, he was thrusting down, she was scratching his back, he was biting her shoulder, pulling her hair, and oh God, she could feel the wetness, she was coming. . . .

'Now, Tom, *now*.'

After a while he said, 'Have you a gasper?'

'They're in the box on the table. Light me one. And poke the fire up. That one, I mean.'

Langorously Alice pointed towards the grate, Tom tipped half a bucket of coal on, prodding away expertly with the poker, before lighting two cigarettes. They lay on their backs, smoking in front of the leaping flames, and Alice decided that for old time's sake she would be discreet. Unlike Louise Claremont. Anyway, she liked Kessie, it was just a mistake that Tom had married her. He would finish with Louise, she would finish with Johnny, and in the spring they could travel to Paris together to see Christabel— and ah, Paris in the spring with Tom! Alice threw her cigarette into the fire and wriggled on top of him, and their bodies were still as slippery as if they had been oiled. In the months and years ahead she would do with him all those things Franklin had made her do, some of which she had not done with Johnny, and truly enjoy them.

Tom was suddenly at home more, very much more attentive when he was. A tiff with Louise? Kessie had no intention of enquiring. Her pride still would not let her. The year 1913 had arrived. Thirteen. The WSPU's once-lucky number, so would it be their year? Not hers, not any more, and resigning had been like losing a loved one, but she did not regret her decision and she was continuing to work for the cause with other suffragette groups.

Then Tom asked her if she would care to hear his final speech on the Irish Home Rule Bill and she accepted the invitation. His speech was good, oh yes, he was developing into a formidable parliamentarian and it was fascinating to hear how he now modulated his Lancashire accent. The Home Rule debate finished, the House about to move on to next business, Kessie was leaving the Ladies' Gallery when the Speaker rose to make a statement.

When he sat down, she sat down, too, resting her head against the panelled walls, close by the space for the grille that had never been replaced after Sarah's padlocking

293

escapade, and she was literally gasping for breath. The unbelievable had happened, the ultimate in perfidious betrayal had just been announced, for the Speaker had ruled that the women's amendments would entirely change the nature of the Franchise Bill, therefore it must be withdrawn and redrafted. Which meant that after all these years, after all the struggles, they had no Women's Bill, no Franchise Bill, no amendments.

Nothing.

It was like Anne's favourite game, snakes and ladders. Move by move they'd climbed up the ladders, and having reached the topmost line, they'd plunged back down the longest snake of all, back to the start. It would be funny if it wasn't so monstrously awful, and to think she had persuaded Mrs Pankhurst to call off her incitement to rebellion because the amendments would not go through if the WSPU violence persisted! Kessie was half-laughing, half-weeping, and she must have stayed immobile in the Ladies Gallery for quite a long time because now Tom was bending over her.

'Come on, Kess, let's go home.'

In the evening Tom persuaded her to accompany him to the Mathersons' reception, saying it would take her mind off things. At the reception the first person they saw, or more precisely heard, was Mrs Asquith, screeching fiercely, 'My husband is dreadfully upset that the Franchise Bill has been withdrawn.'

'I'm sure he's weeping buckets,' said Alice, who was here with her sister and brother-in-law. She was looking absolutely stunning, her embroidered gold brocade evening gown the latest fashion, with a slit at the front and a long train behind, on her corn-gold hair a deep gold turban.

'The only blessing about the Bill's withdrawal is that it has bowled over the suffragettes.'

Kessie looked at Margot Asquith, as she marched imperiously past them. Not for the first time she wondered why she was so violently opposed to other women having the vote. She said to Alice, 'Do you suppose that women like Mrs Asquith are more Anti than the Anti men because

294

they like being the female élite in a man's world and bossing other women about?'

'I do not know and I do not care,' Alice replied, 'I just know I could kill the whole treacherous, conniving, deceitful pack of them, starting with her.'

In fact, it was not Margot Asquith who was commanding Alice's attention that evening, it was Kessie's husband. Since that blissful snowy evening he had not once called upon her, not a squeak or a peep had she heard from him, and when she had gone over to talk to him just now, he had been off-hand, almost dismissive. Just who did Tom think he was and just what was he playing at? Suffering rattle-snakes, Algy Hereford was lolloping towards her, braying like a jackass. Didn't he ever give up?

After supper Kessie saw Mr Lloyd George disappearing into the conservatory. Alone. For a few seconds she hesitated, before making up her mind. If there was one person she really wanted to speak to in private, it was him. Passing Mrs Asquith she overheard her saying (it was not difficult to overhear even a confidential Mrs Asquith), 'My dear child, you must speak to your husband. You cannot keep having babies. Henry has always been good. He always withdraws in time.'

Oh well, that shed light on Margot's problems. And Henry's.

As she entered the conservatory, Mr Lloyd George was very surprised to see her, looking like a startled mountain goat, but he recovered his composure quickly. 'Mrs Whitworth, how pleasant. More lovely than ever. *La belle dame aux camélias.*'

Kessie glanced behind her and she saw she was framed by a tub of the most beautiful camellias.

'Please don't, not this evening, not after . . .'

'Kessie, I assure you, the Speaker's ruling was as big a shock to the Cabinet as it was to you. I assure you the Government did not connive . . .'

'Please save your breath, Mr Lloyd George. I *know* the Antis have been concocting this for a long time, anything to prevent us having the vote. They could not have done *anything* more calculated to enrage *every* woman suffragist in the land. I am so angry I could scream.'

He had forgotten how splendid she was in her anger, the delightful face blazing, the hazel eyes flashing, the husky voice deep with passion. Tom, so he'd heard, was cavorting with Louise Claremont, which he did not imagine a high-spirited woman like Kessie would tolerate. Would she be more amenable? '. . . and what do you propose to do, Mr Lloyd George? You told me—I still have your letter—that if we were again cheated of our right to vote, you would resign.'

'Ah,' he fingered his moustache and gave her a wry smile.

'You're just playing with us, aren't you? You don't give a tinker's cuss about women's rights, do you? You're . . . you're *despicable*.'

'I promise you . . .'

'Ohhh . . . be quiet!' The fury was making the tears smart in her eyes, choking her throat so that she could hardly speak. She was not going to weep in front of him and she turned towards the door, but he caught her hand, pulling her back. 'Don't go like this, Kessie. Can we not be friends?'

His left hand was toying with those tendrils that still escaped even from her most elaborate hair-dos. How dared he? She lifted her free hand to slap his face but he caught at that, holding both her wrists in a tight grip. His other hand was running across the low-cut bodice of her green velvet, Empire-style gown.

'If you don't let go of me this instant, I shall scream.'

'Kessie, just one little kiss, between friends.' His arms were around her, his lips were coming down upon hers, she was back in the street behind Westminster Abbey . . . frantically, Kessie pushed at him and her terror took Lloyd George by surprise. Good God, was she a married cock-teaser? Was that why Tom . . . then he remembered the rumours about Black Friday. So they had been true, poor Kessie, she would need the gentle approach. But her struggles had put them both off-balance and they fell into the huge tub of camellias, Kessie backwards, Lloyd George on top of her.

296

A young woman came into the conservatory, emitting a shrill shriek, 'David!' So that was why he was here, Kessie thought wildly, and behind the young woman she saw Tom. Even more wildly, she thought, was that why *he* was here?

For a few seconds he stayed looking at them, Lloyd George was struggling to his feet but she was lying covered in flowers like the Millais painting of Ophelia. Tom strode across the tiled floor and hit Lloyd George, once, hard on the chin. With a thud he fell backwards into the massed pelargonium.

The young woman screamed loudly.

The commotion brought the guests crowding into the conservatory. Tom rubbed the knuckles of his left hand which were hurting, lifted his wife from the camellias, and without a word half-carried her through the fascinated throng. As the gangway was made for them, Kessie saw Alice looking cross (what had she to be cross about?), and she heard Mr Lloyd George saying, 'An accident, an unfortunate accident. Nothing to worry about, except your poor flowers, Lady Matherson.'

Silently, they sat in the back of the taxi. Kessie was trying hard not to cry—how and why did she get herself into these awful situations?—and Tom thought how vulnerable she looked. Would she ever lose her innocent, childish impetuosity?

After a while she said, 'I'm sorry I went in there like that with him. I shouldn't have. Did you hit him because of me? Because of what happened this afternoon in the House? Or because you were sure he wouldn't bother your wife, seeing you're such good friends?'

'Because of you, Kess.' She had, Tom privately admitted, hit a nail on the head with her last question.

In their bedroom, he watched Kessie unscrewing the marcasite ear-rings he had bought for her twenty-eighth birthday and dropping them into her jewel box, before sweeping into the bathroom. Undressing slowly, he decided he'd been mad, no, just drunk, to have gone with Alice again—that was one thing Kessie would never forgive him, should it ever come to her ears. Louise she might forgive him. She could work out all sorts of theories about aristocratic ladies and working-class men (he wasn't as lacking in self-awareness as she sometimes seemed to think), but with Alice, and for a second time, there was no excuse.

He told himself he had finished with both women, Louise and Alice.

Kessie returned from the bathroom and went over to warm herself in front of the gas-fire. Her long slim legs were silhouetted through the fine cotton of her nightdress. She looked at him. 'Dorothy and the rest of the militants will go berserk now. Who can blame them? Where *do* we go from here, Tom?'

To bed, me luv, Tom thought.

He moved towards her but, giving him a dramatically wide berth, she crossed to the dressing table where she sat down and started to brush her hair. Tom decided it was a moment for positive action. He walked up behind her and took the brush firmly from her hand. For several minutes he swished it through her chestnut mane, watching her respond with a purring, feline pleasure. Then he let fall the brush, lifted her up, turned her towards him and kissed her passionately.

Still holding her tightly he said, 'Would you like to put your "thing" in?'

'I might.'

For a long time after they had finished they lay silently holding each other, then Tom said, 'Why don't we have another baby, Kess?'

'I have no intention of conceiving in the time you have to spare from Louise Claremont.'

The words shot out like bullets and Kessie cursed them because she had sworn that she would never, ever, mention that name. She saw Tom suppress a grin—the remark had been tartly amusing, she supposed—before turning his head away and stretching out his left arm towards his tobacco tin. Kessie gazed at him while he rolled a cigarette between his long fingers, lit it and puffed a smoke ring up to the stuccoed ceiling. This was one of those 'moments of truth' which

298

inadvertently she had brought into the open, but it was up to Tom to say something now.

Giving her a wry, apologetic smile, he finally said, 'I'm a sod, Kess, I know I am sometimes, but I love you and I'm sorry. Truly.'

'You always are,' Kessie felt that if she had not won this particular battle, she had not lost it either, 'about all your women.'

'All is an exaggeration, and I swear to you . . .'

'No, don't swear. Just don't.'

27

Dorothy was at The Grove before the Whitworths had finished their breakfast. Tom gulped down his tea and excused himself, and Dorothy was not sorry because she had never liked him and she could not think why Kessie had married him. He always looked such a mess with that black hair flopping all over the place, he had that terrible accent and he was frightfully outspoken about the wrong things. Still, he supported women's suffrage. Despite her retirement from the WSPU (which probably had something to do with Tom and babies), Kessie herself was a darling and absolutely trustworthy, so Dorothy told her what she was going to do to register her outrage at the ultimate betrayal.

'It's only as an *hors d'oeuvre*. Emily and I have something special in mind for the main course, but it's a good wheeze, don't you think?'

Silently Kessie looked at her, then she said, 'Are you sure you know *how* to do it?'

''Course I'm sure. My brother Georgie's a Sapper and he's keen on military history.'

There was another silence before Kessie said, 'When are you off to Cheltenham?'

'This weekend.'

'Your mother is always inviting me and the children to stay for a few days. Why don't we come this weekend, if it's convenient for her?'

'Kessie, do you mean . . .?' Kessie nodded and Dorothy threw her arms around her neck. 'How spiffing!'

Early on the still dark Sunday morning, Dorothy and Kessie slipped out of the Devonald house in Cheltenham. Dorothy was wearing her knickerbocker bicycling outfit and carrying a large tin, a ramrod, a home-made linstock and a piece of sacking caught at the ends and smelling strongly from the dried cow-dung inside. Kessie had on an old, dark brown two-piece and was carrying a lantern, a banner and a chimney sweep's brush. They walked through the silent streets of sedate Cheltenham, past the sweeping Georgian terraces, along the wide boulevards, through the narrower streets until they came to the park. The gates were locked but Dorothy knew where there was a gap in the railings. Pushing their impedimenta ahead of them, they both squirmed through, before walking across the soggy grass and climbing up the mound.

On the top was the Crimean War memorial and in front of this was the Russian twelve-pounder field gun captured at the battle of Alma. By the light of the lantern Kessie saw the verdigris on its bronze length and hoped to heaven Didi knew what she was doing, because she had not the slightest idea how to fire a nineteenth-century cannon.

'Right. Get the barrel cleaned out.' Dutifully, as the grey dawn lightened, Kessie set to work with the sweep's brush, while Dorothy levered the lid from the tin of gunpowder. 'Fine. Now stick the powder into the barrel and ram it home.' Slowly, Kessie pushed the grey-white substance in and impatiently Dorothy said, 'Hurry up. We haven't all morning and we need all the powder. It's a big gun.'

As fast as she could, Kessie shoved the rest of the powder in and then Dorothy held up the lantern and peered down the barrel. She couldn't actually see anything, but she felt an inspection added the professional touch and it was fun being in charge and giving Kessie orders. While Kessie watched with a baffled expression, Dorothy proceeded to ram in the cow-dung.

'That's what we fire. Makes lovely wadding. I remember Georgie mentioning that. They're very erratic these guns but I reckon the range should be about eight hundred yards.'

Dorothy marched to the other end of the gun, Kessie followed and held the lantern close while Dorothy carefully cleaned out the touch-hole and dropped in her store of best quality powder.

'Now comes the tricky part. I think I'd better light it, don't you?' Her heart thumping with apprehension and excitement, Kessie nodded and Dorothy picked up the improvised linstock. 'Stand well back and cover your ears. These guns have a tremendous recoil and make a lot of noise. I hope!'

Lighting the match wound round the stick, Dorothy held it to the touch-hole, made sure the powder was ignited and leapt back herself. A few seconds later, the gun fired. The recoil was tremendous, there was a deep track in the grass where it had leapt backwards, and in the stillness of the Sunday morning, with the early church bells tolling, the noise was colossal and great puffs of smoke were hanging in the dank air.

Dazedly, her nostrils full of the smell of gunpowder and cow-dung, Kessie looked at Dorothy who was jumping up and down on the plinth of the war memorial, waving her arms. Her mouth was opening and shutting, but Kessie could not hear one single word. The explosion had deafened her! Dorothy was draping the 'Votes for Women *Now*' banner across the field-gun and running towards her. She grabbed Kessie's hand, pulling her down the slope, and by the time they reached the gap in the railings Kessie could hear again and Dorothy was shouting, 'We did it! Oh Kessie, we did it! What a bang! They must have heard it all over Gloucestershire!'

When Kessie and the children returned to London, Tom was at home and Anne ran towards him. 'Daddy, Daddy, did you hear about ve gun going off? I was in bed but I heard it. Mummy heard it, too, and . . .'

301

'I bet she did.'

Tom said he wanted a word with Mummy, in private, he took Kessie's arm and marched her into the sitting-room where he swung her round to face him. 'What the hell did you two imbeciles think you were playing at? You could have killed yourselves.'

'The newspapers say it must have been two lads from the Men's Union, as women could not possibly have fired the cannon.'

'It's me you're talking to, Kess. Remember me? I'm Tom, your husband, who might well be a widower by now.' Kessie looked her husband straight in the eyes, but her lips started to twitch and he was grinning, and then they were both laughing helplessly. He put his hands round her neck. 'If you do anything like that again, I'll strangle you. How *did* you manage it?'

Kessie told him, giving full credit to Miss Devonald. Oppose the policy of violence she might, but firing a Crimean War cannon had captured her imagination and she had not the slightest regret. She hoped it would make Tom realise that wife and mother as she was, she was not giving up the fight, nor was she having another baby straight away just to please him. But she had not forgotten her promise to God, to have four children if He saved Sarah, and that promise she obviously had to keep, in time.

A couple of weeks later Dorothy and Emily Wilding Davison dished up the main course to which firing the Cheltenham cannon had only been an *hors d'oeuvre*. It took Kessie as much by surprise as it did anybody, including Sergeant Brooks who was still, to his chagrin, stuck in 'B' Division of the Special Branch, monitoring suffragette activities.

On a misty February morning he stood among the still smouldering ruins of Mr Lloyd George's new house, close by the golf course at Walton Heath (which the suffragettes had also chewed up). The scientific expert came over with one of those 'Votes for Women' flags in his hand.

'First-class piece of arson, sergeant. No man could have

done a better job. This is only a preliminary assessment, you'll get the detailed report later, but they used coarse-grained powder mixed with percussion caps and nails. Makes for a better explosion. For tinder, it was cloth soaked in wet gunpowder. If you put one end of the tinder in a tin of gunpowder, the other in a bowl packed with more percussion caps and paraffin-soaked wood shavings, and place a slow-burning candle in the middle of the shavings, it gives you plenty of time to scarper before it blows. That's how they did it.'

Muttering 'First-class piece of arson' again and wagging his head in admiration for a thoroughly professional job, the scientific expert returned to prod further among the debris. Sergeant Brooks crushed the 'Votes for Women' flag in his hand. That crazy Wilding Davison woman was behind it and the Devonald girl had planned it. Of that he was certain, since enquiries into Devonald's background had revealed a brother who was a captain in the Royal Engineers.

One day, very soon, Sergeant Brooks vowed that he personally would put a stop to the Wilding Davison and Devonald capers.

High up in the enclosure there was a splendid view of the race-track, and however grim the situation was, however much the odious Government was refusing to budge an inch, Alice refused to miss the English Derby. She swept her binoculars over the moving mosaic of people on Epsom Downs and what an exciting, colourful scene it was, with the sun shining and white clouds scudding in the blue sky.

'I'd have got better odds on the rails, you know.' Johnny was consulting his betting slips.

'Then you should have gone down to the rails, shouldn't you?'

In his grey top hat and morning suit, Johnny played the role of gentleman almost to perfection. If he wasn't Tom, Alice supposed there was much to be said in his favour. Tom! She did her level best not to think about that *bugger*. He had continued to ignore her, but was it entirely his fault? He had made the break with Lady Louise, for her sake, Alice felt sure. Unfortunately, the old bag had reacted badly to his unilateral action, so he'd been forced to turn to Kessie for protection. Frankly, Alice was surprised that she wasn't already *enceinte* again.

Resolutely, Alice returned her attention to the race-track. Today she was here to enjoy herself, to forget about all things unpleasant.

The horses were under starter's orders, the flag went down and they were off! Alice trained her binoculars on the horse she had backed, Nimbus, who was going well, up with the leading bunch. It was a rough race, with much shoving and jostling and brandishing of whips. That most exciting sound, the thud of horses' hooves going at full gallop, was growing louder and she jumped up and down with excitement. 'Come on Nimbus! Come *on!*'

Alice would never be sure what drew her gaze towards Emily Wilding Davison. They'd met her earlier while they had been sauntering round this morning. She had been getting fairly short shrift from the crowds as she had tried to sell copies of *The Suffragette*, and she had said she intended to watch from Tattenham Corner on the unreserved side of the track, and now there she was, tight against the railings by the furthest projection of the bend. The leading horses were thundering past, the noise of their hooves and the roar of the crowds were deafening and Alice returned her attention to the field. 'Come on, Nimbus!'

Her binoculars swivelled back to Emily, who was intently watching the tail-enders. She had her race card to her face and her upheld hand was as steady as a rock. For the rest of her life, Alice never forgot that steadiness, nor the serene expression on Emily's face.

Suddenly, she ducked under the white wooden railings and momentarily Alice could not think what she was doing. Emily raced on to the track, leaping for a horse's head, trying to catch its reins as it pounded past. The horse crashed to the ground, turning a complete somersault as it fell, the jockey was thrown from its back and Emily's body was hurled several feet.

The roar of the crowd stopped abruptly, as if everyone's

throat had been cut, the remainder of the field swerved to avoid the prone bodies, and the thunder of the hooves was the only sound in the awful silence. The fallen horse—Alice suddenly realised it was the King's horse, Anmer—twitched on its side, trying to raise itself, dazedly the jockey hauled himself to his feet, but Emily lay absolutely still. Her hat had come off and her red hair was spread across the ground. Whatever anybody ever asserted to the contrary—that it had been impossible for Miss Wilding Davison to pick out the King's horse in the mêlée round Tattenham Corner— Alice always swore that Emily had deliberately waited for Anmer and deliberately jumped for the King's horse.

The silence lasted a few seconds, then there was pande-monium, people shouting and screaming and running on to the race-track. Alice turned to Johnny whose face was white, stunned. 'Oh my God, Johnny, I'm going to be sick.'

Ten days later, in the late morning of 14th June, 1913, Alice stood in the forecourt of Victoria Station in London. It was a dull, overcast morning, a typical English summer's day, with rain threatening, a chill in the air. Alice shivered but it was not entirely the cold dampness that made her shiver.

Among the crowds that were fast assembling, she saw Kessie, Tom was with her, and Sarah, and little Anne. How sweet she looked in a white muslin dress, long white socks and shoes, a flower-wreathed bonnet, the silky copper-coloured hair hanging down her back. Alice went over to them and Tom smiled briefly. 'Do you want to come inside the station?' she asked. 'I can get you in.'

With Anne holding her hand tightly, Kessie followed Alice inside the station. The train had just steamed in from Epsom and Emily's coffin was being lifted on to the gun carriage. As it was pulled slowly down the platform, Anne's little hand tightened in Kessie's. She had begged to come and Kessie had thought that in later life it might be a day her elder daughter would be proud to have seen.

Outside the station the long lines of mourners were wait-ing, the band struck up Chopin's 'Funeral March', the horses leaned on the traces and the gun carriage rattled up into

305

Grosvenor Place. Immediately behind the coffin walked 'Charlie' Marsh, one of Emily's closest friends, her golden hair hanging loose, a golden cross held high. Behind her Dorothy bore one pole of the banner, '*Dulce et decorum est pro patria mori*', while Alice was one bearer of the banner 'Give me liberty or give me death'—appropriately, because it was her countryman, Patrick Henry, who had uttered those words.

Kessie took Anne to Tom but she begged, 'Please, Mummy, please I come wiv you.'

Kessie shook her head but Tom said, 'Let her. I'll be walking behind you and when she's tired, I'll carry her.'

Behind the girls clad all in white, bearing white madonna lilies, Anne walked between her mother and Aunty Sarah, as the long lines wound through central London towards the church in Bloomsbury where a vicar had been found willing to hold a memorial service. The strains of Chopin's 'Funeral March' rose endlessly up to the grey skies, the tramp, tramp, tramp of feet beat on the cobbled roadways, thousands of women's skirts swish, swish, swished, and the pavements were thick with silent crowds, men doffing their hats, ladies bowing their heads, as the gun carriage rattled by.

They were passing Hyde Park Corner and Kessie thought of the smiling summer days when Emily herself had marched in procession through the streets of London. They swung into Piccadilly and they were passing Hatchett's restaurant, oh dear God, Coronation night, how joyful they had been. Who could possibly have imagined it would have come to this? In Piccadilly Circus a flower seller gave Anne a bunch of violets. 'Bless her little 'eart. It's a lovely turn-out. You've done the poor lady proud.'

They were into Shaftesbury Avenue before Anne's legs gave up, but Sarah carried her piggy-back to the church in Bloomsbury. When the procession reassembled after the service, Tom carried her to King's Cross where, at the request of Emily's widowed mother, the occasion became private. They waited outside the station until five-thirty when they heard the whistle blow and saw the smoke billowing as the Edinburgh train steamed out, bearing Emily Wilding Davison's body on its last journey home to her beloved Northumbrian fells.

Back at The Grove as they had a meal, they were all solemn and quiet until Sarah said, 'I'm glad I came to pay my last respects to Emily. Looking back, I reckon with her something like this was always on the cards. May God rest her soul. We have our glorious martyr, her death has shaken the country, and if Christabel has any sense she'll come back to England, give herself up, and say, look, we've been fighting for our rights for decades now, and this is where you buggers have got us. If she's any sense she'll come back home and rouse the whole country as she roused us women.'

'Christabel no longer has any sense as far as I can make out. So she won't.'

Whenever Tom attacked Christabel, the old loyalty stirred in Kessie. Emily's death had to be a watershed, her supreme sacrifice could not be in vain; Christabel must see that a new initiative had to be taken, that the circle of violence had to be cut. They kept up a correspondence, so would not a visit to Paris be worthwhile?

'Kessie, how lovely to see you, and looking so well.' Christabel kissed her affectionately and she was herself blooming, *très chic* in a pink dress with a hobble skirt and a cherry-red jacket, if plumper, and with her height she could not afford to put on overmuch weight.

Kessie was shown round the spacious *appartement* that Christabel had recently moved into—she wasn't exactly pigging it in Paris—now that the sympathetic French Government had granted her immunity from extradition as a *political* exile.

'*Du thé, Berthe, s'il vous plaît.*'

The maid brought the tea in and Christabel sat with her small Pomeranian dog on her lap. 'How is everything at The Grove? How are the children?'

For the moment she sounded exactly like a society hostess, but then her voice rang with its old pacey tones as she plunged into the topic of the articles she had written in

The Suffragette weekly on such subjects as The Great Scourge of Prostitution, The White Slave Trade, Venereal Diseases and the Sexual Rapacity of Men of All Classes. She was talking, as she had written, in capital letters, and her language was, to say the least, high-flown. How times had changed! Wryly, Kessie thought of the agonies she had gone through penning her letter about sanitary towels to Mr Gladstone, though would Christabel even now write about such a down-to-earth subject, as opposed to her sweeping, over-blown generalisations?

'. . . and I have received hundreds of letters, Kessie, unfolding the most hideous stories of husbands assailing their wives' bodies while they are *enceinte* . . .' Kessie had enjoyed being assailed, sweetly, gently, while she was *enceinte*, '. . . and hundreds more telling of the loathsome diseases men transmit to women and—'

'You wrote that eighty per cent of men are infected with syphilis and gonorrhea. You don't really believe that, do you?'

'Indeed I do.' A flush tinged Christabel's creamy complexion. 'I did not compile the statistics.'

'Where did you get them from?'

'From an unimpeachable source.'

That was no answer, but Christabel had hurried on, saying the best women had always been chaste, that men's base lust was the root of all evil, and that their battle-cry must henceforward be 'Votes for Women, Chastity for Men!' Kessie had not realised until now how deadly serious her friend was about this latest campaign.

'I read an interesting conclusion, based on the researches of an eminent woman expert. She believes that the correct time-span between acts of sexual intercourse should be between two and a half to four years, and . . .'

In the act of swallowing a mouthful of tea, Kessie nearly choked. Solicitously, Christabel patted her on the back. The dog yapped at being disturbed from its position on its mistress's knee. After Kessie had recovered her breath, she took her friend's hand in hers. 'Please, Christabel, listen to me. Forget about purity and lust for the moment. Draw breath. Take stock. You built up the greatest women's movement the world has ever known, don't let it disintegrate, come back home, build it up again on a new base.'

'It is not disintegrating.' Christabel pulled her hand from Kessie's grasp. 'The Cat and Mouse Act is the odious evidence of the Government's legislative bankruptcy and . . .'

How unconsciously imitative people were, Kessie thought. She had heard Tom use almost the same words the day she'd sat in the Ladies' Gallery listening to Reginald McKenna make his astonishing statement about the Government's latest proposals for dealing with the militant suffragettes. Mr McKenna had informed the House of Commons that the Government had no wish to reintroduce forcible feeding. They could not, however, allow an unrepresentative group of reckless women to burn down houses and the like. They therefore intended to imprison the guilty and, if they insisted on hunger-striking, to release them when their physical state had weakened. The release would be conditional, on a temporary licence, and as soon as they were pronounced medically fit, the guilty suffragettes would be returned to prison to complete their sentences.

After Mr McKenna had finished his statement, a silence had settled momentarily over the Chamber. Then Tom had leapt to his feet and said, 'If I understand the Right Honourable Gentleman correctly, and I can scarcely believe that he is proposing such an odious piece of bankrupt legislation, but if I understand him correctly, he intends to play with women like a big fat cat with a mouse, to catch them, to let them go, to recatch them, to re-let them go, on and on and on until . . . what?'

Each time he had said catch-let go, Tom had flung out his left hand, pounced it on the back of the bench in front of him and brought up his hand as if he had indeed caught a mouse. Kessie had not been the only person in the Chamber to gasp at the vividness of the gesture. Since the Liberals had rushed the measure through both Houses of Parliament—how quickly they could get an Act on to the statute book when they wanted—the phrase 'Cat and Mouse Act' had passed into everyday currency.

309

'Our fight has entered its last heroic phrase,' Christabel was saying. 'Only the strongest spirits are in the vanguard. The rest are always followers . . .'

'But they're not following you any more, Christabel. People have left the WSPU in droves. Why do you think the Pethick Lawrences finally left you? Why do you think Sylvia did, your own devoted sister? Why do you think I did? Why . . .'

'Because you are no longer the Kessie Thorpe I cared for. You have become Tom's wife and given yourself over to baby-making.'

There was no animosity or malice in Christabel's tone and indeed it was her very casualness that made the anger surge through Kessie.

Abruptly she stood up. 'And you are not the Christabel Pankhurst I cared for. How can you sit here in Paris while your mother and your members suffer the agonies of the Cat and Mouse Act?'

At the anger in Kessie's voice, Christabel jumped up, too, and the little dog fell unceremoniously from her lap. 'I have given my life to bettering the conditions of women. And when did you last hunger-strike?'

The dog began to bark furiously, running round the hem of Kessie's skirt.

'If your present tactics were likely to sway the Liberals, surely Emily's death would have had some effect?'

Christabel drew herself up.

'Emily would have been with us in our campaign. Controlled violence is the solution—against property not life, for life is sacred to all women—and chastity. Our campaign will purify the world.'

Now the dog was tugging hard at her hemline and Kessie moved her foot.

'Cold baths and continence? Sexual love, real sexual love, is joyous, the root of life itself, not of evil, and I'll tell you what will release women from their *travails* and enable them to enjoy making love to a man—contraception!'

The dog bit Kessie's ankle, she swore softly and gently kicked the animal which started to yelp. Realising what she had done, Christabel bent down and scooped the furry ball into her arms.

'Oh, my poor pet, there, there. Contraception is a licence for lust which no decent woman, no member of the WSPU would indulge in . . .'

'Don't be ridiculous, Christabel!'

Kessie was losing the last threads of her patience, but she made one last effort to turn her friend, her ex-leader, from the path she had chosen.

'Come back home, please, I beg you. See for yourself what the situation is.' Kessie put her hand on Christabel's arm but she shook it off. So she said simply, 'I shall always admire you, Christabel, for the way you roused us and led us so close to victory.'

'You have a peculiar way of expressing your admiration.'

And with that, ignoring Kessie's outstretched hand, Christabel swept from the room, still cradling her little dog.

28

Back in England nothing had changed, except that for their autumn campaign Mrs Pankhurst and her guerillistes hit and ran with greater vigour and violence. Kessie said, 'Oh, Tom, they may be heroic, they may be valiant, but to what purpose? Mr Asquith will not submit to what he sees as the blackmail of violence. *We* have to do something, Tom, we have to take a new initiative.'

'We shall, me luv, but just at the moment you're in no fit state and you shouldn't get excited.'

That was true. Kessie hadn't exactly planned to have another baby, but apart from the fact that she was being horridly sick in the mornings, she didn't mind. With so much occurring that was destructive, baby-making (as Christabel had called it) was at least a creative, affirmative gesture.

Towards the end of October, with the worst of her morning sickness over, Kessie was breakfasting with her daughters when Maggie came in. 'Miss Devonald has just climbed over the back garden fence, ma'am. She's having a wash. Will she be wanting breakfast?'

'I expect so. Set another place, please.'

'Aunty Doroffy,' Anne jumped up, 'how spiffing!'

'*Th*. Do try, darling.'

'May I show Aunty Doro . . . ffy,' Anne tried but did not succeed, 'my new coat and hat? Please Mummy.'

For her fourth birthday, Kessie had bought her elder daughter the outfit she had long coveted and of which she was inordinately proud. 'No, you may sit down and finish your breakfast.'

Scrubbed and shining, looking like an advertisement for Pear's soap, Dorothy bounced into the room to greet them enthusiastically and, with a flourish, to present Anne and Con with a stiff white sheet of printed paper.

'As promised, the "mouse" licence of prisoner 235,649 Dorothy Pauline Devonald, sentenced at Bow Street Magistrates' Court on the sixteenth day of July, nineteen hundred and thirteen, to eighteen months with hard labour in Holloway prison, for malicious damage to property and having the rotten bad luck to run slap into the arms of a village policeman.' She laughed. 'It doesn't actually say *that*, *mes enfants*, but that's what happened. It was a misty morn and I just did not see him. On the twenty-second day of July a conditional discharge was hereby ordered for said prisoner, due to the state of her health. Said prisoner was supposed to report back for hunger-striking duty as soon as her health had improved.'

With a dramatic bow, Dorothy handed over the licence. Con thanked her sweetly and Anne squealed with delight. 'We shall keep it for ever and ever.'

'Just you see you do. I've been offered *fifty pounds* for it, and Mummy can't give you a "mouse" licence, can she? Goody, stewed prunes. I adore them.'

It was time for Anne to leave for her nursery school, but she went reluctantly because she loved being with adults.

Dear little Con, however, trotted upstairs obediently. Kessie watched Dorothy eating her stewed prunes, scrambled eggs, sausages, Vienna steak, piles of hot toast and lashings of Maggie's home-made marmalade. As she paused for a rest she said, 'Honestly, Kessie, Mr McKenna must be stark staring bonkers if he imagines any of us will meekly submit to a medical examination and tamely trot back into prison.'

'What exactly have you been up to, Didi?'

'Nothing in particular.' Dorothy looked sly. 'Well, actually, Olga and I were on a mission last night.' Dorothy buttered the last of the toast and grinned at Kessie. 'I can't go home because the pigs are snooping around at the moment. Mummy found one hiding behind the dustbins the other day and Daddy had a fearful row with a detective. After all, he comes to London to research and write, not to have Special Branch clumping through the garden. Nobody's keeping a watch on your house these days, no reason to . . . you don't mind me coming, do you?'

Kessie shook her head. Didi was still such a child. Being a 'mouse' on the run was only half-fun, whatever she might pretend to the contrary, and in this question of loyalties there was no doubt where Kessie's would always lie, despite the dismissive note that had crept into Didi's attitude towards her.

The detective had just come on duty when he saw the maid taking the Whitworth child down the hill, for Dorothy had been wrong and an intermittent watch *was* being kept on the house in The Grove. Several of Tom's Irish nationalist and Russian Menshevik acquaintances interested Special Branch, as much as his wife's suffragette links. The detective's attention was drawn to a motor car parked near the public house,. by the hens that had settled on its bonnet. (Dorothy had deliberately not parked it in front of the Whitworths', just to be on the safe side.) He went across to shoo them away but something peculiar about the number plate caught his eye. Bending down to examine it, he realised it was false, and that the one underneath was in his book as registered to the WSPU—LS 4587.

In one of the new wooden telephone kiosks, very useful things they were, he put through a call. Sergeant Brooks sounded almost excited. 'The top plate was LR 968? We've got her. It's Devonald. The night-watchman took down the number as they drove off, and from his description of the fleeing figures, one of them was Devonald. You stay put. I'll get somebody round the back of the house straight away. Arrest her if she comes to claim the car. I'll be there as soon as I can.'

After a while the maid and the child returned, and after a further while the Hartley woman arrived, a real stunner she was. Otherwise nothing happened and the detective went on watching.

Vi explained to Kessie that there was an outbreak of chicken pox in the district, so, as half-term was almost upon them, the headmistress had decided to close the kindergarten. With Alice's arrival, Kessie sent Anne up to the nursery, and their coffee was brought to them in the sitting-room.

Kessie poured.

'Dorothy's asleep upstairs. Do *you* know what she's been up to?'

'I honestly don't, Kessie. As long as they follow Christabel's guidelines, those on active service work from their own initiative. My task is to publicise their missions *afterwards*.'

Alice lit a cigarette and Kessie said, 'I actually saw a sight that made me laugh the other day. A group of young suffragettes circling round two policemen, chanting "Syphilis and Gonorrhea, Syphilis and Gonorrhea"! You don't believe this sexual stuff Christabel is dishing out, do you?'

Privately, Alice did not but she was not going to admit this to Kessie.

There was a knock on the door and Maggie came into the room. 'There's a Sergeant Brooks wanting to see you, Mrs Whitworth.'

Sergeant Brooks was right behind Maggie. He apologised for intruding upon the ladies' coffee hour, but would he

314

be correct in assuming Miss Dorothy Devonald was in the house?

Kessie's mind raced. She had to give Maggie time to waken Dorothy, get her out, hide her, do something with her. 'Why should Miss Devonald be here?'

'Her motor car is outside—the vehicle in which she and another young woman were seen escaping after causing an estimated thousand pounds' worth of damage at a timber yard early this morning.'

'Oh.' So that was what Dorothy and Olga had been doing. 'Really?'

At that moment, the door opened and Anne came in, beaming from ear to ear. She was wearing her 'little polar bear' outfit, the soft white fur coat and hat, the white gaiters wrinkling on her legs. Slipping her hands into the fluffy white muff hanging from her neck on a white cord, she said, 'You haven't seen what Mummy bought me for my birfday, have you, Aunty Alice? I've shown it to Aunty Doroffy and she says . . .'

'Oh!' Alice shrieked, dropping the jade holder into the ash-tray, stretching her arms towards Anne, 'It's simply divine. Let me look at you. Turn around. I had a Snow Princess outfit when I was a little girl, but it wasn't half so nice as yours.'

Alice was chattering away, Anne was twirling around, and Sergeant Brooks was watching the scene with great interest. 'My, my what a beautiful little lady you are,' he said. 'Just like your Mummy. But you have a look of your Daddy, too.'

Delightedly, Anne smiled up at him. 'Do you know my Daddy?'

'Yes, I know your Daddy. And your Aunty Dorothy. Just been showing your lovely coat to her, have you?'

Loudly, Alice said she'd simply love another cup of coffee. Sergeant Brooks cut in swiftly. 'Could you wait just one moment, miss. I was asking the little girl a question.'

Kessie cleared her throat.

'I don't think you have any right to question my daughter, sergeant.'

315

'It was a very simple question, Mrs Whitworth.' He smiled down at Anne. 'Is Aunty Dorothy upstairs at the moment?'

Anne was a sensitive child, sensitive to mood and atmosphere, and the atmosphere in the sun-filled sitting-room was as taut as a bow-string. While Kessie held her breath, with a slight frown she looked up at the benignly smiling Sergeant Brooks, then her gaze swivelled towards her mother. But Kessie could make no move. Oh, dear Lord, she didn't want Anne lying to the police, but on her answer Dorothy's freedom could depend. Would Anne remember what she had been told in the past? Not to talk about Aunty Dorothy coming to The Grove? Could she understand anything of what being a 'mouse' meant? She was only four years old.

The silence seemed interminable. Then, very slowly, Anne shook her head. It was Sergeant Brooks' turn to frown and his tone was sharp as he said, 'Are you sure your Aunty Dorothy isn't here?'

'I haven't seen Aunty Doroffy—'

'Since you showed her your coat.'

Sergeant Brooks gave her a tight smile. Bloody hell, they had tiny tots like her trained to lie, and people said Mrs Whitworth was a nice woman and wondered why she had married that working-class Socialist bastard. Devonald was in the house and she was not escaping from him.

When Sergeant Brooks had gone and Dorothy had climbed out from under a pile of blankets in the chest on the landing, Anne said, 'You didn't want me to tell vat man Aunty Doroffy was here, did you, Mummy?'

'No, my darling, I did not.' Kessie wondered how she could explain to Anne when a fib was permissible and when the truth was imperative.

For a few minutes Sergeant Brooks stood outside the Whitworth house, thinking rapidly. He had nourished the faint hope that Mrs Whitworth would come clean and hand over Devonald, but he should have known better. A search warrant would be difficult to obtain because Whitworth was a Member of Parliament, God help the country, and if

316

by any chance they did not find Devonald there would be the devil to pay. But she was not slipping through his fingers this time. Briskly, he walked towards the telephone kiosk to obtain the authority for his plan of action.

It was Alice who first noticed that Sergeant Brooks had not gone away, on the contrary, the number of policemen in front of the house had increased. Then the gardener, Peg-Leg Pete, put his head round the kitchen door.

'They'rn at the back just beyond the fence, too. If they sets foot in my gardin, they'll get the pitchfork in 'em, so they will.'

A crowd began to gather in front of The Grove and the telephone started to ring. The callers turned out to be reporters enquiring if the rumours that Mrs Whitworth had given sanctuary to Miss Devonald were true? Alice dealt with them, dismissing the story as mere gossip. By mid-afternoon there were hordes of children outside, delivery boys leaning on their bicycles, nurse-maids with perambulators, assorted passers-by, all staring at the Whitworth house. A large woman brought her camp-stool, seated herself on it and took out her knitting.

'Talk about Madame Defarge and the guillotine!' said Alice.

'Oh, lordy,' said Dorothy. 'I am sorry, Kessie.'

The evening newspapers arrived through the letter-box. On the front page of the *Star*, underneath the headline 'The Siege of The Grove' were photographs of Dorothy and Kessie, while the *Evening News* enquired whether the most wanted mouse was now in a trap. Within an hour of the newspapers' arrival, the crowd increased, until even with the windows tightly shut the noise outside was like the rush of the sea on the shingly beach below Willow Bank. When Kessie drew the curtains and was momentarily silhouetted against the light, she heard the muffled cheer. At least the crowd was on their side.

'Isn't it exciting?' said Alice, who obviously had no intention of going home.

It was and it wasn't. Should Dorothy be caught, the consequences of harbouring a wanted 'criminal' could be unpleasant, especially since Tom had little patience with Didi or her current activities.

They were having supper when they heard the extra-ordinary whirring, jarring noises. As Kessie opened the curtains, the glare almost blinded her and Alice said, 'Suffering rattlesnakes!'

Two great arc lamps were trained on to the front of the house. It was their generators which were making the racket, and in their vivid bluish light the scene was like carnival night at the Wakes Week fair. The whole width of The Grove was jammed solid, tea stalls were doing a roaring trade, and on upturned boxes men in bowler hats were signalling to each other. Alice turned to Dorothy.

'They must be taking bets on whether or not you escape.'

In front of the house Sergeant Brooks was talking to the neighbours. After a while he disappeared into the next-door house, and the three women went back to the table. Almost immediately, the dining-room door burst open. In came Anne and Con; in her excitement Con tripped over her nightdress as her sister got the news out.

'Mummy, they're putting lights up in Mr Harker's garden.'

Kessie ran into the conservatory and blazing over the hedge to the left were two more arc lamps. She looked towards the Laycocks' garden on the right but that was in shadow, which made sense since the Harkers' disapproval of suffragettes and Socialists was as firm as ever, while the Laycocks on the right had long since become staunch supporters.

'I think we had better have a conference,' Kessie said. 'And you two, back to bed.'

'Oh, Mummy.'

'Bed.'

When Anne and Con had gone they went into the sitting-room, Maggie, Ruby and Vi with them. Kessie chaired the conference.

'We've got to get Dorothy out of here—sooner or later that sergeant is going to come back with a search warrant. It's a cloudy night, hardly any moon, so that's on our

318

side. Escape through the front door is obviously impossible. So is the kitchen or conservatory door. The coal-hole is at the front, isn't it, Maggie?' She nodded. 'That's no good then. Dorothy can't crawl up through that. It has to be the Laycocks' side. Where are the drainpipes?'

Maggie was able to tell them there was a drainpipe close to Mr and Mrs Whitworth's bedroom window. Kessie looked at Dorothy. 'You can climb down a drainpipe, can't you?'

''Course I can. But not in this skirt. I need trousers.'

There was a burst of merriment at the thought of tiny Didi in Tom's trousers, the only ones in the house, but it quickly subsided and Ruby offered to run up a pair from an old black skirt. While she went to the sewing machine, Kessie outlined her scheme for effecting Dorothy's escape once she was beyond The Grove and the back garden.

'What a good wheeze!' Didi enthused and Alice agreed, if with an expression of astonishment, Kessie felt, that she should still be able to devise an escape route.

Shortly before midnight, Dorothy stood by the window in Kessie's bedroom, her hair tucked under a dark beret of Anne's, her face smeared with a burnt cork, wearing a thick jumper of Kessie's and the trousers Ruby had made. Maggie inched up the window and Dorothy blew them all kisses before disappearing behind the curtains.

'Heavens, I hope she makes it!' Kessie breathed.

Crouched on the window ledge, every fibre of Dorothy's being was concentrated on the task of defeating the pigs and making good her escape. Viewed from this vantage point, the whole garden seemed to be bathed in a brightly quivering light. Not a mouse could move without being seen. Oh yes, this mouse could, for there was some shadow down the right-hand side. Dorothy took a deep breath, slid her darkly gloved hands towards the drainpipe, gripped them tightly round it and with one clean, swift movement, swung her body. There were shouts from the Harkers' garden, clinging to the drainpipe Dorothy flattened herself against the wall, and the noise subsided. Swiftly, she monkey-slid down the drainpipe and her feet were on the ground.

Crouching into the tiniest bundle, she started to crawl across the flower beds, hugging the shadow of the bushes. Mew, mew, mew, oh lordy, it was one of Kessie's cats, Amber's elegantly pointed face was brushing against hers, mew, mew, meow, the glare from the lamps seemed like daylight and they would see her any second now. Dorothy pushed at the animal and Amber shot into the middle of the lawn. There was uproar from the Harkers' garden, pinned in the brightness Amber's short fur rose like a brush, her eyes glistened, she emitted the most tremendous yowl, and it was Dorothy's chance. All attention was focused on the petrified, howling cat, and with the sound of the policemen's laughter in her ears, Dorothy crawled to the end of the garden, climbed over the fence and landed in a breathless heap on the other side.

Now she had to get through the woods where there was a dog barking fiercely, so she must move quickly before it picked up her scent. Ducking and running, Dorothy sped from tree to tree and the glow of a cigarette end warned her to change course. Smoking on duty! No woman would do that. Another shape wavered, warning her to veer again, but it was difficult to tell the men from the trees. The barking was way behind her, the trees were thinning, in the distance she could see the lighter surface of the water in the ponds. She had nearly made it . . . oh lordy, the policeman was in front of her and Dorothy could not stop herself from running straight into him.

For a couple of seconds they stared at each other in riveted astonishment, she saw the whites of his eyes, but her reactions were the faster. Dorothy backed off, the policeman grabbed at her but missed, and she was haring down the slope towards the pond. Then she heard the blessed sound, the loud barking noise that did not come from a dog.

'Didi, Didi, over here.'

Right on the edge of the woods, Olga was revving away like a mad thing on her motor bicycle. Dorothy raced towards her, Olga stretched out her hand to haul her into the side-car, with a hard kick on the pedal they were off, careering down the slope towards the ponds, up the other side towards Hampstead and freedom. Clinging to the sides of the car, Dorothy turned her head and the dark shapes of the policemen were lumbering far behind.

She had made it! Hurrah for Olga! And Kessie, too.

In the middle of the morning, in the middle of Hampshire, having decided to drive down to Stephen's cottage in Devon, which was being used as a 'mouse-hole,' a very tired Olga crashed the motor bicycle and side-car into a telegraph pole. Neither she nor Dorothy was seriously hurt, but they were dazed, and despite her being dressed as a boy, the local constabulary recognised Miss Devonald from their Wanted posters.

Both girls were sentenced to eighteen months with hard labour, which meant that Dorothy now had three and a half years to serve. Stoutly, she denied that she had been in the Whitworths' house, saying she had been intending to make for her friends' abode but had been trapped in the woods, until she decided to make the break under the cover of darkness.

A likely tale, Sergeant Brooks thought. But if he was satisfied with his expensive efforts to trap her, then so were his superiors, because the well-publicised furore had re-focused the Home Secretary's attention on the destructive menace the militant suffragettes had become, and the failure of his ludicrous Cat and Mouse Act. Miss Devonald, so Sergeant Brooks had heard, had a surprise in store for her in Holloway.

29

Dorothy was not released again on a mouse licence. After five days of hunger-strike, she was forcibly fed. It was the new official policy for ultra-militants.

Christmas came, crowded streets, carol singers, decorating the Christmas tree at The Grove, wrapping up presents; Anne and Con jumping on Mummy and Daddy's bed at half past six in the morning, look what Father Christmas had brought; turkey and chestnut stuffing, mince pies, plum pudding, Christmas cake . . . while in Holloway Dorothy was still being forcibly fed twice a day.

How long could she endure?

On New Year's Day, Kessie's twenty-ninth birthday, she took the girls to see Aunt Ada. The drawing-room at Thurloe Square had been turned into a bed-sitting room, not that Aunt Ada did much sitting these days but she was in the armchair, wrapped in a rug, when they arrived. How frail she was, but how indomitable her spirit.

After she had kissed Anne and Con and given them her Victorian marble board to play with, she said, 'I hear Tom's been raging again in the House of Commons. Any news of Dorothy's release?'

'No.'

Furiously, she shook her head before looking over the top of her pince-nez at Kessie. 'What's all this I hear about you and Tom and the Pethick Lawrences and the other renegades forming a new women's suffrage society?'

'We're *not* renegades,' Kessie protested. 'The whole idea of the United Suffragists is to get everybody together who's dedicated to votes for women, men as well, everybody from all classes and political parties. We have to make a new initiative. We can't go on like this. Can we?'

'No,' Aunt Ada admitted and Kessie took the wrinkled hands in hers. 'Why don't you join us?'

'Old loyalties die hard.'

'Yes, I know they do.'

'Well, I'll think about it.'

Hetty, the ex-lodger who had become the faithful friend and nurse, brought in a birthday tea for Kessie, the children helped her blow out the candles and afterwards Aunt Ada gave them all presents, an exquisitely crocheted dressing-table set, tablecloth and matching doilies for her niece, a crocheted doll and rabbit for her great-nieces.

'Mustn't forget my little treasures.' Anne and Con hugged her, and what a surprisingly maternal streak Aunt Ada had revealed. Over the tops of their copper and auburn heads she said, 'I'm looking forward to the next one. Another girl for us?'

Kessie smiled and watched Anne appropriate the rabbit. She wanted to say to Con, 'Assert yourself, sweetheart,' but she was happily cradling the doll. If Anne was the stuff of which suffragettes were made, her sister was not, though when her daughters grew up women's emancipation would be taken for granted. Each could follow the path she chose.

It was a happy afternoon and when they left, Aunt Ada looked tired but content. Some time during the night, she died. When Hetty went in to see her at midnight she was fine, but when she took in the early morning cup of tea, Aunt Ada was dead.

A deeply distressed Kessie insisted on going north for the funeral, for her aunt's last wish had been to be buried in Mellordale. It was the bleakest of winter days as they stood in the graveyard clinging to the hillside where Tom's mother lay, the air biting into the marrow, a dank mist rolling across the moors. Kessie broke down as a suffragette piper played the Last Post and the coffin was lowered into the ground, draped in the WSPU's green, purple and white flag.

After the funeral repast, they sat in front of the fire at Milnrow and Papa said, 'You're a rich woman now, Kessie. By the left, our Ada had a good business head on her shoulders, she made her money work for her.'

Bleakly, Kessie smiled. Apart from the Thurloe Square house which she had left to Hetty, Aunt Ada had left everything to her. Kessie intended to give a fair slice of the money—well over five thousand pounds—to Sarah's People's Centre, and Tom could have Milnrow as his base in The Dales.

'It's the blackest New Year I can remember, in every respect.' Tom lifted an eyebrow. Well, yes, there *was* that, the prospect of the new baby. 'Cheer up, Kessie,' Sarah said, 'it's always darkest before the dawn. You'll see, 1914 will be the year the sun comes up.'

In February, Dorothy was finally released on licence from Holloway on medical grounds. She was rushed to a suffragette nursing home, but before Kessie could visit her and never mind what people thought about heavily pregnant ladies appearing in public, Stephen said, 'We've smuggled her to a mouse-hole, old thing; she's in a bad way, worse than she thinks.'

A month later, Kessie was walking slowly past the telephone in the hall at The Grove when it hiccoughed into a ring. 'Dorothy! Where are you?'

'In the telephone kiosk round the corner. May I come and see you?'

'Of course, why ever not?'

'Well, you know what happened last time.'

'Nobody's watching us any more, I assure you. One thing Tom is very good at is making a fuss and, believe me, he created the most enormous stink over "the siege of The Grove". Alice is here. Do come.'

Kessie asked Maggie to send their tea into the conservatory, she told Alice the news, Anne and Con pressed their noses against the glass, waiting excitedly for Dorothy to appear. After a while she climbed over the fence, jumped across the clump of daffodils and came jauntily up the path, but the old bounce was not in her step. As she neared the door, Anne exclaimed, 'Mummy, she's wearing specs!'

'Poor Dorothy!' Alice said, 'They're so disfiguring.'

'Don't make any comment,' Kessie turned to Anne and Con, 'either of you.'

They greeted Dorothy affectionately, while Anne and Con did their best not to stare at her spectacles, and then they asked how she was?

'Absolutely A1. Right as rain again.'

Her voice was slightly hoarse, the clear clarinet edge dulled, which was not surprising, for the feeding tube had been thrust down her throat nearly two hundred times. When her throat could stand no more, they had fed her nasally, sticking the tube up one nostril for the morning feed, the other for the evening feed. The mere thought of that made Kessie feel sick, and how could Dorothy be all

324

right when such monstrous things had been done to her? How could it have happened that the Government of the greatest nation in the world had come to do such things to a child? For Dorothy was not yet twenty-one, not yet of age. When they had finished their tea—Didi had only pecked at Maggie's delectable scones and cakes—she asked the girls if they would like a game of cards and while she was sorting them out, she kept pushing her spectacles up her nose.

'They suit you,' Kessie said, 'You look nice in them. *Distinguée.*'

'Mm.' Dorothy shuffled busily. 'Everything stayed blurred, so Stephen got an oculist to see me and he said it was probably the result of the rotten light in the cells and eff-eff itself.' Old hands referred thus to forcible feeding. 'It's nice to see clearly, so I don't mind what I look like.'

Defiantly she dealt out the cards, she and the girls started to play, while Alice lit another cigarette—how heavily she smoked these days—and said, 'What *do* you hope to achieve by forming yet another women's suffrage society, Kessie?'

Kessie hesitated. She wasn't sure that, in Dorothy's presence, this was a useful topic.

'The whole point about the United Suffragists, Alice, is that we are *not* just another women's suffrage society. We welcome women *and* men, you see, anyone who is dedicated to obtaining votes for women.' She hesitated again. Dorothy appeared to be absorbed in the game, not listening. 'And we have to break the circle of violence. The Liberals won't do it, and Mrs Pankhurst is no longer capable of taking the initiative because she's half out of her mind with the constant hunger-striking. Christabel should take the lead, but she sits in Paris, hearing only what she wants to hear, certain she's the only person marching in step—'

With a sudden movement, Dorothy swept the playing cards from the table, and leapt to her feet. 'I won't let you talk about Christabel like that. You know what a *jehad* is? A Holy War. We are engaged in a *jehad*. Emily knew that and that's why she sacrificed her life. You knew it once, Kessie, but you have forgotten. How dare you from the sidelines criticise *anything* Christabel does, Christabel who was your friend, whom you went to prison with, Christabel who has planned every move of our campaign from the moment she stood up in the Free Trade Hall—you were there to hear her—who knows we must meet brute force with the force of our wills—'

Slowly, painfully, Kessie had risen during this outburst, and in an icily clear voice she interrupted. 'Dorothy, I realise you are not fully recovered from what they did to you in Holloway, but oh . . . oh . . .' She bent forward, clutching her hands over her stomach, before putting out her right hand towards Alice, 'Oh, I'm starting, oh . . .'

Anne ran to her mother's side and cried, 'Mummy, Mummy, what's ve matter?'

Con started to sob and Alice said, 'Go and get Maggie. There's a good girl, Anne. Mummy will be all right. Come on, Kessie . . .'

Alice assisted Kessie into the main part of the house, and Dorothy stood quite still, the rage dying away, the horror at what she had done replacing it. Her temper flared fearfully easily at the moment and Kessie's appearance had embarrassed her—she was simply huge this time, her stomach protruding like a monster gumboil—though she wouldn't have upset her for anything in the world. But she should not have spoken about Christabel like that, she should not.

'Mr Whitworth.' Tom swung round from staring down into the hospital forecourt and dropped another cigarette end into the hillock in the ugly pot ashtray. 'Mr Whitworth, your wife has had twins. A boy and a girl.'

For a few seconds he stared blankly at the sister, whose manner was as starchy as her cap and apron, before laughing delightedly. Twins! That was why Kessie had been rushed to hospital and what the complication had been. He checked his delighted laughter. Twins. Poor Kess. 'My wife's all right? Can I see her and . . . them?'

'Not at the moment, I'm afraid, Mr Whitworth. If you would care to come with me, Mr Merton will speak to you.'

Merton was the obstetrician, a supercilious, uncommunicative, upper-crust gent, though Stephen had assured

326

Tom that Kessie could not be in better hands. He followed the sister to a comfortable office where a weary Mr Merton was standing by the desk. He asked sister for two cups of tea which were promptly produced.

'Cigarette, Mr Whitworth?' Tom accepted one from the elegant silver case. 'Being the bearer of unpleasant tidings is one of the harsher aspects of my profession. The labour was long and arduous and the babies were, as you know, premature, which twins frequently are. The condition of both, the boy in particular, is causing us grave concern. As is your wife's.'

Into the long bleak silence Tom finally said, 'You mean they may not live and my wife may die?' Mr Merton flicked the ash into a crystal ashtray. Whitworth was a northerner and a Socialist which made him doubly distasteful. Calling a spade a spade and digging it into the dirt was unnecessary, but his wife and new-born babies were unlikely to survive. Politely he said, 'We must not look on the gloomy side.'

The next three days were a living nightmare, blurred and shadowy, the only reality sitting by Kessie's bedside. She was exhausted, dark rings under her eyes, a blueish tinge to her skin, and Merton said it was her heart they were worried about, the heart that had been affected by forcible feeding. For God's sake, why hadn't she told him? Had he known, he would never have let her have another child.

At the beginning she was conscious. 'I'm tired, Tom, so very, very tired. You can't imagine what it was like. When they said there was another.'

'It's all over now, Kess. They're beautiful.' With a touch of her old spirit she said, 'I'm glad you think so. I've only seen them once. They took them away. They both look like you, the boy especially. You'll never be able to say they're not your children.'

'Kess, don't. What shall we call them?'

'Kate and Mark.' Her voice had its clearest notes but then she closed her eyes, her head moved fretfully and she put her hand to her neck. 'I want my necklace.' She had several necklaces and Tom asked which one? Her head moved even more fretfully, 'The one you gave me. At the fair.'

327

She became very upset about her necklace, so Tom rushed back to The Grove. He and Maggie searched everywhere in the bedroom. It wasn't in her jewel box, so they went through her drawers, and turning over her neatly piled underskirts, camisoles and stockings, with their fragrant bags of lavender, turned over Tom's heart. While they were still searching, Anne put her head round the door and when she was upset she looked most like Kessie. Tom asked her to help look for Mummy's necklace. Going through Mummy's private things made Anne feel important, excited and just a little bit frightened. She picked up the pile of Daddy's letters that he had lifted from the back of the drawer and left on the dressing table top. She pulled at the ribbon tying the letters and it fell to the floor.

The gilt necklace with the red glass horseshoes that Tom had bought from the diddicoy girl at the Wakes Week fair, as a memento for Miss Thorpe.

Back at the hospital, he fastened the necklace round Kessie's neck and she smiled faintly. 'So tired . . . just want to sleep. . . .' She spoke less and less and much of what she said was incoherent. 'God . . . a sense of humour . . . Sarah . . . promised four . . . two in one fell swoop . . . forcible feeding . . . no surprise . . . Christabel right . . . women stronger . . . very, very tired. . . .'

The babies, Kate and Mark were in a special room by themselves, the staff were working like Trojans to save their lives and the sister's starchiness had diminished. 'They're bonny little fighters, Mr Whitworth. We'll win through!'

Tom sat holding Kessie's hand. Mr Merton came into the room. Underneath that disdainful manner and splintered accent, he wasn't a bad chap, he had let Tom stay without argument. 'Your wife has great will-power, Mr Whitworth.'

'She's a suffragette.'

'Ah, yes.'

Alice drove the Napier up Haverstock Hill. Holding out her right gloved hand she made the turn into Downshire Crescent, continued a short way along and parked the automobile in the forecourt of the Hampstead General Hospital.

What hateful places hospitals were, the sickly smells of antiseptic and disinfectant, of ether and cooked cabbage. Kessie could not be dying, not Kessie, and what would Tom do if she died? He was not the man to live without a woman and after a decent period of mourning he would re-marry. Anne was a handful, but an intelligent one, Con was the sweetest child, and if the twins died Tom would not have a son. The idea of having a baby rather appalled Alice but to give Tom a son . . .

Alice was shown into a waiting-room with ugly chocolate-coloured walls. Sarah was there with Mr Thorpe. He was an old, old man. 'Come in, luv, we're waiting to go in. Tom's with her.' The tears flooded into Alice's eyes and she realised that the enormous bouquet she was clutching must seem ridiculously out of place. She turned to go, saying she'd come back later.

'Nay, stay, Alice luv. Kessie's allus spoken highly of you. She'd want to see you.'

His native Lancashire accent was thick with emotion. Sarah jumped up and walked to the window, and the silence was as heavy as a ton weight. After a few minutes Alice smiled and moved into the corridor. She could not stay in there, silently waiting, waiting, and how she longed for a cigarette.

Tom came out of a room along the corridor and leaned against the wall, closing his eyes. Silently, Alice watched him. His face was grey with tiredness, he hadn't shaved and the stubble was dark on his chin, the tousled black hair falling on to his forehead. She walked up to him and said softly, 'How is she, Tom?'

Opening his eyes, he looked straight at her, but he wasn't seeing her. It came upon Alice like a thunderbolt. Tom didn't care for her. He had never cared for her. All these years she had been deceiving herself, living in a dream world. And she had been jealous of Kessie, yes she had, she who considered jealousy a ridiculous emotion, and how could she have had such terrible thoughts as Kessie lay dying? She didn't want Kessie to die, she couldn't imagine never seeing Kessie again.

An immaculate frock-coated figure came from the room. He bowed slightly towards Alice and he had a frightfully English voice, 'Are you a friend of Mr and Mrs Whitworth?'

Alice said yes, and she meant it with all her heart.

'Can you persuade Mr Whitworth to go home and rest a while? Mrs Whitworth's condition is unlikely to change within the next few hours.'

Vehemently Tom shook his head, and Sarah came into the corridor, moving to his side. Neither of them spoke but they didn't need to: they were from the same nest and Alice felt like the intruding cuckoo. The doctor sighed and said if Mr Whitworth wished he could use his office to rest.

Alice left the hospital and drove down to the Strand, where she sat in the cool calm of St Clement Danes Church, praying for Kessie.

'Mr Whitworth, Mr Whitworth.'

Tom was fighting his way through a dense forest, there was a bright light in the distance which he knew he had to reach because Kessie was somewhere behind it, but he kept stumbling and Kessie was in danger of being blinded by the light, and there were serpents in the forest, their forked tongues darting towards him, and he had to avoid them, otherwise he would die in poisoned agony before he reached Kessie.

'Mr Whitworth, wake up.'

Bleary-eyed Tom stared up at Mr Merton.

'She's sinking fast, Mr Whitworth.'

His mind suddenly as clear as the moorland Mellor stream, he wanted to shout, she's not a ship, she's Kessie, my Kess. 'Can I stay with her?'

Mr Merton nodded.

The blind in the room was half-drawn to shade the bright spring sunlight, but the chestnut tones in Kessie's hair were gleaming. Tom took her hand in his, her skin had lost its blueish tinge, it was as smooth and white and cold as . . . not death, as alabaster, and the veins were a deep purple against its pallor. Occasionally, she made a fretful movement of her

330

head and her free hand clutched at the bedspread but otherwise she lay still.

Sarah and Mr Thorpe came in and her father broke down, sobbing about his little kestrel Kessie. Sarah said fiercely, 'She won't give up, Tom, not Kessie.' But he wasn't really seeing or hearing either of them. They went out and he sat talking to her.

'You can't leave me, Kess, I can't live without you. Anne and Con have been sobbing their hearts out for you. Why didn't you tell me about your heart, me luv? Hundreds of people need you and love you, Kess. The telephone never stops ringing. We could do with our own switchboard. We've so many flowers we could open our own Kew Gardens. We've so many letters and telegrams we could start our own post office. And Christabel's telegraphed. I know you'll be pleased about that, Kess. She has a heart under all that steel. Your babies need you, Kess. They're going to live and so are you, my darling. I love you, I love you, I love you. I've allus loved you, Kess, and I allus will. I swear I shall never, never be unfaithful again. I don't know why I have been. You're the one who likes explanations. You tell me when you're better.'

'Mr Whitworth, dear,' the nurse's gentle Irish voice broke into his soft, steady flow. 'She can't hear you.'

Tom ignored it and went on talking to Kessie. 'Come on, Kess, you're a fighter, my darling, come on, fight as you've never fought before. Live for me, Kess, "For where thou art, there is the world itself, With every several pleasures in the world; And where thou art not, desolation" . . . come on, my darling . . .'

The nurse looked down at him, holding his wife's hand in his, stroking her chestnut hair, running his long fingers along her deathly pale face, reciting poetry to her. Father McCormack said Socialists were terrible wicked people, setting class against class, and themselves against God. He said the suffragettes were as bad, going against God's inviolable law, 'Thou shalt be under thy husband's power and he shall have dominion over thee.' But Mrs Whitworth had been so brave and Mr Whitworth was a lovely man.

How could either of them be wicked and sinful when God was love and they loved each other so much? Perhaps God was speaking to Mrs Whitworth through her husband, telling her to live.

Twelve hours later, at close to midnight, Tom climbed the stairs at The Grove and he didn't know whether he had the energy to reach the empty bedroom. Maggie had left the lamp above the linen chest lit but the landing was shadowy. He saw the dark shape by their bedroom door, those damned cats, Kessie's cats, but he couldn't blame Maggie for not locking them out. God knew, she loved Kessie and she had kept the house going in the last nightmare days.

Hard against the door Anne was fast asleep, curled in a ball, one arm flung across Jasper's thick fur, while Amber stretched sleekly along her back. The tears stung Tom's eyes and he took several deep breaths before lifting his daughter gently into his arms. Half-asleep, she nestled against him. 'I want my Mummy. When's she coming home, Daddy?'

'Not yet, sweetheart. But she will soon.'

The hospital clock had struck nine when Kessie's eyelids quivered, slowly they opened and she looked at him, a tiredly puzzled expression in her lovely hazel eyes. She smiled slightly and sighed. 'Oh Tom, I feel as if I've been on a very long journey. Somewhere into the bowels of the earth. I could hear you calling me.' The eyelids closed but the slight smile stayed on her lips.

Mr Merton came in—he had shown a concern above and beyond the call of duty—and after he examined her, almost disbelievingly, he said, 'I think she's going to pull through, Mr Whitworth.'

They left Kessie in a gentle sleep and had a drink in his room. Then he said, 'We're not out of the woods yet. Her heart will be permanently affected, you do realise that. But if your wife takes care and leads a very quiet life, she could live to a decent age.'

The elation drained from Tom and half of him seemed to

turn to stone. Kess, vital, active, ardent, enthusiastic Kess, an invalid for the rest of her life. Oh God, you bastard, if You exist, You are the originator of the Cat and Mouse Act.

30

'Johnny, something terrible has happened.'

Alice was waiting in his dressing-room at the Criterion as he came off-stage after the final curtain. He was playing in a very successful revival of *Arms and the Man*. Now, anxiously, he said, 'Is it Kessie? She's not had a relapse, poor darling?'

'No it is *not* Kessie. They're threatening to deport me, Johnny, *me*, as an undesirable alien.'

Nobody could be more filled with admiration than she for Kessie's plucky fight for life, for the cheerfulness with which she was accepting her invalid state, but the entire world did not revolve around Kessie. As swiftly as her sleekly tight skirt would allow, Alice paced round the dressing-room, telling Johnny that Lionel had given her the news, and if her brother-in-law was a pompous ass, at least his information was usually correct.

Jonathon nodded to his dresser to make himself scarce, took off his last act jacket, donned his dressing-gown, and sat down at the dressing table. Smearing his face with liquid paraffin, he started to wipe off his make-up. What the hell was going on? Nobody was going to deport Alice Hartley, not with her connections, but if she believed they were, this was his chance. After three years he'd still not persuaded her to back his theatrical company, and Jonathon now wanted golden Alice as his wife or out of his life.

'What am I to do, Johnny?'

'You can marry me, divinest Alice.' His tone was casual. 'As my wife you will have the right to British citizenship and then they cannot possibly deport you.'

She stopped dead. Give up her American citizenship?

Never! Yet she had sworn to stay in England until English women had the vote. She thought about it. Then, looking at Johnny, Alice weighed his debits and credits. He threw his money around, occasionally he drank too much, and he was self-centred, but he was a go-getter, he was a thrilling actor, he made her laugh, and she had to make up her mind quickly.

Ten days later Alice married Jonathon Conway by special licence at Caxton Hall. In keeping with the venue, and the fact that she had been married before, Alice chose a subdued outfit, a blush-rose dress with a fashionable tight, straight skirt, softened by a ruched neckline and bodice, and long flowing sleeves. And her hat was superb, a large one of matching pink satin, with a huge silk gauze bow trimmed with deeper pink silk roses. Johnny sported a very smart lounge suit with a cutaway jacket, neat breast and hip pockets, a low stiff collar, a dashing cravat and a double terai hat. Fleetingly, he reminded her of Franklin at his most casually elegant, but she firmly pushed that memory away.

Many of the people she would have invited to her wedding were unable to come. Christabel was in Paris, Mrs Pankhurst was back in Holloway, Kessie was confined to bed, and Sarah had a crisis at her Centre. Or could she not be bothered to come? Miss Whitworth had grown aggressively working class in recent months.

It was not, however, a dispiriting wedding.

The reception, with an informal buffet wedding breakfast, was in the River Room at the Savoy Hotel. It was the most beautiful of early May days and the long windows were open, a gentle breeze floated across the Thames, and the Embankment Gardens were bright with flowers. Dozens of Johnny's theatrical friends had accepted the invitation—free food and drink always brought them out—and Tom had brought Anne and Con, so sweet in identical polka-dot muslin dresses and cherry-garlanded hats. Johnny wasn't particularly interested in children, though he took it for granted that they would have a baby, and Alice supposed she would have to think about it soon. She would be *thirty* next year, for heaven's sake.

'Kessie sends her fondest love,' Tom wandered over and

smiled amiably, 'And hopes you'll be very, very happy with Johnny.'

He *was* a handsome devil and if neither he nor Johnny had *real* class, each had his own style. Tom's however was natural, you took him as he was, whereas Johnny tried a mite too hard to be a gentleman.

While Johnny and his friends were declaiming reams of Shakespeare, including several of the sonnets (Alice hadn't appreciated how erotic they were until he read them to her, with explanations), she saw Verena and Lionel arriving. They had come, bless them, though they both wore expressions of feigned pleasure.

In truth neither of them had believed the deportation story, but they had seen it as a way of halting Alice in her suffragette tracks. That she would rush into marriage with Jonathon Conway had entered neither of their heads. Blood was thicker than water, however, and somehow one forgave Alice. But dear heaven, what would she do next?

While Alice was celebrating her nuptials, Kessie was not confined to bed. She was walking round the bathroom at The Grove, twelve paces one way, fifteen paces the other. It was like being in her cell in Holloway or Newcastle, and her heart was thumping. Whether this was because it *was* irrevocably damaged or from the half-fear that what she was doing would be disastrous, she was unsure.

When she had first come out of hospital, Kessie was so happy to be alive, so grateful that her twins had survived and were beginning to thrive, that she had accepted everything she was told. Everybody was so loving and kind, there were piles of letters to answer, and dozens of newspaper cuttings that Maggie had collected to stick into scrapbooks. So many people wanted to see her that Maggie had to keep an appointment diary because visitors tired her.

Kessie played her music box, she looked at the photographs of Tom and the children, she fingered the horseshoe necklace, she re-read *The Masque of Anarchy*, and she thought of what the nurse had told her about Tom sitting by her bedside hour after hour, willing her to live. In that limbo between life and death, she had heard him calling, and she was the luckiest woman in the world.

Within a short while it seemed to Kessie that, though everybody continued to be loving and kind, they were speaking to her slowly and loudly, as if she were a half-deaf imbecile. The twins were brought to her bedside each day and they were adorable, but they didn't really know her. How could they? For it was Vi who washed, fed, dressed, changed and played with them.

For the occasional treat Tom carried her downstairs. One evening as he had carried her back, she had said tearfully to him, 'I'm no use to you, am I? If I stay like this, I shall just be a drag on you.'

Gently he had stroked her hair. 'I love you, Kess. You'll get better slowly. Give yourself time.' Even more gently he had kissed her forehead. 'Sleep well, my darling,' and had gone into the separate bedroom where he now slept.

Half the night, Kessie had lain awake. Give herself time. How long? When she had first come home her sexual need for Tom had been dormant, swallowed in the joy of being alive, but it was returning now. And what about Tom himself? How long could she expect him to remain faithfully celibate? Insistently the memory of her Mama was drumming in her head. Was she to become a background figure whom her children grew loth to visit, ringing her little brass bell for attention?

Both Mr Merton and the specialist had warned her that her heart was in an extremely delicate condition and *any* exertion could bring on an attack that might kill her. The only way to find out whether they were right was to test it. Kessie had pleaded to be allowed to go to the bathroom instead of using the hateful commode, which reminded her of the slop bucket in prison. That favour had been granted. While Tom and the children were at Alice's wedding, she had said she wished to go to the bathroom. Maggie and Ruby had assisted her across the landing.

'Mrs Whitworth, you really must not lock yourself in,' Maggie was rattling the bathroom door handle, 'Are you all right?'

'I'm fine, Maggie.'

Dare she take Maggie into her confidence? Kessie decided she had to, because she needed time and space to practise walking if she were to give Tom the surprise she planned.

A fortnight after her wedding day, Alice was sitting in her office at Lincoln's Inn House. They could not have a honeymoon until the run of Johnny's play was finished, and as he had three matinées a week, she was keeping on working, too. There was a ruckus in the corridor, her hand went towards the cigarette box, hastily she lit one and inhaled deeply. Another raid? Yes. Coming through the door was that lowdown rat, Sergeant Brooks.

Alice gave him her golden smile.

'Hello there, can I help you?'

It had been his idea to float the deportation story, because Alice Hartley was about the best asset left to the WSPU, and if he could frighten her off . . . that she would accept the story as gospel, rush into marriage, and take out British citizenship had not occurred to him any more than it had to her family.

'You are Mrs Conway, Mrs Jonathon Conway?'

'Sergeant—you know perfectly well who I am.' What could be coming?

'I have a warrant for your arrest.'

'My arrest? What for?'

'Conspiring to incite women to commit acts of violence contrary to the 1861 Malicious Damage to Property Act.'

'I haven't conspired to incite anybody.'

'Come, Mrs Conway, you run the publicity machine. Very well, too.'

'Thank you. May I telephone my husband?'

'He will be notified.'

Calmly Alice walked to the door, but inside she was in a panic. Her greatest terror over the years, which she had not admitted to a single soul, was the thought of being imprisoned. Nobody had bothered about her not going to prison, her services were invaluable, and by no means all suffragettes had themselves arrested. Now she had to face the terror, the possible shame of breaking at the first test.

Kessie had said that a furious euphoria buoyed you up, and, so far, Alice found that it did.

At Cannon Row police station they treated her decently, but bail was now refused as a matter of course for suffragettes, and Alice was taken along a short corridor with a stained-glass window that looked as if it had strayed from a church. The police constable unlocked a cell door and motioned her inside. Calling upon every ounce of her courage, Alice obeyed, and the door clanged shut.

Oh God, oh dear God, up and down the dimly lit, stinking, cold cell Alice paced, trying to fight off her panic. The hours dragged by, or was it the minutes, because her pocket watch had been taken from her and she had no way of gauging the time. Why had nobody come to see her? Where was Johnny? Or Verena? Or Lionel? Or an attorney? It was a living nightmare. Could she endure weeks or months in Holloway, the hunger-strike, and forcible feeding?

Kessie had endured. Three times.

Like a caged tiger, backwards and forwards, round and round Alice paced, until exhaustedly she sank to the cold stone floor. Oh God, she was so hungry, so alone, and so very, very frightened. In the ceiling the caged light was flickering and spluttering, with tired eyes Alice stared up at it and it was changing colour and shape, dancing stars, juddering stripes. The Stars and Stripes. Her flag. For whatever citizenship she had taken out, she was American and she would be American until the day she died.

No surrender! No siree!

She must have fallen asleep because a Cockney voice was saying, 'You shouldn't be sitting there, Mrs Conway, you'll get piles. Nasty fings piles are.'

The cell door was open, a policeman was holding out his hand to help her up, he was leading her along the corridor, and they were in the Superintendent's office. Johnny was there. She ran towards him and she was in his arms, safe, warm, secure.

'Right, Mr Conway, everything's in order, if you'll just sign here.'

With a reassuring smile, Johnny detached her from his

arms and with a flourish signed the piece of paper on the Superintendent's desk.

Puzzled, Alice said, 'What is that?'

'Your release papers, divinest one.'

Alice frowned and her head was suddenly clear.

'Have you given guarantees on my behalf?' Johnny avoided her gaze. 'You have, haven't you?'

The minute he was informed of Alice's arrest, Johnny had consulted, not Lionel or any of her relations, but Tom, whom he'd always liked. They were two of a kind, outsiders fighting their way to the upper reaches of the insiders, getting a leg-up from their women.

'What would you do, Tom? Can I get Alice out? She's on a conspiracy charge.'

Tom said he thought *he* could get Alice out. Reggie McKenna would have no objection to another of his clay pigeons falling off the shooting range, and he'd certainly get his wife out, however much hell she played. Or pretended to play.

Now, standing by the superintendent's desk, her beautiful face drawn with tiredness, Alice was playing merry hell, and she did not sound as if she was pretending.

She was screaming at him, 'I hate you, I hate you.'

She was rounding on the superintendent. 'My husband has absolutely no right to give any sort of guarantee on my behalf. No right whatsoever. I demand to be returned to my cell!'

The superintendent was fingering the neck of his tunic with embarrassment. Jonathon tried to calm her, but every time he opened his mouth, her voice swept over his like a tidal wave. What should he do? Slap her face? While Jonathon was quailing at that idea, above her shrieks the superintendent suddenly bellowed:

'Mrs Conway, there is nothing you can do. Your release papers have been signed. So simmer down and go off home.'

For a few seconds Alice stood silent, looking from Jonathon to the superintendent, before marching to the door. At a discreet distance, Jonathon followed. She marched across the cobbled yard, out into Cannon Row and up into Whitehall. Johnny had to run to catch up with her.

'I thought we could have supper at the Savoy and then . . .'

'Don't you ever again dare to interfere with my actions or decisions,' Alice cut in. 'I am not your chattel. If you do, I shall leave you.'

As she had left Franklin? Johnny was beginning to have a mote of sympathy for him, but he quoted dramatically, 'O tiger's heart wrapped in a woman's hide.'

Over the next few days, Alice continued to behave like Shakespeare's Queen Margaret, but in her heart she knew she was glad that Johnny had obtained her release, which was partly why she was so angry with him. He had no right to have denied her the opportunity of testing her courage and he had been so *apologetic*. See Tom apologising? Had she made a mistake in marrying Johnny? Was he a shell of a man? Oh well, she had married him, he was good in bed, and she was feeling randy.

On the Sunday morning, finishing the last of a hearty breakfast, Alice pushed back her chair and lit a cigarette. 'You know, Johnny, we have to find somewhere proper to live. I've seen an advertisement for a house in St John's Wood which looks interesting. We could have a look at it tomorrow. And I think we could both do with a change of scenery. As soon as the run of the play is finished, I suggest we have a belated honeymoon.'

He smiled. 'A honeymoon sounds wonderful, darling. Where do you suggest?'

Alice considered. 'In the Fall I thought we should visit the States, but for the time being, how about a Continental tour? I'd like to stop off in Paris to see Christabel.' She paused. 'You see, Johnny, while I was in that cell, I had time to think, and I'm reluctantly coming to the conclusion that Kessie could be right. All this violence is only hardening Mr Asquith's attitude. If I can persuade Christabel to come home and take charge of the United Suffragists, then we might really get somewhere.'

With a dramatic gesture Alice swept her hand up in the air, Johnny caught it and she allowed him to kiss her palm.

The storm had blown itself out, the divine Mrs Conway was back in action, batten down the hatches, prepare for battle stations!

Tom descended from the tram at the top of Highgate Hill. His head was still ringing with the speech he'd made last night in the Free Trade Hall, the main hall, the one he had dreamed of filling since those days when he had stood beneath the black rocks of Netherstone Edge, hallooing to the wind.

'. . . and I pledge that before long you will have the vote you have been so shamefully denied, the right to full citizenship of your country . . . the future is in your hands, men and women together, for the twentieth century is the century of the people. . . .'

How he wished Kessie could have been there to hear him!

As Tom reached the front door at The Grove, Maggie opened it and there was an anxious expression on her face. As well there might be, because behind her, standing at the top of the stairs, was Kessie, looking beautiful in a green velvet skirt, a white lawn blouse and a velvet bolero, her chestnut hair parted in the middle and curled in a thick roll round her face. Tom stared up at her. What the hell was she doing, out of bed, standing there, fully dressed?

Then, as Tom watched, transfixed, Kessie walked slowly down the stairs. She did not quite reach the bottom stair because he moved towards her and lifted her into his arms.

She pummelled his chest, laughing. 'Tom, put me down. I can walk. Can't you see? I can walk. By myself.'

31

'It's nothing short of a miracle, Kessie, a blooming miracle. Sounded the old ticker myself enough times, and it was in a bad way. Off you go marching around when you're told to lie still and what happens? You get better. Interesting that.' Stephen's nostrils twitched. 'But don't you run away with the idea that the ticker's one hundred per cent fighting fit, because it isn't, old girl. Don't you be stupid and undo the miracle. The Good Lord can be a temperamental old so-and-so.'

'I won't.' Kessie giggled and took the broad, capable hand in hers. 'Thank you, Stephen for *everything* you've done for me.'

'Stuff and nonsense,' the nostrils twitched rapidly. 'What are friends for?'

'May I go to Willow Bank, then?'

'Don't see why not, so long as you take care and *don't overdo it.*'

There was little likelihood of that. Tom carried her on and off the boat, Maggie and Vi came with them, while Ruby—who was engaged to a young man who worked in the grocer's shop in Highgate High Street—stayed at The Grove to look after Tom until the House of Commons broke for the summer recess. At Willow Bank, Mrs Dobell and Maggie almost came to blows about who should care for Mrs Whitworth and two men servants were sent from the big house to carry her down to the beach. They were needed because Kessie could not yet manage the steep descent by herself.

It was a heavenly summer and today was particularly shimmering, the gentlest breeze fluttering the sunshades on the beach, the sea a glittering diamond expanse. The twins were up at the house with Maggie, Kessie lay on the chaise longue, watching Anne forge through the water like a little porpoise, and Con in her oilskin paddling drawers trying to chase after her, restrained by Vi.

Lazily, Kessie opened her diary on her knee and started to write:

On the way down to the beach this morning, Anne plucked an overblown dandelion, puffing the seeds of its

342

'clock' which floated on the breeze. Once upon a time, how long ago? oh, some nine summers ago, I thought of life as a well-tended garden, with just a few weeds—such as the inequality of women—that needed to be pulled out to make it perfect. I now know that life itself is the dandelion clock, the spores floating around you, not entirely without a pattern, for there must be a God in Heaven, though as Stephen said, He is temperamental. *And* He has a malicious sense of humour. Nobody can hope to catch all the spores, you can only stretch out your hand to capture a few, to plant them and to trust they grow. Tom is certain he has several within his grasp and I'm sure he will plant them, because he is an exceptional man. I grow more and more convinced of that. I haven't actually asked him if he thinks the price I've paid has been worth the candle, but I believe his answer would be yes, because he has never reproached me for not telling him about my heart condition. Perhaps he feels that as I am the one who is paying the price, I am the one to judge whether it has been worthwhile. Has it? On the debit side, I suppose my heart could conk out any day, or I could be a semi-invalid for the rest of my life, which would be boring, to say the least. But think what my life would have been had I never become a suffragette, had I stayed in Manchester and married a *naice* middle-class man of whom the Thorpe family would have approved. Think . . .

'Aunty Sarah!' Anne and Con were running out of the water. Kessie turned her head and saw Sarah coming down the steep path from the headland. She had been expected for her annual visit to the Isle of Wight—after the usual ritual of Kessie persuading her that the People's Centre could exist without her for a fortnight in the year—though not so early in the day.

Everybody greeted her enthusiastically and then the children said, 'Help us build a sand-castle, Aunty Sarah, a huge one.' Vi joined in and the four of them were digging their spades into the shingly orange sand, erecting a fort,

343

cutting a channel from the water's edge for a moat. Anne called out, 'It's *'specially* for you, Mummy.'

Kessie smiled and putting down her diary, she watched the concentrated efforts. What was it she had said to Christabel in those heady days beyond recall? That she and Tom would transcend all difficulties and forge a true partnership? She supposed you could say they had. Her nearness to death had harnessed Tom's love for her, that she truly believed. They needed each other, they gave to each other, and now, once more, in every way.

There was a cheer from the builders and Kessie joined in as Anne stuck a Union Jack on the topmost sand-pie. Sarah came over and flopped down by her side. 'You've been looking very thoughtful. Penny for 'em.'

Sarah seemed to grow smaller, wirier, yet more determined, as each year went by.

Kessie did not tell her sister-in-law what she had been thinking. Instead, she asked, 'Do you have any doubts, Sarah? That we might not succeed in emancipating women? That too many centuries of history are against us, that . . .'

'Don't be gloomy and don't be insulting. 'Course I have my doubts. Only idiots and maniacs are without doubt. It'll take time, longer than we once thought, I'll give you that, but I know we shall succeed.'

Anne and Con came running up, Sarah had a mock-fight with them and after they'd splashed back into the water, Kessie said, 'Why don't you marry and have children of your own?'

'I wouldn't mind a bairn,' Sarah admitted. 'But there's so much to be done and the husband part is the real trouble.'

'Oh, Sarah!'

For a few minutes she stared silently at the sunlight breaking into a million sparkling fragments on the surface of the sea, then she said, 'Heard anything from Dorothy recently?'

'I had an uninformative post card the other day signed "Tweedledee". That's Dorothy's active service code-name. The postmark was London.'

'Active service! Code-names! They're like a pack of

344

Dervishes winding themselves into greater and greater frenzies, emptying acid into pillar boxes, blowing up cricket pavilions, burning down country houses, cutting telegraph wires, slashing paintings. Do any of 'em know what they're doing any more? And more importantly, *why* they're doing it?'

Later that afternoon, up in the garden at Willow Bank, they had finished their tea and the twins were lying in a double bassinet at Kessie's feet. Kate was a very dramatic baby, already given to watching the effect of her howls and smiles, while Mark could be what his father called him, 'a little bugger'. Was that why Tom was so strict with his only son? Or was it because even for enlightened Tom, girls could be spoiled, but boys could not?

From the bottom of the garden Anne's voice floated up, 'You are ve Queen, Aunty Sarah, so you can't vat way. You are a servant, Con, so you do what I tell you.'

Kessie thought she had better not let her beloved Daddy hear her say things like that, for though Anne remained his favourite—not that Tom admitted to favouritism—his love for his children stopped short of complete indulgence. Maggie came out with the evening newspaper and Kessie smiled her thanks. Dear, faithful Maggie . . . she really should have more life of her own. Or was she content to live what seemed to Kessie a second-hand existence, through her and the children?

The foreign news was worrying. It was a month since the Archduke Franz Ferdinand of Austria and his wife had been assassinated in that Bosnian town. Sarajevo. Recently the murders had dropped out of the headlines, partly because there was a Balkan Crisis every decade, and partly because everybody's attention was focused on the much nearer Ulster crisis. But the Sarajevo affair now seemed to be spreading out of the Balkans. Kessie read the paper carefully. It was emphatic that under no circumstances could or would Britain become involved.

'It's Daddy!' Anne's voice was high with delight and she was running up the slope. 'It's Daddy.'

345

It could not be Tom: until the summer recess he was coming over only for the occasional weekend. But when Kessie turned round, there he was on the terrace, his face sombre.

After he had promised to play with Anne and Con later, Vi had taken the twins inside for their bath, and Mrs Dobell had brought out more tea, the adults sat around the garden table as the shadows lengthened across the grass and the light deepened from gold to amber.

'The Austrians have declared war on Serbia, and we're drifting towards war.' Kessie stared in astonishment. 'That's why I came over, though I have to be back on Sunday.'

'You can't drift towards war,' Sarah jumped up. 'I've never heard anything so daft. The working classes of Europe will not let it happen. Neither will the women. What are you going to do to stop it? You won't do anything sitting here, drinking tea.'

Instantly Tom was on his feet.

'Look, Sal, you know I've fought every inch of the way for peace—'

'And you're giving up now just because this hysterical jingoism is mounting? You're betraying everything we ever believed in. The brotherhood of man, the sisterhood of women.'

'The brotherhood of man has not arrived. Nor has the sisterhood of women. The Germans are determined to have a war. Against us. What do you expect me to do? Let them march through all this?' Tom waved his left arm round the garden which was bathed in the suddenly brilliant light of the dying sun. 'Or tramp through The Dales?'

'I never thought I'd live to hear you mouth such unspeakable rot! Men! You're all the same . . .'

'Don't be so bloody daft, Sal, we are *not* all the same.'

'Stop it,' Kessie cried out, 'both of you.'

The verbal combatants stared at each other for a few seconds, then Tom sat down and took Kessie's hand in his.

'You're the most belligerent pacifist I know, Sal.'

A slight smile twitched Sarah's lips.

'You have to fight just as hard for peace. I know what I'm going to do. I'm going back to Manchester to rally my troops in the battle for peace.'

In the morning they saw her off in Ventnor on the ss *Brighton Queen*. The newspaper hoardings were black with the headlines, 'Germany Declares War on Russia'. The town was seething with excitement, in the steep narrow streets people were clustered in groups, saying it was time the Kaiser was taught a lesson, and three embarrassed soldiers were loudly cheered. On the water's edge the portable bathing machines were decked with Union Jacks, on the sands the pierrot band was playing Boer War tunes— 'Soldiers of the Queen' and 'Goodbye Dolly Gray'. They went into 'Land of Hope and Glory' and Kessie felt tears prickling in her eyes, a lump tightening her throat. On the way back to Willow Bank, she asked Tom to stop the trap. 'Let's have a walk.'

'Kess, you know walking tires you.'

'I'm having a walk today.' Tom sighed, Anne jumped from the trap, racing ahead, and he put his arm round his wife.

'Come on then, very slowly, just to the cliff top. No further.'

They walked through the dense foliage of the Undercliff, with the sun falling in shafts, past the hedgerows garlanded with the sticky fronds of ladies bedstraw, the elderberry bushes thick with ripening fruit, the cow parsley stretching in cream umbrellas over the pink herb Roberts. They came on to the headland and the scent of the sea lavender was sweet. Below them in Steephill Cove the thatched cottages basked in the sunshine, the nets were drying over the lobster pots, in the distance Ventnor was a purple blur, the sea was like rippling glass, and children's laughter echoed in the shimmering stillness. The lump returned to Kessie's throat. How she loved her native land which, despite everything, was the best country in the world.

'Daddy, will you be a soldier, *with* lots of medals?'

Anne smiled triumphantly at her mother as she managed

to pronounce 'th' correctly, and Tom ruffled the child's copper-coloured hair.

Kessie insisted on returning to London with Tom. On Bank Holiday Monday, 3rd August, she sat in the Ladies' Gallery, where she had sat so many times listening to Tom and debates on votes for women, and Sir Edward Grey's speech was one of the most moving she had heard. Not because he was a great orator, he wasn't, but that lent an extra poignancy to his grave, reasoned arguments as he explained why Britain might be obliged to go to war with Germany. He informed the packed House of Commons, so silent you could have heard the proverbial pin drop, that His Majesty's Government had sent an ultimatum to Germany. Unless they respected Belgian neutrality, the two countries would be in a state of belligerence as from midnight, 4th August, when the ultimatum would expire.

Kessie put her face in her hands. Germany had already declared war on France, and her troops had crossed the Belgian frontier. They were virtually at war.

Alice and Jonathon were in Paris. Lying late in bed, sharing the bath, eating sumptuous meals at the Ritz Hotel, being fitted for new gowns at the House of Molyneux, was Alice's idea of bliss. Johnny didn't object, apart from the fittings, and he disappeared during those.

Throughout 3rd August the excitement was unbelievable, thousands of people on the Champs Elysées, jamming the Place de la Concorde, cheering, shouting, singing the Marseillaise. When the news came through that the Germans had invaded Belgium, the bellicose euphoria increased.

'We must get back,' Johnny said, 'We shall be at war tomorrow.'

'Can we return via Brittany?'

'What on earth for?'

'To see the Pankhursts, of course.'

Christabel was not in Paris but enjoying a holiday in St Brieuc with her mother, who was recuperating from her last hunger-strike.

'I want to know what the WSPU will do.'

'What about?'

'*What about*? Johnny, you're not usually so dumb. About votes for women. The war won't last long. Will the WSPU call a truce while it does, or will they not?'

Mrs Pankhurst was looking better than she had in months, some colour back in her cheeks, walking up and down the hotel terrace with much of her old energy, every so often turning towards her visitors, her hands outstretched in a favourite gesture. 'In this hour of peril, we shall lay down our arms, the war of women against men will cease until the Germans are defeated. We are *English* women first and foremost. We have already telegraphed Mr McKenna to that effect. I shall return immediately to London and offer my services to the Government.'

Blinking with astonishment, Alice looked at Christabel who had never been as emotionally inclined as her mother. 'I agree absolutely. I have my affairs to settle in Paris, then I shall return home. They will need us, Alice. Our sex will be ready to play its part in the struggle as never before. This will be a woman's war as much as a man's.'

Which was all very well but . . . Johnny didn't seem in the least surprised by the Pankhursts' passionate volte-face. What else had Alice expected them to do? They were patriotic English ladies, Mrs Pankhurst in particular. All the same, immediately to offer their services to the Government that had been torturing them, abandoning votes for women like last season's hat, seemed to Alice to be overdoing things.

On her return to London she found that Kessie agreed. The United Suffragists had had an emergency meeting and they were *not* giving up.

'Obviously the war effort must come first. But if we are fighting for a better world, for freedom and liberty, which we are, then it is essential that women obtain *their* freedom and liberty, starting with their right of citizenship.'

'Hear, hear,' said Alice, 'I shall join you.'

Kessie threw a small dinner-party. After Dorothy had said it was nice to come through the front door again (the Government had granted an amnesty to all 'mice' and released all the hunger-strikers), she turned to Kessie and Alice.

'I just don't understand you two. Christabel and Mrs Pankhurst are absolutely right. How can we keep on fighting for the vote until the war is won? If we don't support our menfolk and defeat the beastly Huns, there won't be any country left for us to vote in. Do you see them giving women the vote? All they do is rape women and murder children. Have you read what they're doing in Belgium?'

She looked at Tom.

'Are you enlisting?'

Tom said not at the moment. The House of Commons needed people to direct the war effort and he'd have to see how things went.

'I expect you're a bit old, anyway. Are you enlisting, Johnny?'

He said he had been offered the lead in a new comedy, people would need entertaining more than ever, so he had accepted, but like Tom he would see what happened.

'Well, my brother Georgie's a regular, so obviously he's in from the start, but my other brothers are *all* enlisting.'

There was a brief silence before Alice said, 'Momma has cabled ninety-nine times, "Come home immediately". I cabled back. Once. "Home is here." Honestly, I wouldn't be anywhere else at the moment. It's so exciting, isn't it?'

Kessie had to admit it was. There was an incredibly carefree atmosphere, as if everybody's problems had suddenly disappeared in the glory of fighting for England. People were talking together in the streets, on the buses, in the tubes, in the shops, discussing the British Expeditionary Force, following the retreat to Mons and the heroic stand there, saying what a bloody nose the Kaiser would get. Mr Harker from next door burst into conversation for the first time since they had moved into The Grove, bitterly regretting that he was too old to fight, congratulating Tom on his support for the war effort, unlike some of his despicable Socialist comrades.

After the children had come back from the Isle of Wight, Kessie went up to The Dales with Tom, stopping off in

Manchester to see Papa and Sarah. Papa was sunk in gloom, his reasonable Liberal world shattered beyond recall, while Sarah was belligerently preaching pacifism. If the people refused to fight, there would be no wars; it was the rich and powerful who profited from wars, not the working classes. But somebody had daubed 'Votes for Hun Lovers' on the walls of the People's Centre and the warehouse that had previously been swarming with activity was now half-empty.

Old Doctor McPhee was one of the few helpers who remained and as they had a cup of tea in the poky office, he said to Kessie, 'The wee lassie's swimming against the tide this time. She'll need all the strength she possesses not to drown.'

In The Dales the excitement, the sense of uplift, were even greater than in London, long lines winding round the recruiting offices. Tom was mobbed in the streets and cheered to the echo when he said they had to defeat the Huns quickly, decisively, so they could settle down to the task of rebuilding a just, peaceful world. The weather remained heavenly, reproachfully so it seemed to Kessie, and on their last day she said, 'Let's go up to Netherstone Edge.'

'Kess, you can't walk up *there*.'

'Papa says he'll drive us to Crowther's End. It isn't far from there. If I take it slowly . . .'

Her heart was thumping before they reached the summit and Tom had to half-carry her the last few yards. After a while the thudding stopped, they sat between the black rocks of the Edge and the wind blew, as it always did. The high moors were bleak and beautiful, lower down the black stone walls snaked across the grey-green grass, in the valley a train steamed over the high arches of the viaduct and the sun flashed on its windows. Kessie took off her hat, leaning her head against Tom's chest, and silently he stroked her hair.

Tom could not imagine life without Kess at his side. In the past, he had taken her love for granted because she had always given it so freely, so openly. He had cheated her because he had believed in one law for men, another for

351

women. Maybe what he had learned was truly to respect her as he respected not many, but a few, men; to accept her right to lead her own life, in conjunction with his own. How long it would take other men to accept their women as equal partners, he did not know, but then few men had a Kess.

'It won't be over by Christmas, Tom, will it? How long do you think it will last?' The lovely hazel eyes looked up at him, wide with concern. 'A year? Two?'

'Probably.'

Tom was not as old as Dorothy imagined. He was thirty-two and he would fight for his beloved England if he had to, for her, for the children, for the view from Netherstone Edge. Half of Kessie would be proud of him and want him to go, while the other half would be terrified and would hate the war. But it would not come to that. There would be no need for Tom to enlist.

'Do you remember the first time we came up here together on our honeymoon?'

'Yes, me luv, I do.'

'It seems another world. I was so full of hope and now . . .'

'You must never lose hope, Kess. If you do, you might as well be dead. Promise me you'll never lose hope?'

She promised and said, 'I love you.'

Tom kissed her gently. 'I love you, too.'

In silence they sat gazing over their native landscape and the wind sighed through the crags.

'We have to get the vote, you know. War or no war.'

'You will.'

'The girls have to grow up in a different world, a world in which women *matter*.'

'They will.'

They stood up and walked slowly down into the smoky valley.